"I really loved this book. The characters' dynamics and personalities make this book such an exciting and captivating read. I enjoyed following their high school experiences and finding connections within my own life as a sophomore in high school."
~ Joci

"All the feels! Witty charm, young love, family strength, and the perfect addition to the Halsted family series. A great book to curl up with for a dose of nostalgia- remembering the adventure of high school. Or recommended to young readers that will certainly find themselves in one of Gracie's eclectic group of friends and connect with their search for identity, acceptance, and friendship."
~ Danielle

"I appreciated that Gracie's main group of friends were non-athletes and that she got involved with theater and the mystery game nights. It makes her so much more relatable. Her friends were so quirky and fun; it was nice to be invested in their lives as well."
~ Sarah

"Great story! I can't get enough of this series. The characters are real, lovable, unique. It's a plus that in this book they speak American Sign Language for inclusivity at their school. There's nothing formulaic and the action moves fast. Fresh one-liners. So much fun."
~ Tracy

"I've love how this author shows these strong, independent characters to be feeling stupid about something they have done or have self-doubt and how as a reader, you see that others don't see them that way or define them that way. This is such an important part of her characters for young adults and old ladies too - we can all relate to that."
~ Marianne

"I LOVE Gracie! She's bright, witty, and initially an outsider trying to survive her senior year at a new school. Gracie grows up, shows up and outshines those trying to crush her spirit while we cheer her on page after page! Yay for the new girl on the block!"
~ Shelley

"MWARTF was my perfect poolside vacation read! KAH has created an eclectic cast of characters. I enjoyed the witty banter and shenanigans of Gracie's friends and family as we follow her through her senior year of high school."
~ Melissa

"Gracie is someone I want to be with. Hope she and her awesome friends make room for me at their lunch table ;-) because that's where I want to be!"
~ Jody

"Gracie pulls the reader onto her team and into her method for maneuvering the social games ruling high school. This story is as fast and absorbing as the game of lacrosse Gracie plays."
~ Andrea

"Kris Abel-Helwig's skillful combination of current and classic tunes, rock-and-roll the reader throughout this fun-loving continuation of life in a military family; complete with love-struck parents, three military brat siblings, and a year of loveable and endearing ups and downs. Your heart will be grinning madly all the way through."
~ Ellen Filipelli – English Language Arts Educator, Johns Creek High School, Georgia

"... A great culmination of the family story by showing the strength of their bond through endless love, friendships, and indomitable spirits ... I also loved that each of the protagonists were kind, caring to all and also open to making friends with people of all abilities, talents and interests. Great examples for teens to read & learn about the power of inclusion!"
~ Glenda

HERO BOOK 1:
FADE TO BLACK & WHITE

HERO BOOK 2:
I WISH MY WORDS TASTED BETTER

Dedicated to my talented beta readers,
proofing posse, grammar sheriffs,
and critique compadres.

My Wings Aren't Ready To Fly

A NOVEL BY KRIS ABEL-HELWIG

Culicidae Press
PO Box 620647
Middleton, WI 53562
USA
culicidaepress
editor@culicidaepress.com

MY WINGS AREN'T READY TO FLY

ISBN: 978-1-68315-074-9

Library of Congress Control Number: 2023948443

Cover photo, art and design ©2022 Kris Abel-Helwig
kris@kahcreative.com • https://kahcreative.com

Our books may be purchased in bulk for promotional,
educational, and/or business use.
Please contact your local bookseller or the Culicidae Press
Sales Department at +1-515-462-0278
or by email at sales@culicidaepress.com

twitter.com/culicidaepress • facebook.com/culicidaepress
threads.net/@culicidaepress

Acknowledgements

Cori Tanner. Editor extraordinaire. My imagination warden. Locked in my head with characters who kick and scream to escape. Cori makes sure none are released until they are prepared for the outside world.

Grant, for sharing Krutch, Dervis and Hood Snap
Shelley, for medical consultations
Yoda, for the Force you generously share
Laura and Andrew, for military academies experiences
Ed, for small aircraft and aviation information
Colin, for Pokémon intelligence

Introduction

Each chapter begins with or a song to download and listen to as you read. Search Spotify: krisabelhelwig, My Wings Aren't Ready To Fly. The music spans the decades and genres. I did not receive any compensation from the record labels.

If you find something in "MWAR2Fly" that resonates with you, or someone you know, feel free to buy a hundred copies to give as gifts ;-)

Now, download the tunes, hunker down in a comfy chair, and read! When you finish, be a dear, and support indies by writing a review on Goodreads or Amazon. You can also send a selfie with book cover to kris@kahcreative.com. Check out @krisabelhelwig. author.illustrator for ideas or create your own!

Playlist

1　"Natural" Imagine Dragons
2　"Warriors" Freedom Call
3　"No Roots" Alice Merton
4　"The Way I Am" Charlie Puth
5　"The Outsiders" Eric Church
6　"Lean On Me" Club Nouveau
7　"High Horse" Kacey Musgraves
8　"Nobody Does It Better" Carly Simon
9　"Get Your Way" Jamie Cullum
10　"So Am I" Ava Max
11　"Hooked On a Feeling" Blue Swede
12　"Mission Impossible" Dominik Hauser
13　"That's Life" Frank Sinatra
14　"Waking Lions" Pop Evil
15　"Every Little Thing She Does Is Magic" The Police
16　"You Don't Know Me" Ray Charles
17　"Stronger" Kelly Clarkson
18　"Just Like Fire" P!nk
19　"Bad Day" Daniel Powter
20　"Bring It On Home To Me" Sam Cooke
21　"It's Gonna Be Me" *NSYNC
22　"For Whom The Bell Tolls" Metallica
23　"Desperado" Linda Ronstadt
24　"Underdog" Alicia Keys
25　"Sounds of Silence" Disturbed cover
26　"Dream On" Aerosmith
27　"Build Me Up Buttercup" The Foundations
28　"Storybook Love" Mark Knopfler
29　"Get Up" Shinedown
30　"Wake Me Up Before You Go-Go" Wham!
31　"Take A Chance On Me" ABBA

1

"Natural" – Imagine Dragons

"What are you looking at?"

"Don't end a sentence with a preposition," I said to the annoying whine as I squinted to read the high school locker numbers above a cluster of perfectly styled, messy buns. A contradiction of terms, I concur.

The numbers weren't even close to the ones on the slip of paper my curriculum advisor had given me. Wrong hallway.

"*Ex–cuse* me?" The buzz in my ear continued.

"A preposition expresses a word's spatial relationship to another," I said. Modern English has cast this Latin rule aside but I prefer to adhere to it. So much more civilized.

"Are *you* talking to *us*?" The noise persisted.

"Not on purpose, but since you like questions, can you tell me how to get to the senior hallway?" Still focusing on lockers.

"Do I *look* like *Google Maps*?"

Taking a break from my search to locate the source. Ugh. A six-pack of high school divas, wearing so much makeup I thought I was in Madame Tussauds Wax Museum.

"No, because that would be useful." I waved them off.

A gasp emerged from the groupies, then one hissed, "Do you *know* who she *is*?"

Snarky responses raced to my tongue. The winner leaped out, "Do I *look* like a *yearbook*?"

Time to exit before I slip on the newly waxed floors.

"OMG!"

"I can't *even* with her*!*"

Dismissing the entourage, I noticed a guy leaning against a locker across the hallway. Observing. A slight smirk crept across his dark face as he did jazz hands, fingers spread and quivering, which would be strange except – then he signed, "Bravo."

Hold on, of course! The reason I'd chosen this school –the fully integrated deaf student program. I'd been obsessed with American Sign Language as a hobby for years. I tilted my head and wrote with my fingers, "Excuse me?"

"Well done," he answered.

I shrugged, then asked, "Senior hallway?"

His fingers dictated directions in the air.

I signed, "Thanks," and waved goodbye.

"What a *frickin' freak* show!" Laughter.

I turned to the six-pack.

Ten pale pink painted fingernails fluttered like butterflies on a nectar rush, ridiculing me.

"Oh, I'm *so* sorry," I said.

"What?"

Pointing to the silly mocking motions, I said out loud and signed, "About your itchy, bumpy rash. Good luck at the gynecologist appointment after school."

Her heavily made-up eyes squinted as she held out her hands, "Ooooh *gross*!" The other fangirls stepped back as if she were contagious.

I nodded to my silent compadre and went on my way.

Senior year. First day. New school. New state. Oh, joy.

2

"Warriors" – Freedom Call

I walked into the cafeteria at lunchtime. Wow. Nothing screams high school like the prison yard itself. Cheerleaders, jocks, nerds, random friend groups, then the outcasts. Or as I call them, the interesting ones: who look you in the eye, listen to your ideas and consider contrasting points of view.

The room was a large square with mini pods around the perimeter. Each pod had a table that sat eight. I gravitated to one that looked unoccupied. On closer inspection, I saw that it was taken, or at least claimed. It was covered in notebooks and scattered Pokémon cards. Despite the copious amounts of items sprawled over the table, only two backpacks were visible. On one side of the table, there was a large bottle of red Gatorade, half empty. Across from it, its mortal enemy, the same size blue Powerade bottle, half full.

A girl sitting at a nearby table nibbled on a celery stick. She diverted her gaze when I made eye contact.

"Do you know who sits here?" I asked.

"Um, no – they're kinda weird," she said, looking around the room. "I don't *talk* to them; they sit around and play *dumb* card games like *children*. How *immature* is that?" She flipped her hair over her shoulder to show how mature she was. Or not.

Crazy how people here *talk in italics.*

Deadpan, I recited the original 90's Pokémon chant, "Char-meleon, War-tor-tle, Mewtwo, Tentacruel, Aer-o-dactyl, Omanyte, Slow-poke, Pidgeot, Arbok, *that's all folks.*" I'm getting the hang of *this.*

Her blank stare confirmed she had no idea what I was talking about. Could not care less. Her focus returned to the celery.

More curious than ever, I leaned over the gaming table for a better look. There was a set of cards laid down at each of the chairs with the backpacks, as well as a deck next to them. Original, old-school Pokémon up to the latest and greatest. Most of the cards were rare or better, with several holographic and encased shrine-like in plastic covers. And worth a lot of bones. Not that anyone who didn't care would know. Maybe that's why the treasure had been left unattended.

Whoever sat here were huge fans. I looked at the cards placed at the seat closer to me and compared them to the other setup. I smiled. They may be Poké-Fanatics, but they were both amateurs.

The Gatorade bottle next to me shook slightly. I frowned, looking at it closer. There it was again. Another tremor, shaking the liquid ever so slightly. Again. Larger ripples. Something was coming. Jurassic Park anyone?

I looked at the Powerade across the table. It was shaking as well, teetering precariously toward the edge of the table. The ripples suddenly stopped.

I heard a voice murmur, "Biff, look – someone is looking at our stuff." Soft and delicate, like a kitten purring.

"Shhh. I see that, Garth." The wake-up slur of a groggy child.

My eyes dragged across the cards one more time as I turned to the two voices, "Are these your cards?"

Holy mama they were big.

The first guy was wider than I was tall, with a bowl-cut of sandy blonde hair combed neatly just above his eyebrows. His arms were tucked against his enormous body, clutching his lunch tray with shaking hands. I noticed his attempt to hide his Transformers t-shirt, untucked over his tan cargo shorts. Long white tube socks were pulled up to his knees. He looked simultaneously frightened and intrigued, with pouting lips and eyes frozen on me as if I were Aerodactyl – extinct and extremely rare.

The guy behind him was of equal size, his hair nearly shaved down to his pale skin. His mouth was slightly open and he looked perplexed, probably wondering why I stood next to his table. Partially eclipsed by his friend, he sported a Superman shirt and sweatpants.

Sported. Okay – he wore it.

They couldn't stand side by side because the aisle wasn't big enough for the two of them.

"I'm Grace," I said.

The first guy's mouth popped open, closed, and open again, goldfish-like. He glanced from me to his friend, whose eyes never left me.

He approached nervously like I was feral and about to attack, holding his tray close to his body with one hand and wiping off the other. "Umm." Looking back and forth, unsure, he waved short, stubby fingers. "Hi."

Me showing up must've thrown an oodaloop (observe, orient, decide, act, loop) in their entire daily routine. "Is this your chair?" I asked, pointing at Mr. Gatorade.

"Uhh yeah. B-b-but we can move if you want, we don't really need this table. It's cool," he apologized, deflated, shuffling forward with his eyes downcast.

Poor guy. I bet he's been kicked off his share of tables.

"No. I was just wondering about your attack," I said, looking down at the table again. I set my lunch down on an empty chair and pointed. "Your setup consists mostly of fire and water Pokémon. While they're all evolved, you have only water type out. You set yourself up to be countered by electric or grass cards."

Optimus Primeape's (Transformer/Pokémon combo) mouth dropped open as he scanned the cards and smacked his palm on his forehead, knocking his elbow into one of his three cartons of chocolate milk. I jumped in front of him and grabbed it off the tray before it could splash the valuable card weapons of destruction. I set it back upright.

"Whoa. Thanks," OP said. He stared as if I'd teleported.

"Wow. She's quick – and correct," Superman said. His attention had diverted from me to the cards. "Why didn't I think of that?"

They stepped around me, immersed once again in their game and arguing about whether or not the battle was compromised by outside interference.

Forgotten, I picked up my tray and moved on to an empty table. I sat back against the wall to prevent a flank attack (Military Brat 101),

plugged in my earbuds, and listened to the heavy beat of Freedom
Call while watching the impromptu local adaptation of *High School
Musical*.

Without Zac Efron.

Bummer.

3

"No Roots" – Alice Merton

Lakeside High School is within walking distance of our new house. The ethnically diverse neighborhood boasts high academic accolades for the children of diplomats, senators, corporate tycoons, civil service workers, and military folk like my parents – all seeking the best public education their taxes could provide.

Roscoe and Mallory heard the key in the lock and sounded the bark alarm. After hanging my house key on the hook in the mudroom, I sat on the bench to receive kisses, laughed thinking about Doge Meme kisses, then gave tummy and butt rubs as I slipped off my Converse and followed the pups into the kitchen.

Grabbing an apple from the bowl of fruit overflowing onto the granite island, I rinsed it and savored a sweet, crisp bite.

Mom called from her sunroom/guest room/studio. "How was your day, Grace Artemis?"

"Okay," I answered, noticing Roscoe and Mallory had resumed their posts, stretched out across a sunbeam that cut through the window onto the wood floor by Mom's bare feet.

She sat behind a canvas set on an easel. I circled to peer over her shoulder past the blonde hair pulled up in a twist and held in place with a dry paintbrush.

An enigma, Mom shape-shifted from disciplinarian to bohemian. Nurturing, tutoring, entertaining, laughing with and loving on my older siblings and me. First and middle names were an everyday occurrence in our family, not an indication that you were in trouble. She claimed after dedicating nine months of your life to creating something beautiful, you shouldn't abbreviate it.

As for my middle namesake, I like to think contrary to Greek mythology, Artemis, goddess of the hunt, wilderness, animals, and protector of youth, did not demand perfection from others. Rather, like a true, mythical hero, she sought out those who were imperfect as they are much more interesting.

"Talk to me." She turned to study my face, head tilted to the side. Wearing my dad's worn cotton oxford, her irises were clear blue today. Deep crinkle lines on each temple made me think of Dad's comment, 'she smiles with her eyes.'

I pointed to a freshly painted cardinal, perched in a golden maple. "It'll be fine. Grandma stopping by to say, 'Hi?'" Mom believed cardinals were a sign that loved ones who had passed were still with us.

"Yep. Checking on her brilliant granddaughter."

"Visiting Sofi at school?"

She brushed a dot of paint on my nose, "She saw Starlight last night, now it's your turn, Moonbeam." Like I said, our Bohemian Mama, that's what my sister calls her.

***

I could have listened.

Younger, but oh so wiser, I'd rejected my vivacious older sister Sofi's dress-up fashion shows, party-planning skills and popularity do's and don'ts.

Don't get me wrong. Sofi both amazes and amuses me.

Hatched three years before me, she skipped the awkward caterpillar stage I cling to, and emerged from the get-go, an extroverted, glamorous butterfly with a heart of gold.

I climbed two flights of stairs to my attic room to call her. "What's up, Buttercup?" Sofi answered the video chat. Sounding like Mom, her use of the familiar greeting brings a smile to my serious screen reflection. I miss her.

"Nada, Bra," I said.

She pulled the plastic doo-dad out of her ponytail and slipped it on her wrist to free her straightened blonde hair. "Kick'n butt and tak'n names in our nation's Nasty Girl Capitol?"

"Nope."

"Met any drama-free peeps?"

"Few."

"Nice try. Start over. Using multiple-word responses. In this order: any cute guys, potential friends, adorable outfits?"

I laughed. "Couple. Maybe. Didn't notice."

"Wow. Eight syllables. You're on a roll."

A veteran of multiple military moves, Sofi owned it. Walked into each new school, state, country, head held high, a day-planner in hand, introduced herself to everyone and came home with a full schedule of playdates.

Same with Jason, our older brother, both total people magnets, attracting and keeping connections around the globe.

Their positivity and resilience confound me.

I met other military kids, but too soon they moved away. Leaving behind an empty desk to symbolize something missing in my life. With no idea how to sustain a lasting friendship.

I filled the void with books, getting lost in them; swept away with characters on imaginary adventures. But heartbreak waited on the flip side of every painful last page when my beloved fictional friends left in search of someone new.

"Gracie-girl, helloooo, where are you?" Sofi teased, tapping on her laptop screen. "Solving the diminishing bee population problem or shutting down puppy mills?"

I shook my head to refocus on her. "I wish."

"What did you wear on the first day of the first semester of your last year of high school?" Sofi asked. It wouldn't surprise me if she remembered what she had worn three years ago. Back when she was the primo trendy fashionista, even now as a nursing student on an Army ROTC scholarship, she rocked both scrubs and camo.

I looked down to see. "T-shirt, jeans, Converse."

"The purple ones you wore to prom three years ago?"

See what I mean?

I'd been asked by her friend and was allowed to go with their posse. She'd dressed me from hairdo to tea-length dress, but I insisted on kicks instead of heels.

"No, high-top black," I said.

She clapped. "Oooh. Classic! Working the mysterious new-girl angle."

I had to laugh. "Never."

"Never say never, Gracie girl; you have no idea the power you wield as the new kid in town."

"That is an understatement."

She blinked twice, signifying a sudden change in topic. "Is lacrosse a spring sport at your new, brainiac school?"

"Yep."

"So what clubs, sports, activities are you 'falling' into?"

"The Apathetic Introvert Club. No agendas or meetings."

She crossed her arms and leaned back. "Gracie Artemis, you must fulfill your destiny," she teased.

"Whoa, I'm in trouble now, Sofia, goddess of Wisdom." But it was true, proven when she poked a branch into my cocoon three years ago, in the form of a lacrosse stick. Enticing me out of my lofty-loner ideals and make-believe world and onto a team of real characters – not fictional ones. It was a blast.

Opposites on the field, she defended in goal, while I scored on offense. In between, teammates filled a gap I hadn't realized existed. I belonged to something.

Her cell buzzed, she looked at it, "Uh, oh! Gotta go! You're awesome! Go make friends!"

A natural phenomenon, Sofi draws you in like gravity, proves you matter, and lights up every room.

4

"The Way I Am" – Charlie Puth

"Set up the board, Scout," Dad said.

Inquisitive, I reminded him of a character in his favorite movie, *To Kill A Mockingbird*. In addition to Dad's hazel eyes, I'd inherited his love of chess. When I was little, I'd climb up on his knee to observe and absorb techniques when Croc, his aviator buddy, came over to play.

"You need to control the center of the board..." he began.

"And visualize multiple moves ahead," I said.

That is how we formulated my college plan – researching the best women's lacrosse programs and cross-referencing demanding academic institutions that offered financial aid. I like math and science, so we'd come up with my top three that offered both: Northwestern University, Boston College, and the Naval Academy.

It was Croc who'd encouraged my application to the academy, and even wrote my letter of recommendation. Dad had been hesitant, which bothered me, but agreed it was a good backup choice.

I'd applied to each, jumping through all necessary hoops, especially for the Naval Academy, which required a first-place nomination from our district U.S. Representative.

As we hunkered down to play Dad said, "Movie night Friday, unless you have something at school." He moved the white pawn in front of his queen two spaces forward.

I studied the board, then mimicked his move with my black pawn. "I think there's a Spirit Squad pep meeting I'm absolutely dying to join."

One of his eyebrows arched, the other formed a checkmark, a classic supercilious expression.

I lifted one eyebrow in return, mocking him, "Just kidding. How about Sherlock Holmes, *A Game of Shadows*?"

His forehead melted into a smile as he quoted from the movie, "The lady insists."

We played. The silence was natural, normal. A given.

"Lacrosse club tryouts tomorrow," he said, moving a piece.

I scanned the entire board. Formulating an attack. "Yep."

"You want me to be there?"

I looked up at him. "Thinking the needs of our nation outweigh the tryouts of the few," I said, dripping sarcasm like the syrup on our ritual Saturday morning pancakes.

"I know you've got this, but it's the least I can do."

Even the best strategies can be compromised. I was to fly through senior year at my old high school on auto-pilot, play lacrosse, practice karate and then head off to college. In that order.

Then came a request from a former commanding officer, now a three-star general. New scenario. Dad's twilight tour would be at the Pentagon. Out-maneuvered, I tended to withdraw, lacking the ability to improvise, adapt, and overcome.

Dad flew to report with a cargo load of guilt, and my flexible, free-spirited mom plucked me out of the solid, midwestern Oak that I trusted, to plop me into a flowery Eastern Redbud that I don't.

He's following orders. She's anticipating an empty-nest as soon as they can nudge their last fledgling out.

But unlike my outgoing siblings... my wings aren't ready to fly.

***

I stepped into the gladiator arena.

Tryouts. A select team. The elite players from the best high school teams in Northern Virginia, where babies teethed on lacrosse sticks instead of pacifiers.

Teenage girls wearing hoodies from various schools eyed the group confidently brandishing exclusive dark green club warmups.

I stood apart, reading two volumes of body language.

The former flicking ponytails, chewing on lips, checking and rechecking their shallow stick mesh.

The latter laughing, teasing or looking smug.

A muscular man wearing the club hoodie and ball cap approached. "Ladies, bring it in. Take a seat."

The club team members sat at his feet and the rest of us filled in behind. He waited for everyone to get settled as he squinted and scanned the group.

"I'm Coach MacGavin. Rotate your ankles as I talk." He paused, his jaw firm, dark eyes surveying the pairs of cleated feet for compliance. "We'll warm up with a couple laps around the field." He gestured to the sideline and twirled his finger around twice then pointed to the middle of the field. "Do sprints midline to goal, pass and catch exercises, one on one play, and finish up with a mini-scrimmage. Questions?"

A girl lounging back on her elbows in the front row asked, "Do we get new uniforms this year?"

He stared her down. She lowered her gaze and sat up.

"Any questions about tryouts?"

No one dared.

"Okay, everyone up, take two laps."

I stretched my legs, did three quick jump squats, picked up my stick and took off in the direction of his finger circles. Running at a comfortable pace that barely raised my resting heart rate, I stayed outside of the sidelines without cutting corners. After the second lap, I returned to my original spot and continued to stretch, this time using the stick up above my head to loosen my shoulders for passing and shooting.

"Do you always run with your stick?"

Coach MacGavin spoke from behind me, leaning back with muscular arms across his barrel chest.

"Yes, sir," I responded, noticing the rest of the players finishing up. Sans-sticks.

"Why?"

"Habit."

"What's your name?"

"Grace Halsted."

He scribbled on his clipboard. I waited patiently.

"What year are you?"

"Senior, sir."

He looked up from his notes.

"Military family?"

I nodded, noticing his high-cropped gray sideburns above wide, square shoulders.

"Which branch?"

"Marine Corps."

"Let's see whatcha got," he said under his breath, a twinkle in his eye.

Maintaining eye contact, I responded, "Oorah."

He snorted, looking back at the athletes who were finishing up the run. He blew his whistle and shouted, "Line up for sprints. First one at half-speed, jog back, then three-quarters, and so forth."

I trotted to the center of the field.

"Coach, do we need our sticks?" One of the club players called out.

He looked at me, then her. "Seems like a good idea."

As everyone fanned out across the field on the midline, the uniform-question girl stepped in next to me, dead center.

"What do you think you're doing?"

I didn't state the obvious. Why bother? One and done and out of here is my mantra this school year. Not looking for a best friend for life and sure I wouldn't find one on this club.

"What's with you and your stick? You sleep with it too?"

Oh. Got it. Stepped into a hornet's nest. Too frickin' bad.

"Get set. On my whistle, half speed," Coach shouted.

I crouched down to the ground, stick clutched in my fist like a relay baton.

TWEEEEET!

Launching low, I raised up in increments, checked left and right. No one. Apparently, my 50% was above the power curve. Throttling back, I cruised to the goal line, just ahead of the alpha chick on my right.

Sprints. Pass/catch. One v one. Mini-scrimmage. I went through the motions keeping one step ahead.

"Whoa girl, you smoked it!" shouted an enthusiastic girl on my left. Tryouts were over and we were collecting our stuff. I studied her.

"Seriously! No effort! You're frickin' pro! For real."

Scanning her face I saw no malice.

"What's your name?" she asked, adding, "I'm Lanie."

"Hey," I said, as she zipped up a veteran club jacket.

"Grace." Thought for a second, then said, "Gracie."

"You made it for sure, no worries." A car horn blasted. She waved to the impatient driver, none other than Alpha Girl. "That's my ride. See ya soon, Gracie!"

Coach called out, "Everyone good?"

Those of us left, nodded.

"Roger that." He walked toward the locker room.

I waited for everyone to clear out, went to the goal and emptied my backpack. A dozen familiar yellow balls bounced across the green turf. Each had a name on it written in black marker. Signed by former teammates. Sofi's idea, so I could take them with me. One by one, I scooped and shot to fill the empty net. Alone again.

5

"The Outsiders" – Eric Church

Anticipating letters of early acceptance, it didn't matter how I whittled away the remaining academic hours I needed to escape high school. After a wasted week reviewing syllabi and collecting required textbooks, I yearned for parole, but before time off for good behavior, there was an all-school assembly.

"BZZZZZZZZZZZZZZZZZZZZZ"

The not-so-fast dismissal buzz sounded. Proceed to the gymnasium. Do not pass GO. Shouts, insults, and laughter accentuated the teens' stampeding through crowded hallway canyons. I followed on the fringe, dodging slamming locker doors and students diving into the melee to join friends.

"Wait up!" cried a frantic girl.

"Got chu gurrrl!" A hand grabbed and pulled her in.

I remembered a wildlife documentary describing two different herd scenarios. In the first, exemplified above, the stronger surrounded the weaker animals to protect them; in the other, the stronger fought for the center, putting the weaker in between them and potential predators.

School administrators guarded the exits, redirecting wayward inmates to the assembly instead of their getaway vehicles in the parking lot. Sounds escalated in the hot gym, pulsating beat of the pep band drums and students stomping up bleachers to sit in designated year groups.

The tide carried me toward the senior banner on the far side of the gym. In the Junior section, I recognized not-helpful-Perfect-Messy-Bun surrounded by her adoring peeps vying for attention as they crammed together for selfies. Her composed smile was identical in each picture, whereas her friends pursed their lips, stuck out their tongues, and flashed typical two-finger peace signs.

Taking the bleacher stairs two at a time stretched my cramped leg muscles. I reached the last row of the balcony in the corner under metal-bolted ceiling beams. From my perch, I saw Principal Atkins usher in three renegades and point to the junior section.

Captured escapees. The first guy tucked his long hair behind his ears and hit the bleacher stairs. He wore long tan shorts, a patterned shirt, and flip-flops. Following was a shorter, thin guy, dressed in khakis and a bright blue Best Buy employee polo. Last was a hunched-over, six-foot-something dude in a black hoodie and skinny jeans; the epitome of Ichabod Crane. They climbed nonchalantly up, up, past their rowdy peers to the nose-bleed seats, where a smattering of kids lounged, ambivalent to the festivities on the gym floor.

I surveyed.

Populars. Wannabees. Good vibers. And Outcasts.

I imagined this scene being played out in high schools throughout the country, minus the interpreters signing. School principal welcomes students. Warns against the evils of social media and confirms cyberbullying will not be tolerated. Then switches to the rah-rah-rah segment. Band. Cheerleaders. Poms. Team captains. Football first, then the others come down to talk, each group just as monotonous as the last. Until the cross country captains.

Game changer.

A lanky, freckled, red-haired guy in shorts and running shoes sauntered up to the mic accompanied by a girl with skin the color of a latte and form-fitting jeans that showed serious training.

"After you," he said.

She grinned and stepped up to the microphone. "Hello! I'm Sienna. Everyone who participated on our cross country team last year, come on down!"

Both of them waved to the crowd, inviting students to the floor. The rumbling of feet and excited voices erupted as students poured off the bleachers onto the gym floor, high-fiving and fist-bumping as they surrounded the two captains.

"Hi, I'm Josh." The guy introduced himself. He shoved his hands into his pockets, looking at the students. "Everyone makes it, and no bench to sit on to watch others compete. First seven runners are the scoring team, top five finishers in a meet are scored. Everyone else runs for fun!"

"If your sport is off-season, or," Sienna twitched, and reached her right hand back behind her, "... if you want to keep in shape..."

"Or GET in shape!" Josh butted in, finishing her sentence. Amiable. They played off each other well. Sienna's hand flew back and forth again, as Josh continued, "Our first practice is Monday after school. I'll leave you with some t-shirt wisdom." He turned around so the crowd could read the slogan on his back:

We Run Cross Country for the Hill of it.

Sienna shifted but didn't move her hand back. However, she did shoot an annoyed look over her shoulder.

Oh. I get it. Cell phone in her back pocket. Someone is prank dialing. From my vantage point, I could see a guy hiding, looking down at his hands as a buddy blocked for him. It was the dude who signed directions on the first day of school.

"I challenge ALL of you, put down your PHONES, tie on your shoes, and make a run for it!" Sienna shouted.

Right on cue, the now-you-can-leave dismissal buzz.

"BZZZZZZZZZZZZZZZZZZZZ!"

As everyone scrambled to leave, because first to the parking lot won't have to wait forever to get out, I pondered.

Should I – just do it?

***

My phone vibrated in my backpack on the walk home. Surprised, I slid the strap off my shoulder, unzipped the side pocket and grabbed it. Expecting to hear Sofi's cheerful voice I answered. "Mmh, yel-low."

"Grace Halsted?" A man's gruff voice asked.

I bit my tongue to switch off the sarcasm. "Yes."

"This is Coach MacGavin." Pause.

My heart skipped. "Hello, Coach."

"You didn't mention you signed a letter of intent."

My heart stopped. Uh-oh. I've been Googled. Is that a problem for club play here? "I didn't think it mattered."

"That's right, but the fact you didn't, does."

I squinted and grit my teeth. "Sir?"

"Offering you a spot. Practices are six to eight, Monday and Wednesday evenings. Games are most Saturdays."

I exhaled. "Thank you." Another box checked. But – "Um, Coach, thinking of conditioning with the cross country team at my high school. Runs are after school. Is that okay?"

"Only if you don't miss games for meets."

"I won't, I don't have to compete."

He chuckled. "Wait until they see you run. Going to carry a stick?"

I laughed, "Better not; might be considered a weapon."

"Considering how you shot after tryouts I have to agree. It's a skill we can use."

6

"Lean On Me" – Club Nouveau

A sucker for political plots, international intrigue, clever operatives and clandestine missions, the class "U.S. History: Civil War Spies," intrigued me at registration.

On the first day of class we were bombarded by a frenetic elf, our teacher Ms. Davis. New to this school, she introduced herself as a self-proclaimed caffeine-fueled, yoga fanatic with a severe history addiction. Her desk plaque read:

HYSTERICAL FOR EVERYTHING HISTORICAL

In addition, her enthusiasm for espionage and riddles was contagious. "What was the getaway car used in the 2002 movie *The Bourne Identity?*"

Silence. First thing Monday morning and most students were still asleep. She lifted her arms out, hands dangling, shuffled across the front of the classroom moaning like a zombie. "No need to raise your hand, just blurt it out so I know someone has a pulse."

Never the eager brown-noser upfront, or the deadbeat dozer in back, my favorite spot was halfway back in the row closest to the door. Amused, I tapped seconds down with my index finger, then threw her a bone. "A beat-up Mini Cooper."

She nodded eagerly, then stepped up on the empty seat in front of me and hopped onto the cabinet that stretched the length of the room. "That's right! Never underestimate the might of the mini!" She punched her fist in the air.

Startled students woke up and laughed.

Ms. Davis marched down the solid surface, stepping over homework turn-in trays, to point out a brown cardboard box with a gravestone drawn on it that read: "R.I.P. NO NAME, *where your grade goes to die*." Then she said in a cryptic voice, "Travel back in time with me. It's June 1863.

I'm General Meade surveying the battle from Cemetery Ridge outside of Gettysburg." She raised her hand flat above her eyebrows in the classic search pose and paused.

A cell phone buzzed behind me. Several students shifted and provided courtesy coughs to cover until the culprit could silence it. Instead, an excited voice fake-answered, "Hello! General? No sir. Not looking good for the home team! Take a look yonder northwest-a-ways. Best be git'n some of yer blue butt-tallions over to Little Roundtop lickety-split or we're flanked!" Everyone, including Ms. Davis, cracked up.

Not missing a beat, her hand flew to her ear. "Excellent field observation soldier! Soldier? Can you hear me?" She looked at her hand, shook it, then hopped two steps sideways and held it up again. "Can you hear me now?" Applause broke out. She bowed, then asked, "What's wrong with this scenario?"

Students were wide awake and willing to answer.

"Too many trees and hills. No bars."

"Coverage sucks."

"He didn't pay his bill."

"Hardy har har." She hopped down. "Without beloved cell phones, how did the commanders gain intel?"

"Scouts."

"Messengers."

"Spies!" Added an enthusiastic kid in the front row, like she'd discovered the secret to world peace. Apparently, you can lead a horse to water, and make it drink.

Ms. Davis tapped her nose twice in affirmation, pointed one finger at her then held it up in the air to expound. "Who were these spies?" Her fingers spread apart and reached out to beckon to us. "What were their motives?" She crouched down low, searching the room. Students sat up to keep her in view.

She whispered from behind her desk, "... And how did they operate?"

***

At least fifty kids milled around the gym. Co-Captain Sienna stood with freckled Josh on her right, and the muscular dude I suspected was the prank-dialer stood on the left. Animated, she signed back and forth to them; Josh focused on her face, as she turned and tilted her head to listen to him, whereas the incredible hunk followed her hands and lips. I imagined both were crushing on her. A good-natured love triangle with Sienna as the apex. In Forrest Gump's, "a box of chocolates," these three represented sprinkled white, smooth milk and decadent dark.

Watching them interact triggered a craving, but not for sweets. I missed my team. An unexpected and overwhelming desire to belong again washed over me.

An older woman limped up to the trio. The consequence of logging in too many miles over a lifetime? Chopped hair framed her weathered face, a road map of wrinkles that indicated more frowns than smiles along the way. She blew on a whistle from a lanyard around her neck.

TWEEEEEEEEET! The rambunctious horde silenced. "I'm Coach Hudson. Sienna and Josh will take you through practice today. Make sure to get your permission slips in before Friday." She hobbled off. Thinking hobbled, brought to mind *The Hobbit*, and I wondered if she had hairy feet. Very hairy. Sienna's voice brought me back from the Shire.

"Easy run today folks," Sienna said and signed. She spoke in full sentences for the hearing but signed in the abbreviated version. Seamless. Made me wonder what her story was. "Let's start with two laps around the track, then a slow three-mile trail that loops through the woods back to the school."

Josh jumped in. "By slow, she means even basketballer Michael can keep up." He reached behind Sienna to give a friendly shove to Michael, who in turn, signed a common, inappropriate response.

Reading kids' expressions, it amused a few, confused some others, but most laughed like they were accustomed to the casual banter as they spilled off from bleachers onto the floor and outside through the doors.

My ponytail flicked back and forth to the beat of dozens of footsteps trotting up and down the dirt trail. The pace started slow. Groups gradually drifted apart: competitive runners ahead, those less so easing back.

I fell in with the second group. It was easy, comfortable, and gave me a chance to study the woody terrain as well as the group dynamics. The benevolent afternoon sun outlined the trees along the ridge in a golden haze. Once under their canopy, flickering sunlight and shadows filtered through the leaves creating the effect of an old film projector.

Kids chatted and encouraged each other. It was nice, but when I lost sight of the lead pack my competitive nature kicked in and I picked it up. When the faster runners were again in view, I coasted in between the two sets, in control of the center of the board.

Back in the gym, Sienna introduced Michael as our Tunes Chairman; he waved and plugged his cell into the sound system. "We're gonna cool down before rolling out so everybody line up."

Syncopated piano cords introduced the Jamaican-style "Lean on Me." With the volume cranked, the bottom of my feet tingled from the drumbeat vibrations as Michael joined Sienna to lead the line dance. For the first time, I not only noticed his cochlear implants but also that his wide inviting smile was as warm as a Caribbean sunset.

Kids jumped in behind to follow his fluid three steps forward. Clap. Three steps back. Clap. To the right side, clap, then back to the left, clap. Calm ocean waves flowing with the rhythmic tide. Treading in the back row, I eventually let myself be swept into the inclusive whirlpool.

After practice, I wandered back to the deserted, senior hall to grab the book I was reading: a murder mystery that pushed all my mandatory creep-me-out buttons.

The energy-efficient fluorescent lights at low power cast an eerie glow. Oooooooh. Reminded me of a morgue, which I haven't actually been in, but devouring fictional forensics had fed my imagination enough to make me feel like an expert.

I was in a good mood. Not a lightning bolt revelation for most, but for me, an anomaly of late. I walked a half-mile to Mom's car before realizing the keys weren't in my backpack. Using decisive detective work, I deduced they were still in my gym bag. Locked in my new athlete locker. Back to the morgue. Oh well, plenty of time to kill before lacrosse practice.

Someone had propped open the door with a rock. Huge safety violation. I kicked it away and shut the door. The deadbolt set. Deadbolt.

To keep out the bad guys. Unless – they were already inside, I teased myself. Joking aside, my senses kicked into overdrive as I slipped into the barely-lit locker room.

Inhaling, a mixture of various flowery fragrances and dirty socks bombarded my nostrils. Waiting for my eyes to adjust to the darkness, I reached out to locate lockers. Warm fingertips met cool metal, sending chills racing up my arm. Trailing my hand down them, I stepped on the balls of my feet, willing sneakers to sneak and not squeak, haha –

Bam! My lower right shin smacked into the low bench that I remembered, too late, was in the middle of the rows. Sharp pain sprinted up and down the bone as I bit my tongue to keep from cursing. "Smooth move," I chided, lifting my foot up on the bench to press a palm to my throbbing bump. It eased.

Skylights, tinted for privacy, provided little illumination, but I eventually found my locker number. Squinting, I bent over and quietly spun the dial to the right, slowly reversed left, clockwise again, then left again to stop. There was a faint tic as it caught, then –

Sqeeeeeakkkk. Wait a frickin' minute, another door? On the other side of the room? A cool draft blew through my bangs and the hair on the back of my neck stood at attention.

Swhoooooosh. Chunckk. It shut. Me in. With who? Had someone followed me from the parking lot? But I'd removed the rock and closed the door behind me. They had to have a key. This is just like one of my nightmares!

Hunched in an awkward position, I heard a melancholy whistle, a mournful version of "My Favorite Things" but not whistled by a cheerful nanny. "Toowh toowh toowh toowh toowh toowh toowh toowh toowh too-tooooooo..." Each note was stretched out, then released to echolocate off concrete walls, float through the empty air and hang from the cold, dark ceiling.

Caught between fiction and reality, I fought to stay calm. "Get a grip," Logic whispered inside my head.

"Should we run?" Imagination asked.

"Not yet, we need the keys," Logic answered, prying my trembling fingers from the dial.

Then, closer this time. "Toowh toowh toowh toowh toowh toowh toowh toowh toowh too-tooooooo..."

My hand jerked, ramming the release up. "CLICK!"

I pulled open the locker, grabbed my bag and took off. Running along the lockers to avoid the center bench, I reached the door sooner than expected and slammed into it. As my fingers fumbled for the handle, footsteps echoed behind me, coming closer!

I slammed through the metal door and escaped into the deserted hallway. The sound of my footsteps heckled me as I flew out of the haunted school.

7

"High Horse" – Kacey Musgraves

What the heck? I shivered, checking the rearview mirror for the hundredth time. The creepy feeling tailgated all the way to the lacrosse park.

Just the custodian, I reasoned. But then why not turn on the lights? Maybe he likes working in the dark. Because he's a vampire. A whistling, serial-killer vampire custodian. Makes perfect sense. My good mood vanished like Dracula at sunrise.

Lanie waved as she grabbed her gear from a Lexus SUV. She's sweet. Maybe this team won't totally suck. I heard, "Lanie, look, it's the Wildcat wannabe." Alpha Girl leaned back on her expensive ride with her arms crossed. Great. Googled again. For darker reasons.

"She's a 'gonnabe,' Charlotte," Lanie said. "Don't listen to her Gracie, Northwestern is the real deal. Congrats."

I nodded to her and ignored Charlotte, formally known as Alpha Girl, who shrugged and sneered, "Yeah, no doubt a sympathy pickup, to pad the middle of nowhere quota after recruiting out here."

Oh no. I thought back, trying to remember if I'd seen a Charlotte from Virginia on the NU new recruit roster. It would be just my luck. I had to know. "They scouted you?"

Her face flushed, she blinked. Awkward moment. Then she spat out. "Nerdy U? No thanks, probably have to walk around cow crap on the practice fields."

Both the welcoming cross country feeling and the whistling, serial-killer dread disappeared as sarcasm slipped in to fill the void. "Sounds about right," I said. Walking toward her, I faked left, then tip-toed around right in a wide berth.

Lanie caught the subliminal message; her friendly giggle accompanied me to the turf.

During practice, Coach worked his way around to the new players. Asking a question or giving a tip. He is solid. This team was the right choice.

Even though this was my second practice of the day, I coasted two steps ahead in sprints, no matter what percentage effort was requested. Coach called for a water break and walked next to me to the sidelines. Must be my turn. "Do you ever go a hundred percent?" he asked.

"Always." I relaxed and smiled a bit.

His eyebrows arched up. "How's that?"

I shrugged. "I go a hundred percent as fast as needed."

He chuckled and blew the whistle. "Two lines for drills!"

"Quit showing off." Charlotte hissed venom. She'd snuck up on me. I chastised myself for letting down my guard. Whether she liked it or not, I was here to play.

***

"Time for *The Good, the Bad and the Ugly*," Mom said. A game we played at dinner to describe our day, using the title from the epic 1966 Clint Eastwood movie. The Good, we were grateful for, the Bad, we accepted and moved on, and the Ugly was something we could change for the better.

"The Good. Starbucks drive-through was a long line of 'pay it backward.' The car behind me had three creative orders so I was thrice blessed! Afterward, at the stoplight, a car with smiling kids honked and held up their cups. Made my day," Mom said.

"Probably why the line was so long, nobody drinks plain old coffee there," Dad said.

I jumped in. "Sure they do, a plain cold brew, a plain dark roast, a plain blonde espresso." I ticked them off on my fingers.

"I rest my case. My turn, the Bad. I got cut-off by a Tesla on the beltway and refrained from blasting them."

"How magnanimous," Mom said, patting his hand.

He smiled at her. "I thought so."

"I've got two Goods and an Ugly," I said. This was unusual and captured their attention. "My history teacher is entertaining, I joined the cross country team, and picked up litter in the parking lot after lacrosse practice."

"Awesome!" Mom praised.

"Cross country?" Dad asked.

"Yeah, figured it'll be good conditioning for lacrosse season; I don't have to compete."

Dad laughed. "Since when?"

"One touch of nature makes the whole world kin." Sofi's index fingers completed a circle as she quoted Shakespeare on our post-dinner video chat. Her infatuation with the poet/playwright began years before during a semester abroad in England.

"Preach it, Willy," I said, head bowed, palms lifted to the screen.

"Besides British Lit – you're welcome for that suggestion by the way – and Earth Science to save the planet; what else are you taking?" she asked.

"Strength Training for P.E.; to balance out my two cardio teams."

She nodded. "Cool. Congrats on cross country. Proud of you. Any guys with great legs and buns running in front or do they follow to check out yours? Which shorts did you wear? The red ones I left look awesome if your legs are still tan. Double blink. "Have you found a karate studio yet?"

Wow. That train of thought definitely jumped the tracks. "No. Haven't had a chance."

"Well hurry up, your brown belt is so last season. You need to get the classic black update."

"Aye-aye, Sensei." I joked.

Sofi crossed her arms. "So, Mom did her familiar Good, 'glass is overflowing with coffee,' Dad did his normal road rage Bad – but you skipped it."

"Yeah. I had two Goods and an Ugly."

"But?"

I shrugged. "No butts, except for the tight running buns."

"Gracie-girl, you always have a Bad." She stared at me.

I blinked. The locker room. A shiver streaked across my neck from shoulder to shoulder.

"Spill it." Sofi pointed an accusatory finger.

I took a deep breath. "Well, there was an incident involving a whistling, serial-killer vampire custodian."

"What?" Her eyes grew round. "Do tell!"

I described my deserted locker room morgue whistler experience.

"Oh. My. Gosh! That reminds me of your recurring creepy old humming dude with a cane who brutally murdered the last person you thought about before you went to sleep nightmare!" In one breath. My sis has serious lungs.

"I know, right?"

"Didn't you have it every time we moved?"

"Yep."

"Have you had it yet?"

"Nope."

"Dang girl." She sat back.

When we shared a room as kids, Sofi's dreams consisted of princesses riding unicorns up perfect rainbows. Her worst nightmare was discovering a spectacular pair of pink, satin pumps at Nordstrom Semi-Annual Shoe Sale, only to find they didn't have a 7½. She loved horror stories and was the perfect co-pilot on my frequent flights of fancy no matter how twisted or warped the trip.

She glanced at her Fitbit, "Uh-oh, gotta cop some zzzzzs. PT at oh dark thirty tomorrow and ROTC third-years run it." Sofi brought her palms together in prayer pose and bowed her head. "Namasté."

Her chin popped up and one eye opened as the other squinted. "Oh! Think about somebody else before you go to sleep!" She winked and disconnected. Brat. So Sofi, shedding light on my dark side.

It was a moral dilemma – deciding who to think about if the dream returned tonight. A current horrible person? Who am I to judge? Someone already dead? Why make them die again? Perhaps a fictional character? They'd have to be pure evil to condemn them even if it were an unreal death. Not exactly conducive to blissful sleep.

That's the difference between reading and dreaming, you can close the book at a part you don't like.

I thought of my nightmare nemesis – the creepy, old humming dude with a cane – and shivered under my lack of comforter. Drifting off, a haunting lullaby came to mind, and it sounded an awful lot like, "A Few of My Favorite Things."

8

"Nobody Does It Better" – Carly Simon

I eluded the nightmare for the rest of the week, and thanks to duo practices, slept like a baby who was not being pursued by a homicidal maniac. Friday morning, I arrived early to Spies, and as usual, buried my nose in a book.

"Who can name the theme song to the 1977 Bond movie, *The Spy Who Loved Me*?" Ms. Davis asked.

A girl in the front row called out, "It's the same as the movie title, right? Like Adele's, "Skyfall."

"Nope. 'Nobody Does it Better.'" A deep voice behind me corrected.

Ms. Davis flourished her marker like a wand casting a spell, "Fifty points for Gryffindor! Carly Simon's song was the first not to bear the film name since *Dr. No* in 1962." Then she pointed to the girl in front, "But the movie's title was in the song lyrics, so twenty points for Hufflepuff!"

Ms. Davis, an obsessed Potterhead, fancied herself in the Ravenclaw house, because 'wit beyond measure is man's greatest treasure.'

"Now to the task at hand. Who were the daring spies during the Civil War? What motivated them to put themselves and those they held dear in jeopardy? Was it the love of family? Or country? Or were those not the catalysts, but a desire for riches, instead – to take advantage of a tragic situation for personal gain? So many boulevards, avenues, and underground railroads to explore!"

Ms. Davis captivated the classroom, inviting us to delve into the mindset of the time, to cast aside preconceived prejudices and view from different perspectives: Abolitionists, slave owners, politicians, soldiers, opportunists, lovers, husbands, wives, brothers, sisters, daughters, and sons.

"Would it surprise you to know, that many of the most successful spies were women?" Ms. Davis asked.

"Hah." A snort from the back-row sleeper section. Out of range of my peripheral vision.

"Care to elaborate?" Ms. Davis asked.

The same deep voice rumbled in a slow drawl behind me, "Women are fully adept in the art of de-cep-tion."

Ms. Davis feigned shock, her hand fluttering like a fan, "I do declare, I find your insinuation quite perplexing, good sir, please explain yourself." She peeked through spread fingers to read the seating chart, "Mister Kevin." Her voice rang true as a southern belle.

"With all due respect, Ma'am," his voice traveling further south, "my associates, Dervis and Hood Snap, call me Krutch, with a 'K.'" I recognized his voice, the scout on the pretend cell phone call at the Battle of Gettysburg.

"Pleased to make your acquaintance, Mr. Krutch." She curtsied. "Now would you be so kind as to elaborate?"

Curious, I shifted to look. One row over, leaning against the back wall, dinosaur patterned shirt sleeves rolled up the arm draped casually across his desk. A long leg stretched into the aisle, with a flip-flop dangling off the foot. One of the outcasts from the assembly.

Leaning out a little more, I saw his buddies on each side. Best Buy Guy and Ichabod Crane. Both nodded in agreement.

Ms. Davis was clearly amused. I had to admit. So was I.

***

Kids chatted at Friday's cross country practice, thrilled to run away from academics for the long weekend. "First, have a blast today. Second, tomorrow's three mile time-trial will determine the top seven for Tuesday's meet," Sienna signed.

Runners' cheers erupted as Josh and Michael swaggered out of the guy's locker room dressed as pirates. Josh wore Captain Jack Sparrow's trench coat, tricorn hat, and braided wig extensions. A plastic gold-capped tooth and stuffed parrot on his shoulder completed the look.

Josh's serious scowl was no match for Sienna's laughter. It made him grin from ear to fake, hoop-pierced ear as he stood on her right side.

On her left, Pirate Michael's torn brown pants stretched tight over well-defined quads, a white shirt with billowing sleeves and leather laces that couldn't contain his brawny chest. He'd leaped off the cover of a romance novel.

I imagined a fiery, redheaded lady swashbuckler holding him at sword-point, her plunging black smock exposing requisite cleavage, long legs in black tights wearing thigh-high leather boots at the ship's end of a plank.

The title was in a swirly, blood-red and gold font that read "Treasured Chests."

My snort brought me back from Fantasy Island through a sea of laughter. Mortified that I'd made a sound out loud – it was because of the play in front, not my novel narration.

What a hoot! I couldn't wait to tell Sofi.

Sienna spun the two pirates to reveal bulging backpacks with pockets dripping with silver, green, white, and gold Mardi Gras beads. Sienna tucked and zipped the bounty. "Time for Captain Josh and Scalawag Michael to hide their booty."

The crowd roared as the guys bowed and took off.

Sienna gave instructions. "You'll find treasure at each mile checkpoint, grab a strand, put it on, and hustle to the next! Don't forget, 'run for the hill of it.' Questions?"

A tall guy in aviators shouted, "What if we catch 'em?"

Sienna applauded with jazz hands. "You can take their treasure, Nick! Go for it!"

She then explained more rules, obviously buying time.

"Sienna! You're stalling! Let us go!" Nick shouted.

Everyone screamed and signed impatiently. Chasing pirate booty? Heck yes! I visualized a stained, torn parchment and was on it like X marks the spot.

The released runners ran in rabid droves after the pirates, fueled by the prospect of treasures. The competitive front runners quickly pulled ahead. I planned to dog the back of the lead pack led by Nick.

Rounding a curve at mile one, an evergreen bush was decorated in silver beads like tinsel, one strand per branch. Without slowing, kids pulled a string of beads off and threw it over their heads. I ripped one off and put it on. Three steps later it bounced off my chest and smacked me in the eye.

Ouch!

I wrapped it around my wrist. Better.

Up ahead on the dirt trail, four girls trailed Nick's group of guys. Making me fifth. I'd compete at the first meet if I ran like this tomorrow. I checked my six and no one was in sight.

At the two-mile mark, I approached a lone guy, who stopped to untangle a clump of green beads.

"Looks like a cluster of snakes," he said. Freeing two, he tossed me one. Wow. That was nice.

I smiled and caught it, adding it to my silver. "Thanks."

He noticed the bracelets.

"Great idea." He pulled his off and wrapped them around his palms. "It's only fun until someone puts an eye out."

I laughed. Interesting dude. Looked familiar too.

We kept running, side by side. The pace was okay, but he was huffing and puffing and we wouldn't close the gap.

"Do you ever breathe?" he asked, panting. He waved me on, "I bet you can catch 'em."

I agreed, but thought of lacrosse tryouts. Why go for a veteran's spot? I like running with – not against – this team. "I'm good if you don't mind the company."

"You counted, " he smirked. "Prepping for time-trials?"

I shrugged. Busted. "Four ahead, plus Sienna, makes me sixth."

He puffed. "Smart. You play poker?"

"A little. Why?"

"Not showing your hand – yet."

I held both palms out in front, weighing up and down like the scales of justice. He laughed, wasting precious oxygen.

We cruised down a green grassy slope to the three-mile mark. "Great, mud," he said, pointing out the deep footprints in the muck on the creek's bank. It would be slippery. "As if running doesn't suck enough." Pant, pant. "We get to wallow in mud."

He looked familiar. Best Buy Guy! Tidy khaki wearing one from the pep assembly and my Civil War Spies class.

Ahead, the girls splashed into the creek, hands dove down and lifted strands of white pearls. They scrambled up the bank to continue.

"My turn, you jump." I directed. He didn't argue and leaped across, clearing the water and mud. Spotting beads mid-stream, I extracted two and threw him one. He shook the water off, wrapped it around his hand and we carried on to the squish, squish, squish of my soaked sneakers.

"Thanks back."

"Yep." I asked, "Why torture yourself?"

"Square peg."

I caught on. "And the round hole is?"

"MIT. Rebuilding motherboards not enough – coding is only zeros and ones – and croquet's not NCAA sanctioned."

"Was tracking, but you lost me at croquet."

He shrugged, caught his breath. "Krutch, Hood Snap and I play competitive croquet. Krutch is ranked nationally."

What and who? "Hood Snap?" I asked. Cracking up that Ichabod Crane's real name was Hood Snap! Even better.

"We sit behind you in Spies. He's tall, wears only black."

"Then, you're Dervis?" I asked.

"Yeah. How'd you know?" His head tilted.

"In class, Krutch called you two his 'associates.'"

Looking sideways, his eyebrows raised. "Impressive."

"Impressive, excessive, obsessive, take your pick," I said.

He laughed at my self-deprecation. "You say that like it's a bad thing." We exchanged smiles and continued.

Running together, my shoes no longer squished. It was quiet, peaceful almost, except for our footsteps on the trail and his labored breathing.

"Talk nerdy to me," Dervis said, exhaling and inhaling.

"Pardon?"

"Keep mind off lungs that could explode any second."

I searched my brain for a quirky geek fact. "France just recognized Light Saber Dueling as a national sport!"

"I know! Do you fence?"

"Pfffft, seriously trained, with lacrosse sticks." I joked.

"You're the One."

"The... One?" I asked.

Rogue One: Star Wars.

"Hah! I wish. No. Just Gracie."

"Uh-huh. We'll see."

We crossed the chalk line together. Sienna met us with two strands of gold.

"Good job, Dervis! Who's your friend?"

"This is Gracie or Rogue, you pick."

Sienna laughed, "Welcome to the team, Rogue."

"Thanks," I said, and signed. Liking the nickname.

She smiled, "I'm Sienna. Glad you came out."

"Figured I'd give it a shot."

"Have you raced in a meet before?"

I shook my head. "No, play lacrosse, but like to run."

"Like a machine, she's a beast," Dervis said.

"Awesome! Harley and Jazmine play lacrosse too." She pointed to two girls who'd finished ahead of me. "Catch your breath, I'll introduce you when we chat strategy," Sienna turned to Dervis. "Did you do the C++ homework yet? It's messed up. Let me know what you get for number three."

"It's whack. Already texted Mr. Shultz. He'll revise and reassign. No worries."

"Figures. Thanks for the heads up!" She went to greet more finishers.

We watched her go. "Sienna's chill," Dervis said.

"Yep," I agreed.

Dervis is cool too. I read people as well as books and am a good judge of character, real or fictional.

9

"Get Your Way" – Jamie Cullum

Garlic welcomed me home when I entered our kitchen.

"Wash up; the Good is I harvested zucchini and made Veggie Meatless Loaf!" Mom said.

Dad grimaced. "The Bad is we're having Veggie-Meatless Loaf."

Grinning, I pointed out, "What's your pontificate? 'The mind is like a parachute – it only works when it's open.'"

Mom placed her treasured platter in front of us. The cheerful Bobwhite birds, in robin's egg blue and dark brown strokes, were hand-painted by my grandma when she was a teen working at the Red Wing Pottery Factory in Minnesota.

Dad gave me 'the eyebrow,' stabbed a piece, and shoved it into his mouth. He chewed, swallowed, and proclaimed, "Delicious! Tastes like Chickenless Tofu!"

Mom feigned insult, "Okay Mr. Food Critic, what will *you* make for dinner tomorrow night?"

"Reservations at a steak house!" he said.

"No thanks, here on the grill, with veggies and salmon." I countered.

"Only if you're my sous chef," he said.

"Fair enough."

"Watching you two will be my Good!" Mom said.

"Speaking of Good – I made the competitive squad for our first meet."

"That's great, Scout! When and where?" Dad asked.

"Tuesday at the lake outside of town. Starts at five, but you don't have to come."

"We'll be there," Dad said. Mom agreed.

***

The three-day Labor Day weekend flew by. Despite the holiday, I reported to lacrosse practice on Monday evening. The air had lost the heaviness of summer, and the hum from overhead lights replaced both the dreaded buzz of mosquitos and the fading sun.

Coach MacGavin was on the field talking to his clone. Seriously, the nut didn't fall far from the tree. Despite being two inches taller, and twenty-some years younger, the dude in a ball cap and shades was obviously the fruit of Coach's loins. Which I'd rather not think about. However, Clone wore long, black shorts with black mid-calves pulled up to grapefruit-sized calf muscles. Total lax bro.

Watching the two reminded me of my dad and brother. Even though Dad never played lacrosse he read opponents and provided Jason with valuable intel. Another trait we shared.

I noticed the Black Knights Lacrosse logo on the younger man's chest. Wait a sec, as in West Point? I'd buy that, he looks Army Strong. I thought Coach was Corps, like my dad, but then, Jason is Army. Whatever boot fits.

"Don't even think about it. He's mine." Awesome. Flanked again. Dang it. Besides breathing oxygen, I'd done something else to set off Charlotte.

"Excuse me?" I asked.

"Ian. Coach's son. Back off," Charlotte hissed.

"You're dating – him?" I asked. In your dreams.

"Shhh, Coach doesn't know," she hissed.

Bet his son doesn't either. I arched an eyebrow, "Props to you." A potential Ugly for tonight's family dinner, albeit a smidge sarcastic. At least I didn't call her out.

"What's that supposed to mean?" Charlotte asked.

I shrugged, "Well done. It must be hard, with him at school so far away." In New York.

"Annapolis is only, like, an hour drive." She lifted her chin, confident I was buying what she was selling. "I may try to sneak him out this weekend."

A Naval Academy midshipman wouldn't be caught dead in West Point cadet apparel. Ever. Period. Exclamation Point. "Okay then. Wow. Have fun storming the castle," I said, channeling *The Princess Bride*.

It'll take a miracle.

Coach called us over. "Some of you know my son, Ian."

Charlotte coughed, covering her mouth with her palm. She whispered softly, "Some more than others."

Coach continued, "Defense will be with me at goal, and Ian will work with offense at midfield."

Meaning Charlotte and I would be coached by Ian today. Interesting dynamic, except I can't watch people humiliate themselves. This TV sitcom's premise makes me flee with ears plugged until I reach sanctuary, much to the delight of my siblings, who loved to tease me about it.

Lanie waved me over as she put on her goalie gear. "Lucky you! Ian's a sweetheart." Lanie watched Charlotte run to catch him and nodded for me to look. "Watch out, he went to our school and she's crushed on him since we were Juniors and he was Senior class stud."

"Thanks for the heads-up," I said, following her gaze.

Charlotte caught up to Ian and went in for the hug. He greeted her but turned sideways for the block. My brother used that maneuver too when girls fawned over him.

I looked away.

Ian stood on the midline, spinning a lacrosse stick back and forth, switching hands like it was second nature. For thirty minutes, he took us through passing and catching drills, encouraging anyone who messed up. He wasn't a flirt, and his light-hearted teasing put everyone at ease.

I wondered, did he have sisters? I imagined an older one, putting him in his place, and maybe a younger, tagging along as I had with my older brother. Jason played chess with me when Dad was gone, and he didn't send me away when he was hanging out with friends. He teased Sofi a lot, and she slung it back. I made a mental note to call and video chat with them both tonight.

"Line up for workup sprints," Ian said.

Charlotte scrambled next to him, scanning the field until she found me at the end of the line. Satisfied, she gazed at Ian.

He blew a short blast on his whistle and jogged with us. Half speed down, jog back. Three-quarters, jog back. A head taller, he surveyed right and left. On the third sprint, he called for one hundred percent.

TWEEEEET! On the whistle I took off, increasing speed as needed. For the first time, someone was in my peripheral vision. Shifting to high gear, I crossed the goal line knowing only one had kept up. Rotating to jog back, my eyes caught on a heart-stopping grin.

Ian.

Wow. Didn't see that coming.

Five seconds later, a defibrillator death glare.

Charlotte.

Yep. Now that one was expected.

In the last drill, Ian split us into two lines to do one v one ground ball pickups. Two players raced to scoop the ball and shoot.

Charlotte did a victory dance in front of Ian on each win. Undefeated, I jogged to the end of my line. When we were to go head to head, she dropped down to tie a cleat, or adjust her goggles and let the girl behind skip ahead. It was so obvious a player in the opposing line shouted, "Gracie, can you wait a second? Charlotte needs to fix her ponytail, again."

Awkward. "Sure," I said. "Take your time."

Charlotte stared at me, then called over to Ian standing downfield, arms across chest, stick in hand. "How about you show me how." She shot me a snotty look.

Ian thought for a moment, "Gracie, can you help me out?"

"Enjoy the show," I said, loud enough for both lines to hear. Everyone chuckled, except for Charlotte.

Okay, I know, sue me. I won't start it, but I will finish it.

Ian must have heard too. He walked to the front of the opposing line. "All right, Gracie? You're quick, let's see how you handle someone trying to out-muscle you," Ian said.

His one-sided smile looked so much like my brother, I slipped into sibling banter mode and shrugged. "The bigger they are, the harder they fall."

He laughed and tossed the whistle lanyard to another player, "You ref."

Charlotte snatched it away from her. As we crouched down into ready position, he lowered his sunglasses. "Let's see what you got."

I noticed his aviators were a lot nicer than mine. Looking up to reply, I fell into two luminescent blue-gray pools. Buttercup's words echoed in my mind, "with eyes like the sea after a storm."

TWEEEEET! Dang it! By the time I caught him he'd picked up the ball and put it in goal.

Charlotte whooped it up at my expense.

Surrendering the point, I asked for a rematch. He nodded. "This time we switch sticks," I said, tossing him my shallow pocket girl's stick. He caught it and handed me his. He must play middie or attack because it was not the long D-pole like Jason used on defense. When my brother had switched from middie to defense, I'd practiced with his old one. I had a plan.

All set, I avoided his eyes. Because. Well. Yikes.

Charlotte blew the whistle.

Ian was faster, but when he slowed to scoop I slid both hands together in a legal check and crashed hard into him.

The ball bobbled and bounced out of his stick pocket, I scooped it out of the air one-handed before it hit the turf, cradling it low. Knowing he would recover and expect me to raise the stick to shoot, I switched it to my left hand and put it bottom corner as I ran past the goal.

TWEEEEEET! Charlotte's sharp twill pierced the air as she pretended to coach. "Penalty! Throw her out, Ian!" She tossed the whistle up like a yellow penalty flag.

The rest of the players were cracking up.

Ian stood tall, laughing it off.

"Ref or play, bro," I said, lifting my chin. Challenging.

He shrugged, and loudly announced, "It was a legal hit." Walking over, he leaned in and said in a rumbling voice, "That's cold, checking a dude with his own stick."

I snorted, handing it back. "Muscle up to catch up."

"I'll keep that in mind."

He took his back.

I tugged on mine, but he didn't let go. Annoyed, my eyes traveled up the muscular chest, tripped on his square chin and fell into the blue-gray pools.

He winked and let go.

I gasped, to keep from drowning.

***

After a late dinner I got ready for bed and called Jason, he didn't answer so I hung up. Restless, I opened my Apple laptop and shot a video chat to Sofi.

"Howdy!" Sofi's cheerful face popped up on the screen.

"That was quick," I said.

She shrugged. "I'm writing a clinical report and need a break so it's perfect timing."

"How's it going?"

"Good, I've almost started. What's up?"

"Me. Running in a meet tomorrow, but buzzing from lax practice."

Sofi knew the club team dynamics. "Princess Charlotte pitch a fit?"

"Yep. Coach's college kid was home for the weekend and ran the offense. Lanie told me they went to the same high school and Charlotte was all over him. Kind of pathetic."

She leaned in. "Tell me more."

"Charlotte warned me..."

"Not about her – him."

Thinking back, I mentally tip-toed around the blue-gray pools to solid ground on family dynamics. "Reminds me of playing lacrosse with Jason, easy-going, teases a lot, but in a fun way."

Sofi grilled me. "He plays college? Where?"

"West Point."

"Ooh, get some Cadet action, girlfriend. Eye color?" This was expected, she believes, 'the eyes are the windows to the soul,' and provide valuable insight into wardrobe and interior decoration selections.

I hid behind his aviators. "He wore sunglasses and a ball cap most of the time."

"Most of the time, so he took them off?" She tapped the screen cross-examining like a prosecutor.

I sighed and gave in. "Kind of bluish-gray."

She clapped. "Yum. Tell me more."

"That's it." I checked the time on the upper screen. "Probably should jump and cop some zzzzz."

Sofi hung a U-ey. "Not so fast. What's his name?"

"Ian."

"Ian what?"

Grinning, I teased. "No, Ian MacGavin."

"Irish or Scottish? What year is he?"

Pulling my ponytail around to the front, I combed it with my fingers, acting nonchalant. "Not sure, probably first."

Sofi asked. "Ooooh freshman – plebes – can only date other plebes. Bet he's lonely. Did you flirt?"

"No!" I denied it too fast and needed to duck and cover. "He beat me in a ground ball pickup drill, so I swapped sticks and body checked him."

"I bet you did!" She laughed, eyes twinkling.

My face betrayed me and blushed.

"Looks like our borderline vegetarian is having a Big Mac attack."

Reverting to the sixth-grade me, my eyes rolled before I could do the sophisticated eyebrow. "Yeah, right."

"'The lady doth protest too much,'" Sofi quoted Shakespeare. "Three reasons why you can't go for him."

I counted on fingers, "Oh let's see. He's in college. At West Point. In New York."

"Nice use of inflection; you should take a drama class."

I buried my head in my hands. "You're impossible."

"I'm-possible-ly brilliant! Your elder-creature brain and maturity demand you age up! The rest is just logistics and geography. 'Thank U, Next!'" Sofi's head tilted in an Ariana Grande pose.

10

"So Am I" – Ava Max

After talking with Sofi, I needed a fictional villain who exemplified pure evil to think about before falling asleep in case I had "the nightmare." It came down to Star War's Jabba the Hut or Sauron from Tolkien's Lord of the Rings.

Tuesday morning I awoke from a dream featuring me as Princess Leia, wrapped in my white sheets, just as Solo was frozen in carbonite. The silver features on the cast were Ian's, not Han's. I groaned out loud as Sofi laughed in my head. Grumbling, I pulled on jeans and my cross country team hoodie and went to grab breakfast.

"Morning, Scout! Ready to race?" Dad asked.

I grabbed a banana, a spoon, and a jar of almond butter and sat down across from him.

"Sure."

"Just run for fun," he said.

My eyebrow raised; I looked at Mom. "What have you done with my father?"

She laughed, "Don't worry, he'll be back by spring for lacrosse season."

***

In my groggy-morning state, I'd left my uber-healthy Fa!rlife milk in the fridge – so an excruciating wait in the lunchtime cafeteria line to buy regular 2% was unavoidable. Fortunately, Mom had packed my pre-competition lunch consisting of a hard-boiled egg, an apple, and peanut butter and blueberry jam sandwich on whole grain, slightly-toasted, so the bread didn't get mushy.

Thinking about my happy meal, I noticed an unusual salad composition on the girl's tray in front of me. Rather than sprinkled or tossed, sunflower seeds, cranberry raisins, sliced tomatoes and shredded carrots were carefully arranged in triangular sections on the green spinach-leaf bed. It looked like a pie chart. I wondered how she ate it?

She took small steps as the line progressed, keeping a little extra space between her and two big, loud, rowdy guys in front of her. Her narrow shoulders were rigid, and a drawing pad was clamped between an elbow and ribs.

Just then one of the guys shoved the other, he tripped backward, bumped into the girl, and dislodged the pad.

It fell, shedding loose pages haphazardly. Shocked, wide-eyed Anime sketches fluttered helplessly to the floor.

The mortified artist watched, like that person at baggage claim whose suitcase pops open on the conveyor belt spewing undergarments and toiletries for all to see and judge.

Instinctively, I dove for the scattered art, but before I retrieved the last stray, an oblivious kid too busy texting walked across it.

A dusty footprint violated the delicate art.

I heard a sharp gasp and looked up as she winced.

"I can carry it until you have a free hand."

She scurried to the cashier station, set down her tray, and punched in a code.

I followed, offering the pages as soon as she could put her tray on top, place a hand underneath, and vice-grip with the other.

"Thank you," she whispered softly and crept away.

I shivered on the cool and damp cafeteria patio.

"Rogue! Over here."

Surprised, I caught Dervis' wave.

Despite secretly enjoying the nickname, I adopted a poker face. Thinking in military aviator's terms, when a newb pilot despises an assigned call sign, it sticks. Conversely, if they think it's cool, it'll be replaced as soon as they do something stupid. For instance, Two-Bagger, after the novice throws up twice in the cockpit during a training session.

Dervis sat with Krutch and Hood Snap. Not going to lie, this eclectic trio cracked me up.

"Here she is," Dervis introduced me.

I lifted my hand. "Hey."

Krutch gave me the once over, then said, "Ye."

Hood Snap nodded.

Awkward silence.

"She's running tonight," Dervis said.

Hood Snap clicked his tongue through his teeth and gave a thumbs up.

Krutch nodded once.

More awkward silence.

"She's going to Northwestern," Dervis told them.

Hood Snap whistled and held his fist up for a bump.

I did.

Krutch nodded. "Lit."

"She light saber duels with a lacrosse stick."

Hood Snap gathered fingertips to temples then exploded them out. Mind-blown.

Growing tired of the dude audition, and remembering Krutch's real name, I asked him, "So, is the K for Kevin?"

Appraising me, he smirked. "Sure is."

"Why Krutch, if you don't mind."

Dervis jumped in, "Because he uses his croquet mallet as a cane during matches."

Wondering, I asked, "Then why not Kane with a K."

The three silently exchanged looks.

After a moment Dervis said, "Valid argument."

Hood Snap lifted his chin and shook his head. "Ch."

Dervis said, "Krutch sounds better."

Curious to know, I asked, "Why Dervis?"

Before he could answer, Krutch adjusted an imaginary ascot and in a pompous British accent said, "I do say, it's his birthright, m'lady, Jasper Milton Dervis III."

"Jass-purr," Hood Snap said, pretended to lick a "paw" and groom himself.

Krutch added, "Milton, my good fellow, will you attend the polo match today?"

Dervis shot them both dirty looks.

Changing direction, I asked, "Hood Snap, right? How did you get your name?"

Things got interesting real fast, as Hood Snap mimed starting a car, shrugged when the engine failed to engage, unbuckled his seat belt, opened the door and exited. He stood, pretended to open the hood with one hand, while the other jiggled engine parts, scratched his head, rubbed his chin, then came to rest on the imaginary car. He shrugged and let go of the hood. Eyes wide as it shut faster than anticipated.

His face turned into Edvard Munch's, "The Scream," as he jumped back holding the "slammed" hand. He then showed the middle finger was missing the last joint and lifted his palms and eyes to the cloudy sky.

Krutch interpreted, "C'est la vie."

Grimacing, I said, "Ouch."

Dervis added, "Life is pain, Highness. Anyone who tells you differently is selling something." He offered me the quote from *The Princess Bride* and a chair.

I smiled and sat down. "Touché."

Discussion topics bounced from video games to graphic novels to movies. Quotes, plot lines and cinematography techniques were critiqued, destroyed and defended.

The *Gladiator* meme, "Are you not entertained?" came to mind. Raging nerds. My kind of people.

The conversation abruptly stopped. Krutch's carefree eyes narrowed and tracked something behind me.

I raised an eyebrow, imploring Dervis.

"A moment of silence in memory of Krutch's dignity," Dervis said, in a hushed tone.

That earned him a nasty, wicked stare from Krutch.

Dervis lifted his hands up like Spock doing the Vulcan Mind Meld, "Your pain is palpable."

Krutch's gaze shifted, to the distant field and tree line.

I glanced sideways and back to see Perfect-Messy-Bun & Co. emerge through the cafeteria doors. The group turned to parade along the sidewalk and wall of windows. After a quick side glance in our direction, their leader focused forward, her chin held high. The rest checked their reflections, keeping in casual sync.

"Mandi and the Mannequins," Dervis whispered as they walked by us.

Hood Snap struck a series of poses, holding his hand up pretending to shoot selfies: a two-fingered Peace sign, crossed eyes with sucked-in cheeks, stuck-out tongue with rock 'n roll hand sign.

Dervis motioned to Krutch's sullen face, and sighed, "She craves attention from everyone, but one. They used to be..." he stopped mid-sentence.

I looked at Dervis, tracking his line of sight.

A mousey brunette trailing the girls waved to him, then noticed me, frowned, and hurried to get back in stride.

Hood Snap mocked her wave, fluttered his eyelashes and blew Dervis a kiss, making a heart with his fingers and thumbs.

Dervis scowled.

Trying not to grin, I looked away and noticed two dark figures sitting on a bench under a tree. One was the artist girl, or was it? Squinting, I studied the two. They sat facing each other, mirrored images with chin length black hair, tucked behind an ear, crisp white shirts under black cardigans, short pleated skirts, and knee-high black stockings. The only difference was one had on ballet flats, and the other wore black kicks.

Curious, I asked, "Dervis, do you know the two under the tree at your one o'clock?"

He shifted his gaze to the right a notch. "Sure, Scooter and Skater, the Anime twins," he answered matter-of-factly.

My interest peaked. "I saw sketches by the one on the left I think. She's good." Noticing the skateboard leaning on the bench next to the girl in the Vans, I added, "So left to right, Scooter and Skater?"

"Yep. Scooter rides a scooter, but leaves it in her locker so she can carry her art supplies everywhere."

"Everyone has a nickname here," I chuckled.

Krutch rejoined our conversation. "All but Dervis, who creates and bestows them at will."

Hood Snap nodded.

"Fair 'nuff," I agreed.

11

"Hooked On a Feeling" – Blue Swede

Maple leaves fluttered like gold and red banners along the green hills. Gray clouds had surrendered to a vivid blue sky, and the late afternoon sun warmed my face. It was a good day to run for the hill of it.

Before the pre-race warmup, I chatted with Harley and Jazmine, who goes by Jaz, the fellow top seven runners who also played lacrosse. They were thrilled to learn I was on the elite Sharp Shooters squad even though they play for a competitor because we'd be teammates in the spring.

"Coach MacGavin is tough," Jaz said, as she tied her spike shoes. "You must be really good."

I shrugged.

Harley asked, "What position do you play?"

I dodged, "Where I'm needed."

"Cool, but we need a finisher. Can you score?"

"Played left attack last year," I said, a key position to bring the ball to goal, whether to pass or shoot.

Harley nodded then bent in half to stretch hamstrings, palms flat on the ground. "Sweet. Bet Charlotte Winslow is super thrilled. She's such a team player."

I hesitated, not able to read her expression.

Jaz burst out laughing. "'All for One,' as long as she's the One! Rumor has it, she calls teammates her 'assistants!'"

"Total piece of work, her goals to assists ratio is whack," Harley said, standing up to look at me. "Knock her off the leader board, Gracie."

Jaz stripped off her warmups. "But watch your back, playing with or against, she'll be gunning for you, and won't hesitate to throw you under the team bus."

"Thanks for the heads up." Dropping to the ground, I removed my spikes, and slipped into the side splits, right foot in front, switched to left forward, then straddle splits down the middle. I folded to lie my torso and face on the cool grass.

"What the heck, girl!" Jaz exclaimed.

I lifted my chin to look up at her wide eyes. Realizing my position was rather peculiar, I explained. "Karate."

"Killer! You should talk to Michael! He's a black belt," Harley said.

I said, "Figures, he's got the moves."

"So you've noticed?" Jaz laughed.

Busted, I blushed. "Hard not to."

***

Michael jogged up to the team tent as Sienna and Josh finished talking to Coach Hudson. Our vibrant red uniform tank and shorts contrasted well with his dark-skinned muscles. He looked good and confidently smiled at Sienna.

Coach frowned at him, then blasted the annoying whistle and waited, hunched over with her hands on hips, for the team to gather in front of her.

Pondering her crotchety disposition, I decided she hadn't stored enough endorphins to sustain a positive attitude after she could no longer run. Surrounded by runners getting their high on must add insult to her injuries. Those who can, do. Those who can't, coach?

Coach nodded to Sienna and said, as Sienna signed, "In the past, the first home meet has been a bunch of silliness instead of a serious athletic competition. I expect this team to stay on task. No shenanigans. Is that clear Michael?"

Palms shifted up, glorious deltoids raised, he feigned surprise, shrugged then nodded. However, his signed response was a wordplay on "she nanny cams" that raised eyebrows.

But no one dared smile.

Except me.

Coach Hudson caught it, but I held her gaze and lifted one eyebrow as if waiting for further relevant instructions. She doesn't understand sign. Shaking her head, she mumbled something to Sienna, then hobbled away.

Sienna and Josh took over, per usual. "Okay peeps! The powers that be drew straws and it's ladies first today. That means Varsity gals then Varsity guys, JV gals and JV guys.

"For new runners, low score wins. First-place finish, one point, second, two points, tenth, ten points. When our first five finish, place numbers add up to our total score." Her eyes flickered over to where Coach was talking to the referee, then added, "Warm up with a slow jog twenty minutes before your race. What's our motto? When they score high?"

"WE SCORE LOW!" The team chanted.

Runners broke off into groups. Top seven V girl runners, Jaz, Harley, Molly, Tonia, Claire and I jogged with Sienna and the other Varsity girls.

After we'd run a couple hundred meters my taut muscles loosened as my competitive brain kicked in. I asked Jaz, "What's with Coach's Debbie Downer speech?"

"Fans and other runners line the course to cheer. They don't care what team you're on or how slow you go. Some even blast music. It's a party. You'll see."

"Sounds like a Race For The Cure," I said, as we rotated to run back.

"It is! Our team does the Race every fall!" Jaz said. "We dress in tutus and get pink paint powdered when we cross the finish line. Our principal is an eighteen-year cancer survivor so lots of students and staff participate."

I said, "Count me in. I've run with my sister, brother and his girlfriend, in memory of her mom." I wrote a mental note to tell Sofi about it tonight, and Jason this weekend, so he could tell his girlfriend Joan.

Sienna steered us to the starting line.

My heart was thumping. I inhaled and exhaled slowly. Count jerseys, and do the math. On the run. Easy. Calculate. Run for the hill of it. Can do.

I shook out my arms, then one leg at a time, going over the course in my head. Slope, curve, tree line, hill, creek, curve, clearing, home stretch, finish. I'm glad our first meet was at our home course.

Our top three were at the white chalked line, second three next, and the rest behind. The other two teams mimicked us, each team clustered in a patch of trimmed, green carpet.

Sienna knew I was going out quick, but would drop back to observe her and the other experienced runners. "Just don't burn out, we need you at the finish."

"I'll be there." I wasn't going for the win for the first time in an athletic competition. In this race at least. I just needed to override my overachiever competitive nature. Wish me luck.

"ON YOUR MARKS!" The starter raised the pistol to the sky, waiting for the restless pack to steady.

I crouched, fingers tingling in anticipation.

CRACK! I shot forward. Going out fast had been Dad's idea. Less chance of catching a spike in the ankle during the chaotic start.

The half-mile mark was a gnarly oak that reminded me of Coach. Sienna moved up to my elbow. Checking over my shoulder, four red uniforms, five orange, three gold. Like the fluttering leaves above us.

Faces along the sidelines blurred and blended together. Cheers of encouragement roared in my ears as I focused five feet in front of me. We hit the next hill at a mile and a half, Sienna at my elbow. Behind, three red. Two orange. One gold. I checked my watch. We were on pace.

On the downslope, Sienna ran next to me, fist-bumped her chest and pointed two fingers at the top of the next hill. Two-mile mark.

I throttled back and let others pass. Not an easy thing.

At the bottom of a hill, I jumped the creek and heard it.

"Ooh-gah-checka-oohgah-oohgah-oohgah-checka-ooh-gah-oogah-oogah-checka..." What the hecka? A song from the *Guardians of the Galaxy* soundtrack, "Hooked On a Feeling," boomed ahead as I scrambled up the bank and around a curve into a clearing.

Who else could it be, but Krutch. Speakers blasting, dressed in plaid shorts, tank and flip-flops, prancing like a goofball as he serenaded runners. He shouted, "Rock on!"

I just about peed my shorts.

And then Hood Snap. Dressed head to toe in black. Pounding on, no kidding, a frickin' cowbell.

Couldn't help myself, I screamed, "More cowbell!"

He heard, held it high and banged as I ran by laughing.

A glimpse of Coach next to the course, on the other hand, exposed she wasn't amused.

Recalibrating, I returned to race mode for the last mile. Molly, our fifth runner was falling back. I caught her on the home stretch and slowed to match her pace, but she shook her head, waving me forward. "GO!" she gasped.

I nodded once, picked it up, and passed an orange jersey to finish behind four red, a couple orange, one gold, with the knowledge we'd won.

Catching up to my happy teammates for the cool down, they congratulated me, and as my leg muscles shed lactic acid, my heartbeat returned to normal but felt a little fuller.

***

"Tell. Me. Everything!" Sofi gushed through the screen.

"Not gonna lie, it was a lot of fun," I said, shrugging.

"Running? Over hills, and Dale, whoever he is. Poor guy. Talk about issues. 'Feel free to use me like a doormat.' Sofi rambled. Kind of. She's more of a running crazy commentary that you need to jump on and go along for the ride.

"Sort of, yeah. My teammates were supportive, and get this, the fans! Totally into it. Remember the croquet guys?"

"Krutch, Dervis and Hood Snap? Duh! Seriously best callsigns ever!" Sofi said.

"Well Krutch and Hood Snap were at the two-mile mark, lip-synching and dancing to "Hooked On a Feeling.""

"From *Guardians of the Galaxy*?" Starring hunka-hunka burning love Chris Pratt and that green chick?"

"Yes! And get this. Hood Snap was playing a cowbell!"

"No way! For reals? What a hoot! I love them already. Are they bro-in-law material?"

"NO! Friends, and not 'just friends' and especially not 'friends with benefits' so don't go anywhere near there. It was just, well, funny, fun, to compete, with, instead of against, you know?"

"No. Weirdo. But kudos sis. Sounds like you're kill'n it."

"Thanks. Oh. The team dresses up and does the Race like we did, in October, you can come and do with if you want," I said, hopeful.

"I'd love that. Shoot me the date. Carry on my wayward sister, catch you later!" Sofi blew me a kiss and peace'd out.

I love her. For reals and ever and ever.

12

"Mission Impossible Theme" – Dominik Hauser

Early Friday morning, students wandered into Spies of the Civil War to the cheeky mix of old television theme songs. I recognized some of the campy spy shows I'd watched with my family, *The Wild Wild West*, *Get Smart*, and *Mission: Impossible*.

After the buzzer, the music faded and students stared at the open door, expecting energetic Ms. Davis to scramble in late. Instead, we heard a muffled voice shout, "It's a matter of life and death! Name the 2015 spy film based on the 1964 TV series of the same name that featured the collaboration of a CIA operative and his rival KGB agent!"

Front row brown-noser dropped to her knees to look under the teacher's desk as Dervis shouted, *"The Man From U.N.C.L.E.!"*

Ms. Davis burst out of her top-secret, off-limits metal locker. Fortunately, it was vented. "Water!" she croaked, feigning heat exhaustion as she fanned herself and took a long drink from her BPA-free water bottle, the one with a peapod balanced on a globe that read, Peas On Earth.

Our attention was captured.

"We've tip-toed through the whos and whys of Civil War spies," Ms. Davis said, dancing a little jig. "So today we'll try the hows on for size, meaning, dun dun dun dunn – disguise." She tugged a scarf from a wheeled desk chair, causing it to spin, then draped the scarf over her head and shoulders like a shawl. "Now children," she croaked, in a high-pitch, old lady voice. Hunching over, she limped to her chair with the aid of an imaginary cane. "Today we'll learn how to 'inhabit' the look, to 'own' the deception."

Cueing up the whiteboard projector remote with a shaky hand, she clicked on a WIRED video featuring former CIA Chief of Disguise

Jonna Mendez. Using clips of spy movies and tv shows, she identified transformation do's and don'ts. It was fascinating.

Ms. Davis shut it down and announced, "You will have two weeks to create a PowerPoint presentation on a Civil War spy of your choice. Who, where, and how they spied." Pulling the scarf up over her nose, she glanced surreptitiously side to side, and whispered, "Choose wisely."

We sat inside at lunch. It had rained off and on all morning. Dervis scowled at the raindrops racing down the window behind Krutch and Hood Snap. "Running today is going to suck."

Krutch chuckled, "You say that every day."

"Well today is a double suckage day," Dervis grumbled.

"That why you nabbed the last two Little Debbie oatmeal gems?" Krutch said, reaching for Dervis' tray.

Dervis slapped his hand. "Nope."

"Come on bro, you don't need both."

Dervis lifted his chin and surveyed to the end of the windows. "Maybe one is for someone else."

Krutch laughed, "Who you pouring sugar on?"

"Nunyah," Dervis replied.

"Noped and nunyahed, whoa, must be serious," Krutch said, winking.

Entranced, I sat next to Dervis, and bit my lip to keep a straight face, then we all followed Dervis' gaze, zeroing in on the MessyBun crew.

The mousey brunette from the other day was sitting on the fringe watching us. She glanced from Dervis to me, frowned, then looked away.

"Uh-oh, looks like Chloe's jelly," Krutch teased.

Hood Snap struck a pouty face pose, bottom lip out, chin on his fists, elbows on the table.

"Do something. Like, before we graduate," Krutch said.

It was like a doubles tennis match, and my partner was playing defense. The ball was in Dervis' court. He shook his head side to side, "The only time we talk is in C++ when she needs help on homework."

"You mean when you do her homework."

Dervis shrugged. "I don't mind."

"Neither will her GPA."

Down the line zinger. Ouch.

"But if you'd rather tutor Chloe in say, Biology, you best be getting a move on," Krutch said.

"So what, I'm supposed to walk over there, hand her a cookie and ask, 'Would you like to go out?'"

"No! That's the dumbest thing ever!"

Dervis threw his hands up and asked, "Well then, what?"

Krutch motioned for him to approach the net.

Curious, I leaned in as well. Matchpoint.

He whispered, "You walk over there, hand her a cookie and ask, 'Would you like to go out?'"

"I just said that!" Dervis tossed a cookie at him.

"Exactly." Krutch nabbed it out of the air, ripped it open and took a big bite. "That's what I'm talking about."

Hood Snap pointed to the last cookie, then himself.

"Jerks." Dervis waved for him to take it.

Changing the subject, I said, "Thanks for coming to the meet. I tried to find you guys at the finish."

Krutch said, "It's not about the finish, Darlin,' it's about the journey. Stayed to cheer on the other lost vagabonds wandering through the forest."

"Everyone was laughing about you guys, after puking their guts out," Dervis said.

"Speaking of the herd of masochists, most looked fairly miserable, except for you." Krutch's hand stroked a couple day's growth on his chin.

Hood Snap crossed his arms and gave me the side-eye.

Curious. He rarely, if ever, speaks. I shrugged.

"Rogue is a running freakazoid," Dervis said.

"Uh-huh, 'bout that, how'd you end up?" Krutch asked.

I lifted my milk and drank without hurry, then set down the empty container and looked across the court, "It's not about the finish, Darlin.' It's about the journey."

Krutch burst out laughing. Then, in his pompous British accent said, "Well played. I like that, I do. Hood Snap, write that down."

Hood Snap flourished an invisible pen to make a note.

***

After school heading to the locker room, I was borderline giddy for the first time. Ever. My favorite teacher had brought her "A" game, my quirky trio of, dare I say, friends, were a hoot, and I was heading to a Friday practice after a win with a team I enjoyed. Life is good.

"Gracie!" Jaz caught me before I went into the gym.

"What's up?" I asked.

"Coach wants to see you. In her office. Before the run."

I looked left to right. She pointed down the hall past the locker room.

"Thanks."

"Sure, good luck. Let me know if she smiles."

"Will do." Was I going to get a formal "Welcome to the team,' maybe "strong first race," or at least a "well done?" I knocked on the door that read, "Coach Hudson."

"Come in." Her beady eyes squinted, studying me under penciled caterpillar eyebrows. Above them, haphazard salt and pepper hair resembled a bird's nest today. "Close the door, but leave it open an inch, Halsted."

Weird. Not at all what I expected after a victory.

"Sit down." She waved to the corner seat.

Her tone confused me. I sat.

"In all my years of coaching I've never seen such a flagrant, arrogant, weak effort from an athlete."

Her words karate kicked me in the gut. My face flushed warm, then cold. Blood tingled down my arms to icy fingers. I struggled to swallow past a lump that blocked my throat.

All the while, she stared at me.

"Ex- excuse me?" I stuttered. Unable to comprehend.

"No. I won't. There's no excuse, not that I'm surprised, considering you're a big shot, lacrosse star." She twirled her index finger.

Incredulous, words escaped me.

"Quit slacking off and showboating for the fans."

"But –"

"But nothing."

I tried to make sense of it. "Coach, I didn't mean to –"

"Save it. From now on, run to win." She dismissed me with a wave of an age-spotted hand.

Frozen to the chair, my hands gripped the cold metal.

She pointed to the door. "Now."

Willing my fingers to release their death grip, I pushed up and forced my feet to stumble out of the office.

Down the dimly lit empty hall, beyond the exit doors, dark clouds beckoned me. I sought refuge in the storm.

The cold north wind whipped my ponytail and plastered my t-shirt and shorts to goose-bumped skin. Sleet pelted my face. I felt nothing. Numb from Coach's beat down.

My nose was clogged. I gasped air in and out through an open mouth. I choked and wiped my face. My tongue tasted salt. Snot, or tears mixed with rain. I didn't care.

Coach was right. I'd screwed up.

Let my guard down.

Let my need to belong compromise a competition.

In doing so, I'd disrespected a coach, a sport, and myself.

I ran on.

Crack! I jumped. Like when the starter's gun fired. I shot forward. Smoke rose from the gnarled Oak. Another flash of lightning lit the trail, thunder roared close at its heels.

I ran on.

Alone. The raging storm's setting was strangely familiar.

Favorite words leaped across a beloved page in my mind.

"Till I scarcely more than muttered "Other friends have flown before —

On the morrow he will leave me, as my Hopes have flown
before." Then the bird said "Nevermore."
I ran on.

                              ***

The door flew open. I stumbled in. Deranged. Warm dry towels attacked like straitjackets. Appropriate and fitting.

A muffled voice screamed, "Are you crazy?"

Shivering. Teeth rattling. Was the voice in my head? I sputtered, "N-n-nevermore." My eyes blinked at the blurry shadow image surrounded by fluorescent lights.

"Girl, you're whack. We're going to the trainer." Strong arms embraced and guided me.

Muffled voices, I recognized Jaz's. A door closed.

"What the heck? When the worst hit we bailed and came back. How far did you go?"

I sat on the training room table, still wrapped in towels. Lost in my thoughts. An out-of-focus clock ticked.

A firm hand pressed in between my shoulder blades, "What were you thinking? Running in this?"

I shook my head.

"Gracie." A pause. "What did Coach say to you?"

Remembering. I buried my face in a towel.

"Never mind. Breathe. Just breathe."

My heartbeat and pulse returned to normal. I inhaled, scrubbed my face, and sat up to see Jaz's wrinkled forehead.

"You look like shit," Jaz said. "And I mean that as a friend."

Friend. I held her gaze as tears regrouped.

Her eyebrows arched. "Kidding! If anyone can make the puffy eye, snotty nose thing work, it's you!"

I shook my head and sighed.

"Gracie," Jaz grilled me. "What did Coach say?"

Pressing palms over my ears, I recited the contemptuous, cruel words, *"In all my years of coaching I've never seen such a flagrant, arrogant, weak effort from an athlete."*

"WHAT?" Jaz shouted.

I held my hands out to defend Coach. "I deserved it. I dissed her sport." Confessing, my hands dropped to my lap.

"What do you mean, 'her sport?' She hates running."

I blinked. "Come again?"

"Coach! She hates running. Softball's her jam. Rumor has it she tripped running bases in college, screwed up a knee for life and lost her full ride. She only does cross country for the three grand. She has Sienna and Josh run the show."

Clarification. Coach was cantankerous for spite, that's why she abdicated responsibility. The last shiver jolted my neck as warm blood reclaimed my limbs; guilt washed away.

Vindication. I joined this inclusive team to condition and have fun. I hadn't dissed Coach's personal love of her sport.

But, she had mine. My teeth clenched remembering her "big shot lacrosse star" comment and whoop-dee-do finger twirl.

"Come on, they're waiting for us to do cool down."

Affirmation. Touched by this team's supportiveness, my self-sabotaging thoughts dissolved. "Sorry I worried you guys – and Jaz?" I paused to pivot my knees to the edge and scoot off, "Thanks for having my back."

"It's all good," Jaz said, as she collected the discarded towels.

Not all, but a lot more good, than bad or ugly.

She tossed the towels into the hamper. "Don't forget to ask Michael about karate." But after studying my face, she put a hand on my shoulder. "On second thought, you better slow your roll 'til you're not a hot mess."

I laughed.

Words. Funny thing, written or spoken, arrangement and delivery make all the difference.

13

"That's Life" – Frank Sinatra

Trampled leaves, now brown, muffled the crunch of my cleats on the gravel path as I walked to another lacrosse game. Weekend club games had melted together like cheese grilled between buttered whole wheat bread, cut in triangles, not rectangles. Thank you very much.

I'd win the draw, bring the ball down, Charlotte would scream for it, I'd pass, she'd shoot, score and gloat. Whatever. On to the next. If not for the tips and positive feedback from Coach MacGavin, playing lax on this team would be absolute drudgery.

Conversely, except for Coach Hudson, my cross country team experiment continued to surprise and delight me. As did, my Civil War Spies class. Thanks to the theatrics of the spry Ms. Davis and entertaining classmates, now cohorts.

My PowerPoint presentation opened with a slide from the Clara Barton Museum Web Site:

DANGEROUS EMBELLISHMENTS:
FEMALE SPIES IN THE CIVIL WAR
                    Posted on: October 15th, 2018 – Kate J. Armstrong

Nineteenth-century notions about women having chaste and guileless hearts meant that few men saw them as a threat during the Civil War.

"Guileless hearts most certainly not," Krutch declared, once again adopting a rich, southern drawl.

Dervis chimed in, "If you love something, let it go. If it doesn't come back, hunt it down and –"

Ms. Davis interrupted, "Thank you, Master Dervis, for that impromptu poetry slam, meanwhile back to the 1860s. Please go on Mistress Halsted."

Wondering about Krutch's uncivil history, I continued, "Elizabeth Van Lew was a southern lady who led a successful spy ring that fed valuable intel to Union General Ulysses S. Grant. Taking advantage of her nickname, "Crazy Bet," she dressed sloppily and muttered to herself, appearing harmless and mentally unstable to continue her ruse.

"As the war continued, spying became more difficult and dangerous. Miss Van Lew wrote in her diary, 'We have to be careful and circumspect. Wise as serpents and harmless as doves.'"

"Sounds about right, at least the snake part," Krutch said.

After I finished, Krutch slow-clapped me to my seat. I made a mental note to investigate the source of his bitterness. Glancing at the other two, Dervis gave me two thumbs up. Hood Snap silently applauded with jazz hands. The awesome dynamic trio, moody, nerdy and quirky.

***

A couple weeks later, Dervis and I ran side by side at a comfortable pace in between the competitive Varsity and JV squads. Despite daily voicing a desire to collapse, roll off the path into the woods and die a slow, miserable death, his stamina and breathing had improved so much we conversed without him making good on the threat. We were heading back to school.

Out of earshot of other runners, I asked, "If you're not sworn to secrecy, what's with Krutch's acrimony?"

"Not a matter of national security, but keep it on the DL," he huffed. "You know Mandi and the Mannequins?"

"Yep." I slowed down to a trot, then walked it in.

He followed suit. "Well, back in sixth grade, they were neighbors," Dervis said, as he walked in a circle, inhaling through his mouth, arms folded behind his head. "She was shy Amanda then, with a mouth full of braces, chunky glasses, and in the throes of puberty, meaning emerging zits and..."

"Got it. Go on."

He glanced at me and shrugged. "You remember what jerks sixth-grade boys are."

"Present company excluded, of course," I said.

"Of course, and Krutch even more so. He was cool and they hung out."

"What happened?" I asked.

"Military. Her dad got transferred to California for five years where she morphed into Malibu Mandi. She moved back last summer, sans braces, glasses, and zits, with an impressive pair of..."

"Yep. So?"

"Total brush off."

"No way." I couldn't believe it.

"Yep. He got smoked."

"And now she's the jerk," I said, then asked, "What does Chloe say? She's in her group."

"We don't discuss it. She mostly asks for computer help. But, today she mentioned she and Mandi are auditioning for the fall play."

Noticing the shift from Krutch's disappointing past to Dervis' hopeful future, I said, "Sounds like she's interested in you too."

"Probably not. She said they needed people for tech crew. Lighting and sound stuff."

He seemed intrigued but needed a nudge. "Sounds like a creative MIT resume booster shot," I said, opening the door for him.

He went through and held the next one for me, "You think?"

"Sure. Used computer skills to benefit the arts. Check." I drew a box in the air and checked it with a finger.

"Do you know anything about Snapchat?"

I laughed. "Nope, why?"

"Chloe told me to join their Theater Group snap page or pod, or something like that, and I have no idea."

I could relate, and offered, "My sister is social media savvy, I'll call her tonight and let you know tomorrow."

"Thanks," Dervis said. "Also, I need to trace who's posting crap about Chloe."

"Whoa, what?"

"After class her eyes were red and I asked if she had allergies, because I do, and she said no, really softly, then spilled that someone in the group was dissing her with posts."

"And you think that figuring out who it is will make you her hero?"

"Kind of. Lame?"

"Not at all. Noble, actually."

***

"What's up, Buttercup?" Sofi's smile lit up my cell as her positive energy recharged my soul. A strand of pink-dyed hair framed her face. The rest of the golden tresses were swept up top.

"Rock'n a sweet pink streak."

"Thanks! It's for October, matches my outfit," she said, leaning away from the laptop to show me pink scrubs. "And of course, remember these?" She brought her foot up to show me a glittery pink Converse, gifted from me a few years ago. I'm not the only flexible one in my fam. After all, she was a gymnast and PTs like a beast for Army ROTC.

"October, right, I'll figure out when The Race is."

"Hope it's not a field exercise weekend."

"Me too. Got a sec? I need some Snapchat intel."

Her palms flew up, "Hallelujah! It's about time!"

"Cool your jets, Techno Guru, it's for a friend."

Her arms crossed her chest. "Yeah, right. That's what they all say."

"For reals. A theater girl that Dervis likes asked him to join their Snapchat group, and despite the fact he could take apart and rebuild your laptop in the dark he has no knowledge of the social stuff."

"Oh that's right, The Awesome Mayor of Nerdville." She typed on her keyboard. "I'm in, what's her Snap name?"

"Whoa, baby steps, come again?"

Sofi scoffed, "S'not rocket science babe."

"Dude, it'd be a lot easier for him if it were."

Laughing, she ticked off the steps on her fingers. "He needs to download the app, create a profile, let her know it so she can add him to their group chat, which can have up to thirty-one members." She clapped, "Poof. Snap-tisfaction."

"Is there any way to track who's behind a screen name?"

"Difficult. Once received, unless you screenshot it and save it, the snap goes away. Also, it alerts the sender if someone screenshots their message."

"Maybe Dervis can break the code. Thanks, you're the bomb. com.edu.org.net."

"What can I say? It's a gift." Palms together, she bowed her head.

"Yes, you are." To mankind. And sisterhood. I smiled.

"Ah, you're sweet. Speaking of, how's your Big Mac?"

The girl is relentless. I shook my head. "Yo. Not mine."

"Not yet."

"Hah! I'm not even a blip on his radar."

"Then you need to send a bigger signal."

Shifting from Ian to Alex, her hometown honey, I asked, "Speaking of actual boyfriends, how's your Dr. Doolittle?"

Sofi's in love and it showed. Baby blues lit and smile fully engaged. "I'm talking to him about joining the military after undergrad and applying for vet school on the Army's dime."

"Really?" I teased, "Why not Navy or Marines?"

"Army is the only branch with veterinarians, because of the cavalry, which is also why the uniform pants don't match the jackets because back in the day, jackets would get rolled up and placed in their saddlebags and the pants would fade. Makes sense. Cool story, but hello? They still don't match. Drives me crazy," Sofi concluded with flare, brandishing a fingernail polish brush for emphasis.

"Look at you, Miss Military Intelligence."

She blew on her freshly painted nails. "I know things."

I checked my watch. "That's an understatement. Thanks a bil. Gotta bounce. Another race tomorrow," I said.

She blew me a kiss. "Run like the wind, Grace Artemis!"

"Thanks for sharing your wisdom, Sophia Isabella."

***

The early dismissal announcement for the cross country team interrupted fifth period. I packed up my books, nodded to my study hall teacher and left for the athletic wing.

Outside of the locker room, Jaz, Harley, Tonia, Claire and Sienna stood talking. When they saw me, their conversation stopped.

Jaz frowned, "Coach told me to send you to her office."

Great. She'd ignored me since our last little chat, much to my relief. Now, this. I sighed. "Ahhhh-some. Another pep talk, I hope." Despite the heavy sarcasm, dread crawled up my neck. I started toward Coach's office. To my surprise, they followed. Stopping, I looked at them.

Sienna said, without signing, "Figured if she has useful race tips we should hear it, together."

They all nodded in agreement.

Words got stuck in my throat, so I signed, "Thank you."

As we approached the office door, Molly stumbled out, blinking. She tried to smile but failed.

"Hey, you okay?" Sienna asked.

Molly sniffed, and quietly said, "Um, yeah, Coach told me to stay with the lead pack, I've been falling back."

Sienna's jaw muscle tensed. She reached out to squeeze Molly's shoulder. "Don't worry. You'll do great. We'll catch you on the bus."

"Save us some seats, okay?" Jaz added.

Molly nodded, "Sure."

I knocked on the door.

"Come in," Coach said. We entered quietly. Her hunched back was turned away as she looked through a file cabinet. After a moment, she turned, her small eyes flitting to each of us, landing on Sienna last, as the eyebrow caterpillars reared up her forehead. "I just need Halsted."

Sienna's willful gaze locked on Coach. "If you've got a new race strategy, we'd all like to hear it."

Awkward seconds ticked on the large clock... Coach broke eye contact first and growled, "Run hard. This is an important meet. Now go change and get to the bus."

First in, I waited for the others to exit.

Coach's eyes tracked me, squinted, and shot daggers.

Last out the door, the target on my back hardened into a protective shield.

"Best pep talk ever!" Jaz joked. "Run hard!" She made a fist and punched the air.

"This is an important meet," Harley joined in.

"Go change and get on the bus!" Tonia mimicked.

Sienna and I remained silent walking to the locker room.

Jaz tapped me on the shoulder. "Sorry, too soon?"

I shook my head. "Meh, no worries. I'll sit with Molly."

Sienna studied me, then nodded. "Thanks."

14

"Waking Lions" – Pop Evil

"Wow. I had no idea she'd gone after you too." Molly winced as I shared my awful experience. She'd saved rear benches, as far away from Coach as possible.

"Yep." A shiver threatened the back of my neck, but I rolled my shoulders, then tilted my head toward our rowdier teammates and added, "Forget Coach; let's run for them."

After that, Molly and I rode in comfortable silence, ate our pre-race snacks, and enjoyed the undulating landscape on the way out toward Shenandoah Valley.

A damp October breeze greeted us as we disembarked from the team bus in Front Royal, Virginia, only to be befouled by the stench wafting from a row of porta-potties at the end of the parking lot. We pitched the team tent on a hill far away and upwind. In the distance, a giant oak tree stood guard as an army of dark gray storm clouds advanced from the west.

Coach shuffled over from the official's tent and called to Sienna and Josh. Her cloudy face matched the forecast. Our two captains waited for her to get to them. Josh stood tall, his face uncharacteristically serious. Sienna leaned back on one foot, arms folded defiantly across her chest. A double dose of the silent treatment from the interpreter.

Coach muttered briefly to them, then walked away. I was somewhat relieved she didn't repeat her not-so-inspirational speech, but also a little disappointed, contemplating how Michael would have humorously interpreted, "Run hard."

As Sienna turned to the team, her bright smile returned – like the sun emerging from clouds. "Today we're running JV guys, then JV girls, Varsity guys and last, Varsity girls. Find your compadres, warm up and be at the start ten minutes before go time. It's a good day to do great!"

Varsity girls could chill, so we gathered to get insight from the veterans who'd run the course before, then spread out to key places along the route to cheer on other runners.

Dervis had worked his way up to top-six scoring JV, so I stationed myself at the dreaded two-mile point to shout out his time and position. Runners had to cross a creek here, and since it was sprinkling, his mood would be even worse than usual. Fifteen minutes later, I caught sight of his determined red and white blotchy face. My prediction was confirmed. He acknowledged my shouts with a glance and a clenched jaw.

I cut across a field to the finish line, to be there to catch him as he staggered in, or steer him to a trash can to puke.

The rain intensified the bright uniform colors as the runners charged up to the finish against the gray backdrop. Our red, mixed with bright blue and forest green. All soaked from rain and sweat, and speckled brown with mud.

I returned to the creek to cheer on the JV girls. The rain and spikes made a slippery mess on both sides. I noted the tufts of grass to the right that could be used for traction. After our girls splashed past I went to find Josh to let the Varsity guys know.

The rain fell steady now. I pulled up my hoodie, hunched over, and dodged puddles. Rounding the trainer's tent, I bumped into something tall and solid. Peering up from under my hoodie, Michael's bright white teeth were a beacon guiding me through the rainy haze. Being that close to all those muscles caused temporary brain failure, and I scrambled to remember how to sign my intel. He watched carefully as I butchered the beautiful language.

"The creek's a mess. Let the guys know grass to the right best bet for crossing," I signed, hoping it was close.

"Thanks, Rogue. I'll pass it on." Mischief flashed in his dark eyes, "May the course be with you."

My heart skipped. He knows my name. Sort of.

He'd trotted off as I replied, "And also with you."

We yelled for the V guys at their start, then took off for our warm-up jog and stretch. Sienna told us Coach was right about one thing. The two other teams were worthy opponents and a win could set us up for solid post-season action.

Back in our tent, we stripped off our layers and jumped around as the cold air hit warmed-up muscles. Our dry tanks would soon be drenched and clinging to goose-bumped skin. We jogged to the start.

Sienna, Jaz and I were in front, putting Harley, Tonia, Molly and Claire in the second tier. Same game plan as previous races, I'd set a quick pace then drop back a mile or so in. This ignored Coach's edict but fulfilled my desire to assist rather than score.

We were off. Although the rain had stopped, the grassy field was slick and shredded from hundreds of spikes. I settled into a solid pace. It felt good to get up and go after watching the other three teams compete.

At the one-mile mark, I glanced sideways at Sienna, but she shook her head and waved for me to push on. Three blue and four green were hanging tight, as were Jaz and Tonia. Molly was a couple yards back.

Coming up on the creek, the group stretched out into a zig-zag line of random colors. Sienna and I veered right and pounded through, leaping onto the grass and up the gradual slope. Then mayhem ensued.

A scream and a splash.

Sienna and I looked for Jaz, who'd evaporated. Making a split-second decision, I pointed ahead to Sienna and pulled a U-ey. Dashing back through the herd of runners I spotted Jaz on her knees midstream.

Blurred fans lining the banks shouted encouragements.

"Can you stand?" I yelled, reaching for her.

"I think so," she said, arms raised.

Molly and Tonia were coming and slowed down to help.

"GO GO! We got this!" I shouted.

They splashed up the other side and on.

Grasping her muddy arms I slowly pulled. "You good?"

"Not if I can help it," Jaz shouted as we scrambled up the bank and raced on.

In the end, we squeaked and squished by a win. Sienna, Tonia, Harley were in the top twelve, Molly PR'd at fifteenth, and Claire, Jaz and I weren't far behind. Dervis greeted me with open arms and a dry towel. It was a good day to run for the hill, the creek, and the friend of it.

After cooling down, runners returned to pack up our makeshift camp. That's when it hit me. My stomach gurgled and the gurgle traveled south.

For the record, the #1 place for a female to go #2 is in the privacy of her home. However, the bran muffin and raisins I'd snarfed on the ride here, followed by water guzzled post-race, had accelerated the digestion process. Meaning, this aircraft was ready to drop a bomb.

Unfortunately, the tri-meet course was in a public park one hour away from my sanctuary. Sure, the porta-potties were available back by the parking lot, but my nostrils still burned from walking past the retch-inducing reek earlier. Four hundred meters from the bus stood my only alternative, a minimalist concrete block restroom. Weighing both options, I chose to go the distance.

It was dusk, but I didn't bother turning on lights because, well, sometimes it's better not to know. High windows let in enough fading sunlight to see the sink with the plastic distorting mirror and a row of stalls. I checked the first one, no paper.

A time bomb ticked in my lower abdomen. Second stall. Bingo! I had to put my shoulder to the door to shove it closed, as it was a tight fit to the frame. I flipped the metal lock and emptied toilet sheets from the dispenser. Despite Nature's urgent 911 call, I lined the cheap, black plastic U-shaped seat with multiple layers. Saving a hand full, I assumed the position and congratulated myself.

The hollow metal entry door scraped the floor, then shut.

Click. I froze. And heard. *THE WHISTLE!* The morbid version of, "My Favorite Things!"

"Toowh toowh toowh toowh toowh toowh toowh toowh toowh too-tooooooo..."

"NO! PLEASE NO! NOT AGAIN!" Imagination silently screamed as the torturous whistling hung in the air. The first stall door creaked.

"It's the whistling, serial-killer vampire custodian!" Logic whispered, then forced my paralyzed feet to lift just in time. The faint shadow grew on the other side of my door.

The lock rattled but held!

The shadow slipped past; each door's unique squeak cried out. Whatever it was, it searched for prey. A faraway stall door opened. Shut. Click. Then, the encore – "Toowh toowh toowh toowh toowh toowh toowh toowh too-tooooooo..."

Feet down, shorts up, I wrenched the door open and fled.

Trembling in fear, but not scared sh**less, I crab-walked to the closest porta-potty, inhaled deeply and ventured in. With the last ounce of oxygen in my lungs, I punched the hand sanitizer button then burst out, colliding with Sienna as she dashed past.

Discombobulated, I sputtered, "Sorry!"

"No worries." She checked behind us and pushed me onto the bus. "We're the last ones. Let's go."

Logic told me to ignore Coach's glare as I stumbled to the rear bench and peered out the window.

"Somewhere, out there," Imagination whispered, "A far worse demon stalks us."

***

Sofi's excited scream echoed through the laptop screen, "The whistling, serial-killer vampire custodian is back?" Her fingers were spread apart, hands shaking back and forth. She loved scary movies, mystery and mayhem.

"Not only back, but willing to travel," I said, sounding more cavalier than I felt.

"Dang, 'stalk about Halloween! You freaking out?"

Hadn't thought that far ahead. Goosebumps grew on my forearms. I rubbed them and admitted, "Kind of, sort of."

"Did you tell anyone?" She pulled her gray sweatshirt sleeves over her hands then hugged herself.

I sighed. "Yeah, right."

Her hands popped out again, waving around in front of her face. "I mean, the first time was weird, but same song, same whistler, out of town? That's crazy!"

"Exactly. Who'd believe it?"

She shook her head, then tapped the screen. "Be careful! And talk to stud boy Michael about karate in case you need to kick some serial-killer vampire custodian butt."

I welcomed the change of topic. "I bumped into him at the meet. Michael, I mean."

"Oooh, a meet-cute!" she clapped.

"A meet what?"

"A meet-cute, that's when two people destined for love meet for the first time, usually under adorable circumstances." Sofi, forever the hopeful romantic.

"I was drenched, in a hoodie, hardly adorable."

She wagged a finger at me, "Never underestimate the seductive power of a dreamy 100% cotton sweatshirt." She buried her nose into her hoodie and inhaled deeply.

I squinted at the screen. "Is that Alex's sweatshirt?"

"No. It's our sweatshirt. We share it."

"You steal it," I teased.

She shrugged coyly, "And then he steals it back."

Her serene smile could convince even the most steadfast non-believer that true love does exist.

15

"Everything Little Thing She Does Is Magic" – The Police

Color me speechless. The next day, I was surprised to see the Anime twins sitting at the lunch table with Krutch, Dervis and Hood Snap. The fact that I could not only witness this event but also participate cracked me up.

Setting down my tray of yogurt, fresh fruit and nuts across from their identical trays, I bit my tongue. Samzies. Kindred spirits. "Gracie," I said, introducing myself.

"Rogue," Dervis said, correcting me.

"That makes us Scooter and Skater," Skater said, with a glorious, condescending eye roll, waving her hand to her sister, then herself.

I'd assumed as much, as the twin speaking wore sneakers and the quiet artist, in ballet flats, said nothing. Skater's dark pixie-cut hair was parted on the right side, and tucked behind her left ear, whereas Scooter's was parted on the left, tucked behind right. Indicative of classic left-brain logical ideas and concepts in contrast to the right brain's tendency towards the creative? Delicious intellectual tidbits to ponder.

"They're on tech crew with me," Dervis said, bringing me back from my psychoanalysis interpretations. "Scooter's designing costumes and Skater's building sets."

I sat down across from Scooter and asked, "What play?"

"*The Crucible*," Scooter quietly said.

"About the Salem Witch Trials?" I asked.

Skater nodded, "Yep! Fresh version. The public shaming and false accusations are now on social media."

"Makes sense."

"Show her your sketches." Skater directed her sister.

The sullen artist's dark eyes studied my face. After a brief pause, she flipped open her drawing pad. Incredible steampunk wardrobe designs leaped off the page. Black vests, corsets, duster coats, derbies and goggles exuded attitude and expertise worthy of Broadway. Sofi would hyperventilate at the sight.

Krutch leaned in to look. "Righteous."

Hood Snap nodded his head in silent awe.

"These are amazing," I told her.

"Thanks." She gently closed the pad.

I asked Dervis, "Did Chloe get the part she wanted?"

"Yes, she's Abigail, one of the 'bewitched' little girls."

That character wasn't as innocent as perceived; had she cast a spell on Dervis? I wondered if Mandi got a role, but didn't want to ask in front of Krutch.

Skater must be telepathic because she offered. "Mandi Roberts plays Rebecca Nurse, one of the women accused of witchcraft, but she's a teacher in this version, not an old lady because seriously, wow, as if you'd put wrinkles on that perfect face. Her audition was amazing. That girl can act," Skater said.

"Huh. Who'd a thunk," Krutch said, bitterly.

Not catching his sarcasm, Skater continued, "I know, right? But I wanted to scream, 'She's innocent, you fools!' when she read the lines from the last scene, standing on the gallows, about to be hung. Her face was angelic."

"That's why they call it acting," Krutch grumbled.

Hood Snap drummed the table with two plastic knives.

Dervis grimaced, looked at me and changed the subject. "You busy Saturday? We're competing in the United States Croquet Association's Southeast Regional Tournament."

This I have got to see. "Wow. That's a mouth full. Heck yeah, my club lacrosse team is off this weekend. Where are you playing?"

"In the town of Roundhill, in Loudon County – it's an hour away." He shrugged, apologetically.

"That's cool, I like escaping the city now and then."

Skater sat up. "Did you say croquet tournament?"

"Yeah. You play?" Dervis asked.

Skater shook her head. "Nope, but sounds fan-tab-ulous. I'd kill to shoot a documentary." She looked at me, "Can we catch a ride?"

Her artist sister choked, covering her mouth to whisper, "Aspen! Really?"

Skater dropped her chin to whisper back, "Chill Willow, you said yourself, she's cool."

Aspen? Willow? And I thought my mom was bohemian. "Sure. What time do we need to be there?" I asked Dervis.

"First flight at ten, second at noon, and Championship at two," he replied. "If you want to catch Hood Snap and me, you better get there early, Krutch however, will probably make the finals."

Skater whistled, "Dang, really? You a big deal?"

Krutch's face lit up as he shrugged but didn't gloat. The topic change had worked its magic.

Craving a sweet, I went to buy an apple for dessert. On my way back to the table I stopped to check out Biff and Garth's current battle. After Garth played his turn, I nodded in agreement. "Solid."

Totally absorbed, he grunted, "Thanks."

Biff chewed on the fingernail of his pinkie finger. He glanced at me.

"Gracie can't help," Garth warned. Both of us.

Biff studied my poker face and made his move.

"Nice, you guys should go pro," I said.

Biff blushed. Garth grinned like a jack-o-lantern. They'd stepped up their game. I left them with two thumbs up. They didn't make careless newb mistakes like when we first met.

I'd learned from the best, tagging along with my brother Jason at the children's cancer center. He called his community service Checkmate Cancer but played Pokémon and Uno in addition to chess.

I took a bite, savoring the sweet, crisp crunch.

"What's their story?" Skater asked.

"Biff and Garth? Dedicated gamers," I said.

"Savage! What's their jam?"

"Old school Pokémon."

She leaped up. "Do they rage Pokémon Go? I need to add a new friend."

"No clue," I said as she took off, beelining over to launch a surprise attack.

Across the room, their simultaneous wide-eyed faces and chin bobs followed her hand gestures like sumo wrestlers synchronize swimming. Heads shook side to side, up and down, then both guys pulled out their phones as if hypnotized. Shell shocked, they watched her boomerang back to us.

"Cool, Research Challenge completed."

"Rogue, what kind of car do you drive?" Skater asked.

"Mini Cooper."

"Well, that's not gonna work," Skater said.

"Aspen," Scooter admonished.

"Not judging. This weekend's a community event and I offered to Raid with them, but obviously they can't Remote raid with us. But! I have another idea!" She was off.

In more ways than one, I thought. My kind of kooky. Her exuberance reminded me of Sofi.

"Here we go again." Scooter sighed.

Skater returned triumphantly. "Recruited them to help build sets! I have grand ideas for the hanging gallows and need muscle."

I intercepted a look between the twins. Skater nodded and waited for the guys to leave. "Hey, you mind giving some parental digits? Lame, I know, but we're freshmen, Dad's a Langley spook, and Mom's paranoid. Have to clear the ride."

Langley + spook = CIA. "No worries." My parents were the same. I gave her Mom's cell number and wondered if the two Mama Bears would become boho besties.

* * *

Skater exploded out their front door shouting, "I call Shotgun!" when I picked them up early Saturday morning. She popped the seat forward so her sister could climb in, then jumped aboard, buckled up, inhaled and started an hour-long sentence.

Scooter stared out the window. A pencil in one hand, the other on the open sketchpad on her lap. Air pods tucked in; attention checked out. Nodding to whatever she listened to instead of her sister's rambling monologue.

We turned into the park entrance at 9:30. Skater leaned forward to read the banner boasting *United States Croquet Association's Southeast Regional Tournament.* "Let me out to shoot." She grabbed her camera and the door handle as I pulled over to stop. "I'll catch up," she said, jumping out.

My eyes caught Scooter's shrug in the rearview mirror. Modus operandi, I assumed. Skater met us in the parking lot. "The registration tent is on the hill over there. They can tell us how to find the guys."

The hilltop view showed the thirty or so contestants and the setup courts. The eclectic group was a cloud of all-white shirts, vests, a few knickers and cardigans. Except for Krutch, Dervis and Hood Snap. Not one to fixate on fashion but I'll make an exception because the trio did not disappoint. Despite the cold fall breeze, Krutch wore a crazy patterned shirt covered in green palm trees and pink flamingos, beach shorts and flip-flops.

In preppy contrast, Dervis sported a tweed newsboy cap, a bow tie, argyle sweater vest, and his usual khaki pants. Specific details I consider collateral damage attained through osmosis living with a fashionista for many years.

"Check out Hood Snap, representing the dark side!" Skater said.

Indeed. Reminded me of the graphic novel *Abraham Lincoln: Vampire Hunter.* Black tophat, duster, jeans and boots, and his black wooden mallet resembled the axe in the movie poster.

"This is going to be a riot." Skater charged down the hill.

Scooter did a 180-degree panoramic scan, murmuring, "You go on. I like it here."

"Sounds good." I left her to create a pencil and paper memory as her sister captured a digital one.

Skater interviewed them; Dervis answered and explained as Hood Snap nodded and added sound effects.

"Hey, thanks for coming," Dervis said.

I swept my hand across the scene. "This is amazing."

"I know! Record number of contestants! We're playing doubles today. Krutch's first flight is in an hour." He pointed a few courts away.

Skater asked, "Do you send your opponent's ball with a smack when you bump it, and if so, what's with Krutch's flip-flops? Isn't that reckless? Has he ever whacked his foot?"

Dervis laughed. "Yes, yes and not yet, but we can hope."

Hood Snap tapped him on the shoulder with his mallet and pointed to a nearby court.

"That's us. We play last year's champions." He pointed to a middle-aged couple dressed head to toe in white. "Don't let the gray hair fool you. They're wicked good. Got five decades on us. We play best of three; it might be over quick."

Skater filmed the introductory handshakes like an ESPN pre-game segment. Her enthusiastic commentary informed and entertained, contrasting ages, outfits and demeanors. Fearless in pursuit of the perfect composition, she added another dimension worth watching. Climbing a tree for a bird's eye view, or lying in the grass to frame the ball through the wire wicket as it struck the final ringed stake.

I applauded all of the characters at the end of this play.

Dervis and Hood Snap were gallant in defeat. Pretty sure the winning team wanted to adopt them. After wishing the victors well, we launched a quick raid on the food tent and dashed to Krutch's match. He surfed through it, and the next, which set him up for the championship round.

Hood Snap slapped Krutch on the back as Dervis said, "Well done. Let's grab some food."

"We just ate," Skater said, lowering her camera.

"That was brunch, time for lunch. Wait 'til you see it."

"Be honest. You're in it for the food," Skater said.

"Yep. These elder creatures know how to eat."

Hood Snap tapped his hat and rubbed his stomach.

I looked up the hill, "Should we take some to Willow?"

"Scooter," Dervis corrected.

I yielded, "Scooter. She hasn't moved."

"Go for it. I'll interview more peeps," Skater said.

***

Bent over the sketchpad, a dark curtain of hair concealed Willow's face. Her extended legs in black tights were crossed at the rounded ankles, ballet flats arched on point.

"Thought you might be hungry," I announced.

She set her pad to the side. "Thank you."

"Krutch is in the championship match at two."

Nodding, she pulled the tip off the croissant. "An anomaly, that one. Sunshine and storm clouds." She took a bite.

So did I. "How so?"

"The quagmire he and Mandi Roberts wallow in." Her gaze was intense, but not invasive.

Uncomfortable, I shrugged, "I can't say."

"Nor should you. Also not my affair. I prefer fantasy over reality anyway." Profound and weird, but before I could ask, she offered her sketches. The courts below were now a battlefield, croquet morphed into a polo match, where the players rode fantastical beasts instead of horses.

"This is incredible," I said. Surreal, but revealing. An idea formed, reflecting back on my study of Civil War spies. What if one had painted facts like fantasy, framed in gaudy gold, and delivered it to be hung in a home of a general, where perhaps, a well-placed servant deciphered the secret message to pass on? Hidden in plain sight.

Willow brought me back from my reverie. "Interesting, what people expose when no one is looking."

Curious, I glanced over, but Imagination had drawn Willow back into her sketchpad world. Logic wondered, what did my aura betray when no one watched?

***

Our beach boy Krutch won two games to one. Dervis's play-by-play commentary included Krutch's precarious flip-flop look-to-the-side drive as he tapped his opponent's ball away. After hitting the final post, his sprite seventy-year-old opponent shook his hand, then plucked a card from her white cardigan. Handing it to him, she said, "I look forward to receiving your application this summer."

"Yes, ma'am. I'll get right on it," His charming smile engaged. He saw us over her shoulder and excused himself.

"New girlfriend?" Dervis teased.

"Nope. She's Dean of Admissions for St. John's College. It's across the street from the Naval Academy in Annapolis. They play each other in the Annapolis Cup croquet match every year."

"Dang! A croquet subculture, who'd da thunk!" Skater said, sounding like Krutch. A new fangirl. Dervis and Hood Snap exchanged a "here we go again" look.

We collected Scooter, bid farewell to the guys and hit the road. They assumed the same seating arrangement. Scooter's gaze was fed by fanciful landscapes as Skater's devoured her digital screen.

Skater's head resembled a giant fly as she digitally edited in large soundproof headphones. Canceling background noise for her, but increasing it for us, as firecracker bursts of "ooh, sweet, sick, or righteous!" exploded at random, the entire ride home.

16

"You Don't Know Me" – Ray Charles

That night, Sofi's eyes sparkled through the laptop screen. "Check you out! Making friends and taking names! Shoot me a YouTube link as soon as Skater uploads it. A croquet tournament! Those guys crack me up! I'd love to see Scooter's sketches too, but she's probably too private to share with strangers. So funny, identical twins with opposite personalities! Kind of like us, except for the twin thing."

Sofi voiced my thoughts. I nodded.

"Big change, watching instead of playing. Proud of you." She blinked. Change of topic. "When's Homecoming?"

"Football game? No clue. Why?" I asked.

"Yes but no. The dance. Should be soon. You have to go. Have you talked to karate kid stud? I left dresses in my closet. Oh! Better yet! Get a group and go steampunk! That would be awesome."

I followed Sofi's racecar thought process as she switched lanes at breakneck speed, then applied brakes. "We'll see. More important, we've got an Annapolis lacrosse tourney next weekend, so I set up an interview for a midshipman slot, just in case. Coach MacGavin wants me to meet the USNA lacrosse coach too."

"Instead of Northwestern? No word from admissions?"

"Nope."

She tapped clear polished nails. "I despise waiting."

I smiled. "Me too. That's one trait we share."

***

After an all-day pep talk, I summoned the nerve to talk to Michael before practice and found him in the gym. I asked, "Hey, I'm a brown belt, and need to get back into it, can you tell me about your studio?"

He smiled, signed "Kokoro Martial Arts," then placed his palms together in prayer position and bowed.

Courage melted into crush mush as Michael's bulky back provided the perfect muscular anatomy lesson. My face burned as Jaz did a victory dance behind him.

His smile dissolved when he stood up. I tracked his stare to Sienna as she emerged from the trainer room, trailed by Harley, who beelined to Jaz as Sienna joined Josh.

Josh's good-natured grin faded as well. He studied Sienna's face, hidden from the rest of us, and nodded. She smoothed her hair with one hand, squared her shoulders and rotated. Her hands swept across her cheeks then remained silent, tucked in her hoodie pocket.

Josh called out, "Warm up with two laps around track then do the course," he improvised signing by holding up two fingers, swept them around twice, then ran the fingers up his other arm. He pointed to the door. "We'll meet back here for team stretch and roll out. Go!"

Michael excused himself, "Talk later."

I tried not to, but curiosity and a bit of jealousy prevailed. I watched Michael discreetly sign, "What's wrong?"

Sienna shook her head, "Nothing."

Jaz's cheerful mood had tanked. I joined her and Harley and they filled me in as we jogged to the track. My head pivoted side to side between them like a spectator at a tennis match.

"Sienna's college-now-*ex*-boyfriend just broke up with her in a text!" Harley said.

"Jerk!" Jaz responded.

"Never liked him, he didn't deserve her," Harley said.

"She was going to break it off," Jaz explained.

"Why didn't she?" Harley asked.

"Too nice. He promised he'd make it work."

Harley spit out, "Get this, he started with, 'Something important came up, won't make Homecoming.' Sienna said she was worried, and called him but he didn't pick up. Then he texted again, and

Sienna read it out loud. 'With somebody. You should find someone else too.'"

"Are you kidding me? What did she do?" Jaz asked, pumping her fists like a boxer.

Shaking her head, Harley said, "It was weird, she snorted a laugh, choked like something was caught in her throat, then pinched her nose." Harley bit her lip, "I think to keep from crying."

We hung back from the lead pack, running in silence for a bit. The trail was slippery so we concentrated on our footing. Out of earshot, Jaz said, "Sorry Gracie, now that Sienna's flying solo, Michael will get his chance."

I remembered my earlier triangle theory. Looking ahead, the two guys flanked Sienna, the apex, like bodyguards.

"Josh too," Harley said, pointing to the threesome. Sienna's pace was faster than usual for practice. Their backs were spotted with kicked-up mud drops.

Jaz said, "Josh is a sweetheart, but Sienna and Michael have history, not to mention most of the girls, some of the guys, and probably a few teachers are in lust with him. Dude's got it all and then some."

No kidding. Michael's intensity reading Sienna's lips was tangible, despite his playful antics. Josh was subtler, his feelings hidden in friendly banter and finishing her sentences. The revelation of Sienna's now ex-relationship made sense of the dynamics I'd studied for months. My conclusion? This terrific trio's friend zone dance is about to get way more complicated.

And then it did.

Crossing the creek, Sienna slipped and fell. Michael caught her before a total faceplant, but one of her hands landed on a broken branch. We arrived as he gently set her on the bank and pulled a wooden shard out of her bleeding palm. We all stood frozen in the creek bed, staring as blood ran down her arm.

Except for Michael, who pulled off his shirt and gently wrapped it around Sienna's hand. She squeezed her eyes shut, took a few controlled breaths, then looked up at Josh. "Can you go finish up practice? I'll get back as soon as I can."

"Are you sure you're okay?" Josh asked.

"I'm fine, just clumsy. Go on."

He nodded, looked from her to Michael, then took off.

"Hey Sienna, want us to walk you in?" Jaz asked.

Michael glanced at me, "I'll get her back."

I said, "Let's go, they're good."

My foot caught a root as we scrambled up the bank. A tinge of pain stabbed my ankle but I kept going. At the top of the hill Jaz broke the silence, "Wow. Sorry Sienna got hurt but dang that was some sexy first aid."

Harley agreed, "When he tore off his shirt? Right out of a guilty pleasure chick lit. I expected him to beat his bare chest, scoop her up and carry her into the woods. Oh, but did you see Josh's face?"

"Yep. Sienna's not the only one hurting," Jaz said as we jogged into school at dusk.

My ankle ached after stretching and rolling out, so I went to the training room. Sienna sat on a padded table. She waved a wrapped hand to Ms. Smith, who was leaving with her kit.

"Do you need me?" Ms. Smith asked me, checking her watch.

"No, thanks. Just going to ice," I said.

"Okay, you guys lock up when you're done. I need to get to the field hockey game."

"Will do," Sienna called after her.

I filled a towel with ice, hobbled to the table next to Sienna and hopped up. She watched me cocoon my ankle. I leaned back against the wall and prepared myself for the initial "aaahh that feels good" followed by the "ooohh that kinda hurts."

Michael's bloody white t-shirt was folded in her lap. She pointed to my foot, "Is it bad?" Concerned lines creased her forehead; mud freckles on her cheeks reminded me of Josh. The ones under her eyes were smeared.

"No, have lacrosse practice later so I've got time to kill." I asked, "How are you?" Loaded question.

She sighed. "Confused."

We sat in silence for fifteen minutes. Me, because one, I'm the last person you'd want romantic relationship advice from, and two, that's how long you're supposed to ice.

Sienna? No clue. Unless as captain she was obligated to hang out and lock up. She leaned back on the wall. Damaged hand on Michael's shirt, his love letter signed in her blood.

A strain of violin notes swirled in through the open door. "You Don't Know Me," today's cool-down selection by our Tunes Chairman, Michael. Sienna had been absent, getting her hand wrapped, but must have heard it from the training room. Her eyes were closed, but she smiled.

Michael appeared in the doorway. Dang. My heart stopped and he wasn't looking at me. I cleared my throat.

Sienna looked at me, then him.

"Come dance with me," he signed. That grin. Crap. Once again, not for me.

Sienna tapped her index and middle fingers together on the thumb of her unwrapped hand, "No."

"Come dance with me," he persisted. Tilting his head.

She shook hers.

"You'll feel better," he signed. "You always do."

She shook it again, but a bit slower this time. A slight curve grew on the corner of her lips.

I wasn't breathing.

He held out his hand. She glanced at me.

I exhaled way too loud, held my palms up and shoved out, like, what the heck, go already! I need oxygen!

She scooted off the table and placed her bare hand in his. He led her out of the room like freaking Gene Kelly. A buff, really old dude who could seriously dance.

I unwrapped my numb ankle, dumped ice in the sink and hung the towel on the hamper. Bonding with the singer as he crooned about unrequited love, I grabbed my phone, picked up the folded t-shirt, and flicked off the lights.

Expecting a teenager rocking side to side Frankenstein dance, what I got was a glimpse of magic. Like a romantic black and white movie scene that Sofi watched over and over.

Click. The door locked behind me. I leaned back on the cool metal, mesmerized. The lyrical music reverberated off the empty walls and floor, masking the buzz of fluorescents shutting down.

Moving with familiarity in the dim light, teasing at first, with exaggerated motions and mock seriousness, they swept the wooden floor, twirled apart and back together. This must be their "history." Michael pretended to loosen his t-shirt collar, smirking at the "making love" lyrics, Sienna hid a coy smile. He's memorized the words!

They swirled near as the backup singers serenaded the last melancholy refrain. Michael's gaze intensified; Sienna's smile faded. Her lids closed as both arms lifted, the white bandage tracing up and back in a semi-circle arc; his defined biceps and forearms moved behind to support the graceful dip.

Wow. That is quite the pose.

The last notes dissolved as the warning buzz increased.

Oblivious, Michael lifted and held Sienna close.

Ka-chunk.

We plunged into a black void.

From the great beyond, I heard, "Gracie?"

"On it!" But instead of grabbing my cell, I shoved it out the other side of my hoodie pocket. Clunk. "Just a sec." Dropping to my knees I patted, searching the smooth wooden floor.

A giggle. Slap. "S-ssstop!"

Imagination made me blush. Logic relieved no one saw.

My fingers found my phone and grasped it, fumbling to swipe on the flashlight. I stood and held the beacon high to guide them to port.

Michael's white teeth broke through the dark sea. As he entered the faint light his hands appeared hand-cuffed behind. His guilty grin confirmed the transgression was worth it.

"Thanks, let's grab our stuff and get out," Sienna said.

Michael signed, *"Mine's over there."* He pointed to the bleachers. I handed him the bloody shirt.

With one hand tracing our path on the bumpy concrete wall and the other lighting the way, we reached the girl's locker room door. Michael tapped me on the shoulder to sign, "I'll wait out here."

"No way," Sienna said, "you're coming in."

He shrugged and opened the door to reveal nothingness. We ventured in, swallowed by black. My heart skipped a beat. "Sienna, do you know how to turn on the lights?"

"Can't. Need a key. Gonna have to wing it."

Remembering the previous shin-banging, I threw light on the bench in the middle of the aisle on the way to my locker. I gave Sienna the flashlight to grab my stuff, then she guided us to her locker on the other side of the room. When she handed the phone back, a glint of a metal handle caught my eye. I squinted to make out the faint outline of a door.

A shudder racked my shoulders. That's where he came in. The first time I heard the eerie whistling. I stared, wondering where it led. Then froze. A low, slow, drawn-out humming of my least favorite things vibrated behind me. Goosebumps grew in recognition of the mournful tune. Not again!

"Mmm mm mm mmmm mm mm, mmmm mm mm mmmm mmmm."

My phone dropped, bounced off the bench, and belly-flopped screen down. Cement swallowed its illumination. Fear and sweat raced down my neck. Silence pounded my ears. Nobody moved.

I waited. Dreaded, for the spine-chilling refrain to repeat.

Nothing.

I whispered, "D-did you hear that?"

"W-what?" Sienna's meek response quivered.

I crouched to retrieve my phone, and through gritted teeth whispered, "The. Humming."

"The humming?" she whispered, a little louder.

"The creeped-out version of "My Favorite Things.""

Choking sound.

Fearful, but desperate, I swept the floor and found my cell, gripped and lifted, expecting the worst. Meaning a vampire serial-killer strangling Sienna's neck, or biting it.

Not even close. Sienna's eyes sparkled, her hands swiped across her forehead, smoothing creases. "That was me."

"You?" I stared.

She nodded. The phone's glow cast her in ghoulish shadows.

"That song? Do you whistle it too?"

She shrugged. "Don't judge. It's my jam."

Epiphany. I stammered, "YOU'RE the whistling, serial-killer vampire custodian?"

"The what?" She leaned into the faint light.

"My reoccurring whistling, now humming, nightmare! First here, in this locker room, months ago. Then away, at that park, in the concrete block restroom!" Light bounced around as my hands punctuated my explanation.

She gasped, "That was you? Here and there?" Her mouth dropped open, then laughter exploded out, echoing off of the metal lockers. "You scared the crap out of me!"

Michael watched our unexplained hysteria shift from fear to shock, to laughter. He clapped his hands, "What?"

Relief washed away tension as I cracked up and set the phone down.

It took a moment, but at last, Sienna pointed to me, "Rogue's the bathroom stalker!"

I argued, motioning back to her. "No, I'm not! She is!"

Michael squinted. Then his brows lifted. He leaned back, arms crossed. She must have told him.

"Shut up!" Sienna signed, laughing too hard to talk.

"You shut up! You scared the crap out of me!" Remembering the slow, painful crab walk to the porta-potties.

Michael pointed at the side of his head and drew a circle twice. "You're both crazy."

I asked, "Where does that door go?"

"To that inner hall by Coach Hudson's office," Sienna said.

"Figures, she's another one of my reoccurring nightmares."

Sienna placed a hand on my shoulder. "Ignore her. She's all bark no bite."

I gave her a supercilious eyebrow. "Said the vampire."

She smiled wide then whispered, "Let's go, I have to be home before sunrise."

They lived in nearby neighborhoods and usually walked home, but since Sienna was hurt I offered a ride. As we approached the parking lot, Mom's old metallic sky blue Mini Cooper glowed under the alien dinosaur lights perched at the end of their dark gray arched necks.

Michael claimed the back seat, and somehow folded, squeezed, and manipulated all of his muscles in. The rearview mirror revealed him sprawled across the entire rear seat where I used to sit, observing Sofi's and her bff Shelley's craziness back in the day. Now, I had the wheel, and Sienna sat in Shelley's seat, rotated so Michael could read her lips.

"Go down Main past Trader Joe's and take a left at Little River Turnpike. We can drop Michael first."

I parked where indicated, in front of a massive two-story white cube with crisp black shutters. Manicured bushes lined the sidewalk up to a large red door.

Sienna jumped out and popped the seat forward with her good hand to let him out.

Michael's face appeared in the mirror lit by the overhead light. "Thank you."

"You're welcome." I waved as he pushed his way up and out. After a hot sec, Sienna slid in, face flushed.

"Um, okay, we need to go back that way and take two rights. There's a path through the park in between our houses, but I don't want to do it alone in the dark. Sorry."

"No problem." Pretty sure Michael would walk a dark path, through creepy woods, or even fire, for her. Bet she knew too. Too soon. She bit her lip. Maybe not. I wondered if they'd exchanged a quick farewell word via osmosis.

The awkward silence was deafening.

"Nice neighborhood," I said. Lame. The words bounced around the empty back seat.

"Thanks. Mom did research when they joined the National Symphony Orchestra. They are both musicians." Pause. "Because of the deaf immersion schools." Shaking her head, adding, "After an infection knocked out 90% of my hearing in one ear, they worried I'd lose it all. That's why we bought a house in this area."

"Michael's mom facilitated the community support group. She's amazing." Another pause. Her bare hand cupped the bandaged one. "He was born deaf, and she made it her life mission to normalize his experience."

Able to follow and reorder random topics thanks to years of listening to Sofi, I nodded.

"So his mom taught mine while I learned from him. Then our dads bonded over blues and jazz, so we hung out all the time."

That explained Tunes Chairman Michael's taste in music. Our cooldowns were straight-up song dedications. Made me wonder for the hundredth time today why they weren't together, together?

"So you've hung out all these years?" I asked. Implored.

"Except for five years, when they were posted at the U.S. Embassy in London. His folks are Foreign Service. Super fancy. High vis diplomatic stuff."

Bullseye. "When did they come back?"

She motioned for a right turn to a house with her good hand. "The summer before our junior year. While they were gone, my hearing returned, for the most part. That's why I whistle, or hum, that song. Kind of a self-check-up inside my head. Sometimes subconsciously."

Makes sense. And also explains why Michael is on her left reading lips, and Josh on her right so she can hear him. I congratulated myself on this brilliant deduction.

Then I thought, out of sight from ages twelve to seventeen. Sienna moved on, while Michael held on. She read my mind as I pulled into her driveway.

"I started dating Kyle the year before. He was a year older, our star runner. Couldn't believe he wanted to be with me. He graduated and left for Penn State on a full scholarship. I knew it wouldn't work, but he talked me into the long-distance thing." She sighed and confessed.

"And, it made it easier to not have to choose."

I blurted out, "Between Michael and Josh?"

She looked at me like I was the whacko mind-reader.

Awkward thinking I had kind of stalked her with Michael today, I threw her a weirdo bone of my own. "I freaked out in the locker room and restroom because of a recurring dream I have every time we moved. And I haven't had it yet. This move, I mean."

"What is it?" Sienna asked.

I confessed, "The last person I think about before I go to sleep gets viciously murdered."

"That's harsh."

"Tell me about it."

"Do me a favor," she asked, as she opened her door.

I shrugged. "Sure."

"Think about some other whistling vampire whatever, whatever before you go to sleep tonight?"

"Yep. Will do."

17

"Stronger" – Kelly Clarkson

The last two requirements fell into place for my Naval Academy application. The Blue and Gold Officer called to set up our interview for Friday, and Coach MacGavin arranged for me to meet and take the candidate fitness assessment with the USNA coach before the tournament started Saturday.

I was confident about the interview but knew I needed to be truthful about Northwestern. The Naval Academy was my backup. You don't go there because of the free education and stipend you go to serve in the military. Which would be an honor, but I worried, would others follow me? Like they would Jason or Sofi? A delicate juggling act. Northwestern if I get the money, but if not, I commit to USNA, but not because of the money. Make sense?

Sienna said she'd cover if Coach Hutchins figured out I'd skipped practice. We were prepping for regionals so Coach had been around, shooting dirty looks and grumbling when people had the nerve to enjoy themselves. Not that I cared what she thought anymore.

Thursday practice I stretched out on the gym floor next to Jaz but was a million miles away.

"Hellooooh, earth to Rogue."

Folded nose to knees, I lifted my chin. "What?"

Jaz asked, "Are you're going to Homecoming?"

"Um, don't know. When is it?"

"Next week. Friday football game and Saturday dance," Harley answered.

"You can go in our group," Jaz said. "Unless it blows up now that Sienna's free."

"Who're you betting on?" Harley asked.

Jaz studied the trio in a pre-practice powwow. "My money's on Michael. They've been dancing around each other all week since the breakup. Poor Josh."

You should have seen them dance together, I thought but didn't trade on my insider information.

"She may not want to rebound so soon," Savanna said.

Jaz waved it off. "Pffft, Michael plays basketball, he's good at rebounding."

We hit the dirt trail. Previous footprints were frozen into treacherous ruts capable of twisting ankles, so we took it slower than usual.

"Do you want to ride with us tomorrow?" Jaz asked. Vapor puffs escaped as she spoke. She and Harley played for a rival club team.

I coughed inhaling cold air into warm lungs. "Keep your friends close, and your enemies closer?"

Harley laughed. "More like frienemies, for now, we'll be teammates in the spring."

"Yep, looking forward to witnessing your mad skills, as you rack up goals on us," Jaz said.

"Thanks, but I'm riding with my folks." I didn't tell them about the interview tomorrow or the fitness assessment, hard to explain something that wasn't clear in my own head yet. Also, I didn't want to seem arrogant meeting the Academy coach.

My club squad didn't know either. I imagined Lanie's cheerful support but knew Charlotte would be furious, and her toxic waste would spill into the game and poison our play. My strategy was to feed the savage beast assists instead of scoring when we played against Jaz and Harley.

But you know what they say about best-laid plans.

***

"Just be honest," Mom said.

Dad looked at me in the rearview mirror, "They will appreciate your tactical plan of action."

I nodded and exited in front of the admin building. Mom reached out, "Firm handshake, maintain eye contact. You'll be awesome." A jolt of positive energy shot up my arm as I grasped her warm hand.

Dad leaned across and winked, "Dominate."

Exhaling, I pressed my palms together and bowed, "And control the center of the board." Dressed in pumps and a skirt, I rose, pivoted and tried not to march up the sidewalk.

An hour after the interview, we wandered through the cobblestone streets dodging squawking seagulls competing for dropped or tossed morsels around the Annapolis City Dock. Damp, fishy smells mingled with warm, delicious scents billowing out from the open doors of seafood restaurants, enticing hungry and thirsty tourists in from the cold.

In a restaurant bathroom, I swapped skirt and shoes for sweats and kicks before joining my folks in a booth. My empty stomach growled reading the menu. I debriefed them to distract the grumbling as we waited for our entrees. The interview had gone well. The officer shared that he had other options as well, but had chosen the Academy with no regrets.

After dinner we wandered into a historical fiction novel, reading date plaques on the old colonial buildings. Middleton Tavern boasted hosting not only George Washington but Thomas Jefferson and Benjamin Franklin as well! I snapped pictures to satisfy Ms. Davis's "Hysterical for Everything Historical" addiction. We watched wavy reflections of boats floating into the dock at sunset before meeting our host, one of Dad's aviator buddies, and settling in for the night.

The next morning, I pictured Krutch, Dervis and Hood Snap playing croquet in their quirky outfits as we drove by St. John's College across from the Academy. When we got to the USNA gate, Dad showed his I.D. to the guard and followed directions to the track where I'd complete the six physical and motor events in forty minutes: basketball throw, pull-ups, 40-yard agility run, crunches, push-ups and mile run.

Individually, each event was a piece of cake, but doing them consecutively in the allotted time made me regret eating a two-egg omelet and hash browns. Thinking this was my backup school helped, but then Coach MacGavin introduced me to Coach Sinclair and left with my folks.

"Okay Grace, your coach thinks you'll fly through this."

"Yes, Ma'am." I held her gaze, chin up, shoulders back.

She smiled. "Relax; 'Coach' is fine."

"Okay, Coach. Thanks." But her attempt to set me at ease backfired. Now, I had to prove myself to her and live up to Coach MacGavin's expectations.

She motioned for me to walk with her. "For the first five events, you have two minutes to complete with a three-minute rest in between. We'll do the throw on the field, pull-ups at the fitness station there." Pointing back and forth from track to an outdoor workout structure. "Agility on the field, crunches and push-ups here again, then the mile on the track. Stretch for few minutes. Don't get hurt on my watch or Mac will have me drawn and quartered."

Surprised at her calling him by a nickname, I snorted. "Sounds about right." Tension eased during my warmup lap but crawled back up my neck as I kneeled for the basketball throw. Designed to determine strength and balance, it was an awkward way to prove it. But since I threw a lot in lacrosse, and worked upper body in karate, it went pretty well.

After maxing three out of five tasks, I had a couple of minutes to dread the last. A six-minute mile is doable, but this overall assessment's cumulative loading effect sucked. Tortured abs warned wary legs to prepare for battle.

I fantasized ejecting off the track halfway through lap three but punched my inner autopilot button instead. Pumping hard through lap four, I crossed the finish line and got to a trash can in time to throw up, vowing to never put ketchup on hash browns ever again.

"Well done." I heard.

Pulling up the inside of my t-shirt to wipe my mouth, I rested my arms on top of my head and arched back. After a few breaths, I circled back to Coach Sinclair.

She pointed to a couple leaning on a car in the nearby parking lot, "Your folks are waiting, better go reload."

A raspy, "Will do," escaped my throat. I held out my hand to shake, remembered the trash can, and instead made a vague gesture toward the outdoor equipment and the track. "Thank you – for running me through it."

She chuckled, "If this is how you work, I can't wait to see how you play."

Cocooned in comfy sweats back in the warm car I sipped a Coke to settle my stomach, then devoured fish tacos with fresh-squeezed lime, guacamole and coleslaw. Satisfied. I shut my eyes to catch a quick nap before switching from fitness assessment to game mode.

18

"Just Like Fire" – P!nk

"Wake up, Buttercup. Time to rise and shine."

Pushing back my hoodie, the bright sunshine blinded me. I blinked and yawned.

"We'll drop you and go park. Your team is over there," Dad said, pointing toward a gold and red tent.

Groggy, I stretched, grabbed my gear bag and stumbled out. Dressed in thick, gray cross country team sweats instead of the flashy club warm-ups, I moved at a sloth's pace toward my lacrosse club tent.

"There she is!" I heard and saw Lanie waving. She stood twenty yards away, talking to a muscular dude in a hoodie and black sweats. His back view was impressive. You go girl.

But then he turned around.

I squinted. My brain recognized those aviator sunglasses and his high and tight as... my heart skipped a beat. Ian. What the heck was he doing here?

A hand grabbed at his arm, but he deflected, heading my way. Why? His quick departure exposed an arm dressed in our flashy dark green club jacket, belonging to a scowling face, shooting a laser-guided death stare. Charlotte. Awesome.

Wide awake now, I willed my lungs to breathe and heart to beat, not mutiny into full-blown crush mode. Improvise. What would Sofi do? Flirt. What should I do? Not flirt. Definitely not flirt. I suck at it. Why did he have to blow Charlotte off? To talk to me? This will not go well.

Focusing on his approaching chest, I read WEST POINT BLACK KNIGHTS LACROSSE. Seriously? Wearing this at the Naval Academy? Charlotte and Lanie were ten steps behind him.

"How'd it go?" Ian asked when he was five feet away.

"How'd what go?" I asked.

They were closing in.

"The assessment." That cocky smirk. Time for a heart-thumping battle of wits. His dad, my coach, must have told him about the CFA.

"What assessment?" Charlotte asked.

I locked eyes with him.

He read my silent plea for secrecy. "Driving. Around the beltway. On a Saturday. Sucks."

I threw my hands up. "I know, right? Crazy."

Charlotte didn't look convinced.

Lanie shrugged her shoulders and mouthed, "Sorry."

Distract. I pointed to his sweatshirt's logo, a metallic gold knight's armor mask and sword. "So... you're a Knight?"

"A knight in shining armor," Charlotte said, reaching to grasp his bulging bicep.

He deflected her by lifting his elbow and lowering his sunglasses to peer at me. "You tell me."

I remembered falling into those luminescent blue-gray pools. Who's he think he is? James Bond? Close enough. I removed my sweatshirt to hide my blush. What the heck? Two can play this game. Control the center of the board.

I dropped the hoodie on my gear bag. "Probably not a knight, more like a pawn, perhaps? Definitely not a bishop. What are you doing here, wearing that? Got a death wish?"

"He goes here! Obviously." Charlotte huffed. Rolled her eyes. Hands on hips. Whoa dang. Her nasty attitude begged for a dose of comeuppance but I resisted.

Ian ignored her. "We're scrimmaging Navy today. If you get a break, come watch."

Charlotte gushed, "I will! I love watching you play!" She shot me a snotty look. A not-so-subtle reminder that they'd gone to high school together last year.

"Heading to the stadium. We play at noon." For a parting shot, he looked at me and fired, "Anchors away." Clever.

I countered with the rivalry reply, "Beat Army."

He tossed back, "Sink Navy."

I dared to snort. Out loud.

Lanie grimaced.

Charlotte hissed, "What was that about?"

I pulled on my club warmups in silence. Her anger had detonated, words would only stoke the smoldering embers.

Lanie sat next to me in her padded goalie gear as we watched the game before ours. "Don't let Charlotte get to you. She's just jealous."

Shaking my head, I said, "Here to win games, not Ms. Congeniality."

She laughed. "It's about Ian. He likes you, and it's killing her. She's thrown herself at him for two years, then you show up."

Cradling my stick, I kept eyes on the field, but ears tuned to Lanie.

Her attention returned to the game as a player shot on goal. "She's good. I dread playing her."

I shrugged, "Just watch for her 'tell.'"

"Her tell?"

"Yeah, she stutter steps before she shoots."

"Really?" We watched as they set up the draw mid-field.

"Yep. Here she comes again." Same stutter step. Same shot. Another goal.

"Okay, tell me more. How about Charlotte?"

"She fakes a pass, brings it back and shoots right. Every time." I showed her using mini-motions.

"Hah! Like anyone believes she'd go for an assist."

Spinning my stick, I said, "Works for her, she's got the stats to prove it. Goals that is, not assists."

Lanie bumped shoulders with me. "So, what's yours?"

Bumping back, I shook my head. "I never tell."

Tournament format. 19-minute halves. 2-minute halftime. Running clock. Fast and furious. Tourney games were a blast unless you have a vengeful, raging psychotic teammate who might shoot the hard, yellow rubber ball at the back of your skull instead of the goal.

I'd planned on pacifying Charlotte with selfless play, but Ian showing up forced that idea off the runway before it had a chance to take off. So what the heck, calculating our first game would be over by noon, I might be able to sneak over to see him play, depending on our schedule.

That thought crashed too. Our first success put us in the winners' bracket. Second game at 12:30. Against Jaz and Harley. Our somber team stood watching the current game. Lanie figured out another player's tell. Quick learner.

A boisterous laugh erupted on the other side of the field. I spied Jaz and Harley goofing around with a rowdy group stretching in a circle. Thumping bass drum beats and upbeat music from a portable speaker danced across the turf fields, metal bleachers and cement sidewalks. The song wasn't recognizable until Jaz jumped up, swaying back and forth, shoulders, hands, knees and feet lifting up and down, punctuating the rap lyrics part in her favorite, "Just Like Fire."

"Look at that idiot. We're going to crush them."

Stick-cradling stopped as my palms clenched around the cool metal tube in fists. Lanie noticed. She looked from my grip to Charlotte, then followed Charlotte's smug gaze.

"Oh, Jaz's a riot," Lanie said, "You'll have fun playing with her in season."

"Fun losing," Charlotte snorted as the horn blew.

Time to play against friends. With the enemy.

Harley caught my eye and tilted her head to the track behind us. I melted behind my team to meet her.

"Don't hold back. We'd rather you get the goals. Okay?"

Another plan shot down. I nodded, then paraphrased our cross country chant, "When I score high?"

Her conspiratorial grin grew like the Grinch's. "Charlotte scores low."

Jaz and Harley, both on defense, had learned the hard way how to read Charlotte and shut her down at last. I scored enough to keep my team ahead but not humiliate their goalie. When the horn blew both teams lined up. Except for Charlotte, who launched her stick to the sideline like a javelin. I saw Coach point and escort her back to the end of our line.

"Good game, Rogue! The Force was with you!" Jaz said as we moved past each other bumping fists.

Harley was next in line. "Thanks for taking it easy. We'll cheer for you in the Championship!"

I said, "Thanks. Can't wait to play *with* you guys."

"Can't wait to play *against* you, *Rogue*," a sarcastic voice behind me snarled. Charlotte.

Jaz shot back, "That makes three of us."

And there it was, the good, the bad and the smugly.

Clouds rolled across the Chesapeake Bay. The gray water took color cues from the sky, erasing the horizon. White foam crashed up the stone ripprapped shoreline adjacent to the vivid green turf fields. Eliminated teams don't stick around to watch, especially when the damp air threatens rain, so I was surprised to see spectators fill the stands. Butterflies invaded my stomach when I spotted Coach MacGavin introduce Mom and Dad to Coach Sinclair.

Butterflies morphed into hornets when Ian joined them. Wish I could have seen his scrimmage. More handshakes, introductions, then Dad's attention turned back to the coaches. Mom's focus, however, hovered like a momma hummingbird analyzing Ian's sweetness potential. She glanced my way. A slight curve of a smile teased her cheek. What was he saying? Was he talking about me?

"Gracie, watch out!" Lanie shouted.

I ducked as a ball whizzed past my shoulder.

"Get your head in the game," Charlotte growled as she ran past.

I did. Had to, because despite the cold air Charlotte was a hot mess. Her flubbed ground ball pickups, screams after missed passes, and wild shots on goal forced thoughts about coaches, parents, college and Ian to the back burners as the Championship game heated up. Halftime we were down by one.

"Sorry, Gracie! I can't figure out #23! She disappears behind the goal then comes out in my blind spot!"

"Keep your head on a swivel, and remember, she only shoots with her left hand."

Lanie's mouth dropped open before replying. "Wait, what? She's a leftie? How did I not know that?"

"You got a lot going on." I reached for the goalie stick, "My sister was a goalie, she taught me this." I showed her.

"Okay, what if she comes around on my right?"

Moving the stick to her right side, I said, "The angle is awkward, so she takes it out a little farther and has to turn in to shoot it top left. She should switch hands and go to top right, but she doesn't."

Lanie's head tilted, "I've seen you do that. It's wicked sweet. But now that I think about it, you never shoot the same way twice in a row. So when you said, 'I never tell,' you meant it. Because you don't have one."

My fingertips gathered to temples then exploded out. Mind-blown. "Busted."

Lanie sighed. "Can you shoot and not tell a lot this half?"

I nodded. "Yep. I'll try to and not to."

Twenty seconds left, tied score, the clouds cracked open; icy raindrops fell like shards of glass, stabbing exposed skin and coating the rubbery turf.

"Get it to Halsted for the shot," Coach said to everyone but focused on Charlotte, who looked straight ahead; her clenched jaw didn't nod in affirmation.

The ref set up the draw. Everyone held their breath. The whistle pierced the inhaled silence. Clock started. The ball popped toward Charlotte, she scooped it and drove downfield.

I stayed even with her as she ran, her flushed, goggled face didn't bother to glance my way. Charlotte telegraphed the fake pass, then brought the stick back to shoot on goal. Too wild. The ball careened out of her pocket as seconds ticked down in my head. Ten, nine, eight...

The yellow sphere floated across the gray sky in slow motion. Reaching up, pulling it in, using Charlotte as a shield, I crossed behind the goal cradling in my left.

Five, four, three... I switched to my right hand, burst out in front of the goalie and slipped as I fired. The horn sounded. My left knee exploded. Flames seared up my thigh, through my gut into my lungs and roared out my mouth as I fell into oblivion on the frozen turf.

The scream ripped through me. Eyes squeezed shut. Rolling side to side, rocking my tortured limb. Strong arms gathered my writhing body, tucked my face under a solid, stubbly chin. Thick cotton muffled the maddening cry. Warm air burst into my ear.

"Gracie listen. It'll be okay. I've got you."

19

"Bad Day" – Daniel Powter

Trapped. Numb, I shifted.

"Ouuuww-wuh!"

Thump, thump, thump. A wet nose dove into my neck forced my chin up and washed away dried tears with sloppy kisses. I hugged the furry head, inhaling the magical healing properties in the comforting scent.

Using both hands, I took my time sliding up the sheets to a sitting position to assess the damage. My left leg was intact, Velcro-strapped in a constricting black brace from ankle to upper thigh. At least it wasn't an itchy claustrophobic cast. Nothing broken. Okay. It didn't hurt if I kept it straight. Maybe just a sprain? Rest, not run for a few days. Not run? How does one do that? I've never been a not runner.

Nothing against NARPs like Hood Snap and Scooter, aka Non-Athletic Regular Person(s), it's just not my jam. Mom said I skipped from speed crawling to running to keep up with Jason. She also said I listened deeper and faster than most, to keep up with Sofi's constant ramblings. I miss them.

Having performed a successful wake-up, Roscoe and Mallory curled up at the foot of my bed like yin and yang: black with white paws, and white with black spots.

Looking around, I absorbed the chic Bohemian vibe of Mom's guest room/art studio on the main floor. Translucent batik gauze draped the windows for privacy, sunshine filtered through the colorful, paisley teardrop motif. Reminded me of the Kaleidoscope toy Sofi used to play with.

Thump, thump, thump.

My watchdogs detected someone approaching.

"Good morning, Sunshine!" Mom swept in with a tray displaying a periwinkle plate adorned with golden scrambled eggs, a cherry bran muffin, and orange slices. A cobalt blue glass of milk completed the artistic presentation. She put it on my lap, brushed away a lock of disheveled hair and placed her cool, Mom-thermometer cheek on my forehead.

"I'm not sick," I said, sounding grumpier than intended.

A quick kiss replaced her smooth-skinned cheek. "Grace Artemis, seventeen or eighty, you'll always be my baby."

Acquiescing, I took a sip, "This looks good, thanks."

She tucked the gauze behind a curved lizard hook and studied the garden. Still groggy from sleep, her silhouette glowed like an extraterrestrial.

"Time for your anti-inflammatory. Does it hurt?" She handed me a pill.

After popping it in my mouth and taking a drink, I answered, "A little. What'd the doc say? I was out of it. When can I go back to practice? Regionals are this weekend."

She placed a hand on my shoulder and sat next to me. "You hyperextended your knee and need to take it easy for a couple weeks until the swelling goes down. Then they'll do an MRI to see if there's any soft tissue damage."

My stomach dropped as that sunk in. Forget feeling sorry for myself, I couldn't run for my team. Will they be mad? Looking out the window my vision blurred.

Roscoe and Mallory launched off the bed. I clutched the tray; Mom caught the glass. Pain shot up my leg. "Ou-wah!" Appetite lost, I handed Mom the tray to sink into freakish despair just as Dad announced he was sending in guests. Great. Despite the saying, misery does not love company.

"Knock knock! Howdy, don't get up," Jaz said, smiling as she and Harley entered.

Mom laughed. "Come in and have a seat," she said, clearing art supplies from the bench next to her easel.

Harley gushed to Mom, "Wow, this room is the bomb! Is that your work? The colors are crazy!" She studied the canvas. "I can almost smell the flowers!"

My earlier apprehension melted as they admired Mom's work in progress, a hillside vineyard in Italy. They ooh'd and ahh'd as she explained how the artichoke and rose bushes planted at the end of each row protected the grapes from insects. Mom excused herself and left us to talk.

"Need a ride to school tomorrow?" Jaz asked.

School. Hadn't thought about it. How to hobble around? Slowly. Ugh. I don't do anything slowly. Sighing, I replied, "Sure, if you don't mind."

"No problemo. We'll take you to the office to get an elevator pass," Jaz said.

Harley added, "And ride with you to carry stuff."

"Thanks." I hesitated then confessed, "I can't run this weekend."

"No worries, we got your back," Jaz said, a sly grin curved her lips. "And speaking of backs..."

"You've been holding out on us," Harley interrupted.

Confused, I blinked, "What? How?"

"The dude that carried you off the field?"

Squinting, I thought back. The pain. Ouch. Got that. The scream. Didn't stop until my face was muffled under a stubbly chin. Warm words. Vibrating in my ear, *"... I've got you."*

My face flushed vivid red like Mom's painted roses.

"Ian."

They burst out laughing. "Yeah, him."

Looking down to hide my smile, I shifted and grimaced.

They got quiet. Harley's faced scrunched up, "Sorry, it must really hurt."

"Only when I bend it. It'll be okay." *I've got you...*

"So?" Jaz asked.

"So?" I feigned innocence.

"THE DUDE," they answered in stereo.

Twisting my hair into a ponytail, I dropped, "Oh, it must have been Ian. Coach MacGavin's son."

"Well, It Must Have Been Ian fulfilled the fantasy of every player on the field," Jaz said.

"Almost everyone," Harley added.

Looking up at the ceiling, I winced. "Charlotte."

"Yep. If looks could kill, you'd be dead," Jaz said as she drew a finger across her throat.

"Remember when Sienna fell in the creek and Michael tore off his shirt to bandage her bloody hand?" Harley asked, pretending to seductively strip off her shirt.

Jaz flipped her wrist and checked-marked the air with her index finger. "College Boy getting the trainer's approval, then carrying you off the field looked like that scene – on steroids."

Desperate for the visual, I zoned out, trying to picture it.

Jaz stood. "Well kiddo, we better bounce. Rest and recoup, we'll see ya at 7:45 tomorrow morning."

Shaking my head to refocus, I asked, "Does Sienna know?"

"Yep! She wants you to come to practice and hang out in the training room if you're up for it," Harley said.

Jaz added, "She assigned us bodyguard duty if Coach Hudson tries to give you crap."

Remembering Coach's other verbal assault victim, I said, "Not me, *Molly*."

"What about Molly?" Harley asked.

"Protect her, from Coach Hobbit – I mean Hudson." I rubbed my temples. Meds were kicking in.

Jaz cracked up. "Now that you mention it, she does kinda look like a hobbit."

"A grumpy one maybe. You're right though, she's gonna push Molly to take your place in top five," Harley nodded.

Surveying my brace, I said, "I'm bullet-proof. Take care of her."

After they left, I needed to use the bathroom. Decision: call Mom, or put on my big girl pants and go by myself? After an internal debate, I swung my right leg to the floor and lifted my left leg up and over like an automated machine. Bracing my right hand on the side table and the left on the bed, I rose. Wobbled for a second, then balanced upright. So far, so good.

I slid my injured leg forward, then hopped the good one to catch up. Okay. Evaluate. No jarring pain. I can do this. Slide, hop. Slide, hop. Across to the bathroom. Destination achieved.

Washing my hands, I looked into the mirror. OMG. I look awful. Yikes. Next to the sink was the laundry bin. A somewhat familiar, but a little bit different scent lingered over it. Reaching in, I grasped my game pinnie and raised it to my nose and inhaled.

Gross. True. But not now. Because my sweat mixed with Ian's dude/deodorant/cologne combo was intoxicating. How do I know such a thing exists? Because I have a brother. But thankfully it wasn't the same as Jason's, because that would be weird in a Luke/Leia/kiss before they realized in the next movie they were siblings way that made everyone in the theater gag. Thank you very much.

I folded it next to the sink and rested my palm on it. Hmm. Maybe?

20

"Bring It On Home To Me" – Sam Cooke

"What was the occupation of the female lead in the 1997 movie, *The Saint?*" Ms. Davis marched along the classroom storage counter wearing a lab coat with a pair of goggles shoved up on top of her head. Her attire was either a clue or a normal outfit for our eccentric sprite.

"A teacher," the brown-noser in the front row blurted.

"Close, but her occupation pays better," Ms. Davis said.

A shout from the other side of the room. "Pole dancer?"

Ms. Davis's splayed fingers covering her mouth, then pantomimed serious thought, dropping one hand to her hip, and resting her chin on the other thumb as her index finger tapped her cheek. "No. But you may be right about the money, honey." She pulled the goggles down her nose.

"A pilot?"

Ms. Davis pretended to flip switches, extended her arms and prepared to take off, then sputtered to a stop. "N-n-nope!"

Dervis lectured from the back row, "A scientist. Studying cold fusion as a renewable energy source to save the world."

"Eureka!" Ms. Davis punched the air. "Fifty points for Ravenclaw!" The perfect HP house for him and his relentless pursuit of knowledge and academia.

With my leg propped on a stool in the aisle, I attempted an awkward pivot to air bump Dervis. He responded with a silent chin lift, "'Sup."

After class, Ms. Davis was thrilled to see my historic Annapolis photographs. "That would be an awesome field trip option, thanks for sharing." She looked down at my brace. "Bummer, hope you have a speedy recovery."

"Thanks. Me too."

The rest of the school day flew by at the speed of a sloth. It took. For. Ever. To get anywhere. My teammates finished warmups as I lumbered into the gym. Sienna nodded, released the team to run, then came over with Josh.

"Sorry, Rogue. Sucks to be you," Josh said.

Sienna shoved him. "Jerk."

Josh's freckles glowed. "I meant it."

"Then try to mean it nicer," Sienna said.

Josh held out his palms like that annoying "What?" kid complaining to a ref about a legit penalty call. "Okay, what I meant was, sorry you crashed and burned, but I heard it was a wicked shot, and you won the tournament." He looked from me to Sienna. "That better?"

"A little," Sienna said, then added to me. "We want you to come to regionals with us."

"Sure, thanks." Swallowing a sudden lump in my throat, I pointed to the trainer's room. "I'll check with Ms. Smith to see if I can assist her."

"Sounds good, see you in a bit," Sienna said. She and Josh left for the track.

At the athletic trainer's room entrance, Coach Hudson emerged head down and grumbling, almost bumping into me. "Why aren't you running?" Her raspy voice reminded me of a spoon caught in a garbage disposal. Fabulous. Day keeps getting better and better.

Countering her accusatory squint with my poker face, I stepped back and pointed down to explain the obvious. "Hurt my knee." Paused for effect. "At a club lacrosse tournament."

Her disgusted growl was palpable.

"Thanks, Rogue! I assume you've told Coach Hudson the good news?" Dervis asked. An impish grin grew on his cheek.

"Told me what? Another lame excuse why you're not out running with the rest of the team either?" Coach demanded.

"About my quantitative statistical research into the exponential possibilities of your achieving the dubious honor of 'Coach of the

Year!'" We stared at him. His ability to keep a straight face while spewing a butt-ton of verbal diarrhea was impressive.

Coached blinked her squinty mole eyes. "What are you babbling about?"

"Of course the formula to determine if my hypothesis is viable requires further investigation, so since Rogue can't run, she can analyze the essential data." He held up his laptop case. "I've cross-referenced all of our runners' times, splits and points earned throughout the season. Come with me and I'll set you up in the C++ algorithm before I join the others." He ushered me into the training room as I choked back a laugh.

Dervis patted a trainer's table. "Jump up, I'll log you in."

"To what?"

He grinned. "World of Warcraft, you can battle against a character I created. An evil orc named, Attila the Hudson."

I snorted looking past him to the open door. "Sounds terrifying and hauntingly familiar."

He shrugged. "Meh. You can handle her."

An hour of building a warrior civilization later, laughter and footsteps echoed down the hall as the team spilled into the gym to stretch and cool down. I closed the laptop and took my time sliding off of the table to join my teammates.

Michael signed to Sienna, and she relayed it to the team. "Line up. Girls facing guys at center court."

Kids scrambled to obey as Michael cued up, "Bring It On Home to Me," by Sam Cooke. My view from the bleachers confirmed it was another secret song dedication to Sienna. The two lines mirrored each other, swaying, clapping and stepping with various degrees of skill and awkwardness, to the smooth rhythm led by Michael opposite of Sienna.

Watching them challenge back and forth the "yah – yah – yah – yah," lyrics made me smile until I saw Josh figure out he didn't need the Pythagorean Theorem to realize Sienna and Michael were kissing at the right angle, and that he was the hypotenuse at their feet. Poor guy.

"We're gonna have to do easy up-dos or wash-n-gos for the dance after regionals," Jaz said, driving home after practice.

"No big deal, since our group is all runners," Harley said, leaning forward in the back seat. She'd given me her normal place as shotgun for the legroom.

They discussed the team's Homecoming Dance group all the way to my house. I was in and out of the conversation, thinking about the Sienna, Michael, Josh love triangle. Funny, I'd never thought of myself as frivolous, but my Michael crush was gone like Donkey Kong and I was really happy for him and Sienna, besides feeling sorry for Josh.

"'90s Boy and Girl Bands is the theme, so it's way more casual. I'm on Student Council Planning Committee, and we're doing a paint splash black light room so wear a white t-shirt. Gonna be crazy fun," Harley said.

"Too bad Army can't carry you to the dance."

That brought me back. "What?"

"You heard me," Jaz said.

Harley grabbed my shoulder. "Your black knight in Army armor."

"You guys are making something out of nothing," I said, willing myself to be casual.

Jaz glanced over after parking in my driveway. "Yeah right, you didn't see how he looked at you."

A fact I'll regret for the rest of my life. How's that for a rare dose of teen drama? I opened the car door to escape any further inquisition. "Thanks for the ride."

"Same time tomorrow," Jaz called out.

Harley swapped to the front seat. "Next time Army sweeps you off your feet, I'll shoot a pic."

Next time. If only.

***

The rest of the week was exhilarating. By exhilarating, I meant exceedingly dull. This not-running, not knowing when I can run again injury was killing me. Fortunately, when the going gets tough, the tough get going to eat lunch with Krutch, Dervis and Hood Snap.

Sitting at their usual table, my tres amigos were shooting the breeze as I limped up. Well, Krutch and Dervis were, Hood Snap was refereeing the back and forth repartee with his usual silent hilarious expressions.

"So what did Chloe say, when she shot you down and crushed your heart into a million pieces?" Krutch asked. Ouch. Maybe I should walk away? Nope too late. Hood Snap waved me over.

"Cop a squat. We're streaming the new episode of *The Friendship Zone,*" Krutch said. Ouch. Ouch.

Hood Snap facepalmed.

Exasperated, Dervis ripped open a bag of chips and said, "It was the 'oh so sorry, already made plans, but can you help me with this assignment?'"

Hood Snap stood and did the Heisman pose, one knee raised, imaginary football protected close to his chest with one hand, the other stiff-arming players away. Ouch, ouch, ouch.

I riffed for the first time in my life, "Dervis, we've got a cross country group going, how about Krutch and Hood Snap join in, and Skater and Scooter?" Who is this alien creature talking in my voice? Am I channeling Sigourney Weaver? This injury may be way more serious than I thought.

21

"It's Gonna Be Me" – *NSYNC

Harley and Jaz deposited me on the front row of the bleachers in the senior section then dashed off on a mystery mission. Loud, laughing conversations buzzed around me as the rambunctious mob filed in for Friday's Homecoming Skit pep assembly.

Once again, the exponential growth of noise, heat and smells grew as the rowdy, apathetic, excited and bored student body packed in for the mandatory fun required or else event.

What a difference a couple of months make. At the previous all-school assembly I'd self-exiled and conducted a social conformity experiment perched high near the rafters. Turning to search the back of the Junior section, Krutch, Dervis and Hood Snap caught my eye, as did Freshmen Skater and Scooter, who much to my delight, had snuck over to sit with them in the upper-class block. Rebels. The group saluted me with Spock's Vulcan, "Live Long and Prosper" hand signs.

Nerds. I split my paired fingers in the V, extended the thumb, and held it high in response. They smiled and waved, except for Krutch, whose attention was elsewhere. I zip-lined down his gaze to see Mandi and the Mannequins arrive late. With Mandi at point, and Chloe at the longer end of the V-formation. They moved like a cursor toward the Junior section, where the crowd parted to open space in the middle of the first and second rows.

"How could she do that to Krutch?" I asked myself.

"What?" Sienna, sitting next to me, asked.

Oops. I'd said it out loud. "Pardon?"

Sienna frowned, "I couldn't hear, something about a crutch? Does your knee hurt?"

Shaking my head, "No. I'm fine. Just trying to stay out of the way."

EEEEEEEEEEEE! That shrill high-pitched feedback noise pierced through the amplification system. Those who could hear covered ears and grit teeth. Those who couldn't waited for an explanation.

Our principal held the microphone at arm's length as if it had bitten her. She grimaced, then spoke. Her interpreter signed, "Sorry about that, now that I have your attention, welcome to our Homecoming Assembly."

After the announcements about the football game tonight, dance tomorrow night, and tickets going on sale next week for *The Crucible*, the four classes competed in an obstacle course relay race that heavily favored the seniors, much to the disgust of the junior contestants who complained that the referees, who, being seniors, appeared biased. Go figure.

Then came the skits. First up were the teachers, dressed to the Nineties, as in, this year's theme. Pretty sure that their retro graphic t-shirts featuring Metallica, Nirvana, Pearl Jam, and U2 were from personal memorabilia, lovingly saved with concert tickets, playlists and guitar picks.

They parodied the '90's sitcom, *Friends*, drinking coffee and gossiping about "fictional" students while sitting on a couch they'd carried down from their lounge. It got some laughs.

My leg tingled. Too long in one position. I rubbed around my kneecap. The swelling was gone, so I no longer wore the brace. Next week, an MRI would determine my fate. Sitting. Still. Impatient. The only thing I could do was... wait for it... wait for it... wait for... what?

Sienna gave me a sympathetic smile, checked her watch, and looked around. Weird. Harley and Jaz were still MIA, along with co-captain Josh, tunes chairman Michael, aka Sienna's dance partner slash destined to be honey, Nick, and two other top guy runners. Oxford comma fully deployed. Good on me.

Ka-chunk. The lights went out, the crowd hushed. Five cell phone flashlights instantly cut across the wood planks to center court because you really don't want to keep 2,000 teenagers in the dark for too long, if you know what I mean.

Boom. Spotlight bounced around from the back row of the Junior section, hence, explanation of why Dervis is up top with the dudes instead of down with the cross country team. He's head of the tech crew in charge of lighting for the play and knows how to get stuff done.

Spot landed on five dudes frozen in a righteous boy band pose as "Bah bah bah-ahhh" introduced, "It's Gonna Be Me." This is gonna be good ;-)

Oh. My. Goodness, Michael, and the other guys. But, mostly Michael. Good thing my crush is over. Because, dang. Dude killed it. All five were decked out in *NSYNC boy toy outfits from the video but his chiseled arms in a sleeveless black t-shirt dominated.

Harley and Jaz flew down the sideline to join us. "This is so awesome! You're gonna love it!" Jaz fangirl screamed. "Show 'em how it's done, boys!"

"Check out Josh's eyeliner!" Harley said, adding, "I gave him the wing. And his eyelashes! In mascara! I told him he's much prettier than me."

Curious, I tracked. Josh. Harley. Whoa. The plot thickens. Remembering the "which one will Sienna pick" scenarios, Jaz seemed Team Michael, whereas Harley had tipped toward Team Josh. Interesting.

The guy dolls, like in the video, came to life and moved apart, lip-synching, stomping to the beat, crisscrossing their feet and alternating shoulder pumps. The overhead lights gradually turned back on as the crowd screamed for more.

Michael was in front, with Nick and Josh two steps back and a beat behind. One of the other runners was counting out loud and the other's bright red face was on a swivel trying to keep up. No need to worry, all eyes were on Michael. And his were on everyone, except one.

Sienna. Who sat beside me. Laughing. For now.

When the other guys' steps stuttered, counted beats like dashboard bobbleheads, and punched fists at the wrong times, Michael's smooth moonwalk mesmerized. He'd point to a section, and everyone in it screamed, reached out, or did silent applauding jazz hands. His every hip, hop and jump were poetry in motion.

Michael's avoiding Sienna while flirting with everyone else became an awkward problem. For her. And me. Glancing sideways, her frozen smile melted as she slowly sat up straight and stiffened as the temperature seemed to drop fifty degrees.

However, things heated up in front of the Juniors, where Michael stopped in front of Mandi and deployed a killer grin. The Mannequins swooned.

I almost vomited in my mouth. No Michael! Not you too! I wanted to look away for Krutch's sake, but couldn't. Mandi blinked, then a perfect smile grew, but not the posed one hundred selfies a day smile. No. This was sweet, bashful even, and quickly hid behind a cupped hand. The smile Krutch most likely remembered and pined for, I thought.

As the last lyrics rang out, the five returned to the center circle to strike the cheesy, awkward, boy band pyramid pose as Michael pumped his fist over his heart two times, locked eyes with Sienna, and pointed his thumb to his chest on the last "gonna be me." The crowd roared.

Obviously pissed, but equally impressed, her arms crossed her chest in defiance. Oooh. He would pay for his insolence. And most likely, both would enjoy it. I think their past history has caught up to the delicious present and has a promising future if he survives.

The guys joined us. Jaz fist-bumped each of them like a heavy-weight champ. Sienna gave Michael the cold shoulder, but he copped a squat on the floor in front of her with a satisfied smirk. Harley scooted over to make room for Josh.

The last skit featured the pep band playing a mashup of '90's hits while the football players stood planted like trees and the cheerleaders danced around them dressed as woodland nymphs. Random, not quite sure how it fits the theme, but the audience played nice. All righty then. For some strange reason, it brought to mind Shakespeare's romantic mixed-up star-crossed comedy, *A Midsummer Night's Dream*. In a daze, I pictured Sienna, Michael, Mandi, and Krutch as the lovers, Chloe, a magical fairy and featured Dervis, as a clever, mischievous, but unlucky Puck.

Friday night, Saturday day and Saturday night were jammed packed with a lot of stuff to do that I couldn't. Like I wanted to. Skipped Friday's game because of the early regional team bus departure. Perfect conditions for a cross country run that I didn't. Josh lost the girl but won the race. And then got a different girl. Sienna ran well and got the guy and Jaz had a blast being Jaz.

Jaz picked me up for the dance and I got to legit ride shotgun because Harley was going with Josh! We wore white t-shirts and jeans. Jaz, a mini skirt and me, bootcut with my black low top Chucks. We went straight to the splash paint room to accessorize. Splattered and happy we returned to the dance. Even though I wouldn't, but Jaz would.

While she got her crazy on, I sat back in the shadows. It turned out to be the primo view for the spectacular arrival of Mandi and her Mannequins, each in a tight, different colored sequined mini dress straight out of a Spice Girls video. She froze. Mandi that is, noticing the casual paint-splattered attire. Her posse appeared appalled at the informal nature of the surroundings, whereas, Mandi looked mortified. I wondered. What goes on inside that perfect facade?

***

There's always that guy, you know the one, who flails around like a twenty-foot nylon inflatable advertising prop on the curb that you can't ignore as you drive by. Tonight, at the Homecoming Dance, that guy was Hood Snap. Witnessing Ichabod Crane on the dance floor was a sight to behold. Fortunately, he be holding Skater right now, and they be having a frenetic blast.

Meanwhile, at the non-dancing sitting around watching everyone else dancing table, Krutch, Dervis, Scooter and I sat. Watching. Krutch, avoiding looking anywhere near Mandi. Dervis, grumbling as Chloe, in a green shiny mini aka Posh Spice relished her version of "All The Single Ladies" with the Mannequins. Minus Mandi. Who hid in the corner trying not to be noticed for the first time in her life as Scooter captured everything in a woodland fantasy landscape on a sketchpad. Which was a beautiful thing. Dang. The girl can draw. An imaginary world where knees – and hearts – aren't hurting.

22

"For Whom The Bell Tolls" – Metallica

Cold, but resolute, I laid on the molded plastic slab in a thin cotton hospital gown and little else. Descending into the claustrophobic tunnel, cool air flowed around me. I instantly regretted my choice of radio station instead of streaming classical music, as an annoying car dealership commercial screamed into my ears through the padded headphones designed to muffle the ominous CLANG, CLANG, CLANG of the MRI machine. For whom the bell tolls; it tolls for me.

My nose itched. Would it mess up my knee imaging if I scratched it? Probs. So. Ignore it. And the music, or lack of. Try to meditate. Ommmm... No. Brought to mind the Grumpy Cat meme. Don't laugh. Must... not... move. Why am I think talking like that old TV Star Trek captain, what was his name? The one before Piccard? Oh, Kirk. That's it. Captain Kirk. Makes me think of the new movie Captain Kirk. Chris Pine. Wonder Woman's blue-eyed aviator. Now that's an image to meditate onmmmmmm... yum.

Approximately one hundred sixty-eight hours and thirty-seven minutes later, I sat in a sterile room at Dr. Jenson's office with Mom. Waiting for the jury to deliver their verdict. Still no word from Northwestern regarding acceptance or merit scholarship. Meaning, the only monetary aid at the moment, my signed National Letter of Intent, rested on the condition of my leg, connected to my foot, nervously bobbing up and down at random.

Mom placed a hand on my knee. The warm touch stifled the movement but not the uncertainty. I don't like waiting. A fact mentioned before. A trait I share with my sister, Sofi. Along with our warped sense of humor and penchant for sarcasm. The last two eluded me now, as I feared the tolling bells.

A knock at the door announced Dr. Jenson. "Hello!" She greeted us with a tight smile and maneuvered around a stool to wash her hands in the small metal sink. The force she used to tear two paper towels from the wall dispenser made me jump. After drying her hands, she crumpled and disposed of the waste with efficiency.

Her slim athletic frame and running shoes had set me at ease at our initial meeting when we chatted about team sports. She'd played high school lacrosse too, and still made room for long runs in her hectic schedule. Today, however, that kindred comradery was gone, replaced by professional empathy. She patted the smooth white tissue on the examination table. "Hop up and scoot so your legs are straight."

I did. The sheet crinkled as my palms pushed down and butt shifted back. My knees looked pretty much the same, except for the scar on my right knee from when I was learning to ride a bike and crashed into our mailbox.

Dr. Jenson pushed gently on the problem knee. It didn't hurt. Much. A tinge, nothing I can't handle. Studying my poker face, she called my bluff. "Gracie, you tore your ACL."

CLANG. Doubtful, I asked anyway, "Can I play on it?"

Inhaling deeply, then exhaling through her nose, she bent my good knee to ninety degrees, pointing below the kneecap scar. "The ACL is a key ligament that stabilizes your knee joint; it limits the lower leg so you don't hyperextend the knee. It allows you to cut, rotate, fake out your opponent." Taking the joint in both hands she manipulated it to illustrate then put it back down. "If we don't repair it, it'll blow out."

CLANG. Bending in half, I stretched my fingers past toes and rested cheekbones on my inner kneecaps. Strange, they fit like puzzle pieces. Lacrosse tryouts aren't until February. Calculating. I sat back up, sliding hands to knees. "Surgery?"

She nodded. "Yes."

CLANG. Frustrated, I asked the million-dollar, or more like tens of thousands in tuition and fees, question. "How long until I can *PLAY*?"

"With physical therapy, recovery is two to six months."

Formulating. It's almost December... January... CLICK. Decision made. I locked eyes with Dr. Jenson, "You have two months. Clock's ticking."

Dr. Jenson opened her mouth, paused, shut it again. A thin smile grew. She nodded once and said, "Fair enough. Orthopedic knee surgeries are on Thursdays."

I said to Mom. "Next Thursday. Before break. I'll miss Friday. We'll only be watching movies anyway."

Mom scheduled with Dr. Jenson as I rolled backward one vertebrate at a time to lie prone in corpse pose, with fingers pressing in on my ears. Humming. To block out the mocking mental TICK, TICK, TICK of the next two months of wasted seconds.

Numb, riding home in the passenger seat of Mom's Prius with my eyes shut. I feel nothing. See nothing. Hear nothing. Because, when the engine isn't running, like at a stoplight, everything shuts down. I have become a metaphor.

***

While Jaz skied and flirted with chair lift operators in Colorado and Harley played beach volleyball and basked in the sun, I got my knee sliced open and replaced with a tendon harvested from my hamstring. They didn't know. I hadn't told them. Or anyone.

The first few days were rough. Mom fed me healthy soup and pain meds so I could hibernate. When the pain roared me awake, Dad hooked up the circulating ice water machine to quell the sharp fangs gnawing on my leg. Then we'd play chess or binge-watch *Psych* or *Sherlock*, depending on my ability to concentrate.

Saturday and Sunday, I plunged feet first into the river of despair at the bottom of Melancholy Canyon. Clinging to a log tossed about in the rapids, not bothering to dodge the sharp rocks.

Monday, the pain was finally under control. To celebrate, Mom put my hair in a bun and helped me pull a large plastic leg condom over my immobilizing brace. She then excused herself so I could drop towel and hobble into the shower on crutches.

Refreshed but exhausted, dry and dressed in clean sweats by the window overlooking Mom's now barren garden, I eased back into Dad's recliner that he'd brought in from the family room. My chariot, ship, or cockpit, depending on today's genre. Alone. Again. I dove into the pages where I could ride, sail and fly in search of my long-lost but not forgotten fictional friends.

Theft of Swords, *Volume One of the Riyria Revelations*, by Michael J. Sullivan. This time reading, I'll pretend to ride bareback behind Royce, because Hadrian's much bigger, and I don't want to get bashed upside the head by his giant sword. I've missed them, and their charming bro buddy banter.

I'd met them... let me see... groggy from meds, I closed my eyes to think... *six years ago, the summer before sixth grade in a new school, town, state and country. We'd just moved back to the U.S.*

Sofi had sprinkled her typical packet of Insta-Pop Glitter and was off with new friends. But Jason was there for me. Until he discovered the girl next door. Joan Jett Bennett. Dark, quiet and clever, the way he talked made me both despise and adore Joan from afar, until the fortuitous, but also miserable day when Jason asked her to hang out with me when I was home alone.

Fortuitous, because she'd brought a book with her, so we lounged in comfy chairs, devouring delicious final chapters.

Miserable, because I finished first. I'd sighed, and confess, whined. Bemoaning the fact that my beloved fictional friends left me. Alone. Again.

And that's when Joan had shared Royce, Hadrian and the secret with me. They never go. They're here with me forever. Hiding. All of them. My favorite characters. And when they're needed most, like now, I know where to find them.

23

"Desperado" – Linda Ronstadt

Tuesday, despite the pain, my mood tip-toed across a hopeful high wire connecting treacherous cliffs of uncertainty, working up a sweat with my supportive physical therapist. Once home, exhausted, I mounted my recliner/trusted steed to catch up with my favorite assassin and his faithful swordsman as they deciphered myths, magic and legends to determine the fate of humans, elves, wizards and more.

Buzz. An annoying vibration yanked me back to reality. Not recognizing the number on my muted cell, I clicked it off and returned to a simpler, medieval time before such distractions were invented.

Ding. A muffled alert notified me that the caller I didn't want to talk to had left a voicemail I won't bother listening to.

Wednesday, I finished *Rise of Empire, Volume Two of the Riyria Revelations* before lunch. Then Mom took me to get whooped up on by my previous sweetheart now sadistic physical therapist. Back home, sore, I collapsed carefully into bed, cued up a Women of the '70s Spotify playlist, and put on chunky headphones to take a nap.

But didn't. Because...

"'Desperado?' Oh, hell-o no. I'm crashing this pity party. Until further notice, you are hereby banned from Mom's Linda Ronstadt, Carole King, and Carly Simon hippy break up downer, you done me wrong, songs."

Sofi's home for Thanksgiving. Hurrah. She stood beside me, dangling the headphones snatched from my dosing head. I've missed her. But her sparkle hurt my eyes. "Let me sleep."

She sniffed the headphones and pinched her nose. "And when was the last time you washed your hair?" Drawing a squiggly line in the air from my messy bed head to fuzzy socks. "Because you give new meaning to 'Uptown Funk.' Get your bootie outta bed."

"No." Her bossiness annoyed me.

"No?" My obstinance lit her fuse.

"No." I pulled the covers up under my chin.

"NO-WUH?" Control freak mode activated, Sofi's blue eyes flashed as her hands flew into the air like flushed birds.

Flipping a dismissive palm out, she shouted a curt. "NO! What are you, French? Listen, Princess, I'm the Queen of Sassy Talk Back. A giver, not a taker."

Oh, hell no hath no fury like Sofi scorned.

I burst out laughing, which earned me a reprieve.

Sofi flopped sideways into the recliner, one leg draped over the leather arm, pink polished toes kicking up and down. "Spoiled brat. Can't believe Dad dragged this throne in here. Mom making your favorite dinners and special treats?"

"Pretty much." I shrugged. When we were little, being sick had its rewards. Movies, milkshakes and bubble baths.

"Have you talked to Jason?"

"After surgery, but I don't remember much. You?"

"Texts. He and Joan are coming for Christmas. If he doesn't put a ring on her finger, I'll wring his frickin' neck."

I laughed. "How about minding your own business?"

She scoffed, "How about no. Seriously, when it comes to romance, you and bro need the clue bird to fly over and crap on you once in a while. Speaking of..."

"We weren't." I interrupted.

"Well, we are now. What's up with Ian MacAwesome?"

Blushing, I covered my face with a pillow and groaned.

"Just as I thought. You ARE desperado. Did you call to thank him for first responding you off the field?"

Dropping the pillow, "How do you know about that?"

"Pffft. I've got my sources."

"Mom?"

"No!" Repeat of snide gesture.

"DAD?"

"Yep, practically offered your hand in marriage," she said, wiggling her left ring finger. "After you've graduated college and established a fulfilling career worthy of your extreme nerdiness, that is."

I two-handed facepalmed. "Ahhhh, kill me now."

"Not a chance. Can't wait to meet my future bro in law. Let's call him! Maybe he's back too!"

"Let's not and say we didn't."

"Riiigghhht. Where's your phone?"

I swallowed. Remembering. The distracting buzzing. When I was reading. In the recliner. That she's sitting in. "Um, maybe in the bathroom? Could you check?"

Our eyes locked. Sofi squinted, then her angelic pink lips curved into a diabolical smile as she lifted her phone from her pocket, scrolled, and punched.

Buzz. Buzz. Buzz. Reaching down between the arm and cushion, she retrieved mine.

"I don't have his number."

"We'll see. Oh. Password protected. Let me think... six numbers... 235711. Primes. You are such a geek." She sighed and shook her head.

"Sofi!"

"You have seven contacts? Seriously? Let me guess. M: Mom, D: Dad, J: Jason, S: me, Jz: that would be Jaz, I've got hers. Ha: Harley, Si: Sienna. What about Kr: Krutch, De: Dervis and HS: Hood Snap?"

"Why and how do you have Jaz's number?"

"Welcome to social media. School. Sport. Roster. Boom. And we're friends on Snapchat."

"Why?"

"Details. Perspective on Ian. Hold up. You have a missed call and a voicemail." Her excited voice jumped in pitch as I wondered and worried who I'd blown off for Royce and Hadrian.

She put it on speaker and set it on the recliner arm.

"Hey, Gracie. It's Ian. MacGavin." Pause.

Sofi gave me two thumbs up. "Deep voice. Yum."

"Ssshhh!"

He continued, "Heard about the surgery. Dad told me. I won't be back for Thanksgiving." Pause. "I've got field exercises." Pause. "Maybe I can drop by in December?" Pause. "Okay then, take care."

Sofi picked up the phone. Thumbs pummeled the screen.

"What are you doing? You better not be calling him! Or texting! Sofi!"

"Chill-lax bra. Of course not. Or at least, not yet. I added him to Contacts. He got six letters!"

"Sofi..."

She grinned. "BigMac. But a word to the wise? You may want to knock it back to *Ian* before December rolls around. Sometimes these things have a way of circling back to bite."

"Speaking from experience?" I asked.

"Yep." Sofi looked down at my phone. "What's going on with your crew? You have like a billion un-opened texts."

Messing with her, I asked, "My crew?"

"Crew, posse, you know, real humans you hang with."

Shifting to sit up, *Heir of Novron, Volume Three of the Riyria Revelations* got bumped to the floor.

Sofi's quick glance recognized the cover. "Seriously? Those two. Again?"

I ignored her. "Everyone's on break."

"But they're checking on you, right?"

"Why would they?"

"To see how your surgery went, Dufus."

My gaze avoided hers and escaped out the window into Mom's lovely, peaceful, judgment-free garden.

"You didn't tell anyone." She sighed. "Grace Artemis, remember that poem you were obsessed with on Dad's tour when we lived on that remote island? 'No man is an island, no man stands alone?'" She continued, 'Each man's joy is joy to me. Each man's grief is my own?'"

"*We need one another, So, I will defend, Each man is my brother, Each man is my friend,*" I murmured, staring outside.

"NO retreating back to that island of fictional friends. Not on my watch. Books are great for recovering, but you've got a good thing going here. Real people who care about you. So Monday morning you're going to rise up and put yourself out there. Get it?"

"Got it."

"Good. Now, about that shower."

24

"Underdog" – Alicia Keys

Mom waved then closed the door as I crutched to the car.

Harley exploded from the front passenger seat. "What happened? Did you hurt it again?" Her sun-tanned face was cloudy with concern. She adjusted her seat for maximum legroom, took my backpack, ushered me in, then jumped in the back.

Jaz was less sympathetic and more intuitive. "You had surgery and didn't tell us?" Her voice deadpan.

Nothing to do but own it. "Sorry." How do I explain? Fumbling the seatbelt, "I guess, the fewer people who knew, the less real it was. Does that make sense?"

She put the car in reverse. "No. But I'm sure it sucked so you get a pass."

Changing the subject, I asked, "How was Colorado?"

Her face brightened. "Heaven. Too much fun." With that, she skied off on a Rocky Mountain adventure synopsis.

***

I'd missed the question of the day by the time I thump, step, dragged into Civil War Spies class.

"Howdy! Good to see you Gracie, you're going to enjoy the secrets I discovered in Annapolis over break!" Ms. Davis clapped and bounced to the whiteboard, an effective diversion from my awkward entrance.

Hood Snap slipped out from his desk without sound or ceremony to deliver a stool to prop up my leg, then slid back to the last row without making eye contact. Smooth. After getting situated, I blind air-bumped him over my shoulder. Pretty sure it was returned.

As Ms. Davis began, my focus shifted to the row of spy movie posters along the far classroom wall. All of the Bonds, in order, saving the best for last, in my not-so-humble opinion, Daniel Craig.

Three weeks left in the semester, my favorite class and the Civil War were coming to an end. By 1865, women were no longer viewed as inconsequential or harmless, as several female spies on both sides were caught, imprisoned or died for their causes. However, a number persevered and lived to write about their daring wartime exploits. My take from today's documentary was that looks can be deceiving, and conversely, deceiving can be accomplished by knowing how, when, and where to look.

After class, students jostled to get out of the room. The three waited for me. Dervis grumbled, "Can't believe the ruthless woman who survived three husbands and took her espionage act on the stage when the war was over."

Hood Snap slung my backpack over his bony shoulder and handed me my crutches as Krutch added, "Maybe she was addicted to attention."

"Hold up, Gracie." Ms. Davis came over, motioning to my brace. "Sorry about the setback."

I shrugged. "Necessary to move forward."

"If you've got some free time, we could use an extra pair of hands on the play's sound crew." Not tracking for a sec, then I remembered Dervis had told me she was the director.

Suspecting Ms. Davis was throwing me a bone to get my mind off being out of action, I improvised, "As long as no one tells me to break a leg."

Krutch snorted. Dervis grinned. Hood Snap facepalmed.

"Dress rehearsal tonight. Get her up to speed, Dervis. Welcome to the crew. See you backstage in a few!" She gave us a deep, theatrical bow then danced back to her desk.

I didn't know much about theater. Lacrosse fields were my stage and growing up with Sofi had provided enough drama for a lifetime so I'd steered clear. Taking mental notes while Dervis explained that the makeup/costume, prop/scene, and sound/lighting crews behind the curtain must work as a precision machine, I was skeptical. But after the first hour, I was a believer. There were two teams, the actors and the crew, but rather than opposing, they supported each other.

"Of course drama wouldn't be drama without a little bit of backstage stabbing," Dervis said.

"What do you mean?" I asked.

"Remember when you helped me join the theater group's Snapchat?"

"Turns out, after cast list posted, the mean posts stopped. As in, everyone got what they wanted."

"Weird. Or is that par for this alternative reality?"

"No clue. But I'll keep digging."

"Of course you will." I smiled at my friend.

"Rogue!"

Surprised to hear my nickname, I swiveled in my soundcheck chair to discover Aspen jumping up and down on the other side of the stage. She grabbed her twin, Willow, and disappeared behind the hangman's stand prop only to reappear by my side.

"Welcome to our drama-rama-ding-dong! So sorry 'bout your leg, Mate, but happy you joined the crew! Like the sets?"

"Positively bewitching." Laughing, I surprised myself, letting out that pun. Blame it on the pain meds. But it was good to see the two sisters so engaged.

Aspen clapped then threw her hands up in praise mode. "Righteous! *The Crucible*? Bewitching? Gotta love it! Classic thespian humor! Scooter designed 'em, Biff and Garth helped me build 'em! They've been so much help! What 'til you see 'em in action. Stealth ninja prop/scene shifters, they are!"

I looked at Willow. "The steampunk sets and costumes are brilliant."

She gave me a coy smile. Dressed in black head to toe, she stood with her legs and feet turned to a 90-degree angle from her hips like a ballerina. Her constant companion, a sketchbook, pressed tight to her chest. Willow aka Scooter didn't seem to mind that the nicknames had stuck, as Aspen aka Skater delighted in using them.

"And, she's doing everyone's makeup too! Painting faces like canvases," Aspen said.

"Let's get this show on the road!" Ms. Davis stood center stage calling out through an old-school megaphone, "Places everyone!"

"Oops! Gotta skate! Chat later!" Aspen whispered and melted away.

Working the digital mixing console was all-consuming. Controlling church bells, cracks of thunder, and slamming doors. Sounds that reinforced what the actors experienced as they projected their lines to the audience through individual hidden mics. A delicate balance at best, an annoying inconvenience sending screeching feedback shivers down the backs of those who could hear at worst.

After a few of the latter, I achieved enough of the former to take a break so another newb could learn the ropes. I went out to watch the actors act. And did they. Act that is. She. Mostly. Mandi. Wow. Aspen hadn't exaggerated. An enigma, that girl. Beauty *is* a beast.

SparkNotes for *The Crucible* can be summed up like this if you wanted to live, you lied. If you told the truth, you died. Dervis' crush Chloe's Abigail convincingly lied, connived, accused and survived, while Mandi's character Sarah Goode both innocent and truthful, denied, and hung.

***

By the sound of it, opening night was a success. So were Friday night, Saturday matinee and again that night. Four shows and a semester worth of hours culminating in applause, bouquets, and bows.

Even though I'd been a part of it for only a week, the play had provided a diversion from my dismal, sport-free existence. No longer on pain meds other than an occasional dose of sarcasm administered by Sofi via memes, my foul Monday morning mood was obvious. I slumped in my chair.

After class, Ms. Davis called me out. "What now?"

"Pardon?" I looked at her, to Krutch, Dervis, Hood Snap, then back to her.

"What are you going to do to steer clear of crazy town?"

Confirmation. Getting me "to help" with the play was for my sanity's sake. "No clue."

"Yes Clue! Smashing idea!" She swung a fist in an arc across her body.

Leaning on my crutches, I shrugged, which is awkward. "Um. Not. Quite. Tracking."

"An after-school board game club, as in B-O-R-E-D." She spelled it out waving hands in the air. "For those suffering from theater withdrawal, or end of a sport season slump, or in your case, sidelined by an injury. First up, Clue. We need six to play." Clapping, she bounded to her desk, picked up a purple marker and circled a date on her large white paper calendar. "Friday BGC."

Krutch announced, "Colonel Mustard, at your service."

"You'd make a plum professor, Dervis," Ms. Davis said.

"I'm game. That makes you Mr. Green." He gestured to Hood Snap.

Hood Snap studied the ceiling for a moment, rubbed his chin, then nodded. This should be interesting.

"Gracie, you and two more." She counted on her fingers. "To play Miss Scarlet, Mrs. Peacock, and Mrs. White. I will be the butler and host! Now, if you'll excuse me, I have to prepare. It's a matter of life," she dragged a finger across her throat then continued, "and death!" Looking behind us, she gasped, grabbed her throat, then staggered across the room to collapse into her chair; eyes closed, her tongue hanging out.

After a moment of silence, Krutch gave her three slow claps. She opened one eye, "Oh! Be sure to wear costumes!" She winked and played dead. We left her to R.I.P: Rest In Plan-mode.

After we recruited Aspen and Willow to round out the group it was no surprise that Aspen laid claim to Miss Scarlet. Willow's choice of Mrs. White, however, was perplexing.

I'd assumed the artist would choose the creative and colorful Mrs. Peacock. Not exactly my jam. Not that I had a jam – unless it were blueberry, on whole-grain waffles with pecans. It was so far out of my comfort zone, I had to call the all-time queen of theme crusher. Sofi. Of course, in a heartbeat, she remembered Mom's beaded, velvet peacock scarf, easily draped over anything I wore to school. Money in the bank. Her consultant fee was hefty though, a Snap Chat picture of the entire crew, but well worth it.

Friday after school, the six of us admired each other's costumes as we stood outside Ms. Davis's locked room. The lights were out. No "body" home?

"Should we knock? I'm gonna knock," whispered Aspen aka Miss Scarlett's pouty red lipstick lips. Dressed in a ruby flapper dress borrowed from the theater department, she rapped on the door, then jumped back as if electrocuted when the lights flashed on and off.

Thunder cracked inside, then the door slowly creaked open, or at least sound effects made it seem so.

"Stand back, while I investigate," Krutch aka Colonel Mustard's authoritative voice ordered. The golden leaf-shaped "scrambled eggs" embellishments on his vintage Army green visor both matched and contrasted his casual sunshine-colored patterned shirt featuring dancing hula girls.

Aspen giggled and clutched Hood Snap's arm. He wore his usual black long sleeve t-shirt and jeans but had added a cheap, green bowler hat, probably a St. Patrick's Day leftover from the Party Store. His long slender hand covered both of hers, tucking her close as they followed Krutch in.

I held the door for Dervis aka Professor Plum, dressed like a scholar in a crisp white dress shirt, dapper vest, a purple bow tie, and round black-framed spectacles. He, in turn, ushered in Willow aka Mrs. White, wearing a draping white dress, short white gloves, a long strand of pearls, and a satin cap with netting pulled down over her dark, inquisitive eyes.

I now understood her selection and vision, as her outfit was elegant and spot on.

"Good evening," Ms. Davis said, welcoming us in with a low bow. She wore a pleated white shirt, a black bow tie, white gloves, and a short black jacket over pin-striped slacks. Standing at attention, heels together, toes out in V formation, she held a silver platter. Melancholy organ music softly played in the background.

"This is lit!" Aspen gushed, dragging Hood Snap over to our butler/host as the rest of us filtered in.

Offering the tray, in a proper British accent, our host cleared her throat then said, "Please collect your character's piece as well as the envelope on which it stands. Within each envelope, you will find three clue cards. Each card contains either a person – who, or a room – where, or a weapon – how!"

We took our accoutrements, then positioned ourselves around a wooden table laid out with pencils, tally sheets, dice and the previously stuffed, confidential Solution envelope in the middle of the game board. Play commenced.

What a hoot. It was obvious who did what and why based on idiosyncrasies and personalities. Miss Scarlet flitted around the board, guessing at random with abandon and Mr. Green in tow, not bothering to record any information ascertained.

Mr. Green simply moved the weapon and person into whatever room he was yanked into and made a silent guess. They were cute and totally couple-worthy.

Colonel Mustard marched room-to-room, conquering as much territory as possible. Mrs. White closely observed everyone, then ignored the tally sheet side completely and drew an epic climax murder scenario on the back.

That left Professor Plum and me to systematically decipher every clue and diligently record Xs and Os on our respective sheets.

Until Colonel Mustard asked if anyone could stop him. "Professor Plum, in the library, with the wrench." Round the table, it went. A chorus of No's.

"Nope," Miss Scarlet answered.

Mr. Green bit his lip. His eyes looked side to side. He nudged her. She looked at him. His eyebrows rose. She shrugged and shook her head.

Colonel Mustard flourished a fist like a sword high in the air. "Attention! I'm making an accusation. Professor Plum, in the library, with the wrench!"

Our butler/host grimaced, reached for the Solutions envelope, extracted the cards, then displayed them.

Wrench. Library. Colonel Mustard!

Miss Scarlet blushed, as her hand shot to her mouth. "Oops, I've got Professor Plum. Sorry!"

Crickets.

Then Colonel Mustard slapped his thigh and guffawed. "Whootenalley! Golly what a day!"

Gotta love him. Krutch to the rescue. Mistake absolved.

Too much fun and too soon done.

Tuesday morning, I knew the Spy Movie Question of the Day, "Who played the cameo role as Austin Powers in the parody's introduction sequence, *Goldmember*?" Tom Cruise, but I didn't shout it out. Instead, I sat back, observed, and studied the new display on the Civil War Spies class bulletin board above the cabinet next to my desk. Yellowed reproductions of newspapers' headlines in block serif fonts declaring Robert E. Lee's surrender of the last major Confederate army to Ulysses S. Grant at the Appomattox Courthouse on April 9, 1865.

Thinking about Ms. Davis's performance artist dances from whiteboard to the black board to Clue board to keep her students, and lately, me in particular, from being bored got me wondering. So when the buzz buzzed, I told the guys to go ahead and stayed behind to solve another mystery.

After the rest of the students left, I step – slid, step – slid, step – slid, up to her desk, sans crutches. She clapped, "Mrs. Peacock, your injured wing is improving!"

"Yes Ma'am, I mean, Mr. Butler," I said, smiling a bit.

She chuckled and asked, "What can I do you for?"

I paused, considered my next move, then rolled the dice. "Are you worried about me?"

Her head tilted, she frowned, "What? No. You're one of the last people I'd worried about. Why?"

Full speed ahead. "Because – you asked me to 'help' with sound for the play when it was more than covered, then the Bored Game Club to keep me out of crazy town? I see a pattern." I shrugged.

"Oh. Let's just say I can relate. What do you have next?"

"Study hall, no problem."

"I've got a plan period; let's chat."

Taking the brown-noser's front row center seat, it was no surprise when Ms. Davis hopped up on her desk and sat with her legs dangling over the edge.

"Back in the day, believe it or not, I was an extremely competitive gymnast, on track for nationals and beyond. I lived, drank and ate it, which is rare, the eating part, it used to be you had to weigh next to nothing. Thankfully that's changing." She took a breath. "But back then, while others starved themselves, my metabolism let me eat a ton and go full steam ahead." Her hand shot out like a rocket.

Watching how she punctuated her story reminded me of going with Mom to pick up Sofi and being amazed at the pixies in ponytails flipping, twirling and leaping. All things Ms. Davis did in class daily.

She continued her narration. "I was stupid fearless. Until the day I face-planted onto the balance beam, then dismounted with a body slam to the floor. Concussion Number One."

Grimacing, I shifted my brace and rubbed my knee.

"Believe me, it was painful, not only that, I couldn't read, or write or concentrate on anything. I went Bonkers, which is two train stops short of Crazy Town."

I nodded, and despite the serious topic, her tone was so light-hearted I said, "I've been to Bonkers. Visited my sister. She lives there."

Ms. Davis slapped the desk and laughed.

"She was a gymnast too, and a cheerleader, and a goalie for lacrosse. She's the one who got me into it. Lacrosse, that is." My smile faded as my gaze returned to my leg.

She quickly said, "Concussion Number Two occurred when my best friend and I disproved the theory that two headers are better than one, at least when playing soccer."

My hands went to my head. "Ouch."

"Yep, that recovery took me past Bonkers to Boredville. Population: one miserable, frustrated kid. Especially when my parents sat me down for 'the talk.'" She smirked, adding, "Not that talk, the other one. The give up the Olympic dream or face a Concussion Number Three and potential permanent cognitive damage one." With an impish grin, she asked, "Guess which one I chose?"

Despite her attempt at levity, I had to ask, "Any regrets?"

Her mouth scrunched sideways as she looked up in thought. "Honestly, every four years, a part of me turns a wee bit green when I hold my breath and watch the Olympians compete. Coulda, woulda, shoulda, ya know?" She paused, sighed, then added, "But the rest of the time, I get to interact with all kinds of kiddos, not only dedicated athletes, but inquisitive scholars, creative artists, talented musicians, and all-around whack-a-doodles that make the world a better, more interesting place."

"Sounds like you made the right decision."

"Speaking of, what's the next stop on your journey?"

"You mean if I steer clear of Crazy Town?"

She kicked her feet. "It's okay to visit, just don't take up permanent residence."

I snorted, then sighed. "I'm stuck in the waiting zone. On the sidelines. I've signed a Letter of Intent to play lacrosse on an athletic scholarship," I paused, looked down at my leg, then shook my head. "But I need more financial aid to afford Northwestern University." I rambled on. "Both my siblings paid their way through college with ROTC and academic scholarships." Biting my lip, I said, "Everything's up in the air, but I should hear soon." My eyebrows squished together.

Her intense expression grew. "Whoa. That's a truckload of avocados waiting to ripen and be smashed into guacamole. Have you tried meditation?"

Fluent in sudden change of topics and curious curveballs, I actually followed her bizarre train of thought, albeit, hanging onto the railing of the runaway caboose.

"Ommmm. Not really. You?"

"You betcha. You think this weirdo twice concussion brain can run 90 miles an hour 24/7 on caffeine? Don't answer that. But try this." She brought her palms together in prayer pose, then explained her go-to-sleep rainbow muscle-relaxing meditation technique.

"I'll give it a shot." Promising to try it, I got up to go, but stopped at the doorway, looking back at her. "I'm sorry your gymnastics dream got cut short, but you've earned the gold medal for teaching. Thank you."

Her mouth dropped open, then grew into a sweet one-sided smile, sniffing, she murmured, "Best job in the world."

It was both weird and comforting to admit I wasn't 100% locked down in control. I slowly worked my way to study hall thinking, Sofi would be both thrilled and proud.

25

"Sound of Silence" – Disturbed, cover

Can't sleep. My brain won't shut down. Running a mile a minute because my legs can't. Okay. I'll give it a shot. Try to meditate. Relax. Get comfortable. Focus on my breathing.

The pups were two swirls at the foot of the bed until one stretched and kicked my wrapped knee, breaking the bubble of my self-imposed, protective force field. I cringed, waiting for it, but no pain followed. Improvement noted. Calming myself. I released my thoughts to wander again.

Listen. Inside sounds. Roscoe and Mallory's alternating breaths. Relaxed, syncopated with an occasional snort from Roscoe or a yip from Mallory. Dreaming of chasing rabbits. When I stretched my right leg out from under the covers, a tail thumped – puppy Morse code for sweet dreams, sleepy time. Warm breath from a furry muzzle tickled my toes.

Listening. Outside noises. Raindrops on the roof. I love their steady, yet irregular, jovial banter. Wondering, do other senses compensate when another is lost? Does touch tingle to vibrations, beats, and rhythms? Sight, see colors more vividly, with better resolution, and more depth? Hearing intensify to guide through echolocation?

The raindrop's conversation ended, replaced by creatures of the night. Whooot whoot whoot. Ominous pause, one two three seconds, then repeating. Whooot whoot whoot. Hunting? The repetition reminded me of something. Oh! The haunting, in the locker room, then the outdoor restroom! My least favorite whistling things! "Toowh toowh toowh toowh toowh toowh..."

My thoughts raced back to the gym when the lights went out and Michael, Sienna and I, unable to see, fumbled along the cool cement block walls searching the inky black void for the locker room.

She and I, each fearing our own demons, remembered the same situations from different perspectives. When we realized we were in fact, each other's monster, our hysterical laughter ricocheted off the metal lockers while the cell phone flashlight bounced about, casting an eerie gargoyle-like expression on Michael's confused face.

Ms. Davis will crack up when she hears that Sienna turned out to be my whistling, serial-killer vampire custodian and I, her bathroom stalker. Drifting off, picturing my favorite teacher doubled over in laughter, Ms. Davis was the last person I thought about before falling asleep.

***

I awoke to an ominous, cloudy December day. Perfect for sharing Sienna's and my hilarious revelations with Ms. Davis on this final day of Civil War Spies. Not to worry, Krutch, Dervis, Hood Snap and I registered for WWII Spies next semester. Ms. Davis was pumped, which meant a lot of actual jumping up and down, followed by imaginary dribbling between desks and slam dunking as she announced we'd be field-tripping to the International Spy Museum. Cool beans.

The next morning I ducked into the car just as raindrops began to splatter the driveway. "That was close! Don't worry, I'll drop you in front so you don't get soaked," Jaz said.

Harley added from behind, "This stupid weather! Spent a fortune on products and my hair's still a frizzy mess. Might as well pull it back and be done with it like you did, Gracie." She tore a scrunchie off her wrist.

Turning to buckle my seatbelt, I noticed the water streams branching out and racing down my passenger window. I love rain. Despite its bad reputation, a moody, gray day calms my soul. Remembering words I'd written years ago, I recited them to my reflection.

The sky, filled with dark thoughts
Dips a brush in ink
Thick random drops
Splat – – splat – splat splat splat

Rhythm picks up
Crescendo crashes down
Daring to paint
recside the lines

Clouds, barren, above
Canvas, saturated, below
Cleansed air, in between, celebrates

Mesmerized, I heard my name.

"... Gracie?"

"Sorry, what?"

"What are you doing over break?" Jaz repeated.

I registered. "Family stuff. My brother and his girlfriend, Joan, are coming. Sofi will be back, and her best friend, Shelley, who goes to college out here, may stop by before she heads home."

Harley asked, "What about Army?" Ian's nickname.

Incommunicado since Thanksgiving, I deflected. "What about him?"

"Your arms, if you're lucky!" Jaz snorted.

I wish.

"He should meet his future fam jam," Harley teased.

Sigh. "You guys are hilarious."

"We know," they answered in stereo.

Early dismissal today: last block of finals, mandatory blow-off cartoon movie, then don't-even-try-to-escape school assembly. I limped as fast as possible to chat up Ms. Davis before the exam but instead found a slender young man with a trendy short beard and mustache seated at her desk studying a substitute teacher clipboard like it was the Bill of Rights.

Suspecting another trick from our ingenious teacher, I silently questioned my trio of pals in the back row. Krutch held his palms out. Dervis shook his head side to side. Hood Snap shrugged. No clue.

I surveyed the classroom for any strangers or costumed characters, then studied the substitute to decide if it were Ms. Davis in disguise.

The buzzer buzzed.

Sub dude jumped at the sound, adjusted the knot of his red power tie, stood, then walked out from behind the desk to take roll. A good four inches taller than Ms. Davis, I checked the heels of his shoes. Not even an inch. Discarded my incognito theory and went all in on the next plausible play. Skipped town to avoid the holiday rush? Maybe. Had vacation days to burn? Doubtful. Do teachers even get vacation days? Probably not. Notoriously underpaid and overly dedicated. Gotta love 'em.

Roll call was painful as he butchered any name that was not as generic as Mike or Mary, and went with the last name, comma, first name as registered, period. Instead of the preferred nicknames Ms. Davis had adopted whole-heartedly and written with exclamation marks in the margin. As in, Krutch, Dervis, Hood Snap, always in that order, and Rogue, wherever I fit in.

Where is she?

"Clear your desks except for a pencil. Silence your cell phones and put them in your backpacks under the desks," he said, picking up a stack of tests. "I will pass out your final exam face down. Do not turn it over until you are told. No wandering eyes. I will be watching."

Seriously, Dude? Talking in full words no contractions? Subpar substitute is going hardcore disciplinarian on us.

Where is she?

Flying through the test, I smiled at the extra credit question. Who is your favorite James Bond actor? Daniel Craig. I turned it in and limped back to my desk to wonder.

Where is she?

When all the finals were in, Subpar rode the struggle bus until Dervis jumped on to help him cue up the latest Bond flick, instead of a cartoon movie, on the whiteboard projector.

Right at its point of ultimate tension and drama, the classroom door opened. A triangle of light cut the darkness. Principal Atkins flicked on the lights. Subpar's face paled. Dervis snuck up and shut off the projector.

On the verge of tears, Principal Atkins remained poised. "I'm sorry to bring you all sad news, but Ms. Davis has been in a serious car accident. We do not know the extent of the injuries but pray her strength and indomitable spirit prevails. Please know that we care about her, and each of you, and if need be, counseling will be available. As we head into the break, do not hesitate to reach out to your counselor if you require any assistance."

Stunned.

I sat.

Numb.

In silence.

Frozen.

Shadows filtered by.

"Get up." I heard.

"What?" I asked.

"Let's go." A hand gently guided me.

I looked. Hood Snap? "Where?" I asked.

"Away," he answered, in a low, rumbling voice.

We escaped through the Area Vocation Program room, for students who had jobs and left school early to work. I vaguely noticed the AVP teacher give Hood Snap an approving nod as we slipped out the side doors like ghosts.

Floating. Hood Snap's protective hand held my elbow as we weaved through the junior parking lot to his truck. I got in, shivering. He started the engine and cranked the heat on high. Reaching to adjust the vents, my hands trembled like bare branches in the wind.

We parked in front of a generic strip mall coffee shop named Bistro+39. I waited for him to get out and go around to open my door, out of character for the normal I can do it myself thank you very much, revealing how way out of whack I was. The rain had stopped, but the air was heavy. And frigid. The wet kind of cold that scoffs at layers and seeps into your bones. Freezing you from the inside out.

"Coffee?" he asked, as we slid into the red vinyl booth.

"N-no," I answered, shaking.

"Hot chocolate?" he asked.

"Sure," I acquiesced.

He slid out to put in our order, leaving behind a vacuum.

Returning, he quietly sat across from me.

Silence.

He filled the empty air with words.

"I had this pup." Hood Snap began, in a low, anomaly of a voice I never would have imagined belonged to him, but now fit so well. "Gelato. A chocolate lab. Lovable and wild. When we lived in Rome," he said.

"Rome, Italy?" I asked, confused.

"Yes," he said, pausing. "My dad was a diplomat there."

Wow. Why didn't I know this?

"He was a serious turd burglar, ate whatever he sniffed out, but I loved him."

"Your dad?" I asked. Wondering "was a diplomat in Italy," but realizing that's normal here in Northern Virginia, and of course, his dad didn't eat or steal poop.

He shook his head, a sad, understanding smile on his lips. "No, my dog. We were walking in the woods. When we got to the dirt road, I thought to myself, 'should put him on leash now,' as two sparrows attacked a hawk in the sky above us. I watched their midair combat, Gelato charged out of the brush and attacked the front of my neighbor's SUV. They tried to stop but slid on the loose gravel. He shuddered then was still.

"I wrapped him in my sweatshirt and lifted his warm but lifeless body, carried him home, and held him in the car all of the way to the veterinarian, who asked my mom, 'Do you want a vase?'

"And I all could think of was that they were mummifying him in my favorite sweatshirt and burying him with valuable possessions." He paused to explain. "I was twelve. Studying Ancient Egypt in school." His rambling words made total sense. "I was like, what?" Hood Snap recounted.

"'His ashes,' the vet explained. Mom asked me what I thought. 'No. Gelato wouldn't like that. Too fancy. Can you put him in a paper bag?' Just a kid. Trying to make a grown-up decision. The vet told me they didn't have any paper bags. I looked to his receptionist. Eating her lunch. Out of a brown paper bag. She dumped it and handed it over in a heartbeat.

"We mixed his ashes with wildflower seeds and took them on the train to the Amalfi coast and set them free on a breeze overlooking the green-blue sea."

Wow. Just wow. Too much and just enough.

26

"Dream On" – Aerosmith

"Grace Artemis?" Mom called to me. I hung up my key and jacket on their assigned hooks, dropped my backpack, and eased down onto the bench inside our entry.

"Here," I answered, with a heavy sigh.

The pups had learned restraint since my surgery. Instead of jumping up to lick my face, Roscoe climbed onto the bench next to me and dug her nose under my chin as I tried to slip off my shoes. Mallory's tail thumped between the floormat and wall as she rested her furry muzzle on my good knee. Her wise, brown eyes searched mine. Stroking their soft ears comforted me as much as them.

The light dimmed as a shadow reached across the family room floor. Mom appeared in the doorway. "Jaz and Harley stopped by."

Looking up at her worried face, I said, "Oh. I forgot to tell them I didn't need a ride. Hood Snap dropped me off."

She brushed a loose strand of hair from my face. "It's okay, Sweetie, Dervis let them know." She paused, softly adding, "They told me about Ms. Davis. Very sad. Come and get warm. Do you need something to eat?"

"No. I'm fine. Thanks." I dug into my backpack for my cell. Turned off for the final, I held down the button to restart and limped to my room to change. My knee was stiff from the cold. I ran a finger up the closed surgery scar, then gently rubbed small circles along the kneecap. The swelling was almost gone. Unfortunately, so were my muscles. One month to go. Recovery was painful. But doable.

What about Ms. Davis? Would she? Could she?

Gingerly slipping into sweats, I leaned back the recliner to check my phone. The screen showed three texts. Torn between wanting to know, but dreading the unknown, I looked up, inhaled, prayed, exhaled, then punched messages in order.

(*harley*)
You okay?

(*jaz*)
Ms. D is in a coma :-(

(*dervis*)
this sux

I shut the screen. Pushed out of the recliner. Climbed into bed, and pulled the sheet over my head.

Corpse-like. I shoved it off. Morbid thoughts laid bare.

STOP. Think of someone or something else.

Hood Snap. His soothing voice and unexpected story.

Hot chocolate. Whip cream swirls in a chocolate pool.

Remembering my frozen hands wrapped around the thick mug. Runny nose savoring the sweet, warm aroma wafting up. The first sip, infused and flowed out to thaw the rest of me.

Satisfying multiple senses.

But, senses led to meditation.

Meditation, suggested by Ms. Davis.

Ms. Davis, my last thought before sleep.

Last thought, the terrifying, childish nightmare.

Childish nightmare, now a horrifying, teenage reality.

I rolled over to my stomach, squeezed my eyes shut, and silently screamed into my pillow.

***

Skipped dinner. Tried reading. Couldn't concentrate. Can't sleep. Afraid I'll dream. No. Not dream. Afraid I'll nightmare. Specifically, the creepy, humming old guy walking toward me with his serial killer cane one. In the kitchen.

Clue. I'd like to make an accusation. Old Guy, in the Kitchen, with his Cane. Not funny. Well, a little funny. But too soon. I'm sleep-deprived delirious. Maybe if I get a banana. In the kitchen. Because I have to be in the room to make an accusation. And bananas have potassium, magnesium and L-tryp-something converts into a 5-Htp-something that converts into serotonin, a relaxing neurotransmitter, and melatonin.

So I can sleep. But not nightmare.

The house is too quiet. Banging into the stool near the island setting off the bark alarm solved that problem. "Sssh, Roscoe, Mallory, it's just me. In the kitchen. With a banana. Uh-oh. They love bananas. I'll have to share.

Back in Mom's studio guestroom my recovery bedroom, I opened the long curtain. Oh. It's snowing. Curling up in the recliner, I watched the haunting garden nightscape and tried not to think about anything but the quiet, silent, night.

***

"Scoot." Sofi's home.

I scooted. She slid in next to me, taking over as pilot in the recliner cockpit. She unfurled a velvety red blanket across our laps and tucked me in.

"Where to?" she asked.

"Away."

"Check Rog."

Silence. But not for long. Sofi doesn't do silence.

"Mom's garden is magical. A misty fantasy world." Sofi's hands danced in front of us, acting out the scene. "See the snow drifted in swirls around the hydrangeas? If you squint, they look like a group of carolers."

Didn't have to squint, I blinked through blurry eyes. They kind of did.

"And the black leafless tree branches reaching up to the gray sky? A color photograph disguised as black and white. We just need a cardinal. A spot of red would be divine," she paused, sighed. "Tell me about Ms. D."

Where do I begin? "She's a lot like you." I nudged her.

"I like her already." She nudged back.

I smiled. Sofi's home. Rambling. I told her about Ms. D marching on top of the long cabinet and hiding in a tall one. Spy question of the day. Invitation to join tech crew. Inventing an after-school game club to entertain us. Giving up her gymnastic dream and becoming a teacher.

"She's a hoot." Present, not past tense.

"Yep." My head hurt.

"What's her status?"

"Coma." Eyes shut. I winced.

"From the accident, or medically induced?" she asked.

"What's the difference?" I mumbled, drained.

She changed into nursing student mode. "An induced coma decreases intracranial pressure, which gives the brain a chance to rest and reboot."

I nodded. Sighed. Confessed. "The night before, she was the last person I thought about before going to sleep."

"Did you have the nightmare?"

"No."

"It's not your fault."

My sleep-deprived brain wrestled with that notion.

"Another thing, after you had the nightmare, did anything happen to the brutally murdered victim in real life?"

"Well, no." I shook my head.

"So, Grace Artemis, despite being the guardian of woodland creatures and protector of youth, your imagined thoughts aren't automatically manifested in reality. So deal. K?"

I shrugged slowly, stifling a yawn. "K-k."

"Now that's settled, how about copping some zzzzs? We drove all night."

"Alex is here?"

"Yep. Crashed on the family room couch."

As my chin dipped, Sofi eased the lever to tip us back.

"Prepare for lift-off."

"Roger that." Eyes closed, I inhaled deeply through my nose, a whiff of the hoodie she shared with Alex made me smile. Together, their aroma blended into a mix of florals, woods, and a little bit of spice. #relationshipgoals

"Sweet dreams, Gracie girl..."

27

"Build Me Up Buttercup" – The Foundations

Muffled knocks rang the doggie doorbell and interrupted my pleasant dream. "¡Hola Chiquita!" A cheerful voice announced but was instantly shushed. Indistinct mutterings drifted into my subconscious as I fought to return to neverland. Hoping the vision would continue on the inside of my lids like a movie screen. No such luck. It was my other reoccurring dream, the exciting and mysterious not terrifying one. Weird. Must be Sofi's presence. Her energy has this uncanny way of influencing me, even when unconscious.

Peeking through half-closed eyelids, a golden beam cut through the garden window onto the wooden floor like a sundial. Afternoon, if I read it right. Stretching my leg out from under a velvety red blanket, ouch! Leg cramp. Flexing both feet, I reached down to rub the offending calf muscle as the privacy barn door rolled slowly open behind me. Intro notes to a familiar oldie, "Build Me Up Buttercup" increased in volume. Uh-oh.

"Wake up Buttercup!" Sofi shouted as she and her bestie spilled into view, one on each side of my front row recliner seat for the Sofi and Shelley Show.

They danced and sang across me, echoing lyrics back and forth as they alternated leaning in and out. Their mirrored images, complete with synchronized hand motions, shaking hips and shimmying shoulders, indicated years of practice. A friendship five states apart couldn't separate. Nothing for me to do but sit back and be entertained.

As the song ended Shelley reached down for a hug, then twirled to the bed and flopped down. On her stomach, with knees bent up behind, fuzzy socks kicked back and forth. Next to her, Sofi leaned back on the headboard, legs extended, feet crossed at the ankles, wearing a pair of chunky clogs popular with nurses. A far cry from the sparkly pink spiked heels she used to adore and skillfully wear.

"Bravo, I'd give you a standing ovation, but I'm too comfortable," I said.

"Missed you!" Shelley said. "How's the knee?"

"Gett'n better. PT's no fun, but it's helping."

Sofi asked, "When's your next appointment? I'll go with to make sure they're doing it right."

"Like you're an expert," I said.

"Like I'm not! I know things," Sofi said.

"Of course you do, sweetie." Shelley winked at me.

Sofi butted Shelley's hip with a clog. "Whose side are you on?"

"Both! You're you, but Gracie's the little sis I always wished for..."

Sofi and I finished her sentence in unison. "And Jason is the brother you always wanted."

"Truth. This girl had dreams," Shelley sighed. "But he's been taken since he first saw Joan. Speaking of, when do they get here?"

"Any minute now! Mom's on the way to the airport. Their flight gets in around four." Sofi said, adding, "I can't wait!" Shelley is Sofi's best friend/cohort, whereas Joan is her best friend/mentor. Both ground her in their own way, and Alex brings balance to their Force.

Wondering out loud, I asked, "Where's Alex?"

"He went for a run with Dad," Sofi said.

Shelley teased, "Think he's asking for your hand?"

"No, but you're begging for my foot," Sofi threatened, bending her knee back, ready to kick. Alex and Sofi's official two-year dating anniversary was in a couple weeks, thanks to Shelley's intervention in their friend zone dance when the three did a study abroad senior year in high school.

"Jason's the one who should be asking Joan's dad for permission. So I can plan the wedding. Who am I kidding, their entire life is mapped out on a Pinterest board up here." Sofi tapped her blonde head.

"What if they already eloped?" Shelley teased.

"I can't even. Joan wouldn't do that to me. She knows how important this is."

"Because, after all, it's all about you," I said.

"As it should be," Sofi exclaimed, indignant. Her eyes glazed looking out into the garden, adding, "It'll be dreamy." She blinked two times. "Speaking of dreams, did you?"

Startled, I remembered. "Yes. The flying one."

"Fun! Where were you? What were you?" Sofi asked.

"Wait, the flying one? Not the scary one?" Shelley looked over her shoulder to Sofi, then back to me.

I crossed my arms. "You told her about my dreams?"

Shelley said, "Of course she did! Your dreams are straight-up action spy movies."

Which made me think about Ms. Davis. Which made me not want to think about Ms. Davis. I closed my eyes to remember the dream and rambled, "I was a bird," scrunching my face, thinking. "Small, but predatory. A falcon? Floating over a beach, riding winds over the cliffs. I could hear the waves breaking below."

The front door opened and shut. Roscoe and Mallory charged in and jumped on the bed to give doggie kisses. The runners were back.

Shelley hugged Mallory, then pulled away, grimacing. "Ugh. What'd you eat girl? Your breath smells awful."

Roscoe circled twice to make a nest, then curled up next to Sofi. Stroking the black and white pup's silky ears Sofi asked, "Was it that remote island duty station in the middle of Nowhere?"

Odd. It was. Dad's post, two posts ago. She's a freaking, scary psychic, but I'm used to it. Eyes shut tight, I nodded. "Yes. That point where we'd eat lunch, watching the birds float, without flapping, on the updrafts."

"I wanna go!" Shelley said.

"It was beautiful. In a desolate, end of the world, no fashion whatsoever way," Sofi said to her, adding to me, "What happened?"

Picturing it, "I was searching. Looking down the beach."

"Okay hang on the breeze. Look right, in the distance."

"Bird's eye view," snorted Shelley.

"Shush, go with it." Sofi admonished her. "Now Gracie, off where the waves broke on the rocks."

"K," I said. Go with the Sofi flow. It's a thing.

"You see something. Coming towards you."

"Prey?" I asked.

"Sort of."

Shelley snorted.

"Sshhh." Sofi said. "The sea salt's stinging your eyes so squint. It's getting closer. A runner. A muscular dude. Really muscular dude. In military-issued booty runner shorts...."

"Hold up." I opened my eyes and drilled hers.

Shelley laughed. "Is there a United States Military Academy logo on the shorts?"

"Really? You told her about Ian?" I asked.

"I'm going to work for the CIA, remember?" Then added in a really bad over-emphasized accent, "Vee have vays of making you talk."

"Knock, knock." Alex's cheerful voice to the rescue.

"Please, please come in," I begged and tossed off the blanket. Both dogs looked to the door behind me, tails thumping.

"Howdy." A welcome diversion.

"Sit." Sofi drew her knees up to make room.

Tall, lean, and clean after a post-run shower Alex joined the party on the bed. He sat in front of Sofi, next to Shelley. The Three Musketeers reunited. The same easy smile grew across his face, one corner higher. Same brown eyes crinkled at the corners under dark eyebrows. His sandy brown hair was longer though, different from Dad and Jason's short military high and tight cuts. I have a feeling Sofi wants it that way. And what Sofi wants....

"How's Iowa?" I asked.

"Sucks, but Iowa State's great," he said, reaching behind to trap Sofi's ankles before she could clog him. Sofi's an Iowa Hawkeye. Alex, an Iowa State Cyclone. Rival universities two hours apart, but they were solid together, despite the school spirit thing.

***

Twenty minutes later, Roscoe's ears perked up and Mallory woofed. A car engine accelerated into the driveway then shut off. Sofi gasped, "They're here!" She exploded up and out of the room followed by scrambling pups.

Shelley and Alex waited while I eased out of the recliner. A blast of cold air greeted us in the hallway; Sofi had left the front door open. Dad met us in the entryway, shaking his head but foregoing the lecture knowing it would be wasted on Sofi, whose contagious laughter spilled around the corner as she ushered Joan, Jason and Mom in.

Leaning back against the wall to stay out of the melee, I noted layers of family dynamics. Mom's joyful smile having her three-plus bonus two home. Dad pulling Jason in for a dad hug and smack on the back. Sofi and Shelley hugging Joan then rapid-firing questions. Joan's amused smile waiting for them to breathe before answering. Dogs jumping up and weaving between legs. Alex stood next to me. Watching and waiting for our turn to greet.

Embraced by Shelley, Joan peered out from her black CU hoodie. My heart skipped a beat. Seeing her brought out the sixth-grade fangirl in me. So mysterious, but so real. Her sleeve fell as she waved her left hand. A glint caught the entryway light.

Sofi screamed, handcuffed Joan's wrist and held it out to Jason. "YOU PROPOSED WITHOUT ME?"

"Yep, not taking you on the honeymoon either." Jason's one-sided big bro smile egged her on.

"Pffffft." She waved him off. "Sorry, Joan. Hope his proposal wasn't too pathetic." She pulled her in for another sweet hug, missing Joan's smile exchange with Jason.

"He did all right."

"We'll see." Stepping away, Sofi clutched Joan's hand again, lifting it to inspect the ring. "Oh my gosh! A solitaire emerald! To match your eyes!" She shrugged, acquiescing a bit to Jason. "Okay, at least you didn't choke that away." Back to Joan, she touched a white gold band encircling her thumb. "This has the same knot pattern. Is it new?"

"Old. Dad's wedding band. My mom gave it to him. Dad secretly brought it to Jason, along with her matching band, when he came for Thanksgiving."

"Oh." Sofi teared up. The one topic that shuts Sofi up. Joan's mom. Ever since Joan told Sofi that she reminded her of her mother, who'd won years of battles but ultimately lost the war to breast cancer when Joan was in eighth grade. Speechless, Sofi hugged her again.

A lump clogged my throat. Silence.

Jason cleared his throat. "Tell her."

Sofi asked, "Tell me what?" Knowing he meant her.

Joan held her at arm's length. "May. After graduation. Outside. Monument Rock. Colorado. Family. Go."

"As in, me? Greenlight go with it?"

"All you."

"Yay me! Outside? Risky, but doable. Timing is crucial. May? Memorial Day. That can work. I need to see pictures. But." She bit her lip. "Tell me about this." Sofi pointed to the man's ring.

Joan explained. "It's the Celtic eternity knot. Mom's a Downie, from Rosehearty, Northeast Scotland."

"You're Scottish? For the love of tartan patterns and all things plaid!" Sofi clasped her hands together and jumped up and down. "Oh. Heck. Yes. Totally changes everything."

No one else understood but we all knew she did.

"Enough. Why are we inside when we could be playing? Unless, of course, you college kids are out of shape." Jason threw out the challenge.

"Oh. Like you aren't old man?" Sofi smack-talked.

"Been playing a bit."

"Geriatric's league? Using your stick to walk instead of throw?" Sofi teased.

Active duty Army Jason pulled rank. "You learn that in ROTC, Cah-det."

Alex surprised me and injected himself into the sibling throw-down. "You're a D pole," pointing to Jason. "And Sofi," he added with a smile, "Is an amazing goalie." He shoulder-bumped me. "Gracie's on the injured reserve list, otherwise she'd whip all of us. That leaves short-stick civilians Joan and me, on offense. Attacking." He looked to Joan.

Joan picked it up from there. "I believe Alex and I, aka Team Civilian, will smoke, Sofi and Jason, aka Team Hooah."

"I'll referee!" Shelley said.

Dad's face lit up. "Sounds like we've got ourselves a game. Drop your duffle bags and get in gear. Extra pads in the garage. Goal's already set up in the backyard garden."

"I'll get the concession stand up and running. Hot chocolate at halftime!" Mom sang, disappearing into the kitchen.

Not only was Joan assistant coaching at CU Boulder, but Jason coached a kid's recreation league in Colorado Springs near his duty station at Fort Carson, so they were both sticks on. Joan switched with ease from the female shallow pocket to an extra one of our extra deep pockets like she used in high school playing on the guys' team. She and Jason ran and threw warming up, while Alex shot on Sofi in goal. I could tell Alex played tournaments occasionally on the Iowa State club team but knew Sofi didn't have time between nursing school and ROTC at Iowa.

Dad rolled out the garden hose in a squared-off U from the goal line to serve as sidelines. Shelley set up a portable speaker so we could have tunes. And me? I twirled my stick out of bounds, the only play I'll be making is a frustrated spectator one.

But then. As Joan Jett's, "I Love Rock 'N Roll" blasted out of a portable speaker I noticed something amazing. Sofi, the least practiced, was blocking all of Joan's wicked shots.

On the sidelines, I anticipated them along with Sofi! It hit me. Joan, like me, didn't put out "tells." Both of us mixed it up without telegraphing our next move. Sofi picked up on it from playing with me! But how had I developed this way of play? By watching Joan, my idol, or figuring it out on my own? Either way, it was a proud moment realizing I not only emulated my idol, I somehow epitomized her!

The score was tied. Nine blocked shots. Nine scored. Shelley yelled, "I'm thirsty. Next goal wins!"

Alex shot bottom right as Sofi leaned left. Goal. Sofi stood in pissed mode, stuffed, only one padded up since she'd take the most heat in goal. Alex went in for the embrace.

Shelley tossed imaginary yellow referee flags in the air, shouting, "Excessive hugging after the shot, goal dismissed! Still tied."

"No way!" Alex let go of Sofi to complain to Shelley.

Shelley gave as good as she got. Fists on hips Sofi style. "Yes, way. Mouth off and I'll throw you outta the game!"

Everyone, including Mom, Dad and me, cracked up as Joan and Alex planned their next and hopefully final play.

Curious. Both looked at me.

Shelley pretended to whistle and Joan brought it down. Full speed, she faked a pass to Alex. Spun. But. Before she could finish her rotation and shoot, Jason grabbed her around the waist with both arms and lifted her, kicking, off of the ground. Split-second decision, she popped the ball out. It bounced.

Alex scooped it up, advancing to goal, glancing at me. I looked to Joan, who Jason had dropped. She stared at me, then stepped back, over the hose. Out of bounds. I stepped in, onto the field, because in lacrosse, you sub on the fly. As Sofi charged out to challenge Alex, he fired the ball to me. I caught it, drew back and shot behind Sofi to goal. Score.

Shelley jumped up in the air and screamed, "Gracie for the win! Game over!"

Words can't describe how much it meant to have all my people together. If only for a long weekend. Then Sofi and Alex flew to spend some of the holidays with his family; Shelley with them to go to hers. Joan and Jason, back at it in Colorado. Memories created would be stories told, and embellished unashamedly over a lifetime of don't you dare forget me.

28

"Storybook Love" – Mark Knopfler

The house was too quiet. Without the rowdy laughter and sibling teasing, uncertainty and dismal thoughts of Ms. Davis seeped in to fill the void. I took my time climbing the two floors to my attic room now that I could maneuver stairs, bending knees, stepping up, dipping heels low to extend calf muscles then rising to my toes.

I'd missed my fictional friends while convalescing on the main floor. They'd waited for me, in the solid oak bookcase that took Mom, Dad and me thirty minutes to maneuver up here. In the past, running a finger across their spines, each begging me to join in their adventure, had been all the comfort I required. But now, they too were silent, unable to provide solace from reality.

Back downstairs, even Roscoe and Mallory seemed depressed, wandering in vain for the extra hands sneaking them snacks, loving strokes and butt scratches, they gave up and collapsed at Mom's feet as she painted. Thumping tails broke my stealthy sock-footed approach.

Peeking over her shoulder, I admired the solemn garden landscape emerging from the snowy white canvas set on the easel, once again in its rightful place in the studio. A frost-covered tree's dark fingers reached out and disappeared into mist. Like the incomplete train of thoughts in my foggy head.

I drifted back into the hallway, grabbed an apple, passed through the kitchen and dropped into Dad's recliner in the family room. Banished whence it came, reuniting with the black and white blocked chess board on the coffee table. The armies stood at attention, awaiting orders from their respective generals who'd called a cease-fire mid-battle when it got late last night. It was my turn, but I couldn't concentrate much less strategize.

Buzz. My phone vibrated on the side table. A video chat from Sofi. I swept a finger across to answer then took a bite.

"What's up, Buttercup?" Sofi greeted me.

Blinking to adjust to her sparkling enthusiasm, I chewed the crunchy apple, swallowed, then shrugged. "Nada."

"Uh-oh. Why the mood?"

"Kind of discombobulated."

"This will recombobulate you! Guess what?"

"The glitter fairies elected you princess and are throwing you a parade?"

"We can only dream! But almost as fun, Joan called to tell me her brother Jon and his wife Linda are pregnant! Pretty far along too. She'd miscarried before so they waited until six months to announce this time."

I smiled, didn't question how and why she knew such personal information because that's just how Sofi rolls.

"She's due end of March, so itty bitty bambino will be two months old at the wedding. It's a holiday weekend, so, it gives us an extra day off to travel."

When she paused to breathe, I teased. "Have you let the bride and groom know?"

"Yes, and as Wedding Planner and Maid of Honor, I'm cleared to ask you to be a bridesmaid! How cool is that?"

Flattered, a smirk grew as I admitted, "Pretty cool."

"Also, since we've got a short hike on a dirt trail to the dreamy rock locale, you, drum roll please..." She thumped fingers on her desk, "... get to wear flats, maybe even kicks, not sure so don't get your hopes up. I haven't picked the style yet, but the flower colors will include periwinkle." She stopped. Blinked. Spaced out.

Periwinkle. I read her like one of my favorite characters because in reality, she is. Sofi's thinking about Charlie, her little friend who died from leukemia a few years ago, one of the reasons Sofi decided to go into the medical field. I asked, "How far a hike?"

Sofi shook her head, refocusing. "Joan said about two hundred yards from our cars if we park on the frontage road that, get this, leads to the

Monument Helibase. That's where the elite Pike Hotshot Crew firefighters train!" Double blink. "Speaking of hot, have you heard from Ian?"

Took me longer than usual to boomerang. My face tinged pink on screen. "No."

"Have you texted him?"

"No."

"Are you going to? Never mind, we'll come back to that." Her brows furrowed, "Is Ms. D still in a coma? Was it medically induced? If so, they should be easing her out of it."

Her intuition shouldn't surprise me. "I don't know. Should I go to the hospital? Will they let me see her?"

"Unless you're on a no-visitor list, which you won't be, because you're the perfect, brainiac student, and most likely fav. So yes, go."

"Do I take anything?"

"Not flowers, but something fun for her to look at when she wakes up would be good. A toy, or poster. And you could make her a playlist on Spotify. Does she have family there? They could play it on a phone. Or set up an Alexa Echo in her room and play it on loop."

"I know she's married. I think he's an engineer."

"Save it to a thumb drive too, and leave it with a note. He should be able to figure something out."

I smiled. "Thanks for the ideas, and for recombobulating me. What do I owe you?"

"I'll put it on your tab. Now, back to Ian."

Turning my head, I pretended to respond to Mom, "I'll be there in a second!"

Sofi sang. "Gra-cie."

"Gotta go!" I disconnected and put my phone down by the chess set, careful not to dwell too long thinking about my next move with the Black Knight.

***

Checking in at the nurse's station, I learned Ms. Davis was still unconscious, but in stable condition in the ICU. After getting directions, with trepidation I walked amid the calm flurry of staff moving about, machines beeping, and detached monotone announcements over the intercom. The closer I got to her room number, the slower my gait.

Her gift, a set of wooden peg dolls painted like the six Clue game characters plus the butler, was wrapped in the comics section of an actual paper newspaper my parents subscribed to, despite Sofi's technological dismay.

Meaningful and funny when I found it, now it seemed silly and juvenile. Maybe I shouldn't give it to her. What if she wakes up and doesn't remember we played? Or worse. What if she doesn't... wake up? A chill ran down my neck. It's freezing in here. The air conditioning is cranked. Why are hospitals so cold? Probably to keep germs from germinating. That's not right, seeds germinate, germs, microbes, aka bacteria, viruses, fungi and protozoa, grow. And a lot of time, inside humans. Gross, but some microbes are good for you, us, humans.

My scientific discourse was interrupted by wonderful, familiar words from a favorite novel being read aloud with gusto coming from the room ahead. *"... take on some new young pirates. I will sail along for a few days as Ryan, your first mate, and will tell everyone about my years with you, the Dread Pirate Roberts. Then you will let me off when they are all believers, and the waters of the world are yours." Wesley smiled at Buttercup. "So now you know. And you should also realize why it is foolish to be afraid."*

Mesmerized, I stopped just outside of her door and peered in. Next to the lowered bed, a man slouched in a chair facing Ms. D, shirt sleeves rolled up, khaki pants crumpled, his feet in tan loafers propped up on the bedside table blocking her face from my view. He held a large brown book in his left hand. Gold metallic letters flashed *The Princess Bride*, by William Goldman. But I already knew that.

In a higher voice, he continued, *"'But I am afraid.'"*

Lower again, *"'It will all be happy at the end. Consider: a little over three years ago, you were a milkmaid and I was,'"* he lowered the leather-bound novel on his legs, revealing his right hand held hers.

Fumbling to turn the page, the book almost slipped off his lap, but he didn't let her go.

My eyes blurred. I leaned on the door frame.

He lifted the book and continued. "Where were we? Oh, here we go, *'... and I was a farm boy. Now you are almost a queen and I rule uncontested on the water. Surely, such individuals were never intended to die in a Fire Swamp.'*"

Higher again, *"'How can you be sure?'"*

Lower, *"'Well, because we're together, hand in hand, in love.'"* He paused. A lump clogged my throat. He cleared his and went on, high again. *"'Oh yes,' Buttercup said. "I keep forgetting that.'"*

I raised my hand to sweep a stray hair from my face, forgetting the gift tucked under my elbow; it dropped to the floor. The words stopped. Cringing, I bent to retrieve the package, rose, and stuttered, "Sorry to intrude. I'm Gracie, Gracie Halsted, a student of Ms. Davis."

He sat up, set the book on the floor and straightened his scholarly glasses, a weary but warm smile spread across his unshaven face.

An ordinary-looking man behaving extraordinarily.

Stepping into the room, I raised my palm. "Don't get up. Please. I wanted to drop this off for her." My eyes drifted from him to my diminutive teacher, her pixie head, wrapped in a gauze helmet, her pale face, uncharacteristically still.

"How is she?" I said, in a solemn voice. Too melancholy.

"We'll know tomorrow. When she wakes up." His thumb gently stroked her hand in his. Looking back at me, he raised his chin, "I'm James. Kora's husband."

James. Without thinking before speaking, something I very rarely do, I said, "Davis, James Davis."

The corners of his lips curved up. He chuckled, "Spy humor. Never gets old."

Relieved that my poorly-timed Bond joke didn't fall flat, I took another step in and held out the gift. "It's kind of lame," I paused, "They're figures from the Clue game. I thought it would be funny for her to see, to know we're thinking of her."

"Not lame. The after-school game club. She gets a kick out of you all." He looked to his wife, smiled, then back to me. "Your friends, Dervis, Crutch, and – Boot Strap?"

"Krutch, Dervis and Hood Snap." I corrected him automatically and mentally kicked myself.

He chuckled, "That's right, Kora told me you need to say them in order."

"Ms. Davis was, is, the Butler." Purposely keeping her in the present tense. Please.

He looked back at his unconscious wife.

Time for me to go. "Also, I made her this." I pulled the thumb drive out of my pocket. It was taped to a little card. "It's a playlist. Spy theme songs. It's also on Spotify, I put the link on the card with my phone number." Awkward. "In case you, she, needs anything, or someone to read to her, which is brilliant by the way," I said, like a fangirl, paused, blushed. "Or we could all come, and take turns. Krutch is awesome at accents."

He nodded, "Thanks Gracie, she'll love this."

Preparing to leave I pointed to the book. Put on a frown, and said with a serious tone, "Watch out for the R.O.U.S.'s."

Without missing a beat, he waved me off, picked the book up and replied as Wesley, "'Rodents Of Unusual Size? I don't think they exist.'"

I grinned, with one more look at Ms. Davis, I stepped into the hallway, stopped, and leaned back on the wall outside her room to recombobulate for the second time in two days. When the loving words began again, I pushed off the wall, thinking, if you find someone willing to hold your hand in the Fire Swamp, don't ever let them go.

#newrelationshipgoal

29

"Get Up" – Shinedown

Home again. The pups followed me into the studio like they hadn't seen me in a month rather than an hour. I sat on the cream-colored loveseat that stored the guest bed, pulled a cheerful red pillow onto my lap, and waited for Mom to finish a delicate detail as she leaned in with a thin brush.

A wayward wisp of hair escaped her bun held in place by crisscrossed paint brushes atop her head. Her profile matched Sofi's, or rather vice versa. She pulled back to view, and the smile crinkles around her eye told me she was pleased with the addition. She wiped the brush, set it in its place, and came over to sit and give me her full attention.

"Talk to me."

I inhaled. "She's still unconscious, but they're easing her off meds. I met her husband. He said they'll know more tomorrow 'when she wakes up.'" Pausing, I sighed. She waited patiently for me to continue, "When I got there, he was sitting next to her reading aloud from *The Princess Bride*."

"Ooh, how wonderful."

"I know, all the feels. They were in the Fire Swamp, just after she was sucked into the Snow Sands."

"Did you hold your breath like when we watched the movie?" Mom asked.

I snorted, remembering our family fun nights, "No, he was past that part, right before the R.O.U.S.'s attack."

"If they have to go through the Fire Swamp, at least they have each other." We sat in silence. "Look." Mom pointed to the snow swirling like sand on the patio outside the window.

"Do you know where our copy is?" I asked.

"Probably in Sofia Isabella's room."

"Figures, with all of the other princesses."

I dropped into the recliner, dangled my scarred knee over the armrest and tucked the other under me. The words took me on horseback through the forest, sailing over choppy waters, and scaling the Cliffs of Despair. Then at the edge of the Fire Swamp, the image of the Davis's clasped hands gave pause.

Putting aside the book, the chessboard caught my eye. Studying the game in progress, I tried to plan my next move. When the front door opened, excited whines instead of territorial barks meant Dad was home.

"Scout?"

"In here."

Dressed in uniform cami's, Dad entered the family room instead of following his standard operating procedure: Find Mom. Kiss Mom. Change into sweats. He winked and dropped a large, thick purple envelope on the coffee table.

I stared at the packet that could determine my destiny, or at least, a destination. A jolt of adrenaline shot through my murky brain like a double espresso. College early admission decision. I reached for the packet. It was heavy, a good sign. Picking up Dad's crossword puzzle pen, I worked it into the seal and tore along the fold. This is it. Pausing to inhale, I glanced at him. His supercilious eyebrow encouraged me.

I exhaled, then slid a deep purple folder onto my lap. A cover letter fluttered to the floor, landing upside down. Flipping it over, "Congratulations Wildcat!" shouted across the top of the page. Biting my lip didn't stop the corners of my mouth from curving up. I'm in. Devouring the superfluous words in search of magical ones, teeth disappeared behind lips pressed into a firm line. Unless. My brows furrowed as I read the Financial Aid heading. This is it.

Athletic Grant and Scholarship: $30,783 per year. That's it. No mention of additional Academic Merit funding. It was a lot, but only half what I needed to attend. And what if my knee didn't recover, and I lost this too?

Dismay clouded my brain and tears threatened rain. I set the packet on the coffee table and looked up at my dad's solemn face.

"I can't go."

"Of course you can!"

"No. I mean, I won't. We can't afford it." Dropping my head back, I gathered fists full of hair and pulled, eyes squeezed tight. I whispered, "How could I be so arrogant?" What was I thinking? Doubling down on NU.

"Confident, not arrogant. Hard work got you recruited and accepted into a competitive and selective academic institution. We'll figure something out," he said, sitting down in the chair on the other side of the chessboard.

"No, Sofi and Jason did it on their own." At solid state-schools, not an expensive private one. I rubbed my temples. "I won't hear from Boston College or USNA for months, I can't, won't, sit around and wait in case they don't come through." Mentally I sifted through the stacks of college materials we mulled over last summer. Admissions and merit scholarships deadlines twirling in my head.

I sighed. "Only one thing to do."

Three steps ahead, he anticipated my move, leaned his forearm across the chessboard and swept the pieces to the side. "Set 'er up while I change."

Knowing he'd make a studio stop to fill Mom in, I sat back and softly pounded my head on the padded chair. A month ago, fresh out of surgery, this would have devastated me. Having put my hopes and dreams, no, more like assumptions and expectations, into one proverbial purple basket. Now? I wasn't only disappointed. I was angry. At myself. Despite Dad's version, I had been arrogant, and instead of getting my desire, was served a double order of comeuppance with a side of perspective.

Poor, poor Gracie. Not getting everything, right now.

Meanwhile, Ms. Davis and her husband, who have so much, might lose it all, or a heck of a lot of it, tomorrow.

Repositioning a black knight between a rook and bishop, another wave of embarrassment swept through me. What will I tell Ian? And everyone else? Blowing out my knee had jeopardized the Letter of Intent I signed. I have to petition to be dropped to be eligible to play somewhere else. If I can play, that is.

Board set, mind all over the place, I wandered back to the studio. Mom was cleaning her brushes. Done for the day, she wiped her hands, hung Dad's old splattered, light blue oxford on the back of the easel, and reached out her arms. I fell in like a five-year-old who'd run her bicycle into the mailbox. Floral perfume blended with Dad's aftershave, like colors on Mom's paint palette. As I released her, she took my face in her hands and kissed my forehead. Not all better, but a little.

Side by side, we studied her work in progress. Two small pops of color had joined the monochromatic scene, a deep red male and a subtler brown with red accents female cardinal.

"Cardinals mate for life," I said – knowledge gleaned from a wildlife documentary I'd watched with Dad years ago.

"I believe it."

"The male brings seeds to his mate as part of the bonding process." Probably reads to her too.

"That's considerate."

Right on cue, Dad joined us, handing Mom her afternoon cup of chai. She smiled, cupping the mug in her hands. On his way to the family room, he asked, "Ready, Scout?"

"Be there in a sec." I waited for him to go. "Want to tell me what I should do?"

"Nope." She shrugged, "You could ask your sister, then do the opposite. That usually makes you feel better."

"And drives her crazy." I smiled a little.

She reached to brush tousled hair over my shoulder. "You'll figure it out. Now, go whup up on your dad."

"He better not let me win."

"Don't worry, he won't. Remember, 'You learn...'"

"'... more from losing than you do from winning.'"

Mom laughed, took a sip, her eyes drifted to the painting. Head tilted, eyes squinting, she gazed from canvas to garden and back, checking proportions.

***

Dad was reading *The Princess Bride* when I joined him. He put it down and quickly took off his new reading glasses, a recent accessory to his otherwise 20/20 aviator vision. Mom told him he looked handsome and distinguished in them, but he grumbled, "more like old and pathetic."

"Your turn to go first," I said, to give myself a chance to recalibrate into game mode. The NU packet caught my eye; I put it on the shelf under the coffee table. Out of sight, but not quite out of mind. Yet. While Dad contemplated his initial attack, I swiped to Google on my phone.

"Ahem."

I looked up, then at the board. He'd moved his king's pawn. "Sorry." I mirrored his move on my side of the board then went back to my phone.

"Yawn," he said, leaning back elbows out, hands behind his head.

Glancing up again, he'd freed his bishop taking control of the center of the board. True chess nerds have names for this start, like the bishops-scramble or the arch-duke-highlander play. There are too many openings. Why not just call it the move-bishop-forward-three? I advanced my knight forward on the same side and opened a new search window.

Dad drummed his fingers on the board.

I saw he'd moved his queen diagonally two spots, so I moved my knight to threaten his bishop.

"You Googling how to lose in four moves?"

"No, sorry." My mind raced as I read and compared websites. "Got a week to apply to the University of Virginia, in-state tuition not bad. They offer both financial aid and athletic scholarships. Ditto for Virginia Tech, January 15 deadline for applying. Think Coach MacGavin would make calls for me?" I looked at my knee, "If I can get back into playing shape?"

He rubbed his chin. "Interesting. Yes, I'm sure he would. Looks like you've got your next moves planned. In life, at least," he said, sending his queen across to take my pawn and flicking over my black king. "Checkmate."

"What the?" Scowling, I reviewed the board and slapped my forehead, then demanded, "Rematch. Double or nothing."

"As in, Backyard Doggie Doo Doo Duty?"

I nodded once.

"Two weeks?"

I nodded twice.

"I accept," he chuckled.

"Set 'er up," I said, sliding my phone out of reach.

He winked, "As you wish."

30

"Wake Me Up Before You Go-Go!" – Wham

A text message pinged my phone charging next to me on the bedstand. I lifted the pillow blocking the bright morning sun and brought the cell to my face. Squinting, I didn't recognize the number. My heart skipped a beat. Ian? No. Sofi had saved him as BigMac. Note to self, change that.

Who was this?

> Her words, I want a bulldog!
> I will name her Ruth ;-)

I bolted upward, knocking Roscoe off the bed. My legs were pinned under Mallory, who groaned but didn't budge an inch. "Off!" I shooed her. She stood, arching her bottom up in a downward-facing dog pose, then hopped to the floor. I kicked the comforter off and swung my legs to the side. Is Ms. Davis awake? If so, what she said is crazy, and crazy is her normal! My clumsy thumbs weren't awake yet so spell check had a field day, but I managed to type and send:

> (*me*)
> Is this Mr. Davis?

> (*?*)
> Yes! Sorry.
> She's awake!

> (*me*)
> That's great!
> How is she?

(*?*)
Starving ;-)

His light-hearted mood was contagious. I pictured his smile re-energized, holding her right hand in his, Googling "bulldogs for adoption near me" clumsily with his left.

(*me*)
Can I tell the others?

(*?*)
Please do.
She's resting now.
I let you know when she
can have visitors

(*me*)
Okay, thanks!

I tapped the new message box and did the unthinkable, initiated my first group chat message. I abhor them, getting pinged a billion times when everyone responds to everyone. I answer the originator then mute my phone and ignore the rest. But this was different. I looked forward to hearing the return dings like the peal of church bells delivering glad tidings of joy.

Adding the Clue crew names, I snorted, remembering Sofi's definition of crew, "... real humans you hang with."

(*me*)
Ms. D woke up!

Responses trickled in.

(*aspen*)
Hallelujah! Awesome!!!

Can't wait to see her!
When can we go?!?

(*krutch*)
Crikey mates

(*willow*)
;-)

(*dervis*)
Good news

(*hood snap*)
:- O

(*me*)
Will keep you posted

I tapped the new message box for my second group chat.

(*me*)
Need to throw.
You two around?

Instant grief, but in a good way.

(*jaz*)
It's a miracle!
Rogue group texting.
You go girl! ;-)

(*me*)
Ha ha

(*harley*)
Unless she was abducted
by aliens and they are
forcing her to recruit? lol

(*me*)
Busted.
Hiding ship in stadium
2 today. Come alone :-|

I checked the time. Nine a.m. I'd slept late. In the bright morning sun, yesterday's worries were today's memories. Refreshed, I stood, did ten easy sit squats back onto the bed with raised arms out in front for balance. Then twenty heel raises each, feet parallel, in V and teepee positions.

Bending at the waist to palm the wood-planked floor nose to knee, I studied the pale scar, then compared thigh muscles measuring with thumbs and index fingers to see how much muscle I'd lost and needed to find before lacrosse season's first game. Two. Months. From. Now.

Frowning at that thought, I clenched my teeth, jaw tight, then opened my mouth to let out a leftover yawn. No time for that mess. I have applications to attack. Stick skills to practice. And, yes, unfortunately, Backyard Doggie Doo Doo Duty :-|

***

The next day, Clue Crew met at Bistro+39 before going to see Ms. Davis. Scanning the wooden red vinyl booths, I saw Hood Snap's head near an old jukebox I hadn't noticed before.

When I reached them, Aspen, previously hidden by the tall booth, jumped up to hug me. She's quite the hugger. Holds on and squeezes that awkward extra ten seconds that non-huggers like me dread and avoid. But it wasn't so horrible this time. Shared relief was benevolent.

"How ya been? Knee better, no limp! Total Fab! Yay, you! How'd you find out about Ms. Davis? So happy!" She slid in next to Hood Snap.

Sitting across from them, Willow looked up and smiled. Fingers wrapped around a stick of charcoal, her drawing pad opened to an amazing sketch that captured both Hood Snap's magnetic stare and her twin's effervescent personality.

Aspen resumed the pictured pose, hugging his arm, her head tilted onto his chest. Because her dark hair melted into his black sweatshirt, it looked like his chest had sprouted a head. Her baby doll pursed lips formed a lovely heart in front of his actual beating one.

"That's really good," I said, as Willow closed the pad and slid it behind us.

"Thanks," she softly replied and scooted to make room.

"Krutch and Dervis will be here any sec. We're waiting to order," Aspen said as she sat up but remained glued to Hood Snap.

"Been wondering, when we escaped the assembly?" I asked, looking at Hood Snap.

He nodded.

"Why don't you always skip?"

Aspen butted in, "They used to, then Dervis morphed into a jock for MIT and a theater tech for Chloe, so it's rah-rah-rah. Go school spirit. Meanwhile, Krutch, yeah, let's just say, he needs his fix."

Unless Hood Snap was a ventriloquist, it was clear Aspen was now his spokesperson, so I asked her. "What fix?"

"Mandi, and the Mannequins. Krutch has to be the last one in so he doesn't see others watch her grand entrance but can glance at her from his vantage point when she isn't looking."

I asked, "About that, what's her deal?"

Hood Snap shrugged.

"It's complicated," Aspen said, then her voice dropped to a whisper as she looked over my shoulder. "They're here."

"Howdy fellas and fillies, what is going on?" Krutch asked, sitting down on the other side of Aspen, while Dervis sat next to me.

"How many hot chocolates?" Hood Snap asked.

"Oh, so, you're talking now?" Dervis asked. "Great. Once he starts you can't shut him up."

Aspen smiled seductively, "I know how to shut him up."

"As – pen!" Willow whispered.

She shrugged at her mirrored image sitting across the table. "You got filters, I got charm."

Hood Snap nodded, smiling down at her.

"I'd like a ho cho, yo," Aspen cooed, cuddling closer.

"I'll take a barf bag to go and a hot chocolate for here," Dervis said.

Hood Snap snorted and asked, "Willow?"

"Hibiscus tea, thank you," she said.

"Gracie?"

"Hot chocolate, thanks."

He looked over Aspen's head to Krutch.

"Coffee. You fly, I'll buy." Krutch took a twenty out of his wallet and dropped it on the table.

Hood Snap patted Aspen's arm clutching his, picked up the money and unfolded from her and the booth.

"I love everything about this little slice of Italy," Aspen said, plopping her elbows on the table and resting her chin on her hands. She watched Hood Snap order from the woman behind the counter. "He's fluent in l'italiano, ya know. That's how you say it when you are talking about the language, like l'inglese, for English, and you don't capitalize."

"That's right. He lived in Italy," I said, looking across the table at Aspen hoping she didn't mind my contribution. "After Ms. Davis's accident he brought me here, it was kind of a blur, don't remember specifics, other than him telling stories so I didn't have to think."

Krutch said, "Dude doesn't say much, but when he does, he says it all."

***

When we arrived at Ms. Davis's room she was sitting up in bed. Her head bandage was now a band rather than a full helmet. "Hello! Come in cherubs!" Pale, her smile lit up her face. She wore cut-off sweats, arms at elbows and legs at knees to accommodate her bandaged left forearm and left leg in a bright green cast from the knee down. I hadn't noticed those injuries before as she'd been covered by blankets. Driver's side. Must have been T-boned.

Her husband, dressed in jeans and a navy blue George Washington University sweatshirt, welcomed us with a broad smile and a wink. "I'm Davis, James Davis."

"That's on you, Gracie!" Ms. D's gaze found me. Cheeks flushed, I shrugged.

"Goofball hasn't stopped saying it since I woke up," she added, exchanging a true love look with her husband as the rest of us watched in awkward silence.

Aspen filled it with "Righteous pup!" She petted a life-sized stuffed bulldog that stood guard on the bedside tray with the wooden Clue characters and *The Princess Bride.*

"Her name is Ruth," Ms. Davis said.

"Until we get a real pup," Mr. Davis said.

"If you get a puppy, she can be Baby Ruth! My favorite candy bar! Has all the important food groups: peanuts, caramel, and chocolate! Ooh, look! There I am!" Aspen said, pointing to the Miss Scarlett wooden peg.

"That's right! Thanks, kiddos. What game should we play next?" asked Ms. Davis.

"Oh! How about a crime-solving game?" Aspen asked, adding, "We can get one online."

"Sounds good, but how about?" Ms. Davis tapped her bandaged head. "You each are your favorite sleuth?"

"I call Sam Spade," Dervis said.

"Who?" Krutch asked.

"Sam Spade, *The Maltese Falcon.*"

"You mean the Millennium Falcon," Krutch said.

"Crack a book, Han Solo. Dashiell Hammett's novel. But if you must go with Hollywood, Humphrey Bogart played him in the movie," Dervis explained.

A look exchanged between Hood Snap and Krutch affirmed a successful badgering. "I do bee-lieeve," Krutch said in an exaggerated southern drawl, "I'll be Daniel Craig's detective character, Benoit Blanc, from the who-dun-it, *Knives Out*."

"Oh, oh, oh, you can be Sherlock and I'll be Watson!" Aspen piped in, grabbing Hood Snap's arm and jumping up and down.

"That'll work. Gracie?" Ms. Davis asked me.

"Not sure. Need to do some research. You?"

"Miss Fisher, the sassy Aussie private detective," she winced, shifted her leg cast, then smiled at her husband. "And you can be my Detective Inspector Jack."

Aspen clapped. "Ooh, fun. She wears the most fabulous flapper outfits! We're bingeing her show with Mom over break. That and *Murder She Wrote*. Totally opposite vibe but still dope. Willow, you could be mystery writer Jessica Fletcher, but, seriously, rethink living in Cabot Cove because it's gotta be the murder capital of the world. For reals."

Willow sat out of the way with her sketch pad open. She paused to look up from a work and slow-blinked. After a quick glance back to her model, she put her index finger to her mouth and shushed Aspen, then pointed to Ms. Davis, whose eyes were closed. She'd drifted off to sleep with a smile on her pixie face.

Everyone quieted, waved and filtered out of the room. Willow gently tore her sketch from the pad and offered it to Mr. Davis. A grin spread across his now shaven face. He mouthed, "Thank you." It pictured Ms. Davis brandishing a lightsaber, mounted on a giant rearing bulldog, surrounded by an army of doll peg soldiers charging out of a charred, desolate wasteland. The other side of the Fire Swamp.

31

"Take A Chance On Me" – ABBA

"Morning, Scout!" Dad greeted me. I was surprised to see him in civies drinking coffee and reading the paper.

"Three-day weekend?" I asked.

"Nope. Burning leave, the ole' use it or lose it. Thought I'd tag along to your physical therapy session today."

Mom winked at me from the kitchen window above the sink. She was watering her herb garden and humming as Alexa softly played an upbeat ABBA playlist.

I grabbed a spoon, almond butter and an apple and sat down across from Dad. "Sure, but it's pretty basic. Warm-up on a bike, box jumps and hopping on one foot, then the other. Reminds me of kindergarten."

He laughed. "When you either sat in the reading corner or tore around the playground. Zero to sixty."

Mom refilled his mug, topped off hers and leaned back on the counter. "Remember her progress reports? 'Gracie asks to be excused from naptimes saying that is what nighttime is for. Daytime is for reading, running and eating.'"

"That's my girl." He raised his coffee mug to me.

"Hopefully I get cleared to run today." I lifted my apple to him, then dabbed on a spoonful of almond butter and took a bite.

"You'll be up to speed in no time," he said.

"On that note, I submitted both applications to UVA and Tech last night. Regurgitated my, 'How international military moves have influenced and enriched my life experience through exposure to different cultures' essay. I also drafted my petition to be released from the National Letter of Intent. Do you want to read it?" I looked to Mom, who shook her head side to side, then Dad.

"No. You got this," he said, nodding with confidence.

I took a bite, chewed, thought, and swallowed. "Okay. I'll proof it one more time, then hit send." Then hope, hope, hope they let me go and I heal, heal, heal and can play somewhere else.

***

I was given a flexible knee brace and cleared to "jog." A loathsome word for a runner, but I'll take it. Especially since I kind of, sort of, have been, on the DL. Psyched to pick up the pace and make my next move, a rush of energy raced through my limbs. Anxious to get home and get on with it, in the car I said, "I'm going to give Coach MacGavin a call. Just to check in and ask about the UVA and Tech programs."

"Good strategy. Let me know what he says," Dad said.

As soon as he shut off the engine I jumped out, then looked back in, "Thanks for burning leave on me."

"Anytime. Go get'em kiddo."

I took the stairs two at a time, then slowed my roll and paced back and forth in my room rehearsing how to ask Coach to convince the two collegiate coaches to take a chance on me, an athlete re-couperating from ACL surgery. After going over my spiel for the OCDillionth time, I picked up my cell, scrolled through my pathetically few numbers and called. It rang.

"Hello?"

Sounds weird. "Coach?"

"No, this is his son, Ian."

What the heck?

Pause.

"Ian?" I gasped. Is he ignoring caller I.D. or me?

"Yes."

"This is Gracie, Halsted. From his club team." In case you forgot carrying me off the field when I blew out my knee, and on a side note, why haven't you texted like you said you would at Thanksgiving?

"Gracie?"

"Yes, Halsted."

"I know. It's Ian." Pretty much established that point.

"Is this your dad's cell?" And when did you get back?

"No. Believe it or not. We still have a landline."

"Oh. Got it. So do my folks." Awkward silence.

"How's your knee?"

"Um. Better. Just got cleared to run." But not chase you.

"Great. I'll let him know." Awkward silence.

"I need him to call some schools for me." TMI!

"What about Northwestern?" Awkward silence.

"Didn't work out. Gotta go." I disconnected and tossed my phone onto the bed like a kindergarten game of hot potato. My cheeks burned. Was I upset about the merit rejection, having to admit it out loud to Ian, or his lack of follow-through? Regardless, I needed air. I threw on heavy sweats, grabbed my stick and flew down the stairs too fast, but with enough sense to hang on to the handrail.

Dad looked up from his crossword puzzle. "Where's the fire?"

"At the station. Going to wall ball. Be back before dinner."

"Don't overdo – " his voice trailed off when the front door closed behind me and I broke into a "jog."

The fire station was a couple blocks away. I'd asked permission to throw and catch against the backside of the two-story windowless building.

Fitness stations were set up around the grassy lot for the firefighters to train. Dropping to the cold rubber track that circled the field, I stretched. Inhaling, I raised arms above my head then folded over my outstretched legs while exhaling. Hoping the awkward phone conversation would dissipate with the puff of warm vapor into the chilly afternoon air.

After mentally grounding myself, I stood, picked up my stick, scooped up a ball and shot a specific cinder block that I targeted for accuracy. Fifty times I threw right, switched hands, caught left, threw left, switched hands, caught right. Immersed in repetition, my concentration was interrupted when a black stick head intercepted the ball.

"Hey," Ian said. His face was serious in the shadow of a Black Knight hoodie.

I stared. Recalibrated. "Hey." I chopped his stick with mine, causing the ball to pop up. I caught it mid-air and threw it back at the wall but aimed at a block five feet to the right of the target so it angled back to him. He caught it and mimicked the opposite so it rebounded to me.

After a few moments of empty air, he said, "We got cut off. Tried calling back but missed you, so I stopped by. Your dad told me where to find you."

Throw. Bounce. Catch.

Of course, he did. "Uh-huh."

Throw. Bounce. Catch.

"Sorry about NU, it's tough to get into."

Throw. Bounce. Catch. Just say it.

"I got in, but it's too expensive. Petitioned to be released from my NLI."

Throw. Bounce. Catch.

He paused and looked at me. "What next?"

Throw. Bounce. Catch.

"Applying to UVA and Tech."

Throw. Bounce. Catch.

"Solid programs and schools."

Throw. Bounce. Catch.

"Going to ask your dad to make calls to their coaches."

Throw. Bounce. Catch.

"What about Annapolis? Navy coach wants you."

I caught the ball. At least someone does. "Won't go Academy unless I want to serve."

"Respect."

Throw. Bounce. "You going to condition with your runner boyfriend now?"

Duck. Gulp. "Who?"

I rotated as he trotted behind me to retrieve the ball, then shrugged, "Your boyfriend, Davis."

"Dervis?"

He shrugged.

"He's not my boyfriend. Where'd you get that idea?"

"Charlotte."

Throw. Bounce. Catch.

"Oh." My grip tightened as if wringing her neck.

"Was doing last-minute shopping." He paused, shrugged, "Full disclosure, always wait until the last day. I ran into her at the mall."

Hope she didn't get hurt. Too bad.

"She said it was all over social media. So... I trolled you," he sheepishly admitted.

"No way! I'm not even on!"

"So I gathered, but you're tagged. Cross country. Tech crew. And he's with you a lot."

"Because we're friends."

Throw. Bounce. Catch. Silence.

"Think I'm done for today."

"Want a ride home?" he asked.

I searched his face for a clue because I didn't have one.

"Sure."

"Trucks around front."

He clicked a key fob as we rounded the corner. The engine roared on a silver. Jeep. Gladiator. Badass trifecta.

I snorted. "If there's an ARMY STRONG decal on the bumper I'm going to barf."

He laughed. "Not yet."

I climbed in.

Playing it cool. Thinking, what would Sofi do? Say something witty. Clever. Flirty. At a loss, I settled on, "When do you head back to school?" Yawn.

"Tomorrow." He glanced over with a shrug and a slight wince. Apologetic? Regretful? Indigestion?

"Tomorrow?"

"Yep."

I looked through the windshield at the too short, two-block drive to my house and sighed. Out loud. Like the moody, lovesick whiner. Salvage this. I frowned and rubbed my knee.

"Does it hurt?"

My knee, ego, or life's cruel sense of humor? "Meh, just keeping it loose." So nonchalant. "Did you have a good break?"

"Went by quick." Pause. "Have to head back. Running a half-marathon to benefit ALS and Alzheimer's research on New Year's Eve." He pulled into my driveway.

"Good on you. Can't wait to get back into racing."

"With your boyfriend?" he teased.

"Yep, give Charlotte my best." I countered, reaching for the door handle.

"Just a sec." A devious grin appeared above his chiseled chin. "Want to mess with her?"

I snorted, "I do now."

"Come here," he said, putting his cell in selfie-mode. He held in it the center of the dashboard.

I moved in, but seeing wild, wind-blown hair made me pull up my hood. He reached up and brushed it back. "You look great. Natural." He leaned an elbow on the console in between us so our shoulders touched, sending a bolt of lightning, torso to toes.

My heart stopped beating, time stopped ticking, the earth stopped rotating. Defying Ian's gravitational pull I pried my eyes from him to the screen. A stranger with rosy cheeks, tousled hair, and twinkling eyes stared back at me.

"Say hi to Charlotte," Ian chuckled.

I laughed as he clicked the pic. We stayed in the pose for an awkward second too long, looking at us. Him, grinning. Me, drowning in intoxicating dude/deodorant/cologne combo. "What will you do with it?" I moved away, with regret.

"Post it on an old Facebook page, if I can remember how. Haven't updated it in a long time."

"Can you try now?" I asked.

"Sure." He swiped a couple screens and opened the app.

"Here it is." His banner picture was an action shot of a younger, less muscular Ian in a green and gold lacrosse jersey. Don't get me wrong, he looked good, driven, drop-dead gorgeous.

"High school?"

"Yep."

"Any pics with Charlotte?"

"Nope."

"How will she find it?"

"Watch. Your nickname is Rogue, right?"

"Um, yeah," I looked at him.

"Your friends called you that at the tournament when they cheered for you."

Wow. He remembered.

"Since you don't have a page, I'll tag myself." He uploaded our pic, typed 'Re:Laxn' with Rogue,' then clicked 'Post.' "Now I'll turn on my notifications –"

Ding!

"Here we go!" He held up his phone so I could see an instant comment. 'OMG! Gracie?! How are U?!? Hey Ian.'"

I recognized the name. Lanie Moore, the lacrosse goalie on my club team, went to high school with Ian and ride shares with Charlotte. "That was quick."

"Still FB friends I guess. Obviously, her notifications are on. She'll waste no time sharing the good news about your recovery with Charlotte. Probably fired it to her ASAP."

True. Lanie was a sweetheart but she'd be okay knocking Charlotte down a bit after the grief she's endured.

"Middie?" I asked. Pointing to the picture. I thought he played D pole. It was a great shot. Ian's focused intensity in the foreground, his opponent's look of resignation at getting left in the dust, or turf, so to speak, behind him.

"Yep. Played both in high school, but switched to Pole full-time this year, already have two All-American Middies."

"Makes sense." Pause.

"So." He shrugged.

"So." I nodded, opened my door and stepped down.

"Be back spring break. Okay to text in the meantime?"

"Won't hold my breath." I deployed a supercilious eyebrow.

"Because?"

I looked up and around. "Think I've heard that before."

That smile. Dang, it. I was being so clever.

"Check Rog."

"Go Army." I shut the door and waved my stick over my head as I walked away.

Stepping inside, my cell vibrated in my front hoodie pocket, or was it bees buzzing in my stomach? I swiped it on.

MESSAGES

now

BigMac

iMessage

Second Note to Self re: change Ian's contact name in phone. I opened message and promptly forgot note to self, starring at our noteworthy selfie. Exhaling long, ending with a wow. Apparently, I had held my breath. Sofi's going to love, love, heart, heart, XO, XO this.

"Wash up, Scout. Time to eat," Dad called when he heard me greet the pups. Glancing at the selfie for the tenth time in two minutes, I silenced my phone and left it in the den.

"I have two Goods tonight," he said, as in, our *The Good, the Bad and the Ugly* dinnertime ritual.

"I'm all ears," Mom said, as she typically had the Good and he the Bad.

"The first was when Scout got cleared to run today. The second –" he said, grinning madly.

Uh-oh.

"– is the cat swallowed the canary smile on my youngest prodigy's face. Must have been a good wall ball practice."

As my face conceded defeat to a warm, rampaging blush, I retaliated with a Clint Eastwood squint. "I've got the Bad. Which turned out to be not so bad, but still, someone gave out classified intel without clearance." Which I really appreciate.

Holding up his hands in defense, "I thought you could use someone to make a pass to – at," then burst out laughing.

"Daaaad," I growled through gritted teeth to keep from smiling.

"He seems like a fine young man. I was just looking out for your best interests."

"Um. Huh, tell that to the judge." I looked at Mom.

"That leaves me with the Ugly, which is more funny than ugly, for us at least." She winked at me. "A memory. When Jason was a baby and waking up to feed every two hours, I was exhausted. My period started early – thankfully, I was in no shape for baby number two yet."

"Oh no, not this again." Dad slapped his forehead.

Mom continued, "We lived in Naval Postgraduate School housing. I was out of tampons and asked your father to go to the mini-mart on post."

"Please stop," he groaned.

She chuckled. "When he took his basket to the checkout lane, the lady cashier held up the box of tampons in one hand, and a spiral notebook in the other, and announced to the entire store, 'Like to see him take notes with these.' He was still burning bright red when he got home, and to this day, has never purchased another feminine hygiene product."

"Amen."

Mom patted him on the shoulder as she left the dining room. A moment later she called from the kitchen, "Grace Artemis, can you give me a hand?"

"Sure." I cleared some plates. She was reading her cell as I entered and deposited dishes into the sink.

"Where's your phone?" she asked.

Cheeky, I snapped to attention, fingers entwined, elbows out in polite schoolgirl position. "Silenced, in the den, in accordance with proper supper etiquette."

She chuckled, "I received an interesting text from Sofia Isabella." Reading aloud, "'The Good; PICTURE,' in all caps with three exclamation points. 'The Bad; failure to share INSTANTLY,' again all caps." She looked up at me, smiled, then continued. "'The Ugly; she will be punished for her INSOLENCE.' All caps. Tell her to video chat after dinner."

Stunned speechless. What? How? My ears burned. "Excuse me." I rushed to face the silenced, vibrating, music.

32

"Fire" – Bruce Springsteen

"I was today years old when I realized exactly what you are! An elusive, mythical, girl next door/'It girl' hybrid!"

"What?" Confused, I responded to Sofi's video chat revelation. Following her bizarre train of thought hasn't been a problem in the past, since it was all about her, but now that it's about me, I'm clueless. Uncomfortable in my newly-exposed, blushing, "What have I done" skin.

Her hands spun in side-by-side circles on the screen. "Not even gonna reprimand because you are most definitely operating under the influence of intense pheromones, so I'll just say, props to you little sis, well done."

"What does that even mean?" I begged.

"Means welcome to the big leagues. Everybody wants to know who you are, and be who you are."

"Why?"

"Hello? Check out the dude on your immediate left in the pic, Chiquita. Spicy Ian with an extra packet of hot sauce!"

Feeling the burn, I needed to know. "Hybrid?"

"The girl next door, basically Joan."

"Joan literally lived next door." Couldn't help inserting dry sarcasm despite my current dilemma. It's what I do.

"True, but it's a thing. A persona. How a person is seen."

"And the 'it girl' is you, right?"

"Pretty much how Shelley and I rolled."

"Got it. But don't want it. Any chance of reverting back to my obscure bookworm in the attic thing?"

"Not a chance, sweet stuff. You've officially been social-media outed."

I dropped my head into my hands. "Noooooooo." Weird, an image of Mandi of Mandi and the Mannequins popped up. Everyone staring at her, mimicking her every move, what she wore, or how she did her hair. Her glances into windows, checking how she looked, was perceived? Judged? I shuddered. No thanks. "I'll take a hard pass."

"Too late, Buttercup. The list of comments is multiplying exponentially. 'Who is she? Where'd she come from? What school does she go to? How'd he meet her? How can I meet her? She's smoking. I hate/love her.' You're an enigma. A totally, accidentally, what the heck and how did this happen wonder." She blinked two times. "So. What are you going to wear first day back to school?"

I shook my head, palms flipped up. "I don't know. The usual? Jeans? T-shirt? Hoodie?"

"Oh H to the No. It'll look like you're capitalizing on said social blitz. Go to my closet. I left an ECO for you."

"As in eco-friendly outfit?" I hoped.

"Yeah, no. Dufus. Emergency Cute Outfit."

I should have known.

"It's a chunky, turtleneck moss-colored tunic. It'll make your hazel eyes pop. You can wear black leggings and low-top Cons. Dream team accessories that are chic, comfortable and casual."

"Tunic. As in what the queen's knights wore?" I love yanking her chain. It's in our DNA.

"OMGive me a break. Get out of the middle ages girl. A tunic is a long pullover sweater that hits mid-thigh. Have you learned nothing from my tutelage?"

"Apparently not. And FYI, I don't wear leggings, unless running and it's a negative bazillion degrees."

"Note. I am audibly sighing and visually LMAO'ing." She facepalmed.

"Touché." We grinned at each other.

"Now go find it. You can wear skinny jeans if you must. Most important thing is to CYA."

"Cover my ass... why?"

"Because. You're announcing to the world your booty is off the market so don't even."

I pounded my head on the desk. "This. Is. Exhausting."

"Welcome to my world, honey. Get used to 'IT, girl.'"

Closing my laptop, I picked up my phone. The green and white icon screamed 10 unread in the red circle. Sighing, I tapped on it. Ricocheting messages pummeled me from Jaz and Harley. Responding to both, I wrote:

(me)
Throw tmo?
Will update.

Instant replies.

(jaz)
Cha. Yeah. Can't wait!

(harley)
Girrrrrrl. U been holding
out on us ;-)

(me)
Argh

(jaz)
Hahahahaha

(harley)
Hahahahaha
hahahahaha
tmo.

(me)
Be gentle

(jaz)
Nope

(harley)
Not a chance ;-)

***

Twirling my stick, I sat on my front doorstep waiting for them, rehearsing what to say. Explain. Confess. When Jaz pulled in my driveway, I jumped in the backseat. Both of them were grinning like Alice in Wonderland Cheshire cats. I buckled in and began.

"Okay. Data dump." I sighed. "Didn't get the merit money needed to go to Northwestern, so I petitioned to be released from my NLI." I paused to let that sink in.

"Yawn," Jaz said.

"Get to the good part. Hello, Ian," Harley said.

Should have anticipated that what was so devastating to me was next to nothing to them in the grand scheme of things. Noted. "Applied to UVA and V Tech, then called Coach MacGavin to talk about their lax programs."

"Boring. Ian?" Harley asked.

"Well. Ian answered, not knowing who I was. I thought he was ghosting me as he was back but not in contact and didn't recognize caller I.D. so I was a total weirdo. But, it was a landline, not a cell. I got stupid flustered. Asked Ian to have his dad call me and hung up. Left my phone. Went to do wall ball at the fire station."

"Captivating. Go on," Harley said.

"Ian thought it was strange. Called back but when I didn't answer, went to my house. Dad sent him over. We passed for a bit. He thought I was dating Dervis –"

"Wait. What?" Jaz asked.

"Charlotte told him I was dating Dervis."

"Bitch," Harley said.

I shrugged. "We cleared that up, he gave me a ride home and suggested we post a selfie to mess with her."

"Which no doubt rocked her narcissistic world," said Jaz.

Hmmm. Is that why he did it? To get rid of her! Ouch.

"Go on," Harley prompted.

"That's it. Probably wanted to get rid of her once and for all." That thought disturbed me more than I cared to admit.

"Not a chance," Jaz said.

"Playing the NOPE card. I can read fake smiles from miles and this wasn't. It's a true, blue, genuine, All-American, I got it bad and that's good for this girl grin if I've ever seen one, which I haven't, unfortunately, directed at me, but this one at you? Frickin' romance novel dreamy," Jaz said.

"Agree," Harley added.

Hmmm. Maybe? My reflection in the car window smiled back at me. The stranger from the pic. I bit my lip and dared to hope.

"What happened after you posted it?"

"What?" I refocused inside the car.

"He drove you home?" Jaz asked.

"Ah, yeah."

"Well? When are you gonna get together again? Tonight, tomorrow, this weekend?" Harley asked.

"No. He's going back to West Point today."

"Today?" Jaz groaned.

"Today," I sighed.

"How did you leave it?" Harley asked.

"Said he'd be back spring break but would text." A sly grin grew up one cheek, remembering our witty exchange.

"Well at least there's that," Jaz said.

"Then he sent me the pic."

"That's promising, how did you respond?" Jazz asked.

Gunk. I hadn't. Crap.

"Gracie?" Harley asked.

"I didn't. Haven't." My brain froze.

"Better think of something quick otherwise you'll be penalized for delay of game," Harley refereed from the front seat.

We ran, threw, and passed over the next hour. The whole time, only half concentrating on lacrosse. Physically going through the motions. Mentally planning my next move without adequate skills in a game of chance. Romance? Way out of my comfort zone.

***

Back in my attic, I ran a finger along the spines of the trusted titles, mentally searching their pages for clever phrases and witty comebacks. Hoping for insight on how to respond to Ian's amazing selfie share. My index finger paused on an old favorite, *The Count of Monte Cristo*. Full of adventure, deceit and revenge, maybe not the best example of how to achieve the romantic destiny I sought, but at least it ends with, "all human wisdom is contained in these two words, 'Wait and Hope.'" Which pretty much sums up my situation.

Bag it. I pulled out my phone, paused on the screen's new wallpaper image, the sensationalized selfie, then punched the message icon and tapped **BigMac**. Third Note to Self. I really need to change that. Right after I send this.

> (me)
> Thanks for the pic.
> And pep talk.
> Let me know how
> race goes.
> Go Army

I sent it. Phew. Exhaling, I hit the phone icon and tapped **BigMac**, pressed edit, and changed it to **ARMY;-)**

Probably should leave off the semi-colon, hyphen, end parenthesis smiley face, but no one will see it, so I'll keep it for now. I saved and went back to study the screen picture.

My phone vibrated and buzzed. Incoming call, I fumbled, dropped, but nabbed it mid-air and answered without checking I.D. That was quick! My heart skipped.

"Halsted," a gruff voice rumbled.

Coach! "Yes sir," I quickly said, sounding guilty. Of what? My cheeks burned. So glad he couldn't see me. Panicking, I checked to make sure we weren't Facetiming. Not that he would, but accidental butt-face calls do happen. Focus!

"Ian gave me your message. I'm returning your call."

"Oh. Yes. Ian." Glowing brighter. Dang, it!

Pause. Wondering, how much did Ian tell his dad? Does he know we met up? This is getting complicated.

"I petitioned to drop my NLI. I applied to UVA and Tech and wanted to talk to you about their programs," I said.

"I see." Pause. "What about Navy?" he asked.

"It's still in the mix. I'm keeping options open."

"Makes sense, but I know Coach Sinclair is interested."

Navy coach. Ian mentioned that too. They talk about me?

"How's the reconditioning going?" Or, they don't.

"Good! Been lifting, running, throwing." Making passes at your son, thanks to my dad.

"So I hear." So they do. Talk about me. Yikes.

Does Coach mind we hung out? Meh.

Control the center of the board. What's my next move?

"I'm focusing on spring season," I said.

"Keep me posted. After you've got a couple games under your belt we can reach out and see who comes knocking."

Warning: I might not make it back to top competitive shape. Cliché Dash Two Time. Don't put the cart in front of the horse, like all the eggs in the purple NU basket. Message received. I shivered as the warm blush drained from my cheeks. "Okay. Thank you, sir," I said. Holding my breath.

His deep, reverberating chuckle caught me off guard.

"At ease, Halsted."

I exhaled. "Military Brat 101 conditioning. Yes, sir. No, Ma'am. Firm handshake. Look 'em in the eye."

"Not all bad. Worthwhile lessons."

"Yes, Sir."

"Academy might be a good fit."

"I'll keep it in mind, Coach."

"Sounds good."

"Thanks." I hung up. Sighed. Moped a bit. Checked for messages. None. Moped some more. Wandered over to my bookcase. Haunted by what Coach said, "Then see who comes knocking."

If they come knocking. If I get to play again. *"Suddenly there came a tapping – as of someone gently rapping, rapping at my chamber door –"* With that melancholy thought I pulled out the worn, brown, hardbound book with an embossed bronze title, *Edgar Allen Poe Complete Tales and Poems*, opened to my favorite, and read out loud.

> *"But the Raven, sitting lonely on the placid bust, spoke only*
> *That one word, as if his soul in that one word he did outpour.*
> *Nothing farther then he uttered — not a feather then he flutter*
> *Till I scarcely more than muttered*
> *"Other friends have flown before —*
> *On the morrow he will leave me,*
> *as my Hopes have flown before."*
> *Then the bird said "Nevermore."*

33

"Complicated" – Avril Lavigne

Turning sideways, then back to the mirror, I looked over my shoulder to check out my butt in the chunky, thigh-length moss-colored turtleneck tunic that makes my hazel eyes pop. Sofi scores again. Ass totally covered. Incognito even. If only the rest of me could fly under the radar.

I'd hoped the selfie social media drama would subside over the weekend, but Jaz and Harley informed me no such luck. I was still trending on top, with people from my school, Lanie's school, and several in between asking questions, demanding answers and throwing shade. Like I asked for it.

To make matters worse, Ian's ghosting me. Friday race day. Saturday recovery day. Sunday chill day. Now back at it Monday. Yep. No reply to my response. Nothing. Guess it wasn't enough. Or too much. This sucks. Give it a rest. Out of sight. Out of mind-games.

Now, I have to face my demons. Or divas. Samzies.

Dang. Is that how I look like I think I am? Three I's in one sentence? Losing it. Waiting for Jaz and Harley to pick me up realizing they are going to enjoy this so much.

And – they do. Drove up in black shades without smiles. Harley jumped out, opened the back door for me and stood at attention. My Secret Service detail has arrived to escort me to my new annoying role as an It Girl. Oh, joy. Kill me now.

***

"Gracie! Love the look! I follow her too," Chloe said. Chloe, as in the Mannequins entourage member Chloe, who coerces Dervis into doing her computer homework Chloe.

"Excuse me?" I asked. Looking from Chloe to Mandi, of the Mannequins, who stared at me with a what is happening gaze as her rank and file minion changed alliances.

"The influencer. What's her name? On Instagram," Chloe continued as if we were besties.

"I have no idea," I said.

"Gracie doesn't follow," Harley said.

Girl's got my back.

"She leads," Jaz added, with a straight face.

Love it.

"Oh, right. Like when you run. Dervis told me you're a machine. He's gotten better thanks to you. Running that is," Chloe said. Her eyebrows lifted like we shared an inside joke.

Dervis talks to her about me? "Dervis trains hard," I said.

"And it shows," Chloe said, with a lecherous grin.

Ick.

"Ahhh. See ya," I said. Wouldn't want to be ya.

"What was that about?" Harley asked as we escaped.

"About two minutes too long," Jaz answered.

"Did that just happen?" I asked.

"Unfortunately, but not unexpectantly, yes," Harley said.

They dropped me at my first-period class. "Here you go! Have a normal day!" Jaz said.

"That ship sailed," Harley laughed, with a hand drawing waves in the air.

"Thanks. For, being you," I confessed.

"We are who we are," Jaz said, shrugging.

"It's a pleasure to serve," Harley twirled her hand twice as she bowed.

I shook my head, waved them off, and surreptitiously escaped into WWII Spies class.

Krutch, Dervis and Hood Snap were in their usual seats in the back row. I broke my traditional seating chart location and joined them. Go with the flow.

Hood Snap swept his hands, inviting me to sit next to him. I nodded. After sitting down, I leaned forward, looking past him to Dervis. "Chloe talked to me."

He lifted his palms up, "About?"

"My clothes. What the heck?"

"How should I know?" Dervis asked.

"She mentioned us running together," I answered.

"It's weird. She's been all pissed about you, then all of a sudden it's okay, like, you know. We're cool."

The picture. Ian. She thought Dervis and I were. But no.

"Oh," I said.

"Oh?" Krutch said, leaning forward to look at me. "The plot thickens."

"Got something for you." Hood Snap handed me a note.

I looked at him, questioning.

"It's from Aspen. Neither of them got our lunch block."

"Bummer." I pulled the tab marked with a heart and arrow and it magically unfolded onto my desk.

Rogue! So bummed! What the heck!
Banished from the cool table!
Pretty please do lighting and
sound for musical? We miss you!
Parting is such sweet sorrow!

Just then Ms. Davis sailed into the room on her knee scooter. Duct-taped to the handlebar, three blurred red, white, and blue pinwheels made a whirling sound like mini jet engines. Her lower left leg was in a blue cast, left arm in a patriotic tie-dyed sling, and pixie hair cropped even shorter, sporting a headband of white stars on a blue background that covered stitches from the accident.

However, her enthusiasm was unchanged and contagious. Grinning madly, she quizzed, "What was the profession of the wife of CIA agent Jack Ryan in Tom Clancy's book, *Patriot Games*?"

Krutch, Dervis, Hood Snap and I answered in unison, "Doctor."

Ms. Davis shouted, "Hurrah for doctors! Twenty points each for Gryffindor and Ravenclaw!"

Back to normal. Kind of, sort of. But I'll take it.

After class, the four of us stayed behind for a quick chat with Ms. Davis. "Hey, kiddos! Welcome back!"

"Sweet whip, can I take a spin?" Krutch asked, pointing to her knee scooter.

"Sure thing just keep it in the room. Stoke extinguisher busted me in the hallway on my way to class." Ms. Davis tsked, shook her head and looked up at the ceiling.

"Got you. Hate it when fun governors harsh my mellow," Krutch said as he hopped on and pushed off to do a lap.

"Up for a wicked who-dun-it Friday?" Ms. Davis asked.

"Sure, if you are," I said. Everyone else nodded, except for Krutch, who glided gracefully past us, pretending to swim.

"Have you picked your sleuth?" Ms. Davis asked me.

"Kate Warne, a female detective who worked for Allan Pinkerton. She caught killers, found stolen fortunes, and put a stop to an assassination attempt on President Lincoln."

"Love her! Excellent choice." Ms. Davis clapped, then looked at her watch. "Oops. Krutch. I need my ride. I have to hang the spring musical announcement."

"We can post it unless it's classified," Dervis said. "We go by the auditorium."

"Fan-tab-ulous! Here you go, it's *Annie*!" She handed him the posting then looked at me, "You know, now that I've replaced you on the injured-reserve list, I could use a little help on tech crew."

What could I say? Except, "Sure. Count me in."

***

After pinning the *Annie* post we went to our next class. Despite being juniors, Krutch, Dervis and Hood Snap were ninja rock star literature nerds. Working their way up the food chain enabled them to take AP Literature with me, a senior. Apparently, our teacher, Mr. Evans, was fully aware of their prowess having had them for the prerequisite classes. A stickler for his syllabus, rules were meant to be followed without question or comments. No cell phones. No chewing gum. No credit for late homework assignments. This should be fun.

"Sometimes you have to cut a character. It's as simple as that. They can't take up too much real estate if they don't advance the story," Mr. Evans lectured.

"Big brain moment," Krutch said, "But I disagree."

Mr. Evans stopped. Mid stride. "¿Por que?"

Sitting next to Hood Snap, I caught the subtle shift. His phone slid from his back pocket. Thumb tapped camera, slid to video, then cradled in crossed arms, aimed at Krutch to record as he waxed poetic.

"Take Dervis here," Krutch said, lifting both hands into the air then gracefully gesturing sideways to him.

"Why me? Always me. Why not Hood Snap? Or Rogue for a change?" Dervis asked, then leaned forward to thump his head on the desk.

Krutch went on. "A power dweeb. A nerd. A nobody."

"Here we go," Dervis mumbled.

"What good is a world without a Dervis to study along the way?" Instead of cutting experiences or irrelevant people to advance, why not digress? Go off on a tangent? The road less traveled? The path less taken?" Krutch asked.

"Probably because it's filled with poison ivy, or snakes, or creepy spider webs," Dervis muttered.

"Carry on," Mr. Evans encouraged.

"Digressing is what life is all about. An author should tell the character's story and include all their crazy, not follow a formula. Halfway through mini-climax. Three-quarters reveal. Instead, let them jump on and off their own arc, shooting lightning bolts along the way. Random encounters. Acts of kindness or conversely, jerk maneuvers that scar a soul or teach a lesson. Quirky characters that challenge the norm."

"So I'm quirky now?" Dervis asked, lifting his head.

"Not in the least. You have the furthest to go to appeal to the masses to reach your potential. So everyone can cheer."

"Yay me. Go, fight, win. Weirdo," Dervis bemoaned.

"Exactly."

Mr. Evans looked at Hood Snap. "Did you get that?"

Hood Snap nodded.

"Good. Fire it to Krutch." His eyes scanned our row. "Krutch, type it up. I expect it by deadline Friday. Submitting it to the Ayn Rand Essay Contest. If anyone can appreciate an excellent soapbox rant, it'll be them."

Like I said, this should be fun.

***

Jaz and Harley joined our lunchtime table filling the void left by Aspen and Willow. They knew Dervis from cross country; he introduced them to Krutch and Hood Snap.

"You guys are the croquet wizards, correctomundo?" Harley asked.

"We dabble," Krutch said.

Hood Snap nodded.

"Dope," Jaz said, setting down her tray. Hamburger, French fries, packets of ketchup, and a soda haphazardly piled on her tray. A far cry from Willow's carefully arranged salad with accoutrements arranged in artistic wedges. "Gracie! Just heard! We're getting a new high school lacrosse coach."

Harley confirmed after swallowing a bite of egg salad on wholewheat. "Too bad we can't get your club team coach, but I think this new one is legit. She played D1 at North Carolina. Went to high school in this area. I remember watching her when I was in youth league. The real deal."

Here we go. Have to prove myself to earn playing time. As a senior. After ACL surgery. Without a signed Letter of Intent.

"When does she get here?" I asked, nonchalantly out loud, internally crapping bricks.

"Soon. We start workups in February," Jaz said. Her forehead wrinkled as she studied me. "Worried?"

I shrugged. Confessed. "A little."

"Don't be. You're a new coach's dream," Jaz said. "A finisher. Worth your weight in gold."

I leaned my head to the side. "We'll see."

"Chica. You got this. No problemo," Harley said.

Before I could respond, I heard, "Hey Gracie. Did you hear the spring musical is *Annie*? Can't wait to audition! It's one of my favs." Chloe looked around, then whispered behind her beautifully manicured pale pink fingernails. "I'm going for the lead!" She bit her lip. Pretty brown eyes blinked behind a fringe of long bangs. The rest of her mousey brown hair was loose over her shoulders. Perfect-messy-bun-less.

Eyes darted around the table. Eyebrows rose in unison when she tapped Dervis on the shoulder, "Can you grab me a chair please?"

He froze. Krutch's under-the-table kick re-booted Dervis's hard drive. He jumped up and was off on a mission.

"I'll squeeze in here," Chloe said, setting her trendy, multi-sectioned mint green Bento kit next to my reusable lunch sack and beeswax sandwich wraps. She slid into Dervis's chair and scooted closer to make room on her other side for him. Shyly smiling at the other two guys. "You're Krutch and Hood Snap, right? Dervis tells the funniest stories about you." Next, to Jaz and Harley, she asked, "And you're runners, right?"

"Yep," Jaz said, her expression quizzical, but not rude.

"And play lacrosse," Harley added, matter-of-factly.

"Now that we all know who's who, anybody care for a piece of cucumber dipped in hummus? Sliced strawberries? A California roll?" She took off the top layer and placed it in the middle of the table.

"Don't mind if I do, thanks," Hood Snap said, as he reached a long, lanky arm to help himself.

Dervis returned with a chair, sat down, and swept at the cowlick above his forehead that tended to stick up.

I noticed Krutch surreptitiously scanning the cafeteria. Was he too, searching for the wonky parallel universe portal, and wondering if Mandi would come through next?

34

"Karma Chameleon" – Boy George and Culture Club

We'd gone for an easy run after school, with sticks, of course, passing back and forth. On the way home, Jaz and Harley talked about the new coach as I stared out the window, reviewed my recovery, and calculated the chance of earning a starting spot.

"So, what's Chloe's story?" asked Harley. "Isn't she part of The Mandi Mod Squad?"

Another fitting nickname. Forgot they only knew Dervis, from cross country, having just met Krutch and Hood Snap at lunch so they weren't familiar with their Mandi and the Mannequins moniker. I smiled; my friends' circles were merging into a Venn Diagram. The realization I had multiple friend groups increased the grin reflecting in the car window.

"Yep. No clue. Only thing Dervis and I can figure is that she thought we were together, which is weird, but explains her shooting dirty looks until Ian posted the pic."

"I can see why. There are a lot of pics of the two of you on the cross country page. Remember when Jaz wiped out in the creek? You picked her up and finished the race?" Harley asked.

"Vaguely."

"You guys blasted across the finish line splattered in mud grinning like goofballs and he was there waiting with open arms and a dry towel," Harley said.

"Yeah, but," I argued, shaking my head, "That's team stuff, no big woo."

"To us, but if you're not a team player, looks pretty up close and personal," Harley said.

"You looked like an Amazon warrior and Dervis has stepped up his game. Brainy's getting brawny. I can see why she's jealous," Jaz said.

"And, maybe she's not convinced he's not into you. After all, she squeezed between you at lunch," Harley said.

Jaz glanced at Harley, then back to the road. "'Keep your friends close...'"

"'And your enemies closer.' Speaking of friends you want close, still no word from Army?" Harley asked, rotated to look back at me.

"Nope."

"Annoying," Jaz said.

Our gaze met in the review mirror.

Tell me about it.

"Don't read too much into it, after all, that FB post says a lot," Harley said.

Maybe. Maybe not.

Jaz pulled into my driveway. "Thanks." I got out.

"Shor! Catch ya later!" Jaz said.

"¡Hasta la vista, baby!" Harley chimed in.

I cracked up. These two can make any not-so-good situation not so bad.

"See you tomorrow," I said, getting out of the car. I held my lacrosse stick up in a salute as they honked and drove away. My overlapping blue/purple circle peeps.

Roscoe and Mallory were thrilled to see me, but then, if I go out to the mailbox and come back their response is the same as when I'm gone for hours. I love that about dogs.

Mom was in her studio working on a new piece that epitomized the word, "serene." She'd driven the wintery roads of Virginia searching for the perfect scene. A red barn against an immense, dark gray sky in a field of white, surrounded by stark, black, hand-like trees reaching up out of snowdrifts. I could hear the silence. Without speaking, we greeted each other with a smile I left to walk up two staircases to shower.

Standing, robed in front of a steamed mirror, I untangled my wavy, wet hair, mentally traveling step by step back through the day's events. Opposite of planning three steps ahead – checking backward for missteps or to consider other's actions or reactions from a different perspective. Another way to control the center of the board.

My stomach growled. Quickly slipping into sweats and fuzzy socks I padded back down two flights of stairs for dinner. Dad was out of town, so Mom and I chatted as we ate a quick bite, took the pups for a walk around the block, then parted to our respective areas. She, cleaning up in the studio. Me, giving class syllabi for the last semester of my final year of high school a perfunctory glance.

Back up in the attic, I opened my backpack just as it buzzed. Uh-oh. If it were Sofi, she'd be bent that I'd neglected to check for messages for over an hour. I unzipped the pocket and found my cell. The following was stamped on my forehead reflection in the screen pic.

MESSAGES
now
Army;-)
iMessage

What the heck! I punched the icon.

(*Army;-*)
Just got back
from weekend ftx.
Left right after race.

ftx? Sounds familiar. Jason talks about it. Pretend I know? No. Ask.

(*me*)
Ftx?

(*Army;-*)
Sorry. Field training
exercise. Left cell
in dorm

Explains why he's been incommunicado, but not why I'm so inept. Oh well. Carry on.

> (*me*)
> Got it.
> How'd it go?

(*Army;-*)
Freezing rain then snow.
Other than that, kk.
How things there?

Same old stuff, you know. Except I'm uber popular now thanks to you, posting that amazing picture of us.

> (*me*)
> Getting new school
> lax coach. We'll see
> how that goes

(*Army;-*)
Improvise.
Adapt.
Overcome

> (*me*)
> Ha ha.
> Solid.
> Will do.

(*Army;-*)
Tired. Going to
cop somezzzz

(*me*)
Copy that.
Hooah

Well, that was awkward. And awesome. But worth it ;-) Now there's only one thing to do to survive. FaceTime Sofi. Or else, face time with her wrath later if I didn't.

"Mmmmh, yel-low, Buttercup! What's shak'n?" Sofi shimmied her shoulders as her image popped on the screen.

"Salt, hands, James Bond's martini, not stirred." I dead-panned.

"HAH-larious," She laughed, flipping her hair over her shoulder. "So, what's going on?"

"Sending a screenshot of a text exchange with Ian."

"WooHoo!" She grabbed her cell, swiped and punched. Her eyes devoured it. "Dang. Dude was exhausted, chilled to the bone but reached out to warm up. Impressive."

"Considerate. Don't read more into it."

"Said the bookworm."

"Anyway. Knew you'd pitch a fit if I didn't share."

"You bet your sweats bottoms."

"Punny."

"What's your next move?"

"Wait and see."

She sighed. "I despise waiting."

"That makes two of us."

"C'est la vie. Bonne nuit, Grace Artemis."

"Buenas noches, Sofia Isabella."

***

I drove myself the next day, as my final physical therapy session was after school so I couldn't ride to, or work out after, with Jaz and Harley.

First block class, Sunrise Yoga. Yes, you read that right. Yoga. Don't judge. Seriously, if every high school kid started the day wearing comfy clothes in a class that ended with a power nap, the world would be a much better, not to mention safer, place. Just namaste'n.

Since surgery, my flexibility had tanked so I needed to stretch the heck out of every muscle group I used to have and hoped to retrieve.

Speaking of groups. Entering the small gym laid out with rows of mats, I recognized Mandi, front row center facing the mirror-lined wall, perfectly, with two Mannequins on each side and one directly behind her. That one being Chloe. She clapped when she saw me in the mirror, turned and waved for me to take the mat next to her.

I declined, holding my hands up, not in a surrendering way because a Halsted would never, but in a 'thanks but I'm good back here in the back row' kind of gesture.

She shrugged then dropped into yoga's version of the crisscross applesauce pose. For the rest of the class I listened to my inner core and manifested good karma.

After second block was lunch. Arriving last at our table, I was surprised to see a spot saved for me between Krutch and Chloe. Continuing around to her right, Dervis, Jaz, Hood Snap, then Harley, on Krutch's left. Chloe was talking, her hands animated. Approaching from behind, the fluid movement reminded me of something or someone, Sofi perhaps?

The group's attention shifted from the storyteller to me, with varying degrees of raised eyebrows and smiles.

My ears tingled. "Howdy," I said, feeling obligated to announce my presence.

"Hey," Jaz said, her curious downward gaze directed me to a Bento-kit-less reusable lunch sack as Chloe turned to smile up at me, her fluttering hands landed on a sandwich wrapped in beeswax. A closer look revealed au natural fingernails, the opaque, pale pink polish was gone.

I shrugged it off.

"Chloe's telling us how crucial tech crew is to a theater production," Harley said.

Krutch rubbed his chin stubble, striking a profound pose.

Dervis blushed.

Hood Snap nodded.

I set down my lunch and offered, "Dervis is the brains behind every light, sound and action. Like a conductor, he orchestrates all of the elements."

His quick glance expressed appreciation.

Krutch's eyebrow, however, hoisted the BS flag.

Hood Snap gulped a swig of chocolate milk and wiped a smile off his face.

"Are you going to work sound again, Gracie? Or should I say, 'Rogue?' Isn't that what you all call her?" Chloe asked. Her focus bounced from Dervis to me, then ricocheted around the table.

"Yes, from *Rogue One: A Star Wars Story*," Dervis said. "It's the movie that takes place just before *New Hope*," Dervis explained. "New characters attempt to steal Death Star plans."

"What's a Death Star?" Chloe asked.

Dervis's hand froze holding a French fry in mid-air.

Krutch stared at Hood Snap, who blinked, telepathically monitoring Dervis's blood pressure from across the table.

Dervis patiently expounding the spark notes versions of the entire *Star Wars* franchise was like watching Einstein explain his Theory of Relativity to a kitten.

When he paused, Chloe asked, "Was Chris Pratt in *Star Wars*? His eyes are sooooo crazy blue." She looked around for affirmation. "He's also Wonder Woman's pilot boyfriend."

"Chris Pine was in *Wonder Woman* and *Star Trek*. Chris Pratt was in *Guardians of the Galaxy*," Jaz said.

"The one with the raccoon and stick guy," Harley added.

"Oooh, he's really cute too!" Chloe said.

"Super cute," Krutch offered, nodding like a goofball. "And he's Star-Lord," adding insult to Dervis's multiple injuries at the light-hearted, space-related movie comparisons.

In response, Dervis bit the fry and swept his hand back from his forehead, which smoothed down the hair sticking up from the cowlick.

"I'm more of a Chris Evans fan," Jaz said.

"Yummy. Captain America, an Avenger," Harley said.

"He had a star on his uniform," Krutch pointed out.

"And his shield," Hood Snap added.

"The chunky sweater he wore in *Knives Out*? Delicious, amirite?" Jaz said, grinning madly.

"Like a mug of hot chocolate," Harley agreed.

Chloe's face lit up. "The cable-knit fisherman's sweater! I read on Insta it sold out when the movie released. Couldn't keep it in stock."

I knew that tidbit of trivia, thanks to Sofi, but kept it to myself, not wanting to add to Dervis's misery. Circling back, I asked him, "When we first met, we talked about lightsabers, fencing and lacrosse sticks?"

He agreed. "Something like that, you reminded me of the protagonist Jyn Erso, who doesn't take crap from anyone."

"I can see that, but she dies in a big explosion. Kind of a downer," Jaz said.

"Well, yeah, but only after transmitting the Death Star plans," Dervis admitted.

"Worth it," I said.

Krutch snorted.

Hood Snap nodded.

Chloe scanned the faces around the table then shrugged. "So, are you going to work tech crew again for the musical? I can add you to our group Snap."

"Yes, on crew, hard pass on Snap, not into social media."

"What about the picture with your gorgeous boyfriend?"

My turn to squirm, and stammer. "He's just a friend."

"If he wants to stay one he better text," Jaz said.

I glanced quickly from her to Harley and back.

She squinted then asked, "Did he?"

"Last night."

"What the heck!" Jaz said.

"Do tell," Krutch said, as he propped his elbows on the table and dropped his chin onto his fists like a four-year-old waiting for his Dinosaur Eggs oatmeal to cool.

Dervis looked past Chloe to check my reaction.

Chloe noticed. Frowned, following his gaze.

Hood Snap suppressed a grin and did jazz hands.

I took a breath and recalibrated. "It's not a big deal."

"Sure looked like one. How'd you meet? He definitely doesn't go here, I'd have noticed." She grinned.

"He's my club coach's son and goes to West Point."

"A college man," Krutch said, pretending to brush away a tear. "Our little Gracie is growing up."

Hood Snap clasped his hands, fluttering his eyelashes.

"Very funny," I said, squinting with a smirk.

"What about you, Jaz? Dating anyone?" Chloe asked.

"Nope, flying solo," Jaz said, then tossed back. "You?"

"Um, me too, flying solo, that is," Chloe said, moving on to Hood Snap. "You're with the skateboard girl." It was obvious she was going around the table.

Harley stood up, "Gotta bounce, class on the other side of school." She and Josh had split over break. Sore subject.

"Me too," Krutch said. They exited quickly.

Awkward silence. Chloe whispered to me behind her hand, "Are they together?"

"Who?" I asked.

"Harley and Krutch."

"No," Dervis, Jaz and I said in unison.

Hood Snap shook his head side to side.

Chloe shrugged. "Well, they look good together."

"Who's up for the basketball game tonight?" Jaz asked. "Michael's crashing the boards. We've got a winter track posse going." She looked around the table.

"Yeah," Dervis said. "I'm in."

Hood Snap stared at him, then tilted his head ever so slightly toward Chloe. Awkward pause.

Dervis cleared his throat. "Would you like to go?"

Hallelujah!

"Oh. I'm going with Mandi, but I'll look for y'all and come say hi," Chloe said. "Better scoot, see ya later."

Jaz waved and watched her, waiting until she was out of range, then said to Dervis, "Good job."

"What?" he asked, glancing at me with suspicion.

She caught it. "Dude, you know after a race when you need to puke your guts out and your eyes dart for the closest trash can?"

"Yeah," Dervis said, warily.

"That's how you look whenever she's near."

I shot her a silent thank you for not bringing me into it.

"Well done," I said to Dervis, then added to Hood Snap, "Nice work at wingman."

Hood Snap bowed his head.

After the buzzer buzzed, Jaz and I walked together to our lockers. "Harley thought Josh wasn't over Sienna. Turns out, he is." She spun her combination lock.

"And?" I asked.

"Been hanging out with Molly at winter track practices."

"Oh. Bummer."

"Yeah, Molly's a sweetheart, kept her distance from Josh despite liking him, until he ended it with Harley. So Harley is cool with her, just bummed." She paused, then asked, "What about Krutch? Chloe's right, they do look good together."

I shrugged. How much to tell? He's not over Mandi, but would he be open to going out with Harley? And if so, would it be setting her up for second potential heartache? I don't know.

35

"Paparazzi" – Exit Eden cover

A plethora of sights, sounds and scents welcomed us as we entered the gym. Players in our school's bright red and white warmups jogged in figure-eights bouncing basketballs that pounded the wood floor in sync with the beat of the pep band drums. Cheerleaders tumbled down the sidelines, narrowly missing rambunctious students not paying attention as they searched for friends in the crowded bleachers. Energy mixed with perfume, sweat, deodorant and excitement.

Jaz, Harley and I snaked through the masses to the bleachers behind our team's chairs. The winter track kids were piled into four rows. Not claustrophobic, more like, introvert-ick, I scanned the upper stands and found Krutch, Dervis, Willow, Hood Snap, and Aspen, who leaped up and waved both her arms overhead like an air traffic control person directing a taxiing airplane.

Seeing Josh with Molly in the front row with Sienna confirmed my decision. I tugged on the back of Harley's shirt. She glanced back, face flushed, lips in a tight line. Fanning my face with my hand, I shouted, "Too hot, let's go up."

Flashing a look of relief, she grabbed Jaz, pulling her back. Turning, Jaz read my face, shrugged, and acquiesced.

I waved to Sienna as Harley and Jaz climbed the bleachers. An interpreter in more ways than one, she glanced at Molly and Josh, then signed, "Thanks."

"It's all good," I signed back.

When we reached the top, the guys moved their feet from the bleacher bench in front of them. Despite the January weather, Krutch sported his signature flip-flops, Dervis wore typical topsiders with khakis, and Hood Snap, ginormous black biker boots with both laces and zippers.

Jaz cut in front of Harley and walked down the row to Hood Snap, who introduced Willow and Aspen. Was her maneuvering intentional so Harley would be closer to Krutch?

Glancing at him, a frown erased his easygoing smile. I tracked his line of sight. Mandi. Entering the gym with the squad in tow; Chloe bringing up the rear.

Just as Mandi crossed behind a hoop, a basketball missed the backboard and careened straight for her head. A dark flash in red intercepted it before impact. Michael. His actions were handsomely rewarded by a gracious smile. They stared at each other for a moment before he jumped back into formation.

I located Sienna's profile as she witnessed the exchange, but was relieved she didn't appear bothered by it, in fact, Mandi stopped and chatted with Sienna while the Mannequins, including Chloe, stood looking around. Ladies in waiting, waiting. Funny, I'd never seen Mandi actually converse with anyone. An interesting dynamic to ponder. Chloe scanned the rows of runners around Sienna, then continued up and over until she saw us. Her face lit up as she waved then joined her group in the stands.

Bzzzzzzzzzzzz! Starting lineup announced. Cheerleaders flipped. Pom-poms shook. Pep band played. Game on.

The opposing teams pounded back and forth on the polished wood court. Tennis shoes squeaked as players paused and pivoted on offense looking to pass. The preeeeeet of a referee's whistle blasted when defensive play got too rough. The crowd shouted and jeered, some even watched the game.

We were there for Michael, who didn't disappoint. He danced as he dribbled, weaving up and down the court around opponents like notes flowing on a musical score. I wondered if being deaf blocked the noisy chaos? Focusing wholly on taking the shot or rebounding off the board. After each basket, he'd glance to Sienna to see her jazz hands cheering him on. Their silent connection spoke volumes.

I sighed wistfully, wondering about Ian. Buffering the barrage to my senses, I reflected over the last four months, evolving from loner to teammate, to supportive fan with multiple friends and not-so-secret crush.

NEOWWWW, BWOW-CHCKA-BWOWWWowowoh.

A guitar riff jarred me back to the halftime show. Everyone's attention shot to a dark-haired girl standing in the first row of the pep band section. Her cherry red electric guitar teased a twangy cord; its whine reverberating around the packed gym.

Everyone held a collective breath in anticipation. Wait for it. Wait for it. Wait for it. Her head bobbed four counts and then together, the guitar and percussion section exploded into a metal version of "Paparazzi." The dance squad burst onto the court in black leotards, dressed as mimes, their hair slicked back in tight buns, bright red lipstick in hearts painted on their lips, and black stars drawn around their eyes. Swirling red and silver silk strips attached to sticks wiggled behind them like tails that grew into tornados as they spun. Lights flashed on and off like lightning strikes, amplified by crashing cymbals and booming drums.

While ecstatic Aspen jumped up and down punching her fists in the air, mellow Hood Snap sat up, mesmerized, hands assuming the classic air guitar position, the fingers on his left hand played invisible cords. The last note shredded to abrupt silence as the dancers collapsed onto the court. Dang. Impressive.

***

The next morning, arriving early to Spies class I was surprised to see Chloe, not a member of the class, chatting with Ms. Davis. "Hi, Gracie! Guess what? Auditions for Annie are two weeks from this Friday! Can you help me get ready?"

Three completely random simultaneous thoughts hit me. Ms. Davis directs theater productions. Someone, anyone, would be better equipped to assist Chloe. This would make an awesome Good, Bad or Ugly at dinner tonight. "How can I help?"

"Well, I need to rehearse! Do you sing? Or play piano?"

"Not unless forced, and sadly, no. I play chess."

Ms. Davis chuckled, reading my expression.

"Okay, but you can listen." Chloe turned to Ms. Davis, "Thank you *so* much for your advice, I can't wait to audition."

"I didn't realize you two knew each other," Ms. Davis said, eyebrows raised.

"Yep! Gracie's good friends with Dervis, who told me about your class, that's why I signed up for Civil War Spies this semester," Chloe explained. "And now we all hang out at lunch." She rotated, her face hopeful.

For validation or fishing to confirm Dervis and I were only good friends and trying to get to him through me? I can take that bait and cast her a line.

"That's right. And Chloe is not only tight with Dervis, but knows Aspen and Willow as well, because of theater props and wardrobe. How many productions have you been in?"

A grateful smile brightened her face. "Five, so far." She bit her lip and crossed two fingers for luck.

"In that case, you should join Friday's after-school game club," Ms. Davis said. "It's a spine-tingling mystery who-dun-it. The scenario calls for a moderator, so I'll assume that role."

"I'd love to!" Chloe squealed, instantly calming to ask me, "If it's okay with you and everyone?"

I shrugged. "Sure. The more the scarier. You need to select a detective character and dress the part."

"Oooh, fun! Thanks. I'll think about it and let you know." She looked at her phone. "Better scoot!" The second time she's said that, must be her go-to gotta-go. Could also be her nickname if Willow weren't already Scooter. On her way out, she passed Dervis coming in. His surprised expression received a subtle, fingers cupped together princess wave. As bestower of the nicknames, it will be interesting what he creates for her.

As Hood Snap approached our back row, his humorous expression blocked my view of Dervis.

Smack. A slap on the back, then, "Blimey, Milton, I'm gobsmacked!" Krutch said, using his pompous British accent.

It took me a second to remember that Dervis is his last name, and Milton, his middle. Ignoring Krutch, he sat down then leaned forward to ask, "Why was she here?"

I data dumped. "She was talking to Ms. Davis about auditions when I arrived, brought me into the conversation like we were old chums, then Ms. Davis invited her to join our mystery game Friday." A sly smile sneaked out with that last juicy tidbit.

"Brilliant, well played," Krutch said to me.

"Thank Ms. Davis. I'm just the messenger."

"Hang on every word the demure creature utters, gaze into her doe-like eyes, deploy your boyish charm, and Bob's your uncle, you're the lovey to her dovey!" Krutch said.

"Poppycock," Dervis muttered. Following the Brit vibe in a slightly inappropriate manner.

"Don't be miffed, I'm de-lighted for you," Krutch said. His voice rose up and down, syllables drawn out for emphasis.

Dervis growled as Hood Snap sipped imaginary tea, from an invisible cup, while Ms. Davis asked the spy QOD. "In the movie *Fallout*, what do Ethan Hunt and his IMF team need to find to prevent an epic disaster?"

Hmmm. I haven't seen it, but I heard it scored high on Rotten Tomatoes and Cruise did his own stunts. I'll suggest it to Dad next movie night.

"Plutonium?" a student asked.

Ms. Davis lifted her palms up and down like weighing scales of justice. "Kind of, so you get partial credit."

"Nuclear bombs?" another guessed.

"Nice deduction, but more specific."

Voices conversed but no one answered.

"Spoiler alert!" Ms. Davis announced, signaling anyone who planned on watching should cover ears if they didn't want to know in advance. Several students did.

After a pause, she put her hand in front of her mouth to prevent lip-reading, "The detonator. Bombs had to be diffused simultaneously otherwise, KABOOM!" Her uninjured hand exploded out, then grabbed the handlebar to prevent falling off her knee scooter.

36

"Secrets" – OneRepublic

Friday after school, we changed into detective outfits and met in front of Ms. Davis's closed classroom door. As we knocked, Chloe came down the hallway wearing a demure smile, a chin-length auburn wig with heavy bangs and chunky black-framed glasses that emphasized her large brown eyes. The telling details were the bright orange cowl neck sweater, red pleated skirt, knee socks and red flats. Velma Dinkley, the scientific, intellectual character jumped straight out of the comic book and movie *Scooby-Doo*. Adorable.

Dervis was a goner.

I pinched my nose to keep from sneezing after inhaling a hefty whiff of Ms. Davis's floral perfume when she scootered over to welcome us. The scent was out of character with her gentleman butler attire: pin-striped slacks – one rolled up over the lower left leg cast, a crisp white tuxedo shirt, and white bow tie. A black sling held her bandaged left arm.

She motioned to our designated desks arranged in a wide circle. A rusty old fan stood idle between the circle and Ms. Davis's desk, which held a bronze gong and mallet, a silver platter and a blue and yellow can of WD-40, the lubricant used to fix rusty gears or squeaky hinges. A dark grey argyle cardigan sweater hung on her chair beneath the window.

On each student desk was an envelope addressed to our assumed detective identity on top of a black cloth bag. Seated furthest from Ms. Davis's desk, my back was to the classroom door which left me vulnerable to a rear attack. Intentional?

Clockwise sat Sam Spade (Dervis), the down-on-his-luck flawed anti-hero dressed in a shabby suit, shirt unbuttoned at the collar, and a loosely knotted thin black tie. On his other side sat Velma (Chloe). Dervis was trying not to stare at her but failing happily, rather than miserably.

To her left, Jessica Fletcher (Willow), wore a trench coat, a pale blue neck scarf, a tweed skirt, white tights and black ballet flats. It appeared the famous mystery writer had exchanged her vintage typewriter for a charcoal pencil and sketchpad. I anticipated her artistic attention to detail would solve the crime and reveal it in a fantastical drawing.

To her left, Sherlock Holmes (Hood Snap), in a flapped, vintage deerstalker cap they must have hunted down in a consignment store, and a black double-breasted pea coat. He exhaled rather than inhaled into a bowl pipe, resulting in bubbles blowing up in the air, much to the delight of his counterpart, Dr. Watson (Aspen).

She wore a bowler hat, a plaid sport coat with tan leather elbow patches and sported a mustache that cracked me the heck up, and her too apparently, as she wiggled it and giggled, "It tickles!"

Lastly, to my right, slouched and thoroughly immersed in Daniel Craig's laid-back southern-drawl-spewing detective, Benoit Blanc (Krutch). His wide black tie tucked into a gray dress shirt with rolled-up sleeves and black suspenders attached to – are you kidding me – surfer boardshorts with flip-flops. Apparently, Krutch was only top-half in character. Got to love him.

Ms. Davis rolled back past the fan to her desk, spun, straightened her posture and cleared her throat. "Welcome distinguished sleuths! Detective Blanc, if you'd be so kind, please distribute a copy of this photograph to everyone." She held out a silver platter containing a stack of black and white 8 x 10's.

Krutch, a hand to his chest, expounded in a slow drawl, "It would be an honor, ma'am, ahem, sir." He crossed the circle's diameter to collect the tray, traced the group's circumference handing out the evidence, then returned to his seat.

We each analyzed the image of a tarnished, irregular-edged medallion and chain draped on a velvety stand in a glass case. It was engraved with the word: **VERITAS**

"Truth," Hood Snap said, after studying the photo.

"Correct," said Ms. Davis.

"How do you know that?" Chloe asked.

"Snap's fluent in Italian. It's a hop, skip and a jump to Latin," Aspen said, then gasped, "Oh! I mean Sherlock! He knows a bunch of languages as part of his disguises."

"So, in essence, we are searching for truth," Krutch said, to cover her break in character, I thought.

Ms. Davis stifled a smile and continued, "A valuable silver Spanish doubloon from 1715 was found in a sunken pirate ship discovered in the Caribbean. It was displayed in this glass case in a heavily guarded room at London's esteemed Galleria d'Arte last month when rumors surfaced about a potential burglary attempt.

"One week ago, when the museum curator entered the large 24-bolt Diebold vault –" she paused to peruse each of our captivated faces, "she found a six-inch hole in the glass and the case empty." Once again, her gaze interrogated us. "Someone in this room took it! Thus, we begin, *The Case of the Missing Medallion*!

"When directed, open the envelope in front of you, and not one moment before," she warned. "Inside you will find three cards."

I avoided direct eye contact with anyone to maintain a game face and not burst out laughing. Others struggled to remain stoic as well.

"The first, Motive, describes your greatest failure and most guarded secret. You should not divulge it, even if pressed.

"Next, Means. The method for solving the crime. You each received a unique set of questions and a hint that concerns one person in particular that only you are privy to. We will go around the circle twice. The caveat? Each round you may ask only one of the provided questions, then follow up with one of your own. Her magnetic stare moved silently around, drawing us in. Choose wisely.

"Lastly, Opportunity. Your physical location the night the medallion disappeared. This you must answer as written."

Ms. Davis paused for us to nod in affirmation, "At this time, review the satchel contents, but do not let another see."

Instead of looking into the dark fabric sack on my desk, I glanced to review the reactions of everyone else. Dervis's lips moved as if reading, Chloe looked distressed, and Willow met my gaze. Great minds think alike? Exchanging sly smiles, we continued to scrutinize then opened our own.

Maintaining a poker face, I discovered a long, thick strip of black fabric and a plastic pistol, no doubt a theater prop. Wondering if it were incriminating evidence or simply a part of my law enforcement occupation, I closed the drawstrings and casually picked a Mallory hair off my long, black skirt. I'd borrowed it from Mom in addition to a white blouse and short black jacket. A proper outfit for a lady Pinkerton agent.

"In a moment, you will blindfold yourself, lay your forehead on the satchel with one palm facing up, and the other covering an ear. The medallion may or may not be delivered to you. If you receive it. Conceal it. When the deed is done, at the sound of the gong, remove the blindfold, and the quest for the culprit begins."

Ms. Davis cleared her throat, wiped her brow, and said in a deep voice, "My word, it is hotter than Hades in here." She looked at Chloe. "You feel it too, Velma? My apologies, the heater is on the fritz. Do not be concerned. I'll open a window and switch on the fan."

Chloe's flushed, red face clashed with the thick orange wool cowl. Probably itched too. She rubbed her neck and pulled the collar as if loosening a noose.

Ms. Davis pulled the window handle. I noted as the chilly January air rushed in she shivered rather than sigh with relief like one does when retrieving lemonade from the refrigerator on a hot summer day. She quickly scootered to the fan and announced, "Secure your blindfolds, and be reminded, although there is no honor among thieves, you are honorable detectives, so no peeking." A rattling erupted when she switched on the fan.

Blindfolded, I waited for the touch of metal on my palm and formulated a plan to slip it into a deep skirt pocket. I pondered, why would my character steal it? To prevent someone else from doing so?

Straining with my uncovered ear, I heard nothing but the noisy, clicking fan. It occurred to me it faced away from us, blowing the hot air across the teacher's desk and out the open window. I filed the thought as the clatter gradually subsided and the gong reverberated.

Boingggggggg.

We sat up and removed our blindfolds.

Ms. Davis, now wearing the argyle cardigan, closed the window but left it cracked a bit. A knotted rope attached to the handle hung taut outside. Briskly turning, she announced, "Open your envelopes and read the cards."

I complied.

Motive: Kate Warne, you stopped one assassination plot on President Abraham Lincoln. Just not the right one. Ouch.

Means: A list of questions, one for each player. I'd create a second question dependent on their response. Works for me.

Opportunity: You were in Washington D.C. applying for the newly created Secret Service in hopes of suppressing counterfeit currency. Solid alibi.

My fleeting hope to question last to allow consideration of preceding answers was dashed on hearing, "Ms. Warne, please begin."

Contemplating the most likely to spill-the-beans, I asked, "Dr. Watson, please show me the contents of your satchel."

Aspen was thrilled to flaunt a stethoscope. "Tah-daaaah!"

I took a moment to construct a question based on my secret, extra clue. "Are you as proficient deciphering lock clicks, like the ones, say, on a 24-bolt Diebold vault, as you are detecting wheezing lungs?"

She shrugged, "I've got skills."

Well played.

Next, Dervis asked Krutch, "Detective Blanc, what's in your satchel?"

Krutch slouched in his seat with his black sack plopped in front of him. He slowly withdrew a plastic hunting knife, flipped it into the air, and caught it by the handle.

Hood Snap yawned. Aspen snorted.

Dervis squinted, "What's the knife for?"

Krutch pointed it at him, twisting it side to side. "Skin'n and gut'n," he said, with a sly grin.

Chloe blinked, then asked Hood Snap, "Mr. Holmes, where were you on that fateful night?"

Hood Snap paused, his face expressionless, "Alone. At the Gallerie d'Arte, disguised as a security guard."

With wide eyes, she whispered, "Were you hired to protect the medallion?"

"No."

Incriminating. Note to self, don't ask yes / no questions.

Willow gestured to me, "Ms. Warne, what have you?"

I lifted my chin, "In my satchel? A pistol."

She squinted and asked, "Your alibi?"

I regurgitated as prescribed, thereby proving innocence.

Going forward, we cleared Benoit Blanc despite the knife, as he'd been cleaning fish caught on a week-long excursion. And although Mrs. Fletcher had a Galleria brochure with a detailed map, she'd recently returned from biking across Scotland. In addition, the "Get Out of Jail Free" card came in handy for Sam Spade, who'd been held in contempt of court for refusing to divulge the name of a snitch.

Chloe's second turn again zeroed in on Hood Snap, "Mr. Holmes, what is in your satchel?"

"A glass cutter."

Taken aback, Chloe asked, "Why do you have it?"

"In case I need to cut glass," he drolly replied.

Aspen giggled and winked at him.

While everyone anticipated Willow's final interrogation, my attention remained on Chloe. Her satisfactory expression intrigued me. Scanning up from shoes to wig, my attention snagged on the satchel. From my angle, I viewed the end of a rope. Curious. My turns were up; I hoped someone else would ask about it.

"Dr. Watson, where were you that night?" Willow asked.

Aspen's mustache twitched. "On a four-hour roundtrip train journey, tracking down a false tip." She flicked an invisible piece of lint off her lapel.

"Did Holmes send you on this wild goose chase?"

Aspen sighed; her twin knew the answer. "Yes."

Hood Snap's composure revealed nothing. He passed.

Aspen moved on in haste, "Velma, where were you on the night in question?"

Chloe bit her lip, "Outside of the Galleria d'Arte."

Aspen tilted her head. Composing her final question.

"Were you alone?"

Chloe went pale, "No." She offered nothing more.

Out of turns, Aspen's cheeks puffed out as she exhaled.

Studying his cards, Krutch's gaze lifted to Chloe. "Miss, would you kindly share the contents of your satchel?"

Yes! I leaned forward to decipher her reaction.

Chloe retrieved it, pulled out the cord, shrugged, and stated the obvious, "A rope."

Krutch rubbed his chin, contemplating the final question.

She waited, eyes lowered, to study her manicured nails.

He sat forward, set his elbows on the desk, and dropped his chin on one hand grasping the other fist. "Miss Dinkley," Krutch paused, "Did you steal the medallion?"

She looked up and answered quickly, "No sir. I did not."

Boinggggggg.

"It is time to determine who has the medallion and why." Ms. Davis said.

Interesting turn of phrase.

"It's Sherlock. Means, opportunity and no alibi," Dervis said with confidence.

"Codswallop. What was his motive?" Krutch countered.

Dervis flipping through his cards made me wonder if his extra hint was about Holmes. He offered, "Maybe to prove it was fake and prevent insurance fraud."

"Sherlock looks the most guilty, so he must be innocent, that's how it works," Aspen said, defending him.

"Or the exception that proves the rule," Krutch said.

"But I'm right next to him and didn't hear it delivered on either side of me, and I didn't get it, so it must be over there somewhere," Aspen waved a curve from me to Willow.

Hood Snap smiled at her perseverance.

"It wasn't delivered, someone had it," I said.

"Oh! So, it was in their satchel all along," Chloe added with enthusiasm.

"Then why the whole blindfold episode?" Dervis asked.

"So the guilty party wouldn't give it away by accident," Willow glanced at Aspen.

"Thanks for the vote of no confidence," Aspen shot back.

"A distraction, so we'd questioned ourselves, wondering if it'd land on our open palm," Hood Snap said.

I expounded, "We'd strain to hear the scooter despite the noisy fan..."

"Both which, could have been silenced by that there can of WD-40," Krutch interrupted, pointing to the front desk, "My apologies, carry on."

"Exactly. But the fan's purpose wasn't to cover the sound or blow hot air," I said, glancing across to Willow.

She nodded. "It blew the perfume scent, which is lovely, by the way, out the open window."

Ms. Davis smiled and bowed her head in appreciation.

Aspen's face lit up, finishing her sister's thought. "A red herring! We'd have smelled it when Ms. D, I mean Mr. Butler, whomever, came on our side of the fan to deliver it! Smoke and mirrors! Or fan and perfume." She shifted her outstretched palms front and back.

"Still doesn't make sense," Dervis complained.

"Neither does ordering a Whopper combo with large fries and a diet coke, but people do it all the time," Aspen said, breaking character, again.

"Then who has it?" Dervis asked.

Willow turned her sketch around. A charcoal X-ray rendering of Miss Dinkley showed the medallion on a chain around her neck under the outlined thick cowl sweater.

Startled, Chloe whispered, "Why me?" rapidly blinking back what appeared to be real tears.

Really? That's a bit above and beyond.

"She told you she didn't steal it," Dervis shook his head.

"Mr. Spade, your affinity for damsels in distress is admirable," Krutch said, adding, "But I do believe, Miss Dinkley is quite capable of taking care of herself."

Prophetic?

Chloe bit her lower lip.

Acting so innocent. Acting so innocent. What the heck! She's pre-auditioning! Clever girl. Think. Means. The rope. Curiously similar to the one tied to the window handle. Opportunity. Outside of the Galleria. Motive? Her fixation on Holmes. That's it!

"She didn't steal it, but she does have it," I announced.

Chloe's face fell as she clutched her throat.

"Et tu, Brute?" Dervis accused me. "Maybe it was planted, without her knowing!"

"Or, maybe, she's an unwilling accomplice. Isn't that right Mr. Butler, or should I say..." My eyes beelined from Chloe to Ms. Davis, perched on her desk.

"Professor Moriarty?" I challenged.

"Professor Who?" Aspen asked.

"Moriarty, Sherlock Holmes's arch-enemy," I explained, adding a supercilious eyebrow.

Squinting like a hawk, Ms. Davis threw back her head and cackled an evil, theatrical, diabolical laugh.

Chloe sprang from her seat, pointing to the window, shouting, "He made me do it! He dognapped Scooby Doo, and tied him outside the window!"

Dervis and Aspen exploded from their desks and raced behind Ms. Davis. Dervis pulled open the window as Aspen yanked the rope up to reveal a Scooby Doo stuffed animal harnessed at the end.

Krutch smacked his desk and guffawed, "Well done, Professor, I do so enjoy a devious, blackmailing scoundrel."

Dervis presented Scooby to Chloe like a gallant knight.

Hood Snap slow-clapped three times.

Ms. Davis slid off her desk and did a one-legged bow.

Well done indeed.

37

"Go Figure" – Everlife

"Remind me, who's Chloe?" Sofi's nose scrunched up on the laptop screen.

"Dervis's crush."

"The Mannequin? Isn't she persona non grata?" Despite confessing she adored the squad nickname Sofi's loyalty to me is steadfast due to past indiscretions she dearly regretted.

"Not since Ian posted the pic. I think she thought Dervis and I were a thing."

"Gotcha." She clicked her tongue. "That'd do it. We'll get back to Ian in a sec, tell me more about Chloe."

"She's been hanging with us at lunch, played the mystery game with the posse after school, and asked me to help her audition for the school musical," I said.

"Um. Okay. Exactly how?" She bit her thumb and looked sideways. A consummate actor.

"Thanks for nothing."

"Moving along, when did this familiarity occur?"

"First day of the new semester."

"Are any of her previous cohorts in your lunch block?"

I thought a moment. "No. I don't think so."

"That explains it. She's a stray. And you're a sucker for strays. Remember before we got the pups, you'd sneak alley cats into our house and hide them? At dinner, you'd interrupt the conversation, 'Bet I can find a cat faster than anyone.' We'd spread out and do a search and rescue mission all ears straining for a muffled mew."

"I wanted a pet." I plead my case.

"Of course you did, Grace Artemis, goddess of the forest and protector of creatures and youth. And then there was that time when we saw that neighbor kid shoot a sparrow with his BB gun and pick up a rock to kill it."

A visual of a stunned gray, downy-feathered bird cupped in my red mittens came to mind. Only in shock, it recovered after I gave it an eye-dropper of water and set it free. A proud, fulfilling moment.

"You kicked him in the goo-goos."

"Don't remember that part."

"Because you focused on the bird, not the bully. That's why Mom enrolled us in karate. You ate up the 'Kokoro' stuff: attitude, perseverance, fearlessness, virtue, et cetera..." Sofi ticked off the litany on her fingers. "Whereas I just wanted to shop for a new outfit and kick butt like you did. Never saw that little jerk again but assumed he recovered since the police never came for you." Double blink. "Back to your new stray."

"Ms. Davis told the theater kids it'd be a good idea for everyone going for the Annie role to not sing the classic, 'Tomorrow,' as you can only hear it so many times before wanting to 'rip your ears off.' Her exact words."

"Sage advice."

"But Chloe thinks if no one else sings it, and she does, everyone will see she's perfect for the role."

Sofi inhaled through pursed lips, "Risky, going against the director's 'suggestion.'" Air quotation marks employed.

"I thought so too, kind of like ignoring a coach."

"Exactly, but some people think they know best."

"Speaking from experience?" I teased.

"Yep. For instance, you rarely listen to your infinitely wiser sister."

"Because I don't have one."

"Brat." She laughed. Double blink. "Now back to a far more interesting topic, what's up with Big Mac?"

"No idea. Btw, changed his contact name to Army. Suppose he's busy with classes and gearing up for lacrosse season."

She sighed. "You're right. Long-distance is tough. Carry on and keep me posted on both lax and la, la, la, la, la, la, la, laaaaaah tryouts," she sang a scale.

"Will do, O' Wise-one." I bowed my head.

She faked a sniff and a tear. "Too little, too late. TTFN."

Ta ta for now. Tigger from Pooh. A class act. That one.

***

A week after the who-dun-it game, Chloe dropped a new mystery in the middle of Krutch's joke at lunch. With a heavy sigh, she put down the Bento kit, which now alternated with the re-usable lunch sack, and slipped into the empty chair between Dervis and me without greeting anyone.

Dervis's cross-examining, do-you-have-a-clue face asked me over her hunched shoulders. I shrugged. It reeked of a secret drama code I'd not bothered to crack since my brother Jason declared me immune from exposure to Sofi's brief Mean Girl infection years ago.

Hood Snap's fingers drum-rolled on the table ahead of the punchline which Krutch delivered with his usual flair. Harley and Jaz burst out laughing. Much to my relief, Harley shot down Jaz's hints about Krutch, opting to take a break from dating, thereby eliminating the need to share intel about him and Mandi that I don't fully understand.

Seeing Chloe's sullen face prompted a mental note to check on her in private. She'd neglected to follow up about me helping prepare for auditions. Hopefully, she'd realized I wasn't the best person for the job.

Adding to his crushing-hard-for-months credit, Dervis bit the bullet and dumped his half-eaten lunch to walk with Chloe when she packed up hers.

Not going to lie (it's a thing in my family – not lying, that is), I was relieved for the moment, but the upside-down is, if you're going to have a dance, you have to pay the band, DJ, or streaming service. Whatever. Juggling multiple friends' emotions, feelings and relationships is exhausting.

Dervis filled me in later. Someone dissed Chloe on the theater social media chat group. Although he'd joined per her request during the fall play season, he'd never checked posts and missed it. Chloe was too upset to notice the screen name, so he planned to monitor and track the culprit's identity. I told Dervis he was a good friend, inwardly wishing Chloe would stop taking him for granted. He'd shrugged it off.

After school, I caught up with her at the bottom of the stairs. Left took you to the music, choir and theater wing, right to the gyms, weight rooms and locker rooms.

"Hey," I said.

"Oh, hi." She pointed to a small, nearby practice room. "I'm about to rehearse."

"Nice, how's it going?"

"Pretty well," she said, but frowned a bit.

"Anything I can do?" Please say no.

"No, it's all good. The song's going great."

Off the hook.

She checked down the hallway then whispered, "It's just nobody wants me to get the lead."

Navigating around Dervis's information, "Really? You all supported each other like teammates during the play."

"Because we all got the roles we wanted." She paused then brushed wispy bangs off her forehead. "It's obvious; everyone wants Mandi to be Annie."

Uh-oh, green-eyed monster alert.

"Dominate auditions," I said, matter-of-factly. Control the center of the board.

She placed her palms on her temples, "Easy for you to say, you're good at everything, but they're getting in my head. It's bumming me out."

Whoa, that was a weird, random comment.

I skirted and fished. "Who they?"

"I don't know for sure." She crossed her arms leaning toward me. "But someone posted mean memes about me."

"Sure it's not a joke? Kids throw shade all the time, even at their friends, take Krutch, Dervis and Hood Snap."

"No. It's not like that."

"Regardless, Dervis will help you."

Chloe squinted. "What?"

Crap. Deflect.

"He'll see the posts, right? Next time he'll break the code and expose them."

"Oh. That's right. Forgot he's on the group chat." She bit her lower lip. Paused, then reached for the doorknob. "I better get to work. See ya."

Dismissed, I nodded and escaped down the right hall.

***

While conditioning, stretching and lifting consumed my days outside of school, strategizing and anticipating lacrosse season filled my nights. First team meeting with the new coach was on Monday and earning a starting spot played out in my head 24/7. Physically, my left quad muscle was now only a quarter-inch smaller than my right.

Jaz and Harley confirmed my speed was back too. A fact they were a lot happier about since we'd now be teammates instead of opponents. All week, lunchtime conversations gravitated to lacrosse for us, track for Dervis, and croquet for Krutch and Hood Snap. Chloe was introspective – normal for me when gearing up for an important event so I didn't give it much thought. However, after school Thursday when Dervis reminded me her auditions were tomorrow, I inquired about his hunt for the mean meme-er.

He reported no more negative posts, but last night she found a nasty note slipped into her locker. He hadn't seen it, but would share once he did, and that Chloe felt alienated from Mandi and the Mannequins.

Treading in uncharted drama shark waters, I asked what we could do. He said to get Aspen and Willow to sit with us in the front row for support since they were also theater peeps. Hadn't planned to go but agreed, then tracked the dynamic duo down in the auditorium.

"Abso-tootly!" Aspen said, jumping on board the fan club train. "It's a perk of working on school productions."

Willow looked up briefly from her sketchbook, nodded, and then turned her attention back to drawing.

"Don't mind her, she's in 'the zone,'" Aspen whispered. "Almost done designing the sets, which I will use to create magic!" She silently danced around the stage, waving an imaginary wand.

What a goofball.

I didn't mention the negative posts and nasty anonymous note. Waving quietly to not disturb the artist and her muse, I left and drove home.

Roscoe and Mallory greeted me with more enthusiasm than usual. We'd skipped their walks because of below zero temperatures this week.

A text message buzzed from inside my backpack.

(*dervis*)
Took pic of note but
Chloe tore it up

(*me*)
Why?

(*dervis*)
No clue

(*me*)
Literally

(*dervis*)
Will forward pic

> (*me*)
> Kk. BTW Aspen n Willow
> good to go

Photo came through. A purple penned message read:

you suck. give it a rest and forget going for annie

The fact it was written on a corner torn from blue-lined notebook paper provided little evidence since every student carries some in their backpack, except for Krutch who when needed, sponges a piece off Dervis, much to his annoyance and Hood Snap's continued amusement.

It had warmed up a bit. I needed to think and the pups needed exercise so we took off on a run before dinner. Roscoe and Mallory ran off-leash, one on each side; we jogged down the dry, plowed street to the park then crunched through a crust of snow to reach the path that wove through our neighborhood woods.

The stark, silent trees guarding the trail reminded me of protective Dervis. The ominous woods held their breath in anticipation of flurries forecast for tonight. A female cardinal flew to a branch in front of us, its pale brown feathers tinged with red, framed by the snowy-white backdrop. After landing briefly, it flitted away. Like Chloe. Flying just out of reach from branch to branch in a syncopated rhythm with my footsteps.

Halfway point, I slowed, crossing an icy wood bridge – can't risk wiping out with tryouts in a few days. The frozen creek below reminded me of how much Dervis despised running through mud during cross country season. Dervis, who epitomizes the Marine Corps motto, Semper Fidelis, always faithful, I understand, but what was beyond my newly acquired limited scope of empathy was why Chloe gave three craps in a bucket what others thought or said about her.

Granted, since kindergarten, my parents instilled the idea we could be whoever, or whatever, we wanted to be or do as long as we worked hard. Maybe Chloe lacked such support? Perhaps time to give a little grace, Gracie.

Nevertheless, something nagged at me as I exited the woods. Chloe's failure to note the meme poster's name, and then tearing up the note? She's smarter than that. Maybe it drives her, like someone talking smack.

Miscalculating the edge of the pavement my left foot landed on an angle then rolled. My ankle exploded in agony as I rotated to fall on my back in the snow holding my left leg in the air. Crap! Crap! Crap!

The pups were all over me but backed off when I screamed at them and the shooting pain. Whipping off my hoodie and t-shirt, I gritted my teeth, balanced on butt and good leg, covered only in goosebumps and running bra. Not caring I was exposed to the elements and everyone else, I laid the t-shirt beside me, clawed handfuls of snow into it, rolled and wrapped my swelling, throbbing ankle. Shivering in spasms I shook trying to pull the hoodie on, then fell back in the snow, to sob.

Whines, then warm tongues licked tears off my face. I comforted the pups as best as I could, then pulled my cell from the pocket on the right side of my running tights and punched Mom's number.

"Scout?" Dad's voice. Home early, he answered for her.

Recalibrating through pain, I winced. "Yeah. Um. Crashed on ice down at the park. Pick up?"

"Be there in two."

Ankle numb now, I massaged my knee through the running brace. It was fine. Totally fine. Below, the ankle? Not so much. To forget, I started counting one-thousand one, one-thousand two...

One-thousand-one-hundred-ten counts later I heard the rumble of Dad's turbo Jeep. The newer, but just-as-cool version of the '04 scarlet red Wrangler Jason now drove. Both Buckeye alumni, he'd passed it down to Jason for graduation.

"Easy does it, Scout." His warm, calloused hand grasped mine, gently pulling it up and over his head across his shoulders while the other arm reached around behind to lift. I leaned on him and hopped to the car. He opened the door and helped me in, watched as I strained to buckle up, then loaded the pups in back.

"Thank you," I said, sinking into the seat and my fears.

Tryouts in four days.

"No problem, kiddo. You'll be fine."

No judgment, just encouragement, welcome to my world.

"Got bad news," Dad said with a heavy sigh.

"Can't even right..." I murmured automatically.

"Yep. Mom made tofu for dinner."

38

"The Climb" – Jessi Alexander with Chris & Morgan Stapleton

Musical auditions. The last place I wanted to be on this crap happens Friday after hopping around school all day but I'd given my word, and like Horton in *Horton Hatches the Egg*, an elephant's faithful one hundred percent.

Dervis was a pal, scoring a stool to elevate my wrapped, swollen ankle. He sat in the first-row aisle seat to save it for Chloe. I was second in with Aspen two empty seats away to make sure she didn't accidentally bump me, then Willow and other techies. Ms. Davis, casting director, sat in the middle with other auditioning thespians to her left.

Lights were down low except for a single spotlight highlighting a lone chair stage front. The intimate setting buzzed with jittery actors and singers anticipating/dreading performing/vomiting. Garbage cans were placed accordingly.

Five minutes before showtime Chloe joined us, shivering with enthusiasm. Dervis leaped up for her to sit, but first, she flipped one of her messy pigtails, pointed out dark smudges over stage makeup on her cheek and forehead, and twirled in the long-sleeve grunge t-shirt she wore over tights. Updated urban orphan look perfected.

Dervis leaned on the wall in the aisle next to us watching her gush with excitement without a shred of apprehension.

Ms. Davis stood with one leg on the scooter to address the nervous crowd, "Welcome cherubs. We won't be using amplification, so chins up and project!" She checked her clipboard and called first up.

A tall girl shouted, "That's me!" She jumped out of her seat and ran to the steps leading up to the stage, pretending to "accidentally" trip, she slid across the floor then stood and brushed herself off.

The crowd laughed as she smiled and took a seat. I recognized her as one of the Mannequins.

Chloe grabbed my wrist to fill me in. "That's Madeline. She teases a lot and likes to prank. Goes for comedic roles, in this case, the headmistress of the orphanage, Miss Hannigan. Nice voice, solid acting and can handle a ton of dialog," she explained, looking sideways at me.

"Do you think..."

"Sssssshush," she interrupted, as Madeline cleared her throat, reached a hand forward, tightened it to a fist, and pulled the audience into a sassy, you-done-me-wrong song.

As she sang, I wondered, could Madeline have posted the meme as a joke? Next came the nasty note, but what if there were a second one that Chloe missed, with something like – JK LOL XO Good luck Friday!

Mannequin Madeline finished, took a bow, and strutted off the stage. I watched as she joined the M&M squad, sitting together sans Chloe, on the other side of the theater.

My ankle ached, I shifted the stool under my knee.

Performers continued, some earned Chloe's praise, others not so much. She definitely had a preference for the male lead role, dismissing the others like a Hollywood casting director. The other Mannequins tried out for smaller roles, not leads, and she shrugged her shoulders, "They'll be okay. I guess."

Harsh, I chalked it up to nerves and gave her a pass because she was up next. When Ms. Davis called her name she squeezed my arm, blew past Dervis, climbed the stairs and knelt to the floor with forehead to forearm on the chair.

A shout, "Get it, girl!" tracked to the Mannequin section, Madeline.

Chloe began, "Tomorrow" wistful and melancholy.

I glanced to Ms. Davis, who winced, but stayed engaged.

Gradually, Chloe increased volume and sass and sold it without a doubt. After the applause and shouts confirmed she'd killed it she rushed off the stage, down the stairs, and dove into Dervis's surprised but willing arms.

Good for her. But a little weird next as she skipped over and leaned down to hug me, the aforementioned non-hugger. Awkward. Thankfully, she released quickly and sat to watch the final performer. Mandi.

Mandi ignored the audience as she walked up the steps wearing a pale blue sweater cropped to the waist of royal blue chinos and caramel suede ankle boots. She carried a guitar across the stage and sat in the solitary chair under the spotlight. No yells from her posse. Interesting. The sleeves of her sweater were pushed up, one hand grasped the guitar neck, and the other hugged the instrument body close to hers. The spotlight created a golden crown around her perfectly messy blonde bun. With a tilt of her head, she gently brushed a thumb across the strings, inhaled slowly, closed her eyes, and strummed the introductory cords to "The Climb."

Watching nimble fingers caress strings, I noted her nails were trimmed short and left natural. An incongruent memory flashed.

Spectators hushed, evaporating into the silent, darkened auditorium.

Her voice began soft and low.

I leaned forward listening as dreams, disappointments, and self-doubt poured over the guitar, spilling onto the stage. The words increased in intensity as she held a pure, high note.

A chill crept up the hairs on my arms.

Her eyes opened and captured mine.

Her gaze flowed to my propped-up ankle, lyrics creating an invisible current surrounding it, then swirling up around my knee, pulling memories of fear and pain. Reaching up to my heart, sweeping heartaches and loneliness, then climbing to my head, exposing every move, goodbye, and regret.

I was astonished witnessing her ability to connect the row of dimly-lit, awed faces, collecting everyone's sorrows and frustrations to recycle and return as encouragement and hope.

The last phrase was a call to action; her attention washed over me, I leaned back, rejuvenated, then looked at Chloe.

The pain on her face was palpable. Like watching a euphoric Olympic athlete who'd crushed their personal best – only to realize it wasn't enough.

Her eyes blinked back tears that sparkled, reflecting the spotlight. She stood as I reached out for her. She shook me off and stumbled backward. Dervis was behind to catch and lift her up. She turned in his arms and collapsed to his chest in the dark aisle. The roar of applause covered the sound of Chloe's sobs, but the shadows didn't hide her shudders. Dervis held her, his face solemn. They disappeared out a side door before the house lights came on.

Looking back to Mandi, I expected to see a perfect smile basking in the rowdy adulation, instead, her head bowed, a palm rested on her guitar for a moment, she then stood and exited stage right.

Ms. Davis popped up. "Smashing auditions! Well done one and all. Cast will be posted Monday morning on the board outside of the theater. All's well that ends swell!"

***

Mom was reading in the studio. I limped in, greeted the pups, and joined her. She patted for me to sit on the loveseat that faced the garden. "How about some hot chocolate?"

"Special treat before dinner?" I gasped, hopping over.

Answering over her shoulder on the way to the kitchen, "Yep, we've got time. The carnivore's craving green curry chicken so he's getting take-out on the way home."

I settled into the couch, elevated my ankle, and sighed. Normally I'd go for a run, or throw against a wall, or at least lift, but again, I can't even. Coulda, woulda, shoulda.

Moments of reflections later, Mom returned with two chunky hand-thrown sapphire blue mugs on a platter painted in Mondrian's style of black intersecting lines with random red, yellow, and blue squares. After setting it on the coffee table, she handed me mine and lifted hers. I took it and we carefully tapped the two mugs together, saying our family's traditional tea party salute in unison, "Ding."

Blowing across the melting mini-marshmallows I knew there were thirteen, Mom's "perfect ten plus favorite three." We sipped in silence. Out the window, the setting sun cast shadows across the garden. Bare trees anticipated buds, white snow drops and bright pink camellia reached up out of winterized beds, and impatient green tips peeked through the remaining islands of snow in the sea of taupe winter grass.

I inhaled deeply and sighed with a high-pitched "hum."

As if on cue, Mom put down her cup, pulled a bottle of lotion out from a cubby under the coffee table, and unwound the athletic wrap on my ankle on the cushion in between us.

I winced, "What do you think?"

"Lovely shade of purple, like the iris bordering the fence. It'll grow to a leafy green tomorrow, and then mellow to daffodil yellow by Sunday."

My inner sixth-grader eye-rolled. "Thank you, Dr. Rose Colored-Glasses, but will I be able to run on Monday?"

She clicked her tongue like Sofi, tilted her head, and smiled with her empathetic eye crinkles. "With your will? You will, whether you should or not. Should you? No. It needs to rest a couple more days."

I gritted my teeth; disgusted with myself. "Can't believe I lost focus and screwed this up. Again."

"Grace Artemis, your focus is spot on, you've just adjusted your depth of field and increased your perspective, all good things."

"But," I started.

"No butts, it's the journey, not the destination."

I frowned. Then thought, no, it's the climb.

Clairvoyant, she asked, "How did auditions go?"

Not surprised, I launched into Chloe's performance while she examined the bruising, then squeezed lotion on her palms and with extreme care, oh-so-gently massaged the ankle to increase blood flow and alert the body of its need to repair.

"She nailed it. Was sure she'd earned the lead, but then the last one went, a girl named Mandi, and I've never heard or felt anything like it. Took the interpretation of lyrics, emotions, music, and the audience to a new level."

"True artistic expression."

"Yep, and a crushing agony of defeat for Chloe."

"The hard part of a competition, hopefully, she'll get a good part and give it her all."

"We'll see. Cast gets posted on Monday."

"You could call her this weekend, go get ice cream, always cheers you up."

"That and hot chocolate," I said, remembering when Hood Snap snuck me out of the school assembly. I could take her to Bistro+39. Weird thing is, after a month of lunches, I don't have her number.

As promised, Dad brought chow, which was delicious, and even volunteered to do cleanup, which was basically tossing take-out containers and loading a few plates. It was Dad/Daughter Movie night, but since Sofi left for college, Mom had taken her spot. Her choice? *Enola Holmes*.

"I have heard it's really good, and I know how much you like Sherlock, so let's give his sister a chance," Mom said.

We agreed, because one, Dad was outnumbered, and two, it starred two fabulous female actors, the younger from *Stranger Things* and the other from *Harry Potter* fame. Plus, the handsome Sherlock dude who also played Superman.

Win. Win. Win.

39

"High Hopes" – Panic! At The Disco

"Which U.S. military academy was featured in the Tom Clancy movie, *Patriot Games*?" was the Spy QOD Monday morning.

I knew the answer was the Naval Academy because Mom's friend's mother worked at a boutique on the bumpy, red brick street leading to Gate 3 where they filmed. It's my favorite Clancy book and movie; Harrison Ford portrayed the analyst turned CIA agent, Jack Ryan. The heart-attack-inducing, cliff-scaling, boat chase scene near the end is epic.

Dervis was late, he slipped in and back to his seat as Ms. Davis noticed then glanced away as someone called out the correct answer. I didn't see who because he leaned around Hood Snap to report Mandi got *Annie*, but Chloe was okay with it as she got both *Annie* understudy and a sassy orphan with the second most lines.

At lunch, an animated Chloe described every scene her character was in and how many lines she had in each. The rest of us munched our chow, happy to be a captive audience. Her opaque pale pink fingernails reminded me of cherry blossoms fluttering in the breeze along the DC Tidal Basin in April. I made a mental note to check the predicted bloom schedule to plan a bike ride.

She seemed pacified. Relieved, I put the drama in the rearview mirror and looked forward to lacrosse. The rest of the day I practiced walking without a limp.

***

After school, Jaz, Harley and I sat on the front bleacher surrounded by jittery chatter in anticipation of meeting the new mystery coach. Everyone hushed when the door of the training room opened; a dark-haired woman entered carrying a clipboard. She reminded me of Joan before Sofi convinced her to go back to her natural fiery red hair.

"Hello, I'm Gwen Kennedy. You can call me Coach, not Gwen, or Miss Kennedy. I grew up playing here in Northern Virginia, but don't let that scare you." She paused, a corner of her lip curved, adding, "Much." Nervous laughter.

Dry sense of humor. Check.

She continued, "I'm passing around a clipboard for you to write your name, year group, an email address you actually check, and the number for a phone that you'll silence and lock in your athletic locker and not bring onto the field." Her stern squint silenced whispers.

Our coach, not our friend. Got it.

"Today is administrative stuff, you won't dress out until a signed permission slip is turned in to the athletic director's office. No practice until then." She scanned across the front row, noticed the stick in my left hand, then glanced down my leg. I'd dressed out just in case, a long t-shirt, black leggings below the knee, and white midcalf socks that covered an ankle compression sleeve. I crossed my right ankle over it, then blushed. Her eyes met mine.

"Where's your brace?"

"Excuse me?"

"Knee brace."

"Um, yes."

"Wear it."

I nodded.

Psychic?

Half of my brain listened to Jaz and Harley chat on the drive home. The other half questioned how the heck the new coach knew about my knee. I enjoy the thrill of the chase unless I'm the fox. Dang, it.

School took forever Tuesday. Having turned in my permission slip last week, I dressed out for practice and was first to the gym, stick in hand. Well, second, because Coach Kennedy was already sitting on the bleacher.

"Hey, Coach," I said. Her eyes beelined to my running-braced left knee.

"Halsted."

Whoa. She is frickin' psychic.

I spun my stick. "Um... Coach?"

"Yes."

"You know my name?"

She stared for a second, then laughed. "The stick."

I looked at it, then her.

"Coach MacGavin was offered this job."

Of course, he was.

"But instead, he recommended me, saying they needed young blood to keep up with the likes of you."

"Me?"

"You."

"Oh." Awkward, and flattering.

"I played for him on club with his daughter, Ellen, before she concentrated on competitive swimming."

Ian has an older sister!

"Full disclosure. He told me about your ACL, and that you ran with your stick, so I figured it was you since no one else had theirs with them at the first meeting."

Oh. Spot on.

"That's how I knew you should have a running brace."

Mystery solved. Knee, not ankle. Time to elaborate and confess. "Full disclosure," I tapped my left ankle gently with my stick. " Rolled it running last Friday." I winced. Expecting the worst.

"Did it pop?"

I thought. "No."

"Burn?

"No."

"Sharp pain?"

"Yes. But I fell back off of it, elevated and iced."

She nodded. "Okay. Check with the trainer. Have her take a look before practice – and Grace?"

"Yes, Coach."

"Don't push it. You've got time."

Other kids were filtering in, so I quickly said, "You can call me Gracie, or Halsted."

"Sounds good." She tilted her head to the trainer's door.

I complied.

Coach said the first week was about the basics. She reviewed experienced players, used those deemed worthy as examples, then broke us into small specialized skill groups.

Jaz and Harley played in youth and club leagues in the area so they knew a lot of the older returning girls. Since Jaz took the opening "draw" – the girl's version of the guys' much more physical "face off" – Coach had her work with girls who were interested in that skill.

Harley played last line of defense in front of the goalie, so she was in charge of teaching how to defend without getting penalized a ton. Players wear goggles, not helmets, unless they have a history of concussions or were in goal, so officials blow the whistle to protect attackers from headshots, which frustrates defenders, who sometimes have to sacrifice and get flagged to prevent the score.

Coach assigned me the freshmen, sophomores, and brand new laxers for stick skills because I can shoot with either hand. Suspected it also was a way to rest my ankle.

Figured out in a heartbeat who the top dog was in my pack of puppies. Zoë had talent, attitude, and enjoyed showing off. As in, when paired with newbie Emma in a passing drill, if Emma held the stick in her right hand, Zoë threw to her left then vice-versa. Emma missed the ball, but caught the innuendo, blushed and awkwardly laughed. Zoë laughed too, but at Emma not with her.

Not on my watch.

"Bring it in," I called to the two parallel lines of girls. The newbs hustled in too close, apparently hoping to acquire my elder creature wisdom by osmosis. Zoë took her time, stopped on the fringe, her face blank, unimpressed.

"Not a fan of any drill where you stand and play catch, so we're stepping it up. Lacrosse is a game of speed and quickness. The faster you are, the quicker you pass, the more you assist and score, the more you pass, assist and score, the more you win." I paused as Zoë yawned. No, she didn't.

I tossed her the ball. Not hard, this time, but directly to her. She caught it, right hand up, left below.

"Cop a squat," I said. "Zoë, help me out?"

She appeared confident and rather pleased.

Tilting my head away from the group, when we were out of earshot, I said, "That wasn't cool, what you did to Emma."

She frowned, "Just kidding around, no big deal."

I stared at her for a moment before explaining the next drill. Walking back past the group, I told them, "This is why you switch hands." Dropping back ten yards in a diagonal, to show the proper angle needed to defend without drawing a penalty, I waved to Zoë.

She nodded and came at me with the ball and stick on her right side. I angled in, met her in the middle and legally smacked her stick. The ball popped out, I caught it, tossed it to her, and said, "Again."

Zoë caught it, squinted, turned and trotted back. Both set again, she came at me faster, stick still on right. Matching her speed, instead of hitting her stick, I flipped mine, caught the end of hers in my net pocket and pulled, the ball popped again, I caught it in my hand this time, and held it to out to her, "Again."

She snatched it and ran back to her starting point. Rotating to go to mine, I glanced at Emma and the rest of the bright-eyed pups. They fidgeted but were attentive.

This time when we met, stick still on her right, she tried to cut in front of me, as she rotated I saw air space and brought my stick down like a hatchet, sending hers flying end over end. The yellow rubber ball bounced with it.

"Thanks, one more time." I scooped under her stick and popped it up to her. Zoë caught it and shot me a dirty look. I kept a poker face, retrieved the ball and waved for her to walk with me. She fumed all the way to her starting position.

"This time, cut and shift stick to left side out of range. That forces me to redirect and come at you straight on, instead of the angle, so I either draw a penalty, giving you a sweet free shot or let you go past, double back and shoot. Using me to block the goalie's line of sight, with your speed it will be in the back of the net before she sees you."

She exhaled hard through her nose, jaw muscle firm, then nodded.

Turning, I heard, "Sorry, about Emma."

Looking back over my shoulder, "Think she's a natural leftie, figure it out, but encourage her to learn both."

She stared at me for a couple seconds. "How fast do you want me to go?"

With a sly smile, I lifted my chin, "Bring it."

She pointed at my knee brace. "You ready?"

I snorted. "Born ready." Making sure the kiddos could see us both laughing, I jogged to my spot. The moment I was set Zoë took off. Per our plan, she cut early, forcing me to correct. I stalled so she could blow past me.

Returning to the group, noticing Coach, arms crossed, watching from the far side of the field, I shrugged. Oops.

40

"COPYCAT" – Billie Eilish

Last to our lunch table on Friday, I was confused for a tic. Not that we had assigned seats, but as a creature of habit and potentially OCD about order in the universe, the fact that Chloe was sitting in my usual spot next to Krutch, leaving me an empty seat next to Dervis, with Jaz on his right, then Hood Snap, and Harley completing the circle on Krutch's left, threw me for a loop. Jaz and Harley sent simultaneous telepathic, "What the heck?" messages via raised eyebrows, which I returned with my supercilious one, "Above my pay grade."

When I'd settled and taken a spoonful of Greek yogurt, Dervis said to me, much louder than necessary, "Ms. Davis cleared us to work on lighting and sound tomorrow morning – if you can." Since we were in sports, we missed rehearsals after school during the week so she'd made an allowance.

"Sure," I answered, at a normal conversational volume.

"Oh! What time? Can I come too? I'd love to rehearse without the whole crew there," Chloe gushed.

Awkward. I leaned back so they could converse.

"I guess it'd be okay. Willow and Aspen will be there. Finishing up the set plans," he said.

"Awesome!" Chloe said, looking back to Krutch.

The area of the equilateral triangle connecting Jaz, Harley and me was filled with a butt-ton of no clue as we wondered why the world had jumped off its axis and rolled over Dervis.

***

Aspen jumped up and down, clapped, then ran to hug me Saturday morning when I entered the theater hallway. Goofball cracks me the heck up. Willow watched, her beloved sketchbook clasped tight to her chest. Chloe and Dervis stood apart but next to her. Waiting. Ms. Davis arrived on her scooter, opened the theater doors, then left us to do our things as she graded tests in her classroom.

The doorway cast a golden parallelogram into the black theater. Chloe skipped off, disappearing down a dark aisle. Dervis ventured sideways into the void, running his hand atop seatbacks, navigating to the sound/lighting control booth positioned in the middle section, halfway up the sea of rows. He turned on the stage lights.

"Only the spotlight, please," Chloe shouted.

"Check." He booted up the electronic control panel, turned on the spot and cut the overheads. Chloe appeared in the spot with hands raised as if basking in the sun.

Whatever pops her popcorn.

Letting go of the door, I crossed the dim interior to join Dervis. Willow and Aspen sat down in front of the booth for a full stage view to conceptualize the final set design.

"I'll have the sound system programmed for you. Just watch and listen in case someone's ear mic jacks up or falls out. We'll load new batteries for the dress rehearsal," Dervis explained, glancing to the stage, then back to the panel of switches and knobs.

I asked questions to familiarize myself with the console as a precaution for me and a distraction for him, as his focus wandered from booth to Chloe as she moped, danced, and sang softly to herself and the spotlight.

"Will you be with me during the show?"

"Some of the time." He pointed above the stage. "Lights are programmed too, but a few are hidden in the sets and props, so I move around backstage to make sure everything is working and also check on sound out here too. We wear black to blend into the background."

"Because we're cool and tech-spac-ular," Aspen climbed over the seatback to join us in the booth. Next to me, she was quiet for a moment, head tilted, arms crossed, studying Chloe down below.

"Anyone else weirded out with her doing the lead's lines and songs right meow?"

Dervis quickly said, "She's the understudy, likes to do it now instead of during regular rehearsals so others don't judge her."

Aspen snorted. "Sorry. That train left the station, arrived at the dock, jumped on board, in other words, that ship sailed." Her hands pantomimed every step of the journey.

Such a goober.

"Too many words," Willow said. Eyebrows riding up into dark bangs.

Aspen shrugged. "Just saying, everyone's noticed. She's not rehearsing Annie, she's rehearsing Mandi rehearsing Annie. Hides off stage in the curtains watching, memorizing, and mimicking her every nuance. It's super creepy."

Awkward silence. We all inhale, exhale. Look around.

"Guess what? I'm writing a screenplay!" Aspen said.

"Tech-spac-ular," I repeated, relieved we'd moved on.

"I know! It's about William Shakespeare's imaginary twin sisters, Willowmena and Aspenashia."

"Shakespeare didn't have twin sisters," Dervis said.

"I said imaginary, you know, pretend," Aspen said.

"I pretend my twin is imaginary, but she never goes away," Willow sighed, without looking up from her sketch.

Undaunted, Aspen continued, "One's creative and quiet, and the other is clever and fun."

"Guess which is which," Willow said under her breath.

"Can't wait to read it. When will it be finished?" I asked.

"Oh, not for a while. It's all in my head. Kicking and screaming to escape."

"Know the feeling," Willow said, closing her sketchpad. "Dervis, can you turn on the ghost light so I can check the scrim?"

"Sure." He flipped a switch. "I'll go with you."

Aspen watched them go. "The scrim is the backdrop that hangs at the back of the stage. Willow has some sweet scene idea that she wants lit from behind."

"Got it." I watched as Chloe ignored them as they climbed the stairs and disappeared behind the side curtain.

"Guess what dash two?"

"What, what?" I asked.

She giggled. "Oh, how I've missed you, let me count the ways. One gazillion, two gazillions, I do so miss you, in a totally Jane Austin fangirl way. At least I have Biff and Garth in my lunch block, not like they could ever fill the devastating void saved for you in my heart, but we can argue about who's the most badass Saga character. Have you read them?"

"Some. My brother was into the series."

"So epic. Like *Star Wars* and *Game of Thrones* with a dash of *Romeo and Juliet!*" She clasped hands together over her heart and leaned diagonal, wistfully. "Where for art thou, dearest Hood Snap?"

Oh do let's! I've missed her too.

A few minutes later, the thespian and two techies walked up the aisle from the stage. "We're set. I'll cut the lights," Dervis said.

Aspen, Chloe and Willow went out the door. I held it open for Dervis to come through in the dark. He locked it, and the five of us went to drop off the keys to Ms. Davis.

"Are you still with Hood Snap?" Chloe asked Aspen.

"Every delightful chance I get!" Aspen spun in a circle.

"Why don't he and Krutch crew with you?"

"Not with Mandi singing in the spotlight," Aspen said.

Dervis and I momentarily froze, Willow tugged on the back of her sister's shirt.

Chloe stopped, turning to Aspen, eyes wide, "Who doesn't like Mandi?" Her voice an octave higher sounded a bit too hopeful.

"Um, no," Aspen fumbled then gushed, "That's not it, they... don't like musicals, can you believe it? How can you not love it when complete strangers spontaneously burst into song and dance? I totally do."

Nice save.

"Well, maybe I can change Krutch's mind," Chloe said.

Could almost feel Dervis deflate next to me. He returned the keys and we walked out the side doors to the parking lot.

"Gracie, can I catch a ride?" Chloe asked.

"Ah, sure. Anyone else?" I asked. Hoped.

"We're good. Mom's on her way," Aspen said, then read my face, "but I could call and ask since you've been cleared."

She pulled out her cell and stepped away to call.

Dervis avoided Chloe, glanced at me, and shook his head side to side. "See ya." He walked alone to his car.

Chloe opened my Mini Cooper passenger door, popped the seat forward, and stepped back so the twins could climb in. "Cute car. Love the blue."

"Thanks, used to be my mom's."

Leaving the parking lot, Chloe gave me directions to her house, then asked Aspen, "What do you mean, been cleared?"

Aspen leaned forward. "Oh, our parents are super strict and had to approve Gracie to drive us to see the guys' croquet tourney in the fall."

"Croquet tourney? Does Krutch play?" Chloe asked, looking over her shoulder.

"Yep! He's really good, nationally ranked. Hood and Dervis are partners. It's a hoot to watch. New-season starts pretty soon."

"Hm," Chloe thought for a moment. I sensed her eyes turn my way, "Do you think Krutch likes me?"

I shrugged it off. "Sure. Krutch likes everybody."

"But, do you think likes me?"

Here we go.

"I mean, everyone told me he's strange," she said.

"Who's everyone?" I asked.

"Mandi and her friends."

Mandi?

She continued, "They used to be neighbors, Krutch and Mandi, then she moved to California and was in this theater production of, *Sound of Music*." Chloe paused palms out for emphasis. "Played Liesl, the oldest von Trapp daughter, and that led to the TV commercial."

Tracking but confused. "Commercial?"

"Yes. She was the face for Cygnet2Swan's launch."

"What's that?"

"Hello." She held up a thumb and index finger cradling her face like a phone. "Cygnet2Swan! Huge, dream deal." She brought her fists together then exploded her fingers out and waited for my reaction.

"Never heard of it. Circling back. "What about Krutch?"

"Oh, when she came back, so perfect, that was it," Chloe shrugged. "She jumped out of his league."

Harsh and annoying. "Did Mandi say that?" Stopped at a light, I looked at her.

Facing me, she brushed her hair back with her left hand, eyes looked up to the right, triggering a thought CIA wannabe Shelley told me about interrogation tactics. I set it aside for further review.

Chloe continued, "Um... maybe, not sure. Mandi doesn't talk much."

Remembering the save at the basketball game, I fished, "She talks with Sienna and Michael."

"Of course, because they're also perfect and popular." A wistful cloud swept across her face followed by a bright smile. "But now that I know Krutch, well, he's so cute and funny. Quirky, but cool, you know? Like, he wears flip-flops year-round, even in the winter. Who does that?"

Bait her. "Part of his charm."

"I know, right?"

Reel her in. "What about Dervis?"

Chloe shrugged, "We're friends."

I paused, gripped the steering wheel. "Seriously? Just friends?"

She blinked, inhaled, exhaled in a huff. "I just don't feel that way about him, you know?"

Unfortunately, I did. Years ago, my Prom date with Sofi's friend. A sweetheart, but it was one and done as far as I was concerned and an easy out because he was a senior and graduated. Krutch, Mandi, Dervis, and Chloe, however, are juniors. Meaning, a potential re-cast of the main characters that could turn *Midsummer's Night Dream* into a year-long nightmare.

We traveled the last few blocks in silence. When Chloe got out, Aspen jumped in the passenger seat and was quiet as we drove away.

I didn't know how much Hood Snap had told her about Dervis liking Chloe, or Krutch and Mandi's history, but I was soon to find out. We'd gone a mile when she put down her window, leaned her head out and screamed into the cool wind, "AHHHHHHHHHHHHH." She closed it back up.

"Feel better?" Willow asked from the back.

"A little, but she totally sucks," Aspen spit out.

"Maybe she doesn't know about Mandi and Krutch," Willow said, giving Chloe the benefit of doubt.

"Yeah, yeah, whatever, Hood told me she's been playing poor Dervis this whole year. Jerk."

"Nothing poor or lacking in Dervis; it's her loss."

In the rearview mirror, I studied the reflection of Willow's serene face in the car window and wondered.

"Just goes to show, there's all kinds of peeps in this crazy world – The BFDs, BigFrickin'Dealers, like Mandi and you." Aspen flicked her hand toward me, "And Hood of course, but fortunately not many recognize it in him. Lucky for me." She bumped her fist twice above her heart.

I glanced at her, snorted, shook my head, then looked back to the road.

"Next up? The Don'tGiveASchitt'sCreekers, like Krutch, Willow, and me, and come to think of it, you too. You're a hybrid. Sweet!" She jazz-waved her hands. "And then, there's the GiveASchitt'sCreekers, as in Chloe, who kiss up to and copy BFDs, and use and abuse anyone in their wake. What are you thinking, Will?" She looked back to her sister.

Willow, gazed out, silent for a long moment, "Dervis is a BFD, he just doesn't realize it."

Curious.

41

"Say Something" – Keith Urban

"Yell Oh!" Sofi's face lit up my screen.

I snorted. "Sorry. Must be a wrong number, dialing my sista, not a gangsta."

"Haha, Buttercup! Whatzup?"

"Got time to chat?"

"Always, except when I'm in the bathroom, have to set boundaries. What's rocking your world?"

"Relationship drama."

"Lacrosse drama?"

"Negative. Lax is good. Musical drama."

"Score one for good. What about the not-so-good?"

I filled her in on auditions and the aftermath.

Her index finger waved, connecting the invisible dots. "Chloe's into Krutch, who doesn't know it, but Dervis does, and so does Willow, who may be crushing on Dervis?"

"Something like that."

"How I miss high school woes and mayhem."

"Can't wait to leave it behind."

"Soon my precious, revel in the goodness, Gracie-ous." Double blink. "What was Mandi's commercial?"

"Cygnet2Swan. Have you heard of it?"

"Yep! Life-changing. Rumor has it; formula's made from unicorn tears. Would have made my eighth-grade Mount Vesuvius Pimple phase far less painful. No wonder her skin's flawless. Probably scored a lifetime supply."

Hmm. Didn't recall Sofi ever having an awkward phase.

"Have you figured her out yet?"

"Nope. Chloe implied Mandi ghosted Krutch when she moved back but when I pressed her about it she backstroked. Doesn't track with Mandi's heartfelt audition. Also, she's friends with Sienna, the sweetest person ever, unless someone messes with a teammate then she turns into a momma grizzly bear. Then there's the whole Mannequin clone-thing."

"You should know better than to judge a book by its cover, unless the title font is illegible because that's pointless, or the cover image is low resolution, or the colors clash – but I digress."

"More than anyone in the history of digression."

"Lols. So what? Mandi and her Mannequins follow the same influencers and like to look alike? Big woo. Book club members read the same book. Athletes review game clips and coaches scout other teams. It's about searching, incorporating, and sharing ideas."

Stunned that her argument had merit I remained silent.

"Alert the media! Grace Artemis is speechless."

Palms together, I bowed my head.

"Truly a conundrum. Don't you love that word? Used it in multiple conversations today. Sounds so positively British."

"I'll drop it on Krutch, he'll appreciate it."

"Gained insight into his side of the Mandi Mystery?"

"Not a clue."

"Get busy. Inquiring minds want to know, you know." Double blink. "I've made an important decision."

I gasped, "No! You've changed the middle name of your future imaginary first born, again?"

"No. Well, yes," she scoffed. "I can't name her Brooke Brooks, even if I hyphenated, Halsted-Brooks, the name registrars at the Department of Redundancy Department would flag it, but no, that's not today's epiphany."

"Do tell."

"Joan and Jason's wedding. You, Shelley and I will wear flowy dresses – yours is the least girly so don't freak –with delicate tiny blue flowers on white in three different styles. So romantic. Mom's is from the same collection, icy blue with elegant white leaf details trailing across the bodice and down the side, very chic and sophisticated.

You'll get them in a couple days, try them on and we'll video chat with Shelley."

"Aye, aye, Section Leader." I saluted, waited for her to return it, then dropped my hand and signed off.

Lunch turned my stomach Monday. Not the food – the conversation – and lack thereof. Chloe was absent, so Krutch teased Dervis, who fumed more than usual. I assumed Aspen told Hood Snap about Chloe's revelation. We sent mental SOS messages and attempted to intervene. One ear wanted to block out the guys, while the other escaped into Jaz and Harley's lacrosse conversation.

Dervis gulped his food, mumbled and took off. Hood Snap followed, as did Jaz and Harley. Leaving me with cleanup duty.

"Listen, I suck at this but here goes, Saturday, at practice Chloe crushed on you in front of Dervis."

Krutch's jovial face went stone-cold serious, "Bollocks."

"Yep."

"Thanks for the heads up." Leaving together, he spun backward, butted open the cafeteria door, and invited me to go ahead with a sweeping hand gesture that accidentally ended on Mandi's soft, pink cashmere-covered breast. Her face flushed to match her sweater as Krutch surrendered up his hands as if under arrest. "Sorry."

"Oh. Hi," she stammered.

Was that a hint of a smile? It disappeared as her gaze swept past him to me. Her cheeks flushed again. She stepped aside and away with troops, sans Chloe, in tow.

A more considerate friend might've looked away as Krutch morphed from cool casual dude to awkward bumbling fool. Couldn't help but think that witnessing this would've improved Dervis's mood exponentially. "You could have at least bought her dinner first."

Squinting sideways through long wavy hair, he ran a hand back through it and snorted.

"If it makes you feel any better, she seemed amused."

"Yeah, she did." His jaw muscle tensed. "Like when we were punks goofing around in my tree fort."

"Wait," I stopped. "Tree fort? Game changer."

"Yep." Krutch laughed. "We used to hang out there."

Moment of truth, do I dare? Yep, I do. "What happened when she moved back?" Looking at my watch, which is an actual watch, not a Fitbit all up in my business counting steps. Just shows the time. Going to be late for class. Worth it.

"They moved to a different neighborhood, but the first day of school I recognized her, even without glasses. Walked up and said, 'Hey!'" He paused, jaw firm. "She blew me off and Chloe pulled her away."

Full stop. "Chloe?"

He nodded, "Yeah, thought Dervis caught a break when Chloe sat with us. She's got gumption. I'll shut it down." He tapped two fingers to his forehead as if tipping a hat and veered off.

Gumption was not the descriptive word I had in mind.

***

JV and Varsity rosters were posted on the athletic locker room door. Frosh/soph on JV and junior/seniors on Varsity. Coach handed us a slip of paper and pencil as we entered the gym for practice.

"Selecting co-captains for both teams. Cast votes for two names from your designated roster. I'll tally and announce after practice," Coach said.

Without hesitation, I wrote Jaz and Harley's names on my slip, turned it in, and reported to the trainer. She checked my ankle and cleared me to go full speed. Hallelujah.

The late afternoon sun rested on the top bleacher. After jogging a couple laps around the track with our sticks, we broke into the two teams and did running/passing drills. Glancing over to the JV squad, I was pleased to see Zoë and Emma paired up.

Recognizing two Varsity attack players from summer club play, Bailey and Simone, I needed to tell them I'd told Lanie their "tells." Oops. We don't play her and Charlotte's team first game so I can ease into that confession. My plan to feed them passes to garner assists rather than goals would make up for that leaked intel and allow them to switch up their game. Control the center of the board.

Practice over, Coach called us in.

"JV first. Co-captains will be Emma and Zoë." Nice. New and experienced players are both represented.

"Varsity, we have Jaz and Harley..."

As expected.

Cheers interrupted her; she waited a moment. "And a third player who received an equal number of votes, Tri-captain, Gracie."

"Rogue!" Jaz and Harley shouted.

Incredulous, I looked from them to Coach. She nodded.

"Captains lead warmups and cooldowns. Friday you'll hand out jerseys." Coach dismissed us.

"Woohoo! Tri-captains!" They came in for a hug.

This was definitely not expected.

***

Surprised to see Chloe in her previous seat next to Dervis Tuesday, I collected shrugs, eye rolls, and subtle grins from everyone else. Oblivious, she continued an animated monologue with a confused but captivated Dervis. Sitting between Krutch and Chloe again, I heard her ask Dervis, "Do you have a title?"

"A title?" he asked. "To my car?"

"No, silly." She bumped her shoulder into his.

Krutch coughed into his fist. Hood Snap bit his lower lip.

"Drum roll, please?" Jaz asked. Harley complied, with fingers tapping on the tabletop. "Announcement! Gracie, Harley and I were voted Varsity Tri-captains!"

Krutch lifted his chocolate milk. "Sláinte," he said, using his Irish accent.

"Salute," Hood Snap added in Italian, his carton aloft.

"Cheers," Jaz, Harley, and I said in unison, lifting our water bottles.

Dervis leaned in front of Chloe to tell me. "Make sure to add it to college applications. They eat up leadership stuff."

"Good idea, thanks," I said to Dervis. "Kind of surprised me." Didn't think others saw me as a team leader.

"Gracie, you made quite an impression flipping Zoë over from the dark side," Jaz said.

Chloe snorted. "Of course she did." Awkward hush. Everyone looked at her. She blurted out, "Congrats!"

"We get to pick numbers and hand out jerseys Friday," Harley said.

"You should get number one," Dervis said to me.

"Rogue One, savage," Krutch added.

"Fierce," Hood Snap said.

I shook my head. "No thanks." Too vain.

"Truth. Everyone knows it. Can't wait for you to torch Charlotte," Jaz said.

"She leads in goals heading into the season," I said.

"And you're number one in assists because you know how to share," Harley said.

"I call tunes chairman for cooldowns like we did in cross country," Jaz said to Dervis.

He nodded. "We're doing it in Track too."

Chloe squinted, studied Jaz and Harley, then leaned on Dervis and squeezed his forearm. "We can't wait to watch you guys play. When's the first game?"

Gulp. The world slipped back onto its axis? Sort of.

"Three weeks," Jaz said.

"Cool. Better scoot. Walk with me?" Chloe asked Dervis.

"Sure," he frowned but finished his chocolate milk.

The rest of us watched them exit in silence.

"Fickle, much?"

"Which one?"

"Both."

"Not Dervis."

"Never Dervis."

"Then what was that about?" Harley asked.

Chocolate milk shot out of Hood Snap's nose. Krutch shielded me with his empty lunch tray.

"Oooooh."

"Gross."

On either side, both leaned away from Hood Snap.

This should be good.

Hood Snap cleared his throat. "Chloe tried to recruit us for tech crew." Hood Snap tilted his head twice to Krutch. "We declined, Krutch said that Dervis doesn't need help because his techno genius will earn millions before he turns thirty."

"Then, Hood Snap hinted Milton Jasper Dervis III might be related to European royalty," Krutch said, in his pompous English accent. "How was that again, my good chap?"

"Il mio cane scoreggia nel sonno," Hood Snap said in Italian, punctuated with a chef's kiss.

"What's that mean?" Jaz asked as she took a sip.

"My dog farts in his sleep."

Jaz's hand flew up to stop projectile spit water. Harley slapped the table. I shook my head side to side. Stupid funny.

The Krutch/Dervis division problem was solved, but was adding Chloe back into the equation the correct formula? Inconclusive.

Regardless, and somewhat callous, I'm excited to exit relationship dramas and concentrate on lacrosse performances.

42

"We Will Rock You" – Lzzy Hale metal cover

For our game at dinner, I delivered the lacrosse team Goods, Dad's Bad was beltway traffic backup, and Mom's Ugly was that City Hall approved her petition to paint a mural on a tagged and re-painted building wall on Main Street.

After dinner, a ping alerted me as I climbed to my attic. Probably Sofi, she'll get a kick out of my being a tri-captain.

MESSAGES
Army;-)
iMessage

What the heck! I swiped and punched the icon.

(*Army;-*)
Heard about Gwen.

Is he butt texting me?

(*me*)
Gwen?

(*Army;-*)
Your new coach.
Gwen Kennedy

(*me*)
Oh. Yeah

(*Army;-*)
Smart player.
You can learn
a lot from her

Older woman. Speaking from experience? Chill girl.

                                        (*me*)
                                        You know her?

(*Army;-*)
Yeah. Played for dad.
First team all conference
four years

Dang. Legit.

                                        (*me*)
                                        Dang.
                                        Legit

(*Army;-*)
How's the knee?

                                        (*me*)
                                        Good to go.
                                        You?

(*Army;-*)
All good.

                                        (*me*)
                                        Season started?

(*Army;-*)
Two weeks.
Home v Navy

> (*me*)
> Worried?

(*Army;-*)
Piece of cake.

> (*me*)
> Ha ha
> Beat Army

(*Army;-*)
No way. Made a decision?

> (*me*)
> Nope

(*Army;-*)
Have to bounce.
Take it easy

> (*me*)
> Get it

(*Army;-*)
Will. Do

Voted tri-captain. Fixed Krutch and Dervis, and now an awesome Ian text. Talk about a hat trick!

***

We'd received our dresses so Mom and I texted Sofi. She responded to give her five minutes so she could text Shelley to put on hers to video chat.

"Gorgeous! Don't you love them? I can't wait to twirl," Sofi said, stepping back from her laptop to spin.

"Isn't that your motto?" I asked.

"You betcha. You look amazing, btw. You too, Mom."

"They're lovely, Sofia Isabella. What about Joan?" Mom asked, always sensitive to Joan losing her mother years ago.

"Oh, it's soooo dreamy, a simple satin bodice with a floral embroidered ivory tulle skirt so she can straddle."

Awkward pause. Mom and I waited for it.

Sofi blinked. "Coach Cori's palomino. Wait. I didn't tell you? My goodness!" Sofi's hands fluttered in front of her floral bodice like butterflies. "Cori is bringing Phoenix down from Boulder for Joan to ride around Monument Rock to the reflecting pond! Epic! Is that not serendipitous? Joan, with her burning auburn curls fueled by the mountain breeze, astride a golden horse named Phoenix? Be still my frickin' wedding designer heart." Sofi collapsed into her chair.

Shelley cracked up.

"And where will we park the dragons?" I asked, deadpan.

"The dragons?" Sofi sat up.

"That we fly in on."

Sofi laughed and waved me off, "In the dragon parking lot of course, duh."

***

Lip-synching songs using their sticks as microphones during cooldowns was how Jaz and Harley rocked. Me? I rolled through the motions but refused to fully commit. Yet. Three weeks of lacrosse bliss passed as the team bonded. Heading into our first game we were pumped.

In the Midwest, we were lucky to have a few friends join parents in the stands to watch us play. Virginia, however, was a whole new lax universe. Here, girls' and guys' games piggy-backed, alternating who went first game to game. This meant the two teams could support each other for the first half before next up met for pre-game psych sessions. We were excited to be first up for Friday night's opener.

Friday morning, however, dragged... on... forever.

Not hungry, I forced down my game day fuel: PBJ on whole wheat, dark cherry Greek yogurt, and an apple. Jaz and Harley were too hyped to eat. The guys listened attentively to their animated explanation of what to expect.

Chloe gave up trying to steer the conversation back to the musical. She'd been moody again, and I could tell Dervis, despite playing it cool following the Krutch indiscretion, was falling back under her spell.

Like an itch that can't be reached in the middle of your back, it annoyed me. As did the fact afternoon class-blocks took twice as long as forever. After the last buzz buzzed, despite the raging desire to fly across the academic wing and down the stairs, I walked at a determined pace. Aspen was waiting at the bottom T, left to theater, right to athletic wing.

"So, here's the scoop. We've got tech crew, theater nerds, band geeks, and thanks to Dervis, endorphin-pumping runners on board cheering in the stands tonight!" Aspen said, her fists pounded together then exploded into a ten-finger firework. "Redonkulous beyond belief! It'll be epic!" No pressure.

After a quick hug, well, quick for her, held ten seconds longer than most, she skipped to the set production shop. Her exuberance invoked a moment of joyful reflection. It passed and my smile melted into game face in preparation for battle. Two hours until game time.

Antsy, I volunteered to run the playlist up to the stadium press box. We'd gone with metal covers of popular songs – heavy on drums and electric guitar. I took the stairs two at a time, gave the thumb drive to the student running sound, and exited the heated booth. The door closed with a 'chunk.'

Standing on the top bleacher, I relished the crisp, evening spring air crackling with electricity as stadium lights hummed, warming up for a gradual transition from dusk to dark. Below, my favorite stage, white lines glowing on emerald-green turf.

I was surprised at the crowd pouring in from the parking lot and filling the stands. Unlike football, opposing lacrosse team benches share a sideline, separated by the time and scorekeepers table, with fans sitting behind their team's bench. This arrangement is civil during our games, but I remember some loud 'discussions' back and forth when Joan played on the guy's team with Jason, and parents in both sections disagreed with referees and each other.

Jogging down memory lane and the cement stairs I heard a snarky, "Oooh, look, Lanie, it's Rogue."

Crap. She snuck up on me again. Must wear a frickin' invisibility cloak. I looked around. No such luck. Charlotte from my summer club team. Her sneer brought to mind the National Cathedral gargoyles. Next to her, Lanie shrugged.

Scouting mission.

Charlotte pointed to my running knee brace. "Oh, poor Gracie. Blew out her knee. Lost her scholarship. So, so, so, sorry." She paused, palm to cheek, adding a snotty, "Psych."

Lanie shoved Charlotte's shoulder. "Don't be a jerk." Then to me, "Go get it! See you in a couple weeks."

Ignoring Charlotte, I said to her, "Looking forward to it."

"Hope nobody has to carry you off," Charlotte said.

A lightning bolt from Olympus, or Sofi, struck me and I glanced back to Charlotte, "Worth it. Ian's such a sweetheart."

Lanie's eyes about popped out of her head; Charlotte's shot daggers. Despite congratulating myself on my quick burn, Charlotte's words left a mark. I took a moment to flush them down the don't give a crap toilet before heading into the locker room.

Coach went over last-minute strategies, and when we heard our tunes kick-off, she led us out to the field. I kept my eyes off the stands and on our side during drills but glanced at our opponents warming up their goalie to collect and share intel with Joci, our keeper.

New to lacrosse, Joci was a talented athlete and a quick learner. She competed in jiu-jitsu, and her flexibility stretched far beyond my karate skills, pun intended, which helped her defend the entire goal. Jaz and Harley filled her in on last year's squad and I didn't see much to add. Coach called us in.

I jogged to our bench ignoring the crowded bleachers. Time to shed sweats. Dropped pants first. Leaving me in a short black skirt and Spanx. I paused, knowing Charlotte would spy the roaring, crimson red #1 on my bright white jersey. Crossing hands to grab the hoodie hem, lifting it off I heard:

STOMP, STOMP, CLAP. STOMP, STOMP, CLAP. STOMP, STOMP, CLAP.

Boots on metal bleachers echoed across the field to empty stands and back.

Sounds like the intro to – wait, it is, but a metal version of "We Will Rock You."

"ROGUE will..."

What the heck?

Jaz thumped me on the back, "Did you hear that? They replaced WE with ROGUE!"

"Who did?" Rotating, my mouth dropped. Krutch stood on the first row of the bleachers dressed like our school mascot in a red and white striped pirate shirt, black torn rather than cut-off shorts, and his token flip-flops. He sang in a hardcore rocker voice into a headpiece mic borrowed from the musical, with permission no doubt, from Ms. Davis.

Next to Krutch, wearing a black eyepatch, Rolling Stones t-shirt, skinny jeans and biker boots, Hood Snap shredded a black electric guitar licked by yellow and orange flames.

Dervis stood next to them with a one-sided, yep-it-was-me grin. The techno genius behind the epic and much appreciated but never anticipated operation. The dudes never disappoint.

"Friends of yours?" Coach, next to me, asked.

I exhaled. "Yeah."

"Impressive."

"Yeah." Blinking, I rotated, cradling my stick.

"Now get your head in the game."

"Yep."

"Get a couple in from the get-go before feeding assists."

"Sounds good."

I did. Scored two quick goals then fed Bailey and Simone five each. At the final buzzer, the scoreboard's digital red numbers read, HOME:12 – VISITORS:2.

Joci's rant about their goals reminded me of Sofi when someone dared to get one past her.

After exchanging fist bumps with our opponents, Jaz, Harley and I lined up in the middle of the team and lead them in a cooldown jog across the field. The tension melted from my taut muscles as I glanced left then right down the line of celebratory faces.

Back at our sideline, we raised our sticks to the fans. Stick in left, I flashed the two-finger rock n roll sign across my chest with my right hand to the posse, each returned it, except for Chloe, who was engrossed in her cell.

I scanned the crowd, runners mixed in with theater and techie kids next to the pep band. Sienna, Michael, and Mandi? Unexpected. Moved on to Biff and Garth standing next to Willow and Aspen, then Hood Snap, now in a discussion with the band director. Getting in trouble or being recruited? Krutch was reclined in max relax mode on the bleachers, hands behind head, elbows out, legs extended. Dervis and Chloe's heads were together deep in conversation. Up and over behind them in the parent's section, Mom clapped over her head while Dad pumped his fist in the air. All of these people here to support me. It was good to be back in action, but even better to belong somewhere. Can't wait to tell Sofi.

After our post-game talk, Coach released us and we threw on sweats to return to support the guys' varsity. I retrieved my cell from the game locker just as it buzzed.

(*dervis*)
Great game.

> (*me*)
> Thanks

(*dervis*)
Had to leave.
Chloe got another
note

> (*me*)
> And?

(*dervis*)
Same purple ink.
Notebook scrap

> (*me*)
> :-|

(*dervis*)
I'll show you
Monday.

> (*me*)
> Kk

43

"Only a Matter of Time" – Joshua Bassett

"Better leg it or we'll be late," Krutch said as we rushed down the hall to Spies Monday morning. We snuck into the room and took our seats.

Ms. Davis was sitting on top of her desk like she used to before the accident. Her legs kicked back and forth, the injured one in a walking cast. "What world city has the most spies?"

Silence. Some mumbles but no guesses.

"Finally! I stumped you, kiddos! Perfect timing because next Wednesday we invade the International Spy Museum in Washington, D.C., which claims that infamous title! Hard to verify of course, because it's not like people register with a spy directory." She eased off her desk, crouched down and whispered, "They're everywhere and nowhere and where you least expect them. The police directing traffic, your neighbor, perhaps, even your teacher!" She rubbed her hands together under her chin and cackled a diabolical, "Heh, heh, heh, hehhhhh."

The entire class cracked up.

She stood. "Permission slips due by Friday. If you fail this mission, you'll be left behind and forced to watch the original *Home Alone* on repeat, all day." Her hands slapped into parenthesis around the open mouth pose, aka Macaulay Culkin or Edvard Munch, depending on your fine arts preference for film or painting.

On the way to Lit, Dervis showed me the new note:

You still suck

What's the point of this mess? Get a frickin' hobby, jerk. The same purple felt tip ink scribble on a torn piece of lined notebook paper. We were no closer to knowing 'who done it,' and with two away games this week and a big one against Charlotte and Lanie next Wednesday after the field trip, my first, second and third inclinations were to avoid getting snagged in Chloe's drama net again. She'd been distant as far as I was concerned which was fine by me, but Dervis insisted on roping me back into that awkward none-of-my-business territory I used to buck off like a bronco. Whoa, is me.

We finished the week undefeated, and I looked forward to a nice quiet weekend to recuperate and gear up for next. Then at lunch Friday, Dervis reminded me about the sound and lighting run-through at the musical dress rehearsal on Saturday.

"How long will it take?" I asked.

Chloe answered for him, rolling her eyes. "Twice as long as usual, because we'll have to start and stop a lot when amateurs mess up their lines." No one took the bait, assuming she was not one of the 'forgetfuls.'

"You should be back from your field trip in time to catch the player's bus," Jaz said, rerouting the conversation to lacrosse.

My thought process determined the Spy Museum might be a welcome distraction from the typical tedious school day before a game.

"Wish I could ride on your bus," Chloe said to Dervis and only Dervis. "But Ms. Davis said I have to stay with my stupid Civil War Spies because our stupid scavenger hunt is different than yours."

Krutch covered a grin with a cough and pushed away from the table. "Going for another chocolate milk. Don't do anything stupid while I'm gone."

"How can I? You're taking all the stupid with you," Dervis replied.

Both channeled *Avengers: Endgame.* I was relieved their repartee was back to normal.

Hood Snap caught the reference, grinned and nodded.

Jaz, Harley and I cracked up. Chloe? Another eye roll.

***

Saturday the theater was abuzz. Actors scrambling for their turn in makeup and costumes, crew shifting props and sets, techies checking sounds and lights. I dodged the madness and found sanctuary in the booth. Ms. Davis limped to the center of the stage wearing a walking cast.

"Attention everyone, take a deep, cleansing breath," she said.

Mimicking her, open hands closed into fists and lifted as the diaphragms and lungs of actors, crew, and musicians filled with air.

"Now, exhale slowly," she said. Chins lifted, expelling air from O-shaped mouths as fists opened and fingers reached upward, then stretched out sideways and down in a full circle.

"Let's give it a go, cherubs! Places everyone, we begin in two minutes, or as soon as I can gracefully exit stage left," Ms. Davis said, laughing as she limped off. Everyone else darted and disappeared as the curtains closed to conceal the urban skyline on the backdrop.

The orchestra warmed up in the pit.

Dervis came up to look over the soundboard. "Good to go. Replaced batteries in the lights hidden in props too." He paused, then sat on a stool.

Sensing something else was on his mind, I waited.

"I don't get it. She hangs on me around you, upset about the scary notes, but then here," he waved a hand to the stage, "she ignores me."

"Sorry, above my teenage angst emotional pay grade."

"One minute she's paranoid about who's sending them, the next, couldn't care less and babbles on about the musical."

The orchestra began an upbeat mashup of *Annie* songs as the theater seating lights dimmed. Dervis looked left to right, making sure two spotlights lit stools on each side of the stage where interpreters prepared to sign. All good, he looked at me, gave two thumbs up and left to check behind the scenes.

The curtains opened to a dim dormitory room with four bunk beds staggered around a dingy, translucent window. As the window glow became brighter so did the room, revealing bodies under drab blankets in a range of moody blues, tans and grays.

Someone snored loudly on a lower bunk. A body on the upper bunk groaned then covered it's head with a pillow. When lower bunk snored again even louder, upper threw the pillow down at them. Comic relief. The audience would laugh there, and even more when the headmistress, Miss Hannigan, stomped into the room, screamed the orphans awake, and ordered them to clean.

I figured out Chloe was the snorer when she popped up and belted out her first song. Mandi, aka Annie, was slower to rise, stretching out her arms before joining the other orphans as they sang and danced while pretending to clean. The show continued, with a few mistakes, stops and do-overs, as expected.

After a scene that featured Chloe, the curtain closed for a quick set change. She rushed to the booth, her face flushed with excitement. "Oh. You." She frowned. "Where's Dervis?"

"Checking lights behind the scrim."

She chewed her lower lip then glanced away.

Might as well throw her a bone, her timing was spot on, and she projected a ton of lines with confidence. "That last scene went well," I said.

She studied me, head tilted, hair in pigtails, then shrugged and grinned. "I know. I so adore it." Clasping her hands together under her chin, she exclaimed, "It's where I come alive."

Pretending to be someone else. Sarcasm got the best of me but at least I kept it to myself.

The curtain drew back to reveal the next scene. A lone wooden chair was lit by a spotlight in the dorm room set. Chloe slid onto a stool next to me.

Mandi walked out, guitar in hand, and sat down. She strummed the first few chords, then played the infamous, "Tomorrow," singing the lyrics so soft I could barely hear her. I checked the volume levels and equipment, but everything was working properly.

"Don't bother. It's her, not you. She practices her solos when no one's around then at rehearsals she mumbles to that stupid guitar.

Figures the diva would do that to me," Chloe said. She slumped, arms crossed, her profile the epitome of a resting bitch face.

"Do what to you?" I asked.

"Plays the stupid thing! If something happens, not like I'd ever wish it on her, but if I have to take her place, I can't do it as she does. Wouldn't surprise me if she's sending the notes to psych me out."

"Why would she do that?" Psychological warfare I can understand, but idiotic mean girl stuff alludes me. Mandi got the lead, why rub it in?

Again, Chloe backstroked, "Maybe not her, but one of them."

"Assuming you mean your mutual friends, again, why?"

"You wouldn't understand."

"Probably not, but I'll give it a shot. Enlighten me."

She glanced at me, then back to the stage. "Whatever."

There we have it folks, the winner of the most annoying way to end a conversation ever. Fighting a natural impulse to verbally punish, I said, "Maybe the guitar comforts her."

"Like a baby blanket?" She snorted. Her expression shifted from angry to thoughtful to demonic.

What have I done?

The curtain closed. "Better scoot," Chloe said, pigtails bounced as she skipped down to the stage.

Aspen came up the side aisle to join me. "How'd you cheer up Miss Psycho Melancholy?"

"What do you mean?" An uneasy aura hung in the air.

"She's whack. Just say'n." Aspen sat down.

I looked at her, waiting.

"You know Willow does everyone's makeup right?"

"Yeah."

"Well Mandi goes first because she's the star, but it turns out she uses her own makeup not the stage stuff because she's got super sensitive skin and is embarrassed about it." She paused then facepalmed. "Oops. That's a secret, but I know you won't tell." She squeezed my arm and continued, "So, Willow hangs out, and Mandi does her thing." Aspen pretended to draw a smiley face in the air. "But then Chloe insists she's next and wants Willow to do hers exactly like Mandi's but of course Willow doesn't tell her that Mandi does her own because she's much better at keeping secrets than I am." She covered her mouth and giggled.

The world needs more Aspens.

"Willow tells me Mandi goes mental performing in front of an audience. Oops-dash-two, shouldn't have shared that either! What the heck, anyway, Mandi is fortunate to have Madeline, aka Miss Hannigan, a hoot in her own right and in the know about Mandi's out-the-yin-yang-crippling stage fright." Aspen finished and took a well-deserved breath.

"Stagefright?" I asked. A lump grew in my throat.

"Yep. Off the scales. Can't even look at the audience. Madeline holds her hands and talks her off the ledge before she has to go on and perform a solo. Tells her to sing to her guitar. Works like magic." Aspen picked up a pen and waved it like a wand.

I pressed both palms into eye sockets hoping I hadn't screwed up.

"You okie dokie, artichokie?" she asked.

Nodding, "Yeah, busy week."

"Kk. Better head back. Toota lou!" Aspen scampered off.

Did I just expose Mandi's Achille's heel?

***

If in need of the perfect place to hold a scavenger hunt, look no further than the International Spy Museum. So much fun, especially if your partners are Krutch, Dervis and Hood Snap. Talk about the Dream Team. My stomach hurt from laughing from the get-go as we snaked through the entry queue. We split up, Dervis and I took the high road through the air ducts you can climb through to spy on unsuspecting students from above, and taller Krutch and Hood Snap took the low road in search of the fake dog excrement exhibit that transmitted radio signals to direct aircraft to locations for reconnaissance and strikes. Classic spy sh**.

We crawled on our hands and knees through the secret spy ducts praying no one had eaten beans for dinner the night before. I avoided looking at Dervis's khaki butt in front of me aside from noticing the folded scavenger hunt worksheet tucked into the back pocket. We turned a corner and the duct was wide enough for us to peek below to a hallway just as Chloe of all people, entered.

Dervis lifted his fist to knock on the window as she snuck a suspicious look right and left. Something's off. I grabbed his wrist before he could strike the one-way mirror. We watched as Chloe reached into her left jacket pocket and pulled out a short purple pen and a scrap of blue-lined notebook paper.

Dervis's wrist dropped like a brick. "Bloody hel..."

"She didn't," I whispered looking sideways at him.

She un-capped the short purple Sharpie and transferred it to her right hand to awkwardly scribble.

Shelley's interrogation intel hit me. Right-handed people look up to the right when telling the truth, left to make up a lie. She's left-handed, so when she looked up to the right...

Dervis's jaw muscle flexed; he turned and crawled the rest of the way in silence. When we exited the duct and caught up with Krutch and Hood Snap he was business as usual. We completed our scavenger hunt sheet and exited the museum a couple hours later.

Watching our two school buses move at a snail's pace through the heavy D.C. traffic we heard a squeaky, "Dervis!" Chloe weaved through the crowd of students toward us; trembling, she handed Dervis a note.

Krutch and Hood Snap stepped to the curb to board as soon as possible but I stood next to Dervis and read.

Quit while you're behind

Dervis studied the note, then set the stage for her last act, "When did you get this?"

"It was in my pocket," Chloe said, sniffing. "Someone must have put it there when I was in line to get in."

Wow, even blinking back tears.

"Then they have to be in your class," Dervis said like he'd solved a clever riddle. I nodded going along for the ride.

He scanned the note again, then looked at Chloe, "And they have to be involved with the musical, right?"

Chloe paused and squinted.

"Based on these observations, the solution is simple, we determine who in your class is involved with the musical and has a purple pen in their left pocket," Dervis said.

Chloe's face went blank. Her left hand reached for that cropped jean jacket pocket but diverted to her hip.

"You're left-handed," I said.

She leaned in, "So?"

"What's in your pocket?" Dervis's eyes flicked toward it.

She thought, shrugged, then flipped her hand at the wrist. "Figures, you'd believe her. Good thing you're a runner. Have fun chasing the perfects."

Dervis, in his brilliance, snorted, "Busted." He turned and climbed into our bus.

Chloe shot me a dirty look. "Happy?"

"What he said." I pointed up the stairs then followed.

Krutch and Hood Snap studied me. I shook my head and joined Dervis in the bus seat behind them.

Dervis stared out the window. After traveling in silence for a while he muttered, "I'm an idiot."

"Nope. Never. Her loss."

"Should have known she played me."

"Maybs, but...."

"What?"

I inhaled, then this spilled out, "Moving on, I suck at this but here goes, what do you think about Willow?"

He frowned. "What about her?"

My nose scrunched up, "She thinks you're pretty great."

"Me? Willow?" He studied the seatback in front of us as if the answer to a quantum physics problem was scrawled in black marker.

"Yeah."

"Noooo," he groaned.

"Why not?" I asked.

He pointed ahead, whispering, "Can you imagine the grief Krutch would dish out if Hood Snap and I date twins?"

I snorted, shaking my head up and down, whispering, "True, but worth it? She's awesome."

He was contemplative for the rest of the ride.

44

"Feel Invincible" – Skillet

I signed back in and out to catch the lacrosse player's bus to our away game. Jaz and Harley had saved a bench next to them in the front row. "How was the Spy Museum, reveal any cool secrets?" Jaz asked.

I stored my gear. "As a matter of fact, yep. Chloe's been smoke-checking Dervis all semester. Doubt she'll join us for lunch anymore."

"What?"

"How?"

I filled them in.

"That's messed up. Good riddance," Harley said.

"Told you she was fickle. Poor Dervis," Jaz added.

"He'll be fine. Think he's kind of relieved, more of the lazy river type rather than roller coaster guy." I kept Willow and my potential new matchmaking skill set on the DL. My phone buzzed in my gear bag.

MESSAGES
Army;-)
iMessage

Wow! I swiped and punched the icon.

(*Army;-)*)
Big game tonight.

Remembering our previous text session.

> (*me*)
> Piece a cake

(*Army;-*)
That's the spirit

Against his old high school.

> (*me*)
> How'd you know?

(*Army;-*)
My dad will be there.
Watching former
players

> (*me*)
> No pressure :-O

(*Army;-*)
Training over break.
Will try to make playoffs

> (*me*)
> In that case,
> we better win

(*Army;-*)
Get it

> (*me*)
> Will. Do

I tapped off and sighed; Coach MacGavin in the stands to watch
me – coached by his former player – go head to net with two former

teammates and Ian planning on post-season play. Time to get my head into this game.

It was obvious Charlotte and Lanie had an intimidating home-field advantage when our bus pulled into an already packed stadium lot. We bee-lined from team bus to the visitor locker room amidst booming psych up, or in our case, psych out tunes. We dressed in silence. Observing, I nudged Jaz and Harley, "Time to throw out some crazy."

In no time they had Skillet's, "Feel Invincible" blasting and athletes jumping up and down shouting out the lyrics. Coach nodded her approval when she came in to take us to the field. Does she know her mentor is here? Is she as nervous as I am?

My palm tingled as if an electric current ran up from my stick. The three of us met the referee and opposing co-captains Charlotte and Lanie in the center for the coin flip to determine playing sides.

Lanie smiled. I didn't look forward to shooting on her.

Charlotte sneered. Her eyes swept from the cherry red #1 on my black away jersey down my stick to the running knee brace Coach insisted I wear. Despite having double the assists, I was three goals behind and her gloating grin begged to be wiped off every leader board.

A classic Clash of the Titans match-up – being the only two undefeated teams in our conference meant this game could determine seeds going into playoffs. Focus, one game at a time.

We were an even match, trading goals and defending attempts on both ends. Tied at halftime, I was too engrossed in game mode to check the stands for Coach MacGavin. Down by one with two minutes left in the fourth quarter, it was obvious Charlotte and Lanie had shared the intelligence they'd scouted. Their coach had defenders block off my passes to Bailey and Simone.

They scored again. Down by two. We took a time out.

I ran in, muscles wound tight and threatening to spring.

"Bailey and Simone are smothered. Gracie, finish it."

I nodded. A spark ignited in my gut.

"Match sticks!" Jaz shouted, extending hers in the middle of the huddle. Red-netted pocket heads came together forming a cone-shaped circle.

"Light it, Rogue!" Harley shouted.

When mine struck, everyone's exploded out. We took the field. With our intense pump-up tune pounding in my head, two minutes ran off the clock and three yellow blurs flew past Lanie in goal.

I circled behind her after the last shot running down the sideline at the final buzzer to hug teammates knowing I'd face Lanie in the post-game lineup. Sure enough, last in their line, she was a good sport, "Until next time." We fist-bumped both hands then tapped sticks in an X.

"You bet," I said.

Charlotte missed the exchange having skipped the line. A glance to their bench told me her coach wasn't pleased about her poor sportsmanship.

Bummer. Not.

We gathered gear and headed to the bus.

"Halsted," I recognized that deep growl and rotated toward an intimidating figure in the shadows outside of the locker room.

"Coach MacGavin, I presume?"

He chuckled gesturing to my braced leg. "Looks like your knee can run a hundred percent as fast as needed."

"Yeah, the brace is for sympathy."

"Not when you blow by folks. Time to make some calls."

I stood at attention. "If you think so." Too eager.

"At ease. Tech and UVA, then?"

"Yes," I exhaled. "Thank you."

"Keep up the good work, and don't forget about Navy."

***

Practice the day after a game is often low-key. My turn to cook Thursday night so I texted Mom that I'd pick up from our favorite restaurant on the way home. Self-conscious in my practice hoodie and shorts, I paid at the takeout counter and then tried to be inconspicuous. My eyes wandered through potted palms greenery separating me from the dining-in customers.

My attention paused on a woman's profile signing to a small girl wearing glasses. I squinted. Wow, the girl was a mini version of Mandi. Small hands fluttered in front of her sweet face, signing a question to the person blocked from my vision. As the girl focused on the response, one hand swept a golden lock of hair behind her ear, exposing a hearing device. She giggled, both hands flew to cover her mouth, knocking a napkin to the floor. The woman reached to retrieve it, revealing Mandi, whose hands signed faster than Sofi talks after a double espresso. Mandi's little sister is deaf.

Epiphany. That partially explains her friendship with Sienna and Michael – but – not my first impression at the beginning of the school year. I leaned back on the counter with eyes closed, revisiting the memory – I remembered searching the wrong hallway for my locker and meeting the gaggle of perfectly styled, messy buns. Replaying my sarcastic responses, and Michael's smirk when he signed, "Bravo," I snorted, then –

"Gracie? Are you okay?"

My eyelids opened to Mandi's perfect brows arched over ocean blue eyes framed by sea-green tortoiseshell glasses.

"Sure," I said and then backstroked, "Nice specs, new?" Treading in unfamiliar water puns.

"Um, yeah. Contacts feel like my eyeballs are soaked in saltwater."

Sensing a theme. "Well, they look great." Like she needs to hear that from me, the fashion-illiterate, non-conformist.

"Thanks," she said, looking down at my running shoes. "Your team is doing well. I went to a game."

"With Sienna and Michael," I said. So now I'm a stalker.

She nodded. "You're really good."

"Thanks, it's a lot of fun."

Her eyes did another round-the-room then returned. "I'm glad Krutch has you."

"Has me what?" I asked. Blurted.

She blushed again, "Um, to date."

"What? No!" Too loud. Cash register dude handed me our food with a side order of 'thanks now please leave' look.

She blinked.

"We're just friends, buddies, chums he would say, in a pompous British accent," I motioned with my free hand.

She glanced down with a shy smile. "He still does that?"

"Yep. Sometimes it's a southern drawl, and then there's his Irish brogue during croquet tournaments." I'm babbling.

"Croquet tournaments?"

"Heck yes, he's a big deal. Ranked nationally." I set the bag back on the counter and raised my hands up and out in the typical fish story pose. "He, Dervis and Hood Snap have a tournament this Sunday, in Roundhill – it's an hour away."

I gushed. Am I sucking less at this? "You should come, if you're up for it, after closing night."

She scrunched her nose in a cute Krutch heart-melting, self-deprecating you-think-so-? smile. "Really? He wouldn't mind? Because we haven't talked in forever."

Booyah. Climbing out on the limb of the newly planted and growing out of control Tree of Matchmaking, I offered, "Sure, you can ride with Aspen, Willow and me."

She looked through the plants to her family. "I'll think about it." Then back to me, "Can I let you know at the cast after-party?"

Wow. Now all that's left is a graceful exit. I grabbed the brown bag with the stapled receipt in one hand and placed the other under like carrying a football. "Sure."

"Break a leg tomorrow night." I glanced down to my brace then shook my head side to side. "On second thought, don't. Hurts."

Her smirk hinted at an appreciation for sarcasm.

I tried to push backward but the door didn't budge.

"Um, it's a..." Mandi motioned to a sign on the door.

I clicked my tongue through gritted teeth, "Pull, got it." After a step forward, I rotated as someone entered so we did the awkward you go first, no you, dance.

Graceful? Nope, but I nailed Gracie fool.

45

"Tomorrow" – Marisha Wallace

The orchestra played the introduction, the curtain opened to the dormitory room, interpreters signed, and the audience laughed at the appropriate places. We're off to a good start.

With lighting and sound working per plan, Dervis slipped into the booth near the end of the first act. We wore matching black T-shirts with the motto ghosting in matte gray:

TECH MAGICIANS DON'T SHOW & TELL

I doubted his timing was coincidental since Chloe's big scene was next. We watched as she danced with a mop, tossed a bucket full of blue paper confetti "water drops" across the stage and belted out, "It's a Hard-Knock Life."

When the curtain closed to sweep and swap out props, he looked at me, "So, Willow?"

I grinned. He did too, then looked as the curtains opened to the dim dormitory room. The window glowed orange like a setting sun. A spotlight lit a lone chair. The crowd hushed as Mandi appeared, guitar in hand, and sat down. I leaned forward in anticipation. Her thumb strummed the first cord – twang. She frowned, tilting her ear closer. Even I could tell it didn't sound right. She pressed her palm on its rich, wooden body, stood, and gently set the guitar on the chair, then walked forward. Odd. That's not in the script.

Dervis overrode the program next to me, adjusting the spotlight to follow her while fading the lights on the side interpreters. He must be in on it.

Sitting on the edge of the stage, a golden halo surrounded her not-so-perfect messy bun, dirty low-top kicks dangled into the orchestra pit. The crowd murmured then hushed.

Mandi gave a subtle nod to the pit then tilted her head down. A piano played repeating cords that sounded like distant church bells introducing "Tomorrow."

I held my breath.

Eyes closed, she lifted a hand, index finger extended, and rotated it next to her head, the 'sun' sign and opened her mouth to sing and my heart stopped beating because –

NO SOUND WAS COMING OUT OF HER MIC!

My hands flew up, fingers spread bouncing off my forehead, eyes panicking checking levers and dials and lights that seemed to be working – WHAT THE HECK!

Dervis caught my wrist and pushed it down, whispering, "It's okay." My scrunched eyebrows relaxed. I exhaled as a dark shadow flew up the side aisle and sprinted to the booth.

Aspen's eyes were so large I could see white around dark irises. Her hands shot from mouth to ears as her head shook violently side to side.

I held up palms to press pause, and motioned to Dervis, sitting undisturbed next to me. Aspen's forehead creases melted; she crept in behind us.

Watching Mandi's hands write in the air, a visual version of the guitar string twang hit me. Mandi's nails are trim and natural, not opaque pink like the ones that mocked signing in the hallway on the first day of school.

Her hands flowed down tears from her cheeks for 'sorrow,' then an index finger lifted her 'chin' and then two fingers drew a semi-circle up for 'grin.' Her eyes opened and the sun rose in the perfect smile she sent to a small golden head sitting in the front row. Her sister.

My eyes blurred.

Mouth open for 'OOOOO,' one hand pulled the letter across her chest that expanded and decreased as if projected and held out loud. A closed fist thumbed under her chin and extended out twice for 'tomorrow,' and then she pushed out the two-finger and thumb 'I love you' sign to her sister with one more 'tomorrow.'

Other instruments joined the piano and the music swelled. Her gaze swept across the mesmerized audience. When Mandi's flawless face paused on the booth a hand squeezed my shoulder. I looked up to Aspen whose other hand covered her mouth to stifle a sob.

In three breathtaking stanzas, Mandi encouraged herself, then her sister, then everyone hanging on each loving word she painted in the air. On the final verse, Mandi rose and retreated, singing out loud through her mic in a clear, soft plea that grew into the final word held long and strong, her hands lifted above her head, then slowly falling as she and the window faded into darkness.

The entire audience stood as one. Dervis leaned forward maneuvering dials. "She needs to see this." He brought the theater lights up for intermission before closing the curtains so Mandi, standing alone in the tomb-like silence, perhaps wondering if she'd tanked the solo, could look over her shoulder to thousands of fingers fluttering like butterflies in a muted, standing jazz hands ovation.

"Oh my, oh my, oh my, someone deserves a hug." Aspen sniffed, then escaped to backstage before the crowd could rise, stretch their legs, and go wait in the women's restroom for ten minutes.

After the final act, the cast and crew sat on the stage apron to sing and sign "Tomorrow." Dervis told me Mandi had taught everyone to sign the song but only he and Ms. Davis knew she'd perform her solo without the guitar opening night. Interesting.

Mandi inadvertently made it possible for her envious understudy to replicate the crowd-pleasing performance sans guitar. That should make Chloe happy if anything short of switching bodies with Mandi could. Scanning to catch Chloe's reaction, I couldn't find her. Odd.

Later, Dervis and I stood beside our cars. I'd offered to give Aspen and Willow a ride home. He stayed to keep me company while I waited for them.

Aspen was frenetic as they approached, Willow saw Dervis and continued to the other side of my car.

"OMGoodness! Chloe got busted! Maybe," Aspen said.

"What do you mean?" I asked.

"Ms. Davis was talking to her behind the curtains. That's why she missed the bow, encore, the whole ending shebang."

"Didn't notice," Dervis said.

Aspen glanced from him to Willow to him, then me. "Better get a move on!"

Mandi's silent solo was such a huge hit, Ms. Davis asked her to repeat it at both Saturday performances. Following the final show, I grabbed a bottle of water as the cast and crew mingled on stage at the after-party. Dervis was talking to Ms. Davis, but tracking Willow in Aspen's wake as she moved like a speedboat through the crowd.

"Enough is enough. She waved anymore. Remember how Mandi's guitar sounded weird opening night? Turns out, Ms. Davis caught Chloe messing with it! I'd be furious! When the going gets tough, the tough need to plot dastardly revenge that reigns down terror on their oppressor to teach them a lesson," Aspen said.

"Don't hold back, how do you really feel?" Willow gave a slow, sarcastic double blink, and took a sip of her water.

Aspen ignored this, "She denied it, said she was trying to learn how to play, and bumped one of the pegs. Give me a break, on opening night? Ms. Davis didn't buy it and told Chloe to skip the encores so she blew off the cast party."

Crickets. Not going to lie, pretty sure no one cared.

"So! Big tourney tomorrow!" Aspen changed the subject.

"Are you going to be there?" Dervis asked her, glanced at me but quickly shifted his attention to Willow.

Atta boy!

"Yes, and Mandi wants to come too," Willow said. She waved over our shoulders, Dervis's head swiveled, Aspen clapped and Mandi excused herself from a gaggle of fangirls to join us.

"Fab-tab-ulous!" Aspen waited for Mandi to reach us. "What should we wear? I'll ask Ms. Davis if we can launch a raid on the costume storage."

"No, we're spectators not spectacles," Willow said.

"Don't be a fun sponge," Aspen said.

"Costumes?" Mandi asked.

"For the tourney. Hood told me he's dressing as Doc Holiday, and Krutch is wearing a shirt with bucking broncos. What about you, Dervis?"

Awkward pause, as he contemplated Willow's reaction?

"Maybe a saloon keeper with a vest, white shirt, and black tie," Willow said, her voice serene and not sarcastic.

"Sounds good," Dervis said, sounding relieved.

"O.K. Corral then! Will and I have different colored bandanas we can share, because after all, we're their posse. Is that okay with you, fun sheriff?" Aspen asked.

Willow conceded with a brief gaze upward followed by a deep sigh. A mischievous Krutch-killer smile on Mandi's face sealed the deal.

I set a Mandi pickup time of 9am. We'd catch Dervis and Hood Snap's doubles match first, then go to Krutch's singles' flight. Aspen danced off signing, "Tomorrow." Willow and Mandi followed her.

"What just happened?" Dervis asked.

Busted. "Well, I kind of asked Mandi if she wanted to go."

"Genius!" Dervis said.

"Going to give Krutch a heads-up?" I asked.

A devious one-sided grin grew as he shook his head side to side. "Not a chance."

46

"One Thing" – One Direction

I picked up Aspen and Willow first even though Mandi lived closer thinking it would be more comfortable. I was relieved when she climbed in back with Willow, because Aspen could co-pilot, navigate and fill air space with a monologue or music.

Mandi wore her tortoiseshell glasses, a white t-shirt and a pink jean skirt with the pink paisley bandana Aspen gave her tied around her neck. My bandana was sage green to 'make my eyes pop,' Willow's navy blue one matched her cardigan, and Aspen's was red to 'draw Hood's attention' to the bright cherry lipstick on her heart-shaped mouth.

Aspen fulfilled her assigned tasks with her usual exuberance which made the drive go by fast. After a rare moment of silence, Aspen looked at Mandi. "Krutch is positively brilliant, and brilliantly positive, except when he sees you and turns into Mr. Gloomy Gus. Why?"

"Asp!" Willow said, more like hissed.

Funny, and Willow's delivery is spot on.

"Will! Someone needs to be a buttinski or else these two sparkly star-crossed sweeties will be lost in space forever!" Aspen said, then cupped a hand around her mouth to whisper across the seatback. "I liked Krutch first, but realized he was moony for you and then fell head over twinkle toes for Hood."

Mandi's cheeks flushed to match the pink bandana.

"He's mad at me?" She asked into my rearview mirror.

"No," I said, shaking my head focusing on the road. "He doesn't get why you guys don't talk. I didn't tell him Chloe said we were dating."

"Hold your dang horses, Chloe said you and Krutch were together?" Aspen gasped. "What a low-down snake!"

"He'll be glad you're there, Mandi." I glanced in the mirror.

I hope! When did I get so reckless?

Her head tilted down and angled away, fingers combing through the blonde ponytail she pulled over her shoulder and wrapped under her chin.

"Don't worry. He's nutty peanut butter and you're his jam," Aspen said.

Checking the mirror again, I saw Willow reach over and tap Mandi's shoulder, "Dervis told me Krutch sat in the back row all three shows. It'll be okay."

How does she know that? Why didn't I?

From our hillside vantage point, we spotted Gunslinger Hood Snap dressed in black from cowboy hat to biker boots. He was a head taller than the men and women dressed in white slacks or knickers sporting newsboy caps and safari hats. Next to him, dapper Dervis wore a vest per Willow's suggestion with his grandfather's antique watch draped from buttonhole to pocket on a gold chain. Another quirky oddity that added to his unique character.

We spread a blanket out on the green manicured lawn under the Virginia bluebell-colored sky accented with white feathery wisps. Around us, spectators with colorful parasols and umbrellas reminded me of a Monet painting. Or was it a Manet? I leaned over to ask Willow, but she was explaining the croquet rules to Mandi in a soft voice. Her sketchbook lay on the blanket beside her.

Men's lacrosse fans cheered when gladiators smacked each other with their sticks. Croquet audiences, like theater attendees, applauded at appropriate times and hushed when players concentrated.

Our dynamic duo was eliminated in the semi-finals. They hustled up the hill with Aspen, who'd been filming her documentary by the match court.

"Missed Krutch's text. He's about to play in the final round," Dervis said. We grabbed our stuff and scrambled to the other side of the hill to the single's course.

Standing at ease with his final opponent, Krutch listened as the judge explained the championship rules. On his chest was a deputy sheriff star pinned to his short-sleeved bucking bronco print shirt. The holster slung around his hips housed his croquet mallet head; the handle angled down past his long shorts to token flip-flops.

"I see what you mean about costumes. Don't the other players mind?" Mandi asked, squinting as she adjusted her glasses on her nose.

I wondered if she wore the glasses because they were more comfortable than contacts, or if she was thinking back to when she and Krutch were kids.

"Nope! They love our guys and the 'youthful energy' they bring to the sport." Aspen smiled up at Hood Snap and squeezed his arm. "And Krutch is being recruited by serious and some not-so-serious colleges – much better fit if you ask me – so he's kind of a big deal, but you already knew that," Aspen said, giving Mandi a double elbow nudge.

"Look, they're starting," Willow said, diverting attention to the course.

"You draw, I'll shoot, partner!" Aspen said to her sister. "Hood, pretty please boost me into that tree down yonder? Want to start from a bird's eye view." She grabbed her GoPro and tugged him down the slope, leaving Dervis, Willow, Mandi and me to set up camp.

Watching the match was a blast. Krutch and his opponent were jovial and we could hear laughter, as he was both charming and respectful.

Equally entertaining was Aspen hanging off a branch, then stalking unobtrusively on foot, occasionally lying flat on her stomach shooting for the ball's perspective. Krutch tipped his hat to her at one point, so he saw some of us were here, just not all of us that were.

Observing Mandi watching Krutch, Dervis chatting up Willow, and Hood Snap assisting Aspen, I realized that I was the seventh wheel in this scenario, which was fine by me.

Dervis moved us closer to the course as Krutch hit his ball toward his opponent's which blocked his final task, the Rover hoop. It found its mark and stayed in contact, setting up the chance to drive his and send the other ball in any direction.

Again, Dervis ushered us, this time next to Krutch as he focused down, placed his left flip-flop foot on his ball, and prepared to do his signature send-away shot. At the height of his backswing, he turned his face, saw us, and jerked up just as the mallet swung down and struck. Crack!

"Owuuh-shhhh!" Krutch dropped his mallet, sat down and rolled back clutching his injured foot and setting in motion an EMT-worthy chain of events.

"We need ice!" I looked around.

"Here," Willow tipped her large lemonade onto her hand and strained it through her fingers.

"Use this." Mandi tore off her bandana and cupped it in her hands. Willow dumped the ice into the scarf, and we ran to Krutch. Mandi kneeled next to him. "Sit up." Her voice was quiet but firm.

He froze mid-roll, opened wide eyes in disbelief, and watched her gently place the ice packet on his swollen ankle.

Avoiding their 'moment,' I concentrated on securing the ice-packed handkerchief to his ankle with my green bandana. A giant shadow clouded over us, and the red and blue scarves fluttered down as well.

Dervis hurried over. "You've been granted a five-minute medical time out. Think you can finish?"

Krutch nodded, looking at Mandi with a dazed grin.

Awkward silence.

"Man, oh man!" Aspen said from behind her mini cam.

Willow reached over to push the camera down. "Let's get some more lemonade."

"Sounds good," I said, standing up.

"We'll bring you some," Aspen said over her shoulder as Willow pushed her away. Dervis and Hood Snap followed.

Sipping lemonade next to the concession stand Aspen gushed, "How awesome was that!"

"Krutch getting hurt or you turning crazed paparazzi?" Willow asked, her eyelids half-closed, fluttered, then finished in her classic slow, sarcastic double blink.

"No, silly. The adorable, re-meet-cute moment. I should bury it in a time capsule for their kids to dig up for the 50th wedding anniversary." She took a sip and passed her cup to Hood Snap.

"He's okay. Krutch is a finesse player. It was a tap to put his opponent out of position, not a smack to drive her into next week." Dervis looked at his watch. "Better head back, it's play or forfeit."

"Shoot!" Aspen scampered back to the course.

The match had resumed. His opponent's ball was at least two hits away. Krutch used his mallet up-side-down as a crutch to limp to his ball.

"Ironic," Hood Snap said, not needing to elaborate.

I smirked.

Willow delivered a drink to Mandi on the sideline.

Krutch had an easy shot through the Rover hoop to peg out. Aspen was again on her belly recording. The crowd applauded when his ball clicked the final peg.

Afterward, at the award ceremony, his spry, elderly opponent extended her hand. "Congratulations on your skillful win." She winked and added, "And your talented medical team."

Krutch gave her his 'aww shucks smile,' and sneaked a peek at us in general and Mandi in particular.

I suggested we leave Mandi and Krutch at the food tent and drive back to pick them up. Mandi agreed; I'd yet to hear Krutch utter a word, with or without any of his goofy accents.

Aspen, Hood Snap, Willow and Dervis were in good spirits as we walked to the parking lot.

"That look on his face when he first saw her? Glorious," Aspen sighed, danced two steps forward, then spun back to Hood Snap.

"And the silence since, priceless," Dervis said. "If I'd known how to shut him up, I'd have dropped the Mandi bomb months ago. Thanks, Gracie."

"Not me, Willow deserves the credit."

"I encouraged her after you suggested it," Willow said.

"Thanks just the same, and for coming," he said to me, then Willow. We split off to find cars in no particular hurry to give the two reunited friends space to reconnect.

47

"Never Gonna Give You Up" – Rick Astley

"Oh, oh, oh, I love this oldies station!" Aspen squealed, cranked the volume and bounced to the steady beat. After hearing the chorus once, she sang along acting out the lyrics, shaking her head while pushing her hands up, down and pumping them back and forth as if running. Next, she twisted her fists near her temples as if crying, waved goodbye and crisscrossed hands in front of her for the 'never' lyrics.

Goofball gave me an idea to tuck away for later.

In my rearview mirror, Willow and Mandi's chins nodded in unison, similar smiles resting on profiles facing opposite directions. Green-leafed trees blurred along the highway as the car weaved through the rolling hills on our way home.

Willow's sketchpad lay open on her lap, the white page empty, pencil poised but motionless. Awaiting inspiration or lost in reflection?

***

Over the next few weeks, it was a relief to leave the theatrical dramas and enjoy the comedies acted out by the eclectic cast of characters I now call friends. They balanced the uncertainties surrounding what university to attend, which STEM program to major in, and whose team to play for, so I could focus on finishing the lacrosse season strong and keep all options open.

Our team remained undefeated and was the number one seed going into playoffs. The number two seed was Charlotte and Lanie's team with only one loss to us, so we'd go up through different flights.

Antsy, Coach told us to take one game at a time, as did theirs I bet. Both won in the semi-finals, so we'd meet in the championship game. Clash of the Titans 2.0.

Nerves on edge –Tuesday before the championship, this:

(Army;-)
Big game!

> *(me)*
> Woohoo

(Army;-)
Tough team to beat twice

Ya think?

> *(me)*
> MOTO

Master of the Obvious. See if he gets it.

(Army;-)
Ye. Ha

He got it.

(Army;-)
Got someone for
you to meet

Why?

> *(me)*
> Okay

(*Army;-*)
Bringing her to
game

HER?

>   (*me*)
>   Really

(*Army;-*)
Ye. Heard VT n UVA
scouts will be there

>   (*me*)
>   Greaaaat

(*Army;-*)
Get psyched.

You get psyched

>   (*me*)
>   Ye. Ha

(*Army;-*)
Get it

>   (*me*)
>   Will. Do

What the heck? Who the heck? Classmate? Wife? No, not a wife. Pretty sure he can't get married right now. What did Sofi say about him dating? Time to video chat.

"'Sup, Buttercup?" Sofi's face popped in sideways on the screen. Ponytail spilled to the side as an arm stretched over her ear.

"Argh," I said.

"Uh-oh." She turned her desk chair/pseudo ballet bar backward, straddled it and rested her forearms on the back. "Go on."

"Ian texted he is coming to the playoff game."

"Woohoo, Dawg. Get it!" She air fist-bumped.

"Um. He's bringing a 'her' to meet me."

Pause. Arms dropped and lips scrunched to the left. After a thoughtful moment. "Hmm."

"Beep, beep, beep, is that the sound of a dump truck I hear? Then again, since we never had an actual date, I can't get dumped, right?"

"Inconceivable. Another conundrum."

Despite lack of insight, seeing and hearing her improved my mood. "Look who's using big brain words."

"Yep. Speaking of big brains what's going on with Dervis, et al?"

"Oh wow. Tons." I data dumped the diabolical Chloe reveal along with my successful matchmaker skills regarding Willow/Dervis and Mandi/Krutch.

"Kicking backstabbing Chloe butt and matchmaking like it's your job! Well done, you!"

I bowed my head. "How could I not, under your tutelage."

She fluttered her eyelashes and flipped her wrist to wave me off. "Stop, please."

She cracks me up.

"One more thing." Double blink.

"Go on."

"Circling back to Ian."

I groaned.

"Why bring a girl back to his hometown to watch a high school girls' lacrosse game? Doesn't track. I bet it's West Point's lacrosse coach, and he told her Navy's interested so she wants to check you out."

I sat up. That makes sense.

"So, now that's solved, what else?" Sofi blinked.

I shrugged. "Pretty much covers it. Except for how to beat a tough team twice."

"No worries. You put the pro in improvise."

"Since when?" I asked, my sigh ended with a hum.

"Always." She thumped her fist over her heart, then held out two fingers for 'peace out,' and the screen went dark.

***

Coach decided to pull a couple of JV players up to give them post-season experience and asked us tri-captains for our opinions. It was unanimous: Zoë and Emma.

We filled them in on Lanie in goal and warned them not to show too much in warmups because she'd have scouts looking for 'tells.'

"Charlotte's goal tallies slowed down and assists were up the second half of the season," Jaz said.

"Maybe she's nice now and has learned to share," I said.

"Doubtful. Heard their coach told her to pass or ride the bench. She's behind in assists, but is two goals ahead of you," Harley added.

"It's her last chance to shine for recruiters," Jaz said.

Mine too. "Weird no one's picked her up," I said.

"Would you want to coach that hot mess?" Harley asked.

Jittery, nerves on edge, team practices leading up to Saturday's game were a cluster of epic disasters. Dropped balls, failed pick-ups and missed passes. We needed to calm down and pump up our teammates so I borrowed a page from Aspen's playbook, shared my idea with Jaz and Harley, and we put it into action during warmups on Friday.

Jaz and Harley started per usual, lip-synching with their sticks as mics, but when I channeled Sofi, jumped up and jammed on my stick like it was a guitar, the team went crazy. Following that practice was productive, stress-free and fun.

We were ready.

My stomach growled when a delicious aroma of cheesy, night-before-competition pasta greeted my nose.

Mom and Dad were excited when I told him both Tech and Virginia coaches and maybe another, would be at the game tomorrow night.

"Coach Sinclair is coming?" Dad asked.

I winced. "Forgot about Navy." Four potential coaches. I'd lost my appetite.

48

"Be Legendary" – Pop Evil

The music blasted our warmup tunes as we burst out of the locker room.

"The game is afoot!" Aspen shouted to me, channeling Enola Holmes, she jumped up and down holding on to the metal handrail in front of the bleachers. I saluted our posse as we jogged past them to drop off gear.

They were here. For me.

I scanned the crowd above the student section and saw my folks... then Ian. Wait a second – in between him and his dad, aka Coach MacGavin, was an athletic, young woman wearing aviators. Her wavy shoulder-length light brown hair shimmered under the stadium lights. She kind of looked like the West Point coach I'd Googled. Shoot. Who is she? Why is she sitting between them? Forget her and focus.

I shoved Ian back into his who knows what the heck he is compartment and escaped into game mode.

Team captains met again center field for the coin toss.

"Looks like Ian brought a girlfriend to watch you lose. Poor Rogue. Yesterday's news," Charlotte said, with a sneer.

Nope. No change. Still a jerk.

"I know, right? So pretty. Good for him," I said.

Her mouth dropped opened, then shut, without a word.

Glorious.

She and Lanie won the coin toss and picked which side and we went back to our bench and huddled up.

"Pirates! Oooh argh on three! One... Two... Three..."

"OOOH ARGH!" The team shouted.

Game on.

My heart beat in my throat as Jaz froze like a statue for the draw. When the referee blew the whistle the yellow ball arched in slow motion across the indigo sky then spun to real-time as my stick instinctively snatched it and sprinted to goal. From that moment on the game moved on fast forward.

As before, we traded and defended goals. At half-time, we strategized in the locker room. We knew they'd adjust their play, so we did. Attacks play on the offensive two-thirds of the field, Defenders, the defensive two-thirds, and Midfielders get to go where ever the heck they want. I love that. Coach gave me license to switch from attack to middie on the fly to mix it up. We'd worked on different scenarios shifting multiple players, including Zoë and Emma.

Third-quarter when we modified, they countered, fourth they switched from a zone defense to man-to-man, more like men-to-man, as three players stuck to me like Gorilla glue.

Minutes ticked down to seconds on the clock. Thirty to be exact. Our ball. One last goal or go to overtime.

Time out. I sprinted to the sideline. Coach told me to implement the least expected, and riskiest play. Bandit.

I found Zoë. "It's time," I said, picking up a water bottle.

"Okaaay," Zoë said, pulling her goggles down from her forehead. Her eyes wide.

"You ready?" I squirted water into my mouth.

"Born ready."

I choked and coughed, spewing water.

"Match sticks!" Jaz shouted.

"Light it!" Harley shouted.

"Get it," I told Zoë.

Together, we popped our sticks to ignite the bonfire.

Control the center of the board.

I lined up left, Jaz, center middie, nodded to me and prepared to take the draw. Zoë jogged to right Attack. The whistle blew, but instead of coming in my direction, it went opposite toward Zoë, who bobbled but scooped it up.

Hang on, you've got this!

Drawing my oppressive guardians toward the sideline, over my shoulder I watched Zoë cut diagonal, stick in right hand, her eyes on me. Holding my stick out, I shook it to signal for the ball. At the top of the white-lined arc, she pump-faked the pass then drove straight to goal. Her defender let her go by instead of taking the penalty, probably banking on her inexperience. Zoë switched hands and fired top corner above Lanie's shoulder. Nothing but net.

Zoë dropped her stick as if it'd burned her.

BZZZZZZZZZZ!

Red match sticks rose up and rained down, bouncing off the green turf. Zoë flew and launched onto Jaz and me, and the rest of the team enveloped us to create a human ball of sweat, tears, and screams.

Postgame, Lanie squinted and nodded her head as we double-fist bumped, "You told your clone to hide her left."

I shrugged. "All's fair in lax and war."

She nodded. "Yeah, right."

"Are you playing next year?"

"Yep, William and Mary. You?"

"Hope so. Not sure where." I looked at the stands.

"Good luck with that, let me know where you land."

"Will do. Take it easy."

Both the rowdy team cooldown jog and salute to our fans were bittersweet. The realization hit me, this was the last time I'd play with the first and in front of the second. I blinked away unexpected tears and waved to Aspen and my posse, then let my gaze wander up the bleachers. I smiled at my beaming folks then shifted higher to see Coach MacGavin talking with a couple of strangers. Ian and mystery woman nowhere in sight.

Zoë sprinted, hugged Emma then grabbed and squeezed my arms, "Thanks for letting me take the shot!" She let go and waved her hands in the air. "It was so amazing! Like super-slow motion awesome. Did you see me pretend to mess up picking up the ground ball?"

"Convincing," I said, "They'll know better next year."

"We'll keep 'em guessing, right Coach?"

Coach Gwen nodded.

"See ya!" Zoë grabbed her gear and took off. I watched her and Emma cross the deep green turf under the overheads.

"Going to miss this," slipped quietly out.

"Yeah," Coach said, wistfully, "But you've got a lot of play ahead of you."

I hope. "Maybe. Wasn't my best showing tonight, but props to you. First-year coaching and you took it all," I said.

"You played a role in that..." she paused, her attention shifted over my shoulder. "Look who's here..."

I did. Ian, and the mystery woman, aviators pushed back on her head, her grin oddly familiar. She was a little shorter than Ian and obviously athletic as she cut across the track – lifting her hands? Is she going to hug me? I froze.

"Congrats!" Mystery woman said, embracing Coach.

"Right back at you, First Lieutenant!"

Confused. Ian's a plebe cadet.

Coach released the woman. "This can't be, little Ian?"

Little Ian?

"Yep. Howdy, Gwen." Ian grinned, then looked from her to me to mystery woman, "Gracie, this is Ellen, my sister."

Sister. Ellen. Swimmer. Duh. Her shiny hair should have been a clue – chlorinated highlights.

On auto-pilot, I stuck out my hand and made eye contact. "Nice to meet you." She gave mine a firm shake then dropped it but held my gaze, "I hear you're something of a GOAT."

I blushed, "Not even."

"My dad thinks you may be, no offense Gwen."

"None taken, those days are in the past."

"I know another goat, his name's Bill," Ellen said.

"Okay..." I gave Ian a supercilious eyebrow.

"Ellen swam for Navy," he said.

First Lieutenant. Bill the Goat. USNA mascot.

***

"Ellen, Coach MacGavin's daughter, took a unique route, a special request for permission to commission into Medical Service Corps and go to a physical therapy doctoral program," I explained to my folks. They'd invited my posse to celebrate with ice cream and we were last in line watching everyone order.

"Kids at rival military academics, I bet that makes for a rowdy Army-Navy football game day," Dad said.

"It's too bad they couldn't come with us," Mom said.

I shrugged. "Ellen has to report to her new duty station and Ian's driving back to New York early tomorrow."

"Bummed! Was hoping to hang with him," Jaz said, nudging me.

I winced. Me too.

Jaz changed the subject. "Thanks for treating all of us!"

"Anytime," Mom said.

It reminded me of sitting in the background watching my folks enjoy Jason and Sofi's continuous flow of friends, and how the atmosphere and noise level changed when they left for school and I retreated to my silent books.

49

"Kokomo" – Leo metal version

Saturday, I gave Sofi play-by-plays of both the game and meeting Ellen. She cheered listening to the exciting rivalry takedown, applauded my sharing the glory with Zoë, and then interrogated me about Ian's actions and my reactions.

"When he texted he'd be at playoffs, I was excited, but then he had someone for me to meet, so I was confused. It turned out to be his sister, and the real reason he was back was for her promotion ceremony. She's a USNA alum, so, maybe, he figured she could answer questions since I haven't made a decision." I paused, my sigh ended in a hum.

"You know who you sound like?"

I snorted. "You. A couple years ago."

She laughed. "Yep. 'To be, or not to be.' You'll figure it out sooner or later, most likely later, because for now, the academy owns him. That's why you should do ROTC at UVA or Tech. You get the normal fun college experience, a stipend, and graduate the same rank as the academy kiddos." Double blink. "So, what's next?"

I shrugged. "Pick a college, I suppose."

"No. I mean end of senior year fun stuff. When's prom?"

"No clue."

"Are you going?"

"Not sure."

"What will you wear?"

"To the event I may not attend?"

"Permission granted to raid my closet: recycle, reduce, repurpose. Save the bees."

"How would wearing a worn dress save the bees?"

"How should I know? You're the nature girl."

***

(*dervis*)
Should I ask
Willow to prom?

> (*me*)
> Yep

(*dervis*)

Prom?
```
       *
 *         *
 \_(")_/
  [ *]
 _/   \_
```

> (*me*)
> Nerd. No.
> In person.

(*dervis*)
    :-|

"You're awfully cheeky today," I said to Aspen as she bounced up to me in the parking lot after school.

"Beg your pardon, I'm awfully cheeky every day!"

"Truth," Hood Snap said, his long stride matched three of her skips.

"Guess double what?" Aspen asked, standing on tip-toes, mini-clapping her fingertips.

"What, what?"

"Dervis met Willow in the hallway with a bouquet of Tootsie Pops to ask her to prom!" She placed her hand next to her mouth and whispered, "A little bird may have hinted they're her favorite." She dropped her hand, "Then Krutch offered another bouquet made up of strands of black licorice, yuck, of all things, tied with a red ribbon, and asked Mandi in a pompous British accent, 'Would you do me the honor?' But it gets even better! Mandi plucked a piece out, tore a bite off, and answered in a hilarious cockney accent, 'Be my pleasure, Gov'nor.' Adorable! A *My Fair Lady* moment minus the creepy, double-decade, sugar-daddy age difference."

"What about you two?" I asked.

"Oh, I asked him ages ago," Aspen said, waving her hand about in the air. "Technically he should have because he's a junior and I'm only a freshwoman." She winked.

Hood Snap grinned.

"The theme's Tropical Nights, "It'll be epic! Steampunk Pirate Prom, whaaaaaaat?" She danced her version of a jig.

"I'll bite. What?" I asked.

"We'll borrow *The Crucible* costumes! Because Willow designed 'em and my mom sewed 'em."

"Why steampunk costumes?" Why any costumes?

"Because, why the heck not?"

What's not to like about this girl? Absotootley nothing.

***

Sofi will be proud. I went big instead of staying home with the steampunk theme: Vintage leather aviator helmet, old school goggles, Sofi's white puffy peasant blouse, a wide brown leather laced corset belt, Mom's riding breeches and knee-high equestrian boots.

Watching Mandi and Krutch, Willow and Dervis, and Aspen and Hood Snap made me the seventh wheel until Jaz and Harley grabbed me to line dance with an eclectic group of athletes, band members and theater friends that had merged over the past year.

When the metal version of Kokomo cued up, I found myself doing an awkward Hula dance in between the never-awkward Sienna and Michael! So fun.

I took a break and joined my posse who were in the middle of an intense philosophical discussion.

"You're turning this conversation into a confrontation," Krutch said in his gentleman's drawl.

"And you're a hyper dufus, power-dweeb," Dervis said.

"What's up?" I asked.

"Krutch thinks that if Hood were a vampire, and he had a mirror on the inside of his adorable pirate eye patch," Aspen flipped it up, then folded it back in place, patting his cheek. "He could look into the mirror and see behind himself."

"Interesting hypotenuse," I said, joking, grasping my chin to ponder. "As a self-proclaimed expert in vampire lore, do we all agree that their reflections do not appear in mirrors?" Looking around the table I collected affirmative nods except for Dervis, who appeared deep in thought. At last, he sighed heavily and with reluctance agreed. "Well then, the definitive answer, is yes." I love these weirdos.

Aspen had turned Willow's Assorted Tootsie Pop bouquet into clever corsages and boutonnieres for the posse, and as the dance progressed the suckers were taken apart, unwrapped and devoured. Willow then folded the different colored wrappers into a flock of origami cranes and set them around the sand and palm tree centerpiece at our table. Tropical delight.

Last call for group photos was announced. We scrambled to get to the pirate ship backdrop and found the Mannequins sans Mandi plus Chloe and their dates. The ladies wore the traditional prom garb, dresses like those in Sofi's closet, with the guys as accessories in tuxedos and matching ties and vests.

Krutch dove into the props bin and pulled out a sea captain's jacket to put over his pink flamingo embroidered shirt, Dervis tucked a foam sword under each suspender strap, and Hood Snap perched a stuffed parrot on his shoulder next to the eye patch.

We girls were already set. Mandi had added a laced-up black corset over her sweet Sarah Goode *Crucible* outfit, Aspen wore a short jacket with a ruffled mini skirt over knee-length pantaloons, and Willow was elegant in a black netted face veil, elbow-length gloves, and multiple strands of black pearls over the lacy dress she'd worn for our mystery game.

From the sneer on Chloe's face it was obvious she didn't agree with our fashion choices. Madeline on the other hand, was ecstatic when she saw us. Rushing over after their pics, she reached out hands to Mandi, who grasped them in hers.

I tried not to listen or watch them, but I'm human.

"Hey you, you look happy."

Mandi glanced at Krutch goofing with his chums, then back to Madeline.

"Hey you. I am."

"It's about time. Looks good on you. And this corset? Killer. You go girl," Madeline said.

The tired photographer laughed when she turned and saw us. After a long night of typical prom poses, she waved us to the set. When I grabbed one of Dervis's swords, smacked his arm, and challenged him to a swashbuckler slash lightsaber duel, she shot continuous action pics as we fenced to a hysterical play-by-play commentary from Krutch while the rest of our motley crew shouted hardy 'oohgs,' 'arghs' and 'avast ye bandits.'

***

Sunday afternoon, Roscoe and Mallory took me for an easy run on the neighborhood trail while I reflected back on last night's crazy prom, and looked ahead to graduation in a couple days. It was hard to believe the school year I couldn't wait to be 'one and done with' was over. My cell buzz startled me. It was strapped to my upper arm so I tapped my right earbud to answer not knowing who was calling.

"Halsted?" A gruff voice growled.

Coach MacGavin. I stopped, almost tripping over a branch. "Yes, Coach. On a run." Such a suckup. I joked, "Trying to get in shape." Shaking my head, I inhaled.

"About time," he chuckled. "Got some news."

Holding my breath in, I watched the pups tree a squirrel.

"Both Tech and UVA scouts were impressed, and asked if you'd heard from admissions."

I exhaled. "Not yet, soon I hope. Was a little worried."

"About getting in?"

"No, about the game. Wasn't my best." I kicked a rock off the trail.

"Don't beat yourself up. Coach Sinclair appreciated your obvious leadership qualities, so much so, she wants you to visit a team practice this Thursday."

"This week?"

"It's a busy time. Think about it. Send her an email."

"Thanks, Coach."

"Sure. Now quit dawdling and do something."

"Will do, Sir."

His deep snort sign-off made me smack my forehead.

Dad was playing chess with Croc when I got home. Originally, "Crockpot," because his name, Stew, brought to mind a 'crockpot.' But over the years it had shortened because he didn't mind it and didn't do anything stupid to earn a worse one. Dad's was Snake; he didn't like it but wasn't as savvy so it stuck and we still didn't know how he got it. Sofi was relentless trying to get Croc to tell, but he'd say, "Mum's the word because your Mum would kill me if I told you."

Croc was retired military and flew for an airline now. That, however, hadn't stopped Sofi, who thought as a retired captain he could officiate Joan and Jason's wedding. When he informed her he couldn't, she got him certified online in Colorado. He got such a kick out of it, and her, he agreed.

I sat down on the ottoman and studied the chessboard.

"What'd ya think, Spitfire?" Croc's nickname for me, also a British WWII single-seat fighter aircraft in the Royal Air Force.

"No helping," Dad said.

"Wouldn't dream of it." I waited for a minute to add, "Coach MacGavin called, Tech and UVA are interested, and Navy invited me to meet the team Thursday."

Dad's attention shifted to me. "What do you think?"

"Can't do Thursday, we're flying to Colorado."

"Check with Coach Sinclair about another day."

"Tuesday is graduation and Wednesday is Mom's gallery show."

"You can fly with me Friday. We could leave first thing, gas up in Illinois, then touch down in Colorado Springs late afternoon," Croc said.

"In your Diamond?" I asked. The sweet single-engine airplane he leased with a couple of pilots.

"Sure," Croc said. "Scheduled it for the weekend."

"Can I?" I asked Dad. My heart skipped a beat.

"Go clear it with Mom," Dad said.

"Check," Croc said.

"Check, what?"

"Check, you." Croc pointed to the board.

"Not so fast," Dad leaned forward, studied the board then blocked and the game continued as I flew to Mom's studio.

50

"Shower the People" – James Taylor

Our senior class sat alphabetically in red caps and gowns in two sections facing the temporary stage on the gym floor. Some paid attention to the inspirational stories, others scanned the stands for friends and family, and a few nodded off. Floral perfumes and sport deodorant aftershave combos permeated the warm air.

Ms. Davis sat on stage in the section reserved for favorite teachers. She wore the traditional black cap and gown, but instead of her curriculum-colored sash she sported a scarlet and gold Gryffindor scarf.

When I walked across the stage to pick up my diploma, she made a funny face. I swooshed an index finger and mouthed, "Wing-gardium Levi-o-sa."

She grabbed her cap and pretended to struggle to keep it from rising off of her head.

I'm going to miss her crazy positivity.

Last up, Sienna and Michael were our chosen speakers. They walked up opposing stairs and met at the microphone.

"We know everyone is ready to celebrate, so instead of writing a speech, we're going to let this song do the talking, while Mandi interprets for us." She waved to Mandi who was already on her way up the stairs – her sleek, blonde hair gathered in a low ponytail at the neckline of a sleeveless blue shift. Elegant and perfect, as was the smile she shared with Sienna and Michael.

Both discarded caps and gowns to reveal Sienna's sparkly red-fringed dress and Michael's striped pirate shirt and black slacks. We erupted in shouts and whistles as the upbeat, "Can't Hold Us" began. The crowd clapped to the beat as Sienna and Michael exploded into a fast-paced salsa routine, interpreting the lyrics into moves as Mandi tried to keep up with the signing.

Their bodies flowed wicked fast to the frenetic rhythm. Sienna shimmied, spun out and back, then together they wove in and out around the stage. Near the end, Michael lifted her to sit on his shoulder so she could 'burst' through Macklemore's invisible ceiling. She dropped into a cradle in his arms, then popped out to land and high-five Mandi after the rapid-fire words gave way to instrumentals. Sienna and Michael then split down the side stairs and grabbed the closest grad at each end of the front row to lead us in a rowdy, celebratory dance line. Led out by two of my good friends, I enjoyed the moment with fellow classmates, now chums.

***

Mom left early to finish setting up for her show at the Peaceful Tea Gallery. I watched her 'eye crinkles smile' when Dad surprised her by wearing the paint-splattered light blue oxford she'd painted in for years. We'd washed and paired it with an Escher print tie featuring bright red and blue- gray birds merging together in opposite directions of flight, as my folks had for much of their married life: Dad deployed around the world, Mom nurtured three children at home.

The show featured some of her landscapes and all of the feels, especially when my posse arrived. After greeting them, I observed as they wandered off in pairs to view Mom's art.

Krutch snuck glances at Mandi's profile in front of a pair of cardinals perched in a golden maple with a chorus of red and orange oaks, green pines and deep purple plums.

Dervis and Willow's heads tilted slightly toward each other as they studied the misty fantasy world where leaves swirled around buried hydrangeas and the frost-covered tree, whose boney fingers disappeared into a melancholy fog.

At the next painting, Aspen hugged Hood Snap's arm and waved at the red barn standing on the snowy hill and then circled her palm up to the immense, dark gray sky.

Sienna and Michael's animated hands discussed the painting where dark trees, no longer bare, were speckled with tiny purple buds. Impatient white snow drops and bright pink camellia reached out of dormant beds and eager green tips peeked out of the last islands of snow.

Jaz stood with Harley in front of the work-in-progress they'd seen, the sun-drenched Italian hillside vineyard, and admired the beautiful rose bushes and artichoke plants at the end of each row protecting the grapevines from insects.

I wandered ahead to the last painting, one I'd never seen. The beach scene captured a young girl with windblown hair running barefoot in the sand racing her shadow as waves erased footprints behind her. A long-sleeved white shirt billowed behind like a cape; her outstretched arms prepared to take off with the flock of seagulls that rose before her. Next to it, a small white card read:

Testing her wings (Not For Sale)

My phone buzzed. Startled, I pulled it out of my pocket.

(*Army;-*)
How's it going?

> (*me*)
> Good. At my mom's
> gallery show

(*Army;-*)
Cool.
Video chat?

For real?

> (*me*)
> Sure

I stared at my cell, waiting. It buzzed a couple minutes later, I accepted the call, because, who wouldn't? Ian's gorgeous grin appeared. "Hey. Sorry for the delay. Reception is sketchy on The Point. Had to search for a hot spot."

He definitely succeeded.

"Who is it?" Jaz had snuck up on me.

"Ian," I said, my eyes wide, I held it up so she could see.

"Army! This is Jaz. Let me introduce you to the posse." She grabbed it and was off as I stood stunned with my ears burning. Ten minutes later she returned, fanned her face and mouthed, "WOW."

"That was fun. What are you looking at?" Ian asked.

"Don't end a sentence with a preposition." Deja vu.

"Who are you, the grammar sheriff?"

Nice comeback. Change subject.

"A beach scene."

"Let me see."

I punched the symbol to flip the camera view.

"Is that you?"

"Apparently."

"Thought so. Recognize the wild hair."

I blushed, thinking of our selfie post. "Going to watch Navy practice tomorrow."

"Whaaat?'

"Yep."

"Let me know how it goes."

"Will do."

I heard a shout behind him. He turned to acknowledge. "Gotta bounce." His face disappeared.

"Seems like a good bloke," Hood Snap said, clearing his throat.

"If by a good bloke, you mean a smokin' hot, sweetheart, gentleman, then yeah, he's okay," Jaz said.

"Who's up for ice cream? Dervis is buying," Krutch said.

"Why me?" Dervis asked, incredulous.

"To celebrate your Best Buy Geek Squad promotion," Hood Snap said.

"You got a promotion? Sweet! Congrats!" Aspen said.

"I'll catch up, thanks for coming," I said.

"It was our pleasure viewing your Mum's works of art," Krutch said.

As they walked away I heard Hood Snap say, "'Earth' without 'art' is just, 'eh.'"

Dervis responded, "'Fart' is mostly 'art.'"

"Mine are," Mandi said, with a nonchalant shrug.

The guys stopped and stared with open mouths while Aspen burst out laughing. Willow locked arms with Mandi and they exited together.

51

"Hit Me With Your Best Shot" – Pat Benatar

I dropped Mom and Dad off at Baltimore BWI for their flight to Colorado, then drove south to Annapolis. Perplexed, wondering why I'm considering an academy knowing how restrictive it is to one's life? Ian's life? I should have looked into ROTC like Sofi and Jason had. By the time I showed my I.D. card at the USNA gate I was convinced this wasn't the right fit for me.

Then I observed the team practice. No evidence of rival high school drama queens, instead, seasoned athletes performing quick draws, accurate passes, clean catches, generous assists and a butt-ton of rocket shots on goal.

After practice, Coach introduced me. A few midshipmen stuck around to chat, a few were from military families like me, and used to moving around. Others came from private school backgrounds, and appreciated the regimented lifestyle. All of them sung Coach's praises, about her work ethic and drive for them to succeed as a team as well as individuals.

She knew my ACL history and was willing to take me on. I had a decision to make with a drop deadline looming large, six days from now.

Time to oodaloop (observe, orient, decide, act, loop).

***

Croc picked me up at 5 am and we were at the airport with the pre-flight check completed by 6. I stowed my lax gear because Sofi had texted me to bring it. Mom took my wedding stuff so I could travel light.

The interior of the DA40 NG was simple, sleek and comfortable. We sat side by side, me on the right, each of us with a control stick between our knees. Croc told me to handle it like an egg, meaning, don't grip too tight as it took only the slightest nudge to maneuver. I studied the two screens and quizzed Croc about the switches, dials, and crisp electronics display. So cool.

The turbo-charged engine took us up to cruise at 9,500 feet and was quieter than expected. I enjoyed listening to air traffic chatter on the headphones. The flight required a refueling stop mid-trip; I was surprised that an hour and a half had gone by so fast. Croc switched off the autopilot and hand-flew us into the tiny Willard Airport in Champaign, Illinois. The runway was so narrow it looked like we were landing on a two-lane highway. I held my breath until we touched down and taxied in.

We grabbed a quick bite while refueling then took off on the second leg. Visibility through the large canopy had been incredible, but when the Rocky Mountains came into view, they took my breath away.

Croc warned about drafts coming off of the mountains as we began our descent. He coached me to radio in, *"TOWER, VICTOR ZERO ZERO SEVEN BRAVO, AT THE INITIAL, FULL STOP."* I smiled, 007– really? Thinking Bond, James Bond, shakin' not stirred, just as we hit turbulence. The tower's calm response gave me goosebumps and I exhaled slowly when we touched down smooth as icing on a cake.

My cell buzzed. Sofi. "Yel-low," I answered.

"Dad is waiting for you guys in the parking lot! Hustle! We've got a pickup game with the Buffs and it's gonna be spicy!" Sofi said, then hung up.

"Dad's here to pick us up," I said to Croc. He'd finished signing out and had grabbed our gear.

"Ready when you are, Spitfire."

"Is that my call sign now?" I asked.

"Do you like it?"

"Not one bit."

"Well then, Spitfire it is." He chuckled.

I grinned. Wait until I tell Sofi. She's going to pitch a fit because he calls her Squirt.

CU's Coach Cori had arranged with the president of the local youth league for her team to hold a clinic at the district stadium the week before the wedding, so we got to use the stadium and press box sound system. When we arrived, Joan Jett's "I Love Rock 'N Roll" was playing. I geared up to jog onto the turf.

They'd split up the Buff's team, with Dad coaching Sofi in goal, Jason at long pole D, and Sofi's honey Alex at attack. Cori coached the Buffs with Joan at middie and her brother Jon, the other long pole D, playing for the Buffs to make it even since women don't use long poles on defense.

After studying the field, I decided to counter Alex at attack and play against my siblings with Joan and her brother, who I never met but instantly bonded with, much to the delight of our referee, Shelley. Game on!

Too much fun. Dishing up incredibly fast action lacrosse, with a hilarious side of goofing around and showboating craziness, thanks in part to the guys and their antics. We loved it. Shelley, Cori, and the CU Buffs loved it. Dad on the sidelines and Mom in the stands with Joan's dad loved it.

Pat Benatar was singing, "Hit Me With Your Best Shot" when Joan got the draw and we flew toward Sofi in goal. "Fire away!" she shouted, which sounds like "fruwir waw" through a mouthguard. Joan pumped faked right, switched to left, and passed to me. I caught and put it away top left corner as Sofi screamed, stomped and pitched a diva fit, then laughed and pulled Joan and me in for a goalie padded embrace.

"Illegal group hug without me!" Shelley shouted, as she pelted us with penalty flags, and then joined for the quad hug.

Mom and Dad ordered pizza and salad into the hotel lobby for the unofficial rehearsal dinner because the lacrosse game was the only practice we were doing for the wedding tomorrow. Booyah!

I showered without washing my hair because it takes forever to dry, threw on the super comfy black and gold CU Buff flannel jammies Joan had given us for bridesmaid gifts, and crawled into the double I was sharing with Sofi. She and Shelley wore samzies pjs and were going over details for tomorrow's pre-wedding 'Morning of Beautification.' Yawn.

"Not so fast, Grace Artemis, no copping zzzs 'til you've data dumped yesterday and today." Sofi jumped on the bed.

"Who did you like, Navy or Buffs?" Shelley asked, bellyflopping across the foot of her bed to face us.

I studied the ceiling for the answer, like in the television show *The Queen's Gambit*, but minus the drug-induced hallucinations. "Toss-up I guess. Both were really talented, Navy was more structured, but it was a real practice, whereas CU was a goofy scrimmage with the guys putting on their comedy show."

"But where do you picture yourself?"

Rubbing my tired eyes, "That's a whole other enchilada." I ticked off bullet points on my fingers. "Academy offers free tuition, plus a stipend, and multiple career options."

"Boulder has mountains covered in gorgeous, sometimes shirtless, snowboarding hotties," Shelley said.

"And a ginormous buffalo running through the stadium with five handlers hanging on for dear life. Hooves down, straight up, best collegiate mascot ever," Sofi said.

"I see what you did there," Shelley snorted, they laughed even harder.

"It's expensive, no academic scholarships and even if they want me to play, meaning lacrosse, not the snowboarding hotties, the athletic ones, still talking about scholarships, are gone by now. Oh, and it's too late to apply. Good night." I covered my head with the comforter.

Sofi pulled it back. "Valid points." She was silent for a moment, "Navy dress uniforms are sweet, and they got rid of the blue camouflage for everyday use because that totally didn't make sense if someone fell overboard."

"Word," Shelley agreed, nodding her head.

Time to recalibrate. Reset the board. Pick a new opening and plan multiple moves ahead.

"So, it's Navy then?" Sofi asked.

"Yep. You mad?" I shrugged.

"Me? Why?" Sofi scoffed.

"Because I'm being different, again," I said.

"Different is what you do best, Buttercup. Don't ever change," Sofi said.

"Stay as cute and sweet as you naturally are, and you'll go far!" Shelley chortled, mocking their favorite high school yearbook quote.

Double blink. "Any weird dreams lately?" Sofi asked.

"Not really." Hadn't noticed until she mentioned it.

"Um. Interesting."

"How's that?"

"Could be your real life's so active that you don't need fantasy anymore."

"Too bad; they were entertaining. I never remember mine," Shelley said.

"How's your dream world with Alex?" I asked.

Sofi sighed, "Lov-er-ly. Talked him into applying for Veterinarian school on the Army's dime. If he's accepted, he'll get commissioned after graduation and start the program while I train to be a nurse anesthetist. Can you imagine? Me, putting people to sleep?"

"Nope," Shelley and I replied in unison.

Double blink. "How was the flight out with Croc?"

"Can't believe you got him to officiate," Shelley said, her loud yawn ended in a burp. One of her many endearing traits. She crawled under her covers.

I sat up, wide awake. "It was amazing. We did the precheck before take-off; I got to fly some and switch the flow from the wing fuel tanks to keep them balanced every fifteen minutes."

"Wow. Geek Alert. You sound like Alex nerd-raging online with Jason and Jon." Sofi switched off the lamp.

The room was black except for the glow of our charging cell phones. Sofi's breathing slowed, Shelley snored, and I stared at the dark ceiling and imagined flying among the stars.

52

"Girl On Fire" – Alicia Keys

When I told my folks about the decision to accept the USNA nomination at breakfast, Dad's reaction was difficult to decipher. Like when I used a new defense playing chess, he studied my face and the gameboard. I wanted to discuss it with him, but Sofi flew in and whisked me away to get beautified.

Mom volunteered to watch Linda and Jon's baby girl so Linda could come to the spa with us girls, and Jon could go golfing with the guys. Mom confided in me that she planned to finish her wedding gift during naptime, a sketch of the outdoor setting, to be displayed at dinner after the ceremony. I wished her luck and a long, productive slumber for the infant.

We had appointments for manicures and pedicures: Joan, to make Sofi happy, Shelley and Linda, to be pampered, and me, under protest. Next, we'd get our hair and makeup done. I blew a strand out of my face. I'd washed it an hour ago, and it was still damp. It was humid in the spa, which is weird since Colorado is typically awesome and dry.

Half-listening to Sofi go over today's schedule for the umpteenth time, I stared at the calendar on a bulletin board as we waited, trying to recall everything USNA alum Ellen had data dumped on me after the championship game. Plebe Summer lasts for approximately seven weeks, we get to call home twice, and it's stupid hot when you're not out learning how to sail on the Chesapeake Bay. Oh, joy.

Next to the calendar was a poster for Locks of Love. I squinted to read the donation requirements. At least ten inches past ponytail twisty. I reached back, pulled my hair forward, and ran my fingers through it. At least that if not more. Hmm. I picked up a magazine featuring short hairstyles and leafed through it. My hair grows about a half-inch every month, if I cut it super-short now, it'll be out of my eyes and carefree all summer.

I tapped Sofi's shoulder. "I changed my mind."

"About the Academy?" Her eyes wide, eyebrows arched.

"No. Instead of getting my nails done, I want to cut my hair and donate it." I gestured across from us.

Sofi and Shelley tracked and read the poster.

"I did that senior year, remember, Sofi? Before prom." Shelley said.

Sofi bit her lip, glanced at Joan, then back at me. "Do it. Get the Emma Watson pixie. You can slick it down or spike it up. Adorable. Google it."

The spa was pure chaos, one side for nail technicians and the other, for hairstylists. Sounds of whirring machines, laughing guests and blowing hair dryers blasted my ears, while harsh chemicals for applying or removing polishes combined forces with the perm and hair dye products to conquer the fragrant, more delicate and appealing lavender and sage scented lotions, shampoos and conditioners.

Over my shoulder reflecting in the mirror, Joan sat between Sofi and Shelley, listening to their back and forth banter while Linda relaxed next to them. Joan's Mona Lisa smile found mine as a foot-long ponytail was draped across my lap. Gulp. I really did this.

"Your beautiful gift will make someone very happy," my stylist said, "Would you like to dedicate it in memory or honor of someone?"

"Um, sure." She handed me a notecard and pen, picked up the thick hair, and gently laid it on pale pink tissue paper in a long white box to be delivered to the wig company.

My cheeks flushed as I stared at the blank card. Joan's mom. I don't know her name. After a moment, I wrote:

Sending strength and perseverance. You've got this.

I slid the card into the box. Glancing back, Joan's focus was on Sofi and Shelley's animated conversation. I used to study the threesome like a social dynamics experiment. As a lonely, twelve-year-old introvert, their tangible comradery was an enigma, as foreign then as following an influencer on social media is to me now.

53

"Scotland the Brave" – Northunder

Per Sofi's vision, the Colorado weather was glorious, the Monument Rock location stunning, and the bride serene, if not exactly lady-like, as she hiked her full-skirted dress up over her knee, stuck her pink-laced, white high top Converse into the stirrup, and hoisted herself up to float down like a gauze cloud atop golden Phoenix.

Sofi squealed, clapped and did a victory dance with Shelley. Phoenix snorted. Joan laughed. Her dad wiped away a tear. I sighed. Cori went ahead of us to cue the music.

As we waited, a woman hiker and a young girl wearing a ball cap came around the scrub oak thicket. The little girl looked up at Joan and gasped, "Is she a princess?"

"Sort of, kind of a warrior princess," Sofi said.

"Cool. I like her shoes," the little girl pointed to them.

"Of course, you do." Sofi laughed, then looked up at Joan and tilted her head toward the hikers.

"Care to join us?" Joan asked.

"We don't want to intrude," the woman shook her head.

"Please! You can show us the way to the pond." Sofi said, holding out a bucket of flower petals. "And scatter these along the trail? Like this." Sofi took a handful and tossed them into the air. The little girl giggled and looked up to the woman, who nodded permission just as the classic violin chords from "Canon in D" floated on a cool, mountain breeze.

The girl and the woman walked slowly around the giant white limestone rock outcropping that reached skyward into the deep blue. Her small hand dove into the bucket, grabbed petals and tossed a fistful onto the packed, white dirt trail.

I followed her, behind me, Shelley, then Sofi. We each carried bouquets of Forget-me-nots to symbolize fidelity, truth and long-lasting connections between friends and lovers that can't be broken or shaken. Sofi had done her due diligence.

Behind me, I heard her invite another group of surprised hikers entering from a converging trail to join us.

Shelley laughed and shouted, "The more the merrier!"

I glanced back over my shoulder and saw Joan astride Phoenix. Her confident composed face looked like the cover of a fantasy novel about a warrior princess prepared for battle. I snorted. That's one way to look at marriage, at least she has a solid army supporting her.

At the pond the little girl stopped, I gestured for her and the woman to join my folks and Joan's sister-in-law, Linda, who sat with her baby on a wooden bench.

I continued across the land bridge trail next to the pond per Sofi's directions.

Retired Captain Croc wore his Navy dress blues uniform decorated with ribbons and medals. Above them, his gold aviator wings glimmered in the late afternoon sun. Standing next to him was my brother, Jason, and his best man, Greg, in Army dress uniforms. They joined us on the land bridge as the recorded music transitioned from soothing violins to the whine of ceremonial bagpipes announcing the bride.

Sofi's huge smile was contagious, "Wait until you see this!" She tilted her head toward the other side of the pond.

The solemn bagpipe rendition of "Scotland the Brave" echoed off the mountains as Jon and Alex emerged from opposite sides of a scrub oak grove, wearing serious game faces, tartan kilts, dark blue jackets, tufted knee socks and shiny dress shoes. A line of CU Boulder lacrosse players in snazzy black and gold uniforms followed each of the guys. Parallel reflections marched along both sides of the pond. They carried lacrosse sticks like parade rifles.

The pace picked up as snare drums joined the bagpipes, but when electric guitars jumped in, the stoic march broke into a cocky strut.

What a riot.

"Oh, brother," Shelley said. "Are you kiltin' me?"

"I know, right? That's the Downie tartan!" Sofi giggled.

Any excuse to get Alex in a kilt.

The grinning guys joined us on the land bridge and the players stood at parade rest along both sides of the pond. When everyone was in place, the music stopped. Sofi nodded, the guests on the pond bench and hikers seated beside them on the hill stood.

Joan arrived. A hush fell as Phoenix pranced to a halt. Joan's dad stepped forward as she dismounted. Cori took the reins, and father and daughter walked toward us arm in arm. Their image reflected into the pond. I watched Jason's eyes follow Joan as they passed. He gazed at her the way anyone in love forever, and ever, should.

Joan's dad released her and swept a wayward copper-colored strand off her cheek to join the mass of curls flowing free in the wind, wild and natural down her back. Like her mom's had.

Sofi had seen a photo of Joan's mom when it fell out of Joan's Jeep glove box, back when Joan dyed her hair black to spare her father the painful reminder of what he'd lost.

Must be ten years ago, I thought. Sofi told me she'd convinced Joan to go back to her natural color. When Joan emerged from years of guilt-ridden dark despair 'to live out loud and in color.' Sofi's words were emphasized by air quote marks.

Joan's dad kissed her forehead. In response, she fist-bumped over her heart twice, kissed her closed hand, then released it up to heaven.

I blinked, swallowed past the lump in my throat, then reached up to push my hair behind my ear, then realized it was too short. The cool breeze tickled my bare neck and activated a shiver that ended in a shoulder shake.

Jason reached to shake Joan's dad's hand but was pulled in for the hug. Joan's dad stepped back, wiped his face, and walked away toward the guests.

Seems everyone needed a moment.

Croc cleared his throat, "How do you follow that?" He then delivered a funny, heartfelt matrimonial ceremony. As the couple shared private vows, Croc checked his watch and then the sky to the north.

A couple of seconds later, he did it again, then shot a look sideways to Sofi. She twirled a hand in a subtle faster, funnier motion aviators do when a speaker talks too long.

Something's up.

When Joan and Jason finished, Croc checked his watch a third time, then announced in a booming voice, "By the power vested in me by the Great State of Colorado, and Squirt here," he winked at Sofi. Everyone laughed. "I now pronounce you, husband and wife. You may kiss the bride!"

Jason buried one hand in curls behind her neck and wrapped the other around her waist. Joan took his face in both hands, traced his one-sided, Kevin Bacon smile with her finger, then kissed him. He never closed his eyes.

Thunder roared off the mountains. Was Croc concerned about the weather? Wait, no – I squinted. Six specks appeared above the pines.

"Here they come!" Sofi shouted. Everyone watched the specks increase in size, speed, and sound as the Air Force Thunderbirds roared overhead in a tight delta formation.

Awesome. How the heck did Sofi pull that off?

54

"I Love Rock 'N Roll" – Joan Jett & The Blackhearts

The informal reception was held in Monument at the Black Forest Cafe, an eclectic little deli with delicious food and an outside patio for the band, Pourly Edukated, to set up. The band members were talented local teachers/musicians who played instrumental covers of the requisite 80's songs while the crowd sang the revered and rowdy vocals, including Joan and Jason's first dance song, "I Love Rock and Roll."

I loved everything about that.

Next, when a slow song played, Joan and Jason melted together. It was easy to picture them, thirty years from now – they were the mirror image of my folks dancing next to them.

When the beat picked up, Sofi and Alex joyfully showed off their mad dance skills. I smiled, drawing a parallel to Sienna and Michael's maneuvers on and off the dance floor.

Shelley and Greg, Jason's buddy, epitomized the phrase, dance like no one's watching as they flailed like crazy goofballs, reminiscent of Aspen and Hood Snap's abandon at Homecoming and Prom.

Leaning back on the patio wall to observe soldiers' and lacrosse players' interactions I was reminded of a mating rituals documentary about the Laysan Albatross. Birds that practice standard moves to impress, nicknamed 'sky snap' and 'bob strut.' The polar opposite of Willow and Dervis's sweet, new something, and Mandi and Krutch getting reacquainted after a year of misunderstanding.

My attention meandered away from dancers to guests at tables. A setting sunbeam sparkled off the wisps of copper penny hair on Joan's baby niece as her brother Jon rocked his daughter in his arms.

Seated next to them, Coach Cori chatted with Joan's dad. A widower since losing the love of his life, I wondered if he would ever be open to loving again.

My phone buzzed, I jumped, and caught my reflection on the screen with Army ;-) stamped on my exposed forehead. Self-conscious, I smoothed back my spiked, short hair and wondered if he'd like it. Or not. Then wondered if I cared if he didn't, then realized it was dumb to not answer. So, I did.

"Howdy."

"How's the wedding?" Ian said.

"Amazing. The Thunderbirds flew over at the end."

"What? How?"

"Sofi heard they practiced over the wedding site on the weekend before Air Force Academy's graduation flyover. She got Croc, Dad's pilot friend who officiated the ceremony, to find out practice times and coordinated it.

"That's crazy!"

"That's Sofi," I laughed. "And since a lot of people wore uniforms, the two civilian groomsmen, Sofi's boyfriend and Joan's brother, wore tartan kilts from the family crest.

"Kilts?"

"Yep. Sofi's obsessed with them."

"What about her sister?"

"It's a good look, on the right legs." Did I say that out loud?

"I'll remember that."

His laugh caught my breath. MacGavin. Is he Scottish? Irish? Delicious? Stop.

"So, why Colorado?" Ian brought me back to the States.

"Jason's field artillery at Ft. Carson and Joan finished her masters at CU. She played there and was assistant coach, so the whole team is here."

"Soldiers too?"

"A few from his unit."

"Behaving?"

Are we flirting? "Define behaving; one just proposed."

"To you?"

"Me, Shelley, the waiter, and maybe a chair." I shrugged.

"What about the rest?"

Is he worried? "Dude. The CU women's lax team is here in black and gold shorts, aka Army colors. Nobody's paying attention to a recent high school grad in a long girly dress."

"Who picked it?" he asked.

"Sofi." My eyebrows furrowed.

"Thank her for me," he said.

We are definitely flirting.

Sofi and Alex magically appeared. She mouthed, 'who?" I showed her the screen, Army ;-)

"BigMac?" She mouthed.

I nodded to her and said, "Tell her yourself."

She took the phone. "Ian? Sofi here, we need to talk."

"This may take a while, care to dance?" Alex asked.

I sighed, "Be forewarned, I don't follow."

"What is it with you Halsted women?"

"You've heard, 'Lead, follow, or get out of the way?'"

"Yep." He did that lop-sided grin Sofi loves.

"Dad stopped at 'lead.'"

"I like that about your dad."

"Of course you do, brown-noser."

"Here you go, she's all yours," Sofi said into the phone then handed it to me with a wink.

"So – Going Navy," Ian said. Sofi told him.

"Yep – Beating Army." I squinted, how will this work?

"That's awesome."

"It is?"

"We're both in the Patriot League."

"So?"

"We can see each other at the rival games."

Wow. "Cool."

"When do you get back?" Ian asked.

"Monday... and then report for Induction Day, Tuesday." My nose scrunched up. Think. No, act. "Want to drive me?"

"To Annapolis?"

"Yeah, I have to be dropped off by 2 pm, so if you take me, Dad can go to work, and he and Mom can bring the rest of my stuff to the Oath of Office ceremony at 7 pm."

"Okay, it takes an hour, depending on the beltway traffic. Pick you up at noon?"

"How about ten? Just to be on the safe side." And allow more time together.

"It's a date."

"A date, date?" I inhaled and held it.

"The perfect date – 'because it's not too hot, not too cold, all you need is a light jacket.'"

No, he didn't. Exhaling with a snort, "Did you just drop a line from Miss Congeniality?"

"Busted. Ellen and Gwen made me watch it."

"I can't even...."

"Hey! Sandra Bullock's smoking hot!"

"Are you a cougar crusher?"

His deep laugh sent an electric current from ear to toes.

"Have a type: smart, athletic, sarcastic."

I bit my lip and wondered, long hair on that list?

"Have fun, but not too much," Ian said.

"I'll try to, and not too."

We disconnected.

Not great, but dang, I'm getting better at this.

55

"Wind Beneath My Wings" – Bette Midler

I craned my neck to peek into the cockpit as I boarded the commercial airline for our return flight. Croc warned that I'd be disappointed. He was correct. The Diamond's double screen panels were more intricate, interesting, and way cooler.

My window seat was over the wings. Mom and Dad sat together across the aisle. I plugged in my headphones and searched through the channels on the armrest for air traffic chatter. Croc told me you could listen in sometimes, but after not finding any frequencies, I pulled up a chill playlist instead.

Listening to the song that Joan and her dad danced to, "Wind Beneath My Wings," I watched the flight attendant run through the safety instructions because most passengers were ignoring him. When he finished with his props and hand motions I looked out the window as we taxied and took off.

Rising through the clouds, my thoughts returned to the dance. I'd hung back against the wall, watching Joan with her dad, and our dad with Sofi, his oldest daughter. Waiting for my turn. Croc had found me there and handed me a bag.

"What's this?" I asked.

"Take a look."

I lifted out a ball cap with the Diamond Aircraft logo on it. "Wow, this is awesome! Thank you!" I put it on.

"To remind you of your first Diamond flight."

"This is so cool. When did you start flying?" I asked.

He told me he'd crop-dusted fields as a teen. After college, he was accepted into the Navy aviation program and later selected for the Blue Angels flight demonstration squadron. Now retired from the military, what he missed most was camaraderie. Knowing your wingman had your back.

When it was my turn to dance with Dad, they had shaken hands, set up their next chess match, and said goodbyes as Croc had an early flight.

Back in the here and now, I snuck a look over at Dad as he studied the emergency safety card that shared the netted pocket on the airline seatback with the puke bag. He hated flying commercial. Never trusted planes without parachutes and didn't trust ones that did because there's a reason. He hadn't talked much about his pilot career, opted instead to make our family time a priority. Left work at work to spend quality time at home with us.

Reflecting on last night, I recalled Sofi danced with Mom after Dad. Sofi's hair was pulled up in a twist and held in place by two ballpoint pens. Their profiles matched as they chatted and swayed back in forth, Sofi's arms around Mom's neck and Mom's hands resting on Sofi's waist.

I replayed my conversation with Dad as we'd danced. It began with chess; I thanked him for the beautiful set he'd given me for graduation. The black pieces, my preference to play, were made of obsidian, the white pieces, his favorite, were moonstone. Symbolic perhaps, since my middle namesake, Artemis, was the mythological goddess of the moon.

Our discussion had gravitated to my decision about the Naval Academy. "You're intelligent, strong, and driven to excel. I thought you'd make an excellent scientist, engineer, or doctor."

"But not military-material like Sofi and Jason."

"Not necessarily. You're not outgoing like your siblings, but your perseverance after shredding an ACL proved you're resilient, your decisions as a team captain showed leadership skills, and your chess prowess confirmed you're capable of strategizing. 'A good plan violently executed now is better than a perfect plan executed next week, General George S. Patton.'"

I bit my lip and blinked back tears. Inhaling, I lifted my chin and gave him a supercilious eyebrow. "As long as I control the center of the board."

"That's right, Scout," he chuckled, "Don't ever forget it."

56

"Something Just Like This" – Coldplay

Too hyper to sleep, I rose with the sun and took Roscoe and Mallory running. Their sad puppy eyes had tortured me ever since I started to pack.

It had rained overnight. The vivid green woods smelled fresh, and a gust of wind sent a shower of residual droplets from saturated leaves to rinse me as I ran in silence. The damp sandy path muffled my footsteps.

Back home, I forced myself to chew and swallow my post-run breakfast. Dad had gone to work. Mom drank her coffee next to me in silent solidarity. Ian was due to pick me up at ten. I ran fingers through my short hair, wondering what he'd think of it. Still not sure whether I cared if he liked it or not. Pretty sure if I wondered this many times, I did.

He drove up at 9:55. I put on my Diamond ball cap, tucked wisps of hair behind my ears and hugged Mom, "See you tonight."

She squeezed me tight, "Love you, Grace Artemis."

I picked up lacrosse gear, took a deep breath and left.

The aviators hid his reaction to my lack of long, wavy hair. When he smiled through the windshield I exhaled, opened the truck door and climbed in. "Hey."

I turned away to buckle up and calm down, "Thanks for the ride." Looking back at him, I paused, took off my cap, lifted my chin and ran my fingers back through my pixie cut.

Lowering the aviators, his blue-gray eyes followed my hand. "Nice hair. Looked good at the wedding too."

Wait. What? "How did you –"

"Sofi shot me a pic."

Of course, she did. When I gave her my phone.

"Smart. Low maintenance." He rubbed his tapered cut. "Cool that you donated it too. Ready to Go Navy?"

I nodded. He pushed the start button, put it in reverse, then grabbed the compartment between us to look over his shoulder to back out. His warm forearm brushed mine and doubled my heartbeat.

Whoa, Army. I need a moment.

"Went to Best Buy when I got back," he said. "Dervis upgraded my graphics card and got me into their World of Warcraft guild."

Thank geekness. Hello, nerd rage comfort zone.

"Nice! Dervis created a Rogue One avatar for me after I wrecked my ACL so I could play," I said. This led to thirty conversational minutes of super online warrior civilization battle strategies that got us around the beltway.

As he rambled on about online gaming I gave my quirky friends a mental assist for this game-changing relationship goal. Had a sneaking suspicion Jaz strategized Ian meeting them on that video chat at the gallery to strengthen our connection. Well played, my friend.

"They are crazy insane but also chill," Ian said.

"Yep. Krutch might go to St. John's College across from the Naval Academy. The two schools play a croquet match every year and spectators dress up like the Kentucky Derby. I'd love to play against him as a midshipman."

"What about Dervis and Hood Snap?"

"Dervis wants MIT, Hood Snap's looking at American University for political science and international relations."

"After MIT, Dervis should start up a cyber company. I'll go to work for him when I get out at twenty." Ian checked the rearview mirror. I checked Ian's chiseled profile then mentally shook my head to focus back on the conversation.

"You're going cyber?" I asked.

"Yep. What do you want?"

Is that a trick question? "Excuse me?"

"Surface, submarine, aviation?" he asked.

As in a career focus, not a relationship status.

"Not sub." I shivered. Lack of control issue. Prefer flying high or making waves rather than submerging low.

Awkward pause. Running out of time, ideas and miles.

"Tunes?" Ian asked.

"Sure," I said. Relieved.

He swiped a thumb up his phone screen, held it up to his face to sign in, then punched Spotify, "Knock yourself out."

Wishing Sofi's clue bird would crap sense into this mess, I scrolled through his playlist. Boom. The exact dose of spicy sauce. I tapped Coldplay's "Something Just Like This." It started playing and I pressed the volume up button.

With eyes on the road, Ian turned down the volume on the steering wheel. "You'll have to rank your preferences eventually."

Preferences? I'm thinking someone with a military haircut, "with eyes like the sea after a storm." Get a grip, Gracie. I turned up the volume and hoped he listened.

He turned it down again, "You don't have to decide now. You've got time."

Not really. We're almost to our exit.

Inhaling, I turned it back up. Here goes something.

I pointed to the stereo, "This."

Forehead furrowed, he looked at the radio and listened. His eyes opened wide, and his mouth started to smile, then formed a stern line as he bit down on the inside of his lips. His expression was mock-serious. "You want – this?" he pointed to the console.

Mimicking his look, I gestured an equilateral triangle to him, the radio, me, back to him.

His head cocked, "Did I hear something about a 'kiss?'"

I smiled. "I believe you did."

"Got anyone in mind?"

"Meh." I shrugged and waved him off. "Someone smart, athletic, sarcastic." His list of Sandra Bullock qualities.

"I play lacrosse," he said, deadpan serious.

"I play lacrosse," I said, with mock enthusiasm.

He rotated the wheel to change lanes.

Honk!

The car behind us didn't appreciate the quick maneuver. Ian swerved back into the middle lane, waved as they passed us, lifted the turn signal and checked over his shoulder.

"Hope you kiss better than you drive," I said, monotone.

"You be the judge."

"If I live that long."

"I guarantee delivery."

"Same day? If the army doesn't work out, you can work for Target." I shot him a poker face.

He glanced at my mouth. "Funny, got a target in mind."

I turned away, lowered the window and let the incoming air cool my flushed face. I surfed my hand in the wind like a dolphin. Sofi would be proud.

I'm definitely getting better at this.

He tapped my shoulder and handed me his phone. "Jaz told me my contact name. Make this song your ringtone and change Rogue to Navy."

I scrolled through his contacts and found Rogue. Our selfie pic was the background. Why hadn't I thought of that? "Keep the same pic?"

"For now; we'll take a new one."

I looked ahead. Seeing our exit, I quickly typed a search for 'parks near me,' because seriously, don't want our first kiss to occur in crowded, touristy downtown Annapolis!

Quiet Waters Park popped. Sounds like a sweet place. I punched Directions and let Siri do her job.

"Detour?" Ian asked.

"Yeah, we made good time." Heck yes, we did. "We can hang a bit, maybe grab lunch." Or each other.

"Sounds good."

Heck yes, it does.

As luck would *not* have it, we pulled into the not as quiet as the name implied Quiet Waters parking lot as three huge buses vomited chatty middle-schoolers to coagulate under a giant banner that read, "Welcome to Science Camp!"

Ian parked. We stared. Looked at each other and burst out laughing. Then, a smile spread across his gorgeous face. "You know. It *is* science camp." He shrugged, "Biology?"

I smiled and leaned onto the console. "Chemistry..."

A wonderous minute later we came up for air from our first kiss and noticed multiple pairs of wide-eyed middle schoolers learning a lesson in natural selection.

Giggling, I grabbed Ian's aviators from the top of his head, put them on, buckled up and scrunched down, knees to chin. He saluted our enlightened science campers, punched the start button, and slowly backed out of our 'parking' space.

It was time. We drove in silence and turned into a short-term parking lot across from USNA Visitor Gate 1. Ian parked and pressed the engine button off.

I inhaled his aphrodisiac aftershave scent, committed it to olfactory memory then exhaled a sigh ending with a hum. Looking at him, I leaned in for one last kiss. A moment or multiple awesome ones later, three knocks rapped on Ian's window. We disengaged and smoothed back short haircuts.

A gray-haired man wearing a short-sleeved city uniform shirt and a ball cap that read PARKING pointed to the Short Term Parking sign.

Ian started the engine to lower his window.

"Need to move along," the man said.

"Thanks. Will do."

The man leaned down to look across to me, his head tilted toward Ian.

"Brave, foolish or both?"

"Excuse me?" I asked.

"His bumper sticker. Beat Navy. In front of USNA gate."

I glanced from him to Ian and crinkled my nose. "Both?"

The attendant chuckled, tapped the bill of his cap and left us with a "Hooah."

Wait. What? Army's version of the battle-cry? I laughed. He must relish ticketing all of the Navy visitors.

"Better go before you get thrown out of town," I said, pulling off his aviators.

"No," he placed them back on me. "They look good on you and we need to shoot a new pic."

"Then you need this," I said, putting my cap on him.

Logic questioned how and why I was shooting another selfie with this gorgeous human; Imagination wondered what could become of us as we leaned together and took a pic that was a combination of real and fantastical.

"Send it to me," I said, grabbing my gear.

"Done," he said, tapping on his phone.

I inhaled and held my breath.

He exhaled and shrugged.

I reached for my cap. He leaned back. "Not uniform plebe. I'll keep it until next time."

Lowering his aviators, I shot him a supercilious eyebrow. "Then I'm keeping these."

"Aight," he said, with a teasing grin.

"Until next time." I got out and walked toward the gate.

A horn blasted behind me. I heard him yell, "Go Navy!"

I held my lacrosse stick up and shouted, "Beat Army!"

Showing my I.D., walking through the gate, I nodded to the guard who tried not to smile.

57

"Born to Fly" – Sara Evans

Walking takes too long. I want to run. Or fly. To get to what's next. After the swearing-in ceremony, I bid farewell to my folks and took my duffle bag to Bancroft Hall, nicknamed Mother B, my home for the foreseeable future.

My room was in the first of eight connected dormitories. I set the bag on the bed and unzipped it. On top was a framed Steampunk Pirate Prom picture. I sighed. Mom knew these friends were important. My reflection smiled in the glass as I studied my motley crew and realized the borders of my close-knit family had expanded to include them. I set it on the desk at the foot of the bed.

Next, I lifted a rectangle package wrapped in brown paper. A book? No. Too light. Unwrapping it with care, I blinked as my vision blurred.

The beach painting. I read the title out loud, "Testing her wings," and carried it to the window. I looked out at the rising full moon with a bird's eye view of the courtyard below.

Grace Artemis. Moonbeam. Rogue One. Spitfire. Navy.

Studying the painting, I inhaled deeply and held it, then exhaled a sigh that emptied my lungs and ended in a hum.

Memories of that day washed over me, running on the sand, climbing the path to lunch atop the cliffs, watching the falcon float on the updraft as I had in my dreams.

Not yet ready to fly, but when it's time, I will soar.

And my wings will be made of gold.

Kris!

ABOUT THE AUTHOR

Kris is a graphic designer, author, and illustrator of six children's books, a young adult novel series and is currently working on a modern crime fiction novel. She enjoyed substitute teaching for more than ten years in Virginia, Colorado and Iowa. Originally from Illinois, she and her husband Mike moved coast to coast and a few states in between while he was in the military, then an analyst. After eight years in colorful Colorado, they followed their youngest to Iowa State University in amiable Ames where Mike taught for nine years, including summer abroad classes in Europe, giving Kris the dream opportunity to wander, photograph and write. They recently moved to Manhattan, Kansas, where Mike will teach at Kansas State as they build a mountain home in Monument, Colorado. They are owned by a herd of cats and dogs and enjoy visits with their three dashing sons, two amazing daughters-in-law, two darling grandsons, and fabulous friends near and far. Diagnosed with breast cancer in March 2001 and a benign brain tumor in 2022, Kris advocates early detection, aggressive treatment, and thriving happily ever after.

Children's picture books written and/or illustrated by the author:

"I love you I love you I love you I do. If you were a sock ... then I'd be your shoe"
"I love you I love you I love you I do. If you were purple ... then I'd be blue"
"We love you We love you We love you We do. If you were a pirate ... then we'd be your crew"
"Any color in the rainbow, and then some ..."
"Any dinosaur that's been discovered, and then some ..."
"Any place you've ever imagined, and then some ..."
And newest, by debut author Connie Kotnik-Abel:
"I wish I were a firefighter instead of a little girl"

Follow Kris Abel-Helwig for events and new releases:
Facebook: @krisabelhelwig.author.illustrator
Twitter: @krisabelhelwig
Instagram: @krisabelhelwig
Email: kris@kahcreative.com
Web: kahcreative.com

 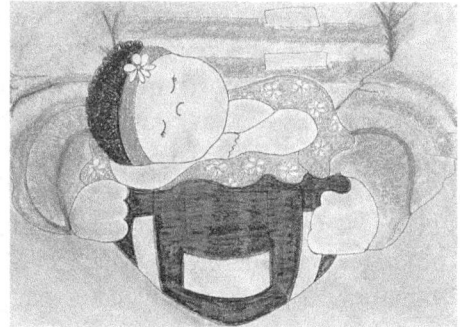